ANOMIE

A NOVEL OF 21ST CENTURY AMERICAN EXISTENTIALISM

ANOMIE

RICHARD FENDRY

NORTHPAW PUBLISHERS
2023

Anomie

Copyright © 2023 by Richard Fendry

Northpaw Publishers LLC

www.northpawpublishers.com

Printed in the United States of America

Publisher's Cataloging-in-Publication data

Fendry, Richard.

Title : Anomie / by Richard Fendry.

Identifiers: ISBN 978-1-7364416-2-6 (print edition); ISBN 978-1-7364416-3-3 (ebook)

1. Psychological thriller -- Fiction. 2. Technothriller -- Fiction. I. Title.

First Edition

10 9 8 7 6 5 4 3 2 1

PART ONE
THE CUTE GUYS

A CHUBBY GIRL pedals her bicycle in ovals on the vacant tennis courts. I observe her maneuvers as I cut across the athletic fields on my way to sensitivity training. Outrageously good fortune has placed a mental health option nine and a half blocks from my home so I leave the motor skateboard in my garage and hoof the short distance. This is to be the fourth of my twelve scheduled sessions. I can attest that I've already detected a subtle improvement in my neuroplasticity.

I break into a jog crossing the busy street in front of a car that shows little interest in reducing its speed. I enter the office and find that the waiting room of King Kryczek & Rohr-Kisslinger Counseling Solutions LLP features a new addition. A chattering African grey parrot occupies a large cage in the corner. The bird screeches "Meow raowww raowww!" The young African-American woman behind the partition would seem to be the receptionist. She has offered no more than three words and a cold gaze on any of my previous visits but today she cracks a smile and volunteers information about the parrot. His name is Ivanhoe K. Petrovich, known to familiars as Ivan the Terrible. Apparently, Dr. Arthur King's brother is a veterinarian, and Ivan bit someone at his office, necessitating emergency removal from the practice. No Tippi Hedren, the vet's wife refused to tolerate a dangerous animal at their residence, so the office of the family psychotherapist became Ivan's default temporary sanctuary. Ivan bears a slight facial resemblance to my childhood friend Gayle Spaatz. The bird screeches "Why can't birds talk?"

My therapist is Dr. David Rohr-Kisslinger. I have informed the doctor that I find his hyphenated surname pretentious and I refuse to acknowledge the segment before the hyphen. Cognitive behavioral sensitivity training a la Kisslinger is conducted in the dark with the client in a float tank in order to lift depression and enhance therapeutic immersion. Evanescent images of fast-moving cumulus clouds with periodic rifts of blue sky are looped across the ceiling every ten minutes. "I owe everything to my formal education," I follow Kisslinger's suggestion to embrace the past. "In high school I learned that I was ugly and awkward. In college I learned I was stupid and lazy."

"You derived takeaways that you can apply to the rest of your life," the doctor consoles me. "But the blur of generalization is a mark of a cowardly person trying to elude specific memories." I can hear him force a condescending smile. "Speak if you will of particular figures and events."

"I liked my seventh-grade science teacher," I confess, "but as a typical hard-core nerd suddenly handed authority, he overdid the discipline bit and became a browbeater. It damaged his effectiveness and eroded his credibility."

"I feel his frustration," Kisslinger remarks, "so how much more, speaking with the voice of experience, should you? More telling though is your continued refusal to discuss your nuclear family. I imagine you'll contend you're unaware of this avoidance."

"Here's my great childhood epiphany." I lower my guard to confide an actual historical tidbit. "I'm about eight and a half years old and I crave comics and candy. I've saved my allowance for just such an occasion, but I must cross a lighted intersection to reach the drugstore where I might procure the desired items, and I'm not permitted to cross busy Bluemound Road alone. My mother balks at letting me go, and I protest that she's treating me like a baby. She finally relents with the stern directive that I abide by the traffic light and obey the walk signal. So I hustle to the corner in question, diligently wait for the walk signal, cross north and purchase the targeted spoils. I return to the street, wait for the walk signal again and start crossing south toward home. A blue pickup truck traveling north barrels around the corner to head west and finds me in the crosswalk directly in its path. The driver slams on the brakes, squealing to a stop so his bumper barely tickles the fuzz on my forearm. For just a couple of seconds, I stand frozen with the realization of how close my promising young life had come to being blotted out. Yet not content to have nearly splattered my guts across the concrete, the driver lays a protracted blast on his horn. I scurry the rest of the way across the street with my eyes fixed on the still beckoning walk signal."

"That's life in the big city," Kisslinger resolves the trauma. "The incident probably affected the truck driver more than you. He perhaps went home and cried."

"I can't imagine what city you live in," I counter with unfluffed petulance. "That's not how people process events. By the time he finished relating the tale twice, I would've flung myself blindly into traffic and only his supernatural peripheral awareness and lightning-quick reflexes saved me. I'm not a violent man, but even 25 years after the fact, if I discovered his identity, I'd break his jaw for his extraordinary contribution to the miserable trajectory my life subsequently took."

"We're all relieved you're not violent," Kisslinger scoffs. "You need to let it go. After all, your life trajectory didn't take you on an ambulance ride. He did stop. And he didn't hit you."

"Maybe as a routine practice," I suggest, "I should thank everyone I encounter for letting me live. I'll say 'I have no good excuse for existing; I appreciate your restraint in not taking the opportunity to snuff me.'"

"Such a course might demonstrate an improved attitude," Kisslinger mutters. "Sincerely, I'm surprised that you recognize how selective memory can be and how subjective perception is. Perhaps in your excitement you failed to discern the green turn arrow or you became engrossed in your comics as you waited for the light to change and were moving through the crosswalk at a snail's pace with your nose buried in outlandish adventure. The driver tapped on his horn, and his presence startled you."

"It happened precisely as I described it." I slap my hand in the water to create a splash. "You sound like the truck driver's insurance agent. If I achieve psychoanalytic transference from the driver to you, I'll pluck your scraggly beard." I can feel the counselor sneer in the dark. "Anyway, I reported the traffic incident to my mother, and she threw a fit. She told me she knew I couldn't handle the heady responsibility of crossing busy Bluemound alone."

"Ultimately, she was proven correct, hmm?" Kisslinger snickers. "If it remains a problem, I'll take you to any bustling intersection in the area and walk you through the protocol of safely crossing the street until you're comfortable with it."

"I don't believe I ever really discussed another serious issue with my mother after that," I conclude.

Kisslinger emits a protracted sigh. "I've withheld judgement to this point in order to get a solid handle on where you're coming from, but as today's session completes the first trimester of your program, I must observe that your self-absorption is off the charts. Your critical thinking skills are grossly underdeveloped. Your concept of accepted and demonstrated knowledge is so naïve. You're the sort of individual who would perpetually moan and mope about each and every trivial setback that clouds your life from cradle to grave. If your mother had sent you to ninja camp, you'd complain that she ruined your summer. If she didn't order you to go, you'd lament that she cheated you out of your most basic opportunity for self-enrichment. Your passive-aggressive tendency always points you in the direction of playing the luckless misfit; it always leaves you as the consummate outsider."

I'm disoriented by the light when my session ends, and I struggle back into my clothes. As I reach the door to exit the King Kryczek & Rohr-Kisslinger office, Ivan screeches

"Bowwow rarf rarf!" I march home slowly. Sensitivity training is a joy. It's paid time away from the job.

After packing a full day's work into the afternoon, I head to Pfixx's Inn, a hospitably gloomy gothic conventicle east of Eagle in western Waukesha County, where I'll meet with my old school chum of over thirty years Gayle Spaatz and my former fellow research associate of almost seven years Delmar Vecsey. I haven't seen the former in a few months and I've seen the latter twice since he was escorted from our building six weeks ago after being fired. I've exchanged brief messages with each in the respective interims.

Gayle has arrived first and claimed our corner table. He savors a sip of his ice wine mojito as I join him with my Guinness draught and orange juice. "I'm sorry it's been so long," I offer. "This trail of minor tragedies I've been dealing with-"

"So she dumped you," Gayle needles me. "She moved out and took your new car? What kind was it again?"

"Charger," I utter. "It was her early birthday present. How pathetic would I have looked if I demanded it back?"

"You've already zoomed way past pathetic, goombah." Gayle sips his mojito. "Pathetic has shrunk to a tiny dot in your rearview mirror." I grin because he doesn't know the half of my personal futility. "The last time I saw fair Morticia, her fool's-gold flaxen hair flowed down to the crack in her ass cut in back to a point. I interpreted that as a barb destined straight for your heart."

"How's Vito?" I inquire about Gayle's longtime on-again-off-again partner.

"Wanting." Gayle shrugs. "I'm sorry these affairs always leave you such a whipped puppy."

I catch a glimpse of Delmar at the bar. "Maybe sensitivity counseling is the missing ingredient that'll reverse my fortunes, hmm?" I raise my beverage and take a long, hard swallow. "By the way, I've invited Del Vecsey to meet us here." I've brought Gayle and Delmar together previously with no particular esprit de corps developing. "That's another of the tribulations I've had to endure."

"A trail of trials." Gayle takes a series of sips. "Tell me again how Delmar got himself offloaded."

"He produced a one-woman show starring our boss Nancy." I employ a subtle roundhouse wave to attract Del's attention. "If he can find his way over here, he'll give you the inside analysis."

Vecsey wanders to the table with an unpretentious rail Irish whiskey on the rocks. He would've ordered it as crushed emerald ash borer juice across windshield shards. He stares blankly. As full as he is of quips, he rarely smiles and almost never laughs. But when he does express delight, he discharges an uncontrollable billow of sound and saliva. He's gotten his hair clipped as short as Spaatz's. "You look great," Gayle greets him, "trim and sassy."

"Working 70 hours a week for 10 years has helped me maintain my youthful disposition." Delmar plunks himself into a chair.

"Allusion had just been made to the rare event which led to your dismissal," I advise him. "Shall we recap the highlights for sports fan Spaatz's benefit?"

Delmar displays a self-effacing grimace. "Rare events are diminished by familiarity."

I raise my glass. "One more recap for our own forbidden self-indulgence." Del has always required prodding so I begin. "Nancy was scheduled to be out of our humble little lab for a week-long conference on intellectual property rights in the Galapagos Islands. On that Wednesday, I receive a cryptic memo to move a tray of spent mutant culture samples from a particular storage tower and shelf to Nancy's desk." I fix my eyes on poker-faced Vecsey. "I fetch and pack the tray, get the key to her office and open the door. Motion triggers some dim corner lights, and I'm startled to find Nancy seated behind her desk. She says 'What took you so long?' and rises. She's holding a bottle of Killian's Red and she's nude except for three strategically placed ice cream cones, perky points protruding forward. She says 'Shut the door, dummy.' Her chest bears an imposing *FANCY NANCY* tattoo with a hummingbird on her left breast. I spit out 'I, I, I didn't realize you're back.'" Del's lips begin twitching. "She says 'I've wanted to get you alone' and I realize it's a frighteningly authentic artificial Nancy – a fematon, a gynbot."

"It's trademarked as a Companion Piece!" Hearty spasms of raucous laughter escape from Delmar. "They have security applications for house-sitting! They respond to motion or light triggers and can stand, sit, swivel, talk! You just furnish a few photos and voice recordings, and they're made to order, so anyone who peers in your window can't tell that's not living, breathing DNA!" Gayle and I giggle along with Del. "I couldn't procure photos of Nancy's more personal attributes so we gave her the full benefit of the doubt."

Gayle rubs my shoulder. "It sounds exactly like what our Constable of County Cuck here needs to fill all the empty hours he has in the wake of his bitter breakup."

"Trish asked me to hand over or delete all the photos of her in my possession," I lament. "So I only retain a couple. Anyway, I don't think a dollbot would offer quite the same ceiling of emotional fulfillment."

"Before you reject, give your Companion Piece a name." Vecsey takes a bold belt of whiskey. "Consider your heartbreak history. Give the process a chance."

"So Executive Frau Nancy found out and took executive action," Gayle infers.

"What happened was Lisle panicked." Delmar rocks in his seat. "One of our peers, research associate Kelly, poked her pretty head inside the Duchess's office to see what Lisle was howling about. She laughed and said, 'You guys are sick!' Lisle swore her to secrecy and got rid of her. He tells me we have to dispose of Nancy 2.0 immediately."

I nod. "Del insists, 'No, it's a treat for the whole office!' I try to reason with him: 'There are going to be a few people who won't appreciate this quite as much as we do.' He waves his hand. 'Ahhh, after all the trouble I took, it has to have a half-life of at least a couple of days. On Friday, I want to put out some mint ice cream and cookies on the side.' I keep working on him throughout the afternoon and finally convince him that the ersatz Nancy has to go."

"At the end of the day," Delmar seizes the narrative like a seasoned co-anchor, "Lisle has the brilliant idea to dump the body down the freight elevator shaft, so there's no chance security catches us taking it out of the building. But we can't quite pry open the door, so we convey her down to the basement and dump her in a corner bin of compact storage. Lisle leaves, but I'm not satisfied with the stunted yield I got from the gag, so I return to compact storage and wedge improved Nancy in between two contiguous shelves, positioning it so just her head and one extended arm protrude into view." He shakes his ice. "And biochemist extraordinaire that I am, I mixed a chocolate-syrup and tomato-juice concoction that looked just like blood and I rigged slow-drip flows emanating from her mouth and hand." Del emits a wicked cackle. "It looked as though she'd been crushed between the sliding shelves."

"Lillian from H.R. spotted it, fainted and bumped her head when she fell," I finish the account. "Proto-Nancy cut her conference short. She left her rudimentary sense of humor on the Santa Cruz beach, waded back into the office morass and took Del and me to task."

Spaatz squints at me with mock indignation. "Accessory after the fact."

"Guilt by association," Vecsey advises him. "The Duchess was never more frustrated by anything than me taking sole responsibility for the exhibit. As you might extrapolate, she and I share a proud history of strife. You see, I'm deliberate and painstaking and I don't like to be rushed, so it doesn't look like I work very hard." He empties his glass. "But ask Amonor – I would spend more time in the stinkin' lab than anyone. So sometimes I'd be there in my sweet potato sweat pants and lucky mukluks, and she'd take issue with my degree of *casualty*." Del narrows his right eye. "She said she couldn't interpret this 'dummy incident' as anything less than a not-so-subtle threat against her and the last straw in an escalating series of insubordinate acts, so she fired me." He waves his arms and forces the self-conscious chortle of a morning shock jock. "In the final analysis, if Lisle hadn't coaxed me to move the dummy from the Duchess's office, where the carpet is much thicker, and Lillian's fainting episode occurred *there*, the bump on her head might've been a bit smaller, and I might've gotten off with sensitivity training like he did."

"Del, you tend to push your point a little further at times than the light of day can bear." I soften my tone to that of a funeral director. "You'd do well to accept that deploying the dream isn't often worth the material cost to the dreamer."

"Nancy is a ripping bar of a woman," Delmar asserts. "She has a rare personal depthlessness. She's one of those women with a pug nose, jug ears and no sex drive whose tainted excuse for libido manifests itself as pick-pick-picking people to death while acquiring a fancy job title in the process. The pose she'd most like to strike is to put a bad hurt on some good people, if she could find any. Her idea of personal growth is to become a greater threat."

I chuckle. "I think she's already aware of how much the lab misses you. In a few weeks when it's obvious she's feeling the crunch of your absence, I'll broach the idea of letting you rehab through sensitivity training and bringing you back-"

"I don't want that shitty job back!" Vecsey slams home any remaining whiskey drops. "Getting fired should be the best thing that ever happened to me! Dreams, ideas and visions are nice, but at some point if you haven't taken action on them, don't you have to conclude that your life was nothing but a trail of hot vapor? You need to get out of there too, Lisle. A man makes the world feel the weight of his being."

"If Nancy is anything like *my* supervisor," Spaatz offers, "she chews up weakness. You never whine to people like that or beg them, even if they're threatening your life."

I allow Delmar to rescue me from the indignity of another turn with commercial transportation and drive me home. It's proven to be a much later night than I'd anticipated. Del and I tentatively arrange to meet again in a week, and I shuffle into the house. I fix light chicken and rice dinners for Maynard and myself. "Is the world mad," I challenge him, "or am I? My friends always chide me for how little I have, but what I have seems to be better than what they have. You would indubitably agree?"

"GUYS LIKE ME cling to a myth," I confide to Dr. Rohr-Kisslinger in the heat of our fifth session. He has implied that my lack of a romantic bond is the crux of my presumed personality disorder.

"You're an erratically shifted narcissist," he interrupts me. "Your behavior tends to vacillate between smarmy and snarky depending on what you believe at any given moment is more self-serving. We often see a megalomania present in those that society at large would deem least entitled to it."

"I'm the sort of fool who tends to glorify women," I persevere. "We like to believe that if they took the time to get to know us, they'd prefer a kind, compassionate, devoted man to the pompous, blustery jerks toward whom they typically gravitate."

Kisslinger snorts. "My wife is a real peach and I'm nothing like that. I could've attained an M.B.A. faster than a Psy.D.

in clinical psychology and easily be pulling down five times what I'm earning here, but I felt it was more important to pursue a career in helping challenged people." He sighs irritably. "What you call a myth is mistaking an overall social paralysis for virtue. Can you honestly be mystified that the projection of personal power, commanding social standing, showing some balls, is going to attract more babes than being weak and needy? When you look at a woman through your desperate, pleading eyes and she looks through you like you're not really there or she blatantly avoids making eye contact, are you devastated by her lack of response? Perhaps in your heightened degree of vulnerable instability you perceive this casual slight as a hard rejection which merits your contempt, your full-blown hatred?"

"I'm not going to hate all women for what one did to me," I intercept Kisslinger at the pass. "Or two or three or four."

"So you've had many women?" Kisslinger scoffs arrestingly.

"I've had many women disappoint me." I paddle closer to the doctor and attempt to splash him. "I've recognized for some time that leading a stunted existence beneath a cloud of despair because some prospective romantic partner doesn't want to be with me is the height of idiocy."

"That's a disturbingly over-intellectualized insight for you," the counselor snarls. "About ninety percent of the happiness you'll experience in life will be based on your ability to make other people approve of you. It's a crazy little thing called charm. Ever heard of it?"

"Persona's poor cousin?" I try to suppress my disgust with Kisslinger's operant superficiality. "If you feel the need to change outwardly to win the admiration of others, even that special someone, I believe you're misframing the problem. The solution is to change inwardly so you don't need the approval of others."

"That is the most pathetically arrogant perspective I have ever heard!" Kisslinger's Notemaster lights up with his need to preserve a point or check the time. "Relationships are the root of satisfaction, the basis of all that's worthwhile. If you don't give anything to other people, you can't lead a life of significance."

"Doesn't doing no harm count for anything?" I challenge. "That should win you more points than most have."

Kisslinger rises with a pronounced peevishness. "You're courting an attitude that can easily evolve into that of the proverbial troubled loner. Tightening your social connections will help maintain your thinking skills and reduce the risk of rapid cognitive decline."

As I leave the King Kryczek & Rohr-Kisslinger office, Ivan screeches "Why can't birds talk? *Ayyak!* Why can't birds talk?"

No sooner do I return to work than Chief Operating Officer Nancy Buetow-Detweiler summons me to her office for the first time since the series of cross-examinations she conducted to investigate the Companion Piece incident. As the spouse of Dr. Aaron Detweiler, the University of Wisconsin molecular bigshotologist who launched our little biotech startup Ideal Allele LLC (a.k.a. I Deal Anele LOL), Nancy is easily the most dangerous person on the premises. (After acquiring licensing rights to commercially apply the protein-shaping method he developed in care of U.W., Aaron remained on the Madison campus to conquer other proteomics challenges and perhaps other female graduate students.) Since relieving Delmar Vecsey of his senior research associate duties, Nancy has acted pettier and more aloof than usual. I believe she applies radium to her fangs each morning for authoritative emphasis.

"I'm taking everyone in the lab aside," she discloses, "to inform them that I've promoted Gene Napolitano to the position of senior research associate. I'm confident you'll extend him your full cooperation."

"I guess there's nothing quite like being named 'Gene' to predestine one for success in biotech." I make a minimal attempt to conceal my lingering low morale. "Good ol' Sleepy Gene."

Nancy narrows her eyes. "We don't use disparaging terms to refer to fellow employees in this company."

I snort. "Sleepy Gene and Skinny Jean refer to themselves as such; it helps avoid confusion."

"That doesn't give you the right to make references which might be interpreted as offensive." She leans forward. "You can't be surprised that you weren't considered to be drafted for the lead job. Are you upset about it? You can't still be acting out about Delmar? If you are, power through it."

"In case you haven't noticed," I huff, "the lab has been in some disarray since its Del-ectomy. He was the most productive worker you had. Put him through sensitivity training if you must, but you need to invite him back. I wasted two hours yesterday afternoon searching for cell-culturing tools-"

"I still can't fathom why he so adamantly protected you,"

she interrupts me. "Off the record, didn't you have a more significant involvement in that despicable escapade? I asked Delmar 'Did he pay you off? What does he have on you?'" She flashes her cloying smile and rises like the Nancy gynbot but in business togs instead of cones. "He's demonstrated violent tendencies, and this workspace could not be secure with him here. Further, anyone who'd provide him with physical or electronic access to our property will be dismissed as surely and swiftly as he was."

"We're rather out of methyl cellulose media," I counter.

"Reagent? Aw, what can we do about that?" She taps her cheek. "How about: Submit a request to Gene to order more."

I tap my cheek. "It appears that he just did. The old bottle only contains a few drops. The new bottles are designated 'Mouse' or 'Human,' but I'm working on the rat line."

"You're setting up a CFC assay and aliquoting the media now?" She offers a moue. "You must know the 'Murine' media is used for both mouse and rat."

"The label on the old bottle said *Murine*, but the new bottle is marked *Mouse*. The 'Human' media is fortified. Would you recommend I try using *it* or should I miniaturize the assay?"

"Do you have any reason to expect that the 'Mouse' reagent won't be adaptable to rat cells?"

"I thought we tried that crossover a while back, and the media wouldn't support any cytokine stimulation. Del introduced some additive that finally worked, but I can't find anything that seems like it would be applicable now."

"I get your point, Lisle." She reseats herself. "An assay is too time-consuming and expensive to shortchange, so I'll recommend that Sandee postpone it and review best supply acquisition practices with Gene." She sighs. "Dissension is the first sign of a struggling enterprise." I take my cue to exit her chamber of the hive. "I liked Del too, but even you must recognize he had some personal issues."

"Who doesn't?" I place my hand on the doorknob.

"One last thing, Lisle." She waits for me to turn and face her. "Can I ever expect to receive any kind of apology for your part in the incident? A genuine one would be nice."

I pause for a moment. "You sound like my sensitivity shrink."

The Duchess's wry grin dissolves into a glare. "I guess you haven't progressed far enough in your training. We'll see what your counselor ultimately says about it."

"I do my job," I assert. "I earn my money. I tell the truth." I leave her office.

My immediate supervisor Sandee Perwadananya-Sridharan reports directly to Nancy. Like the Duchess, Sandee fashions herself a research scientist at heart and always seems to be steeped in projects of her own. She is currently completing a gene-drive study which requires her to flash-freeze fruit flies. Most of my interaction with her is electronic and terse.

I have a nervous tension headache when I arrive home. I fix Maynard and myself a dinner of sirloin and asparagus tips. Afterward, I recline on the living room davenport and turn on the jumbo TV but pay no attention to the programs. Trish coaxed me to replace all of the living room furniture except the coffee table shortly after she arrived. Maynard takes a worn bone and lies on the carpet beside me. I rub his back as he chews.

I reflect on my place in the universe. "The 27 credits I need to complete my B.S. saved me from getting a headache that wouldn't be gone when I wake up tomorrow. Nancy would've loved to dangle Del's old job under my nose until she enticed me to express my inner opportunist."

I review the day's session with Kisslinger objectively. I open the coffee table drawer and remove my high school yearbook. I remove the printed copy of my final letter from my first serious girlfriend Amie Ballard and reread it for the first time in several years. I'd remembered my official permanent rejection as unfair and unnecessarily harsh, but it now strikes me as insidiously calculated to inflict lasting emotional devastation. It succeeded spectacularly, as the wound remains tender 13 years later. In Amie's final analysis, I developed into a nuisance, I bored her and I was hopelessly inferior to at least two other men with whom she maintained relations. She could "hardly express how over we are."

In the immediate aftermath of Amie, I'd languished in the shifting shadows of my gloomy bedroom for many brutal hours. My viscera bore the burden of an increasing weight. The walls kept closing in tighter and tighter. All capacity for feeling beyond suffering faded; I felt my life force slowly oozing out and leaving me with no resistance. I was a shell, a hollow, indifferent onlooker at my own existence. I abided on the verge of tears, and though I didn't attempt to prevent myself from crying, I rarely did. I had trouble uttering a sound. I could hardly move. I was paralyzed with grief.

It was my first mature lesson in what sort of mercy the real world shows its innocents. I kept wondering how she could abandon me. Did she fail me or did I fail myself? Certainly, I'd failed to avert a state of complete misery. I could understand how the suggestion that she might love me would engender resentment, but why did she find the idea that I was worthy of loving her so insulting? For months after our breakup, I prayed that Amie would come to her senses, reconsider her values and beg me to take her back. The prayers continued even as I gradually stopped going to church to launch them.

Maynard returns me to the present with a whimper. I invite him to sniff the three pages of the misery missive before I slip them back into the yearbook. "Why do I keep it, old buddy? Because like everyone else, I sometimes revel in feeling like prince of the poor victims, and this provides me with documented justification." I return the yearbook to its drawer. "Beyond that, I thought it might be a useful reference tool in the future whenever I faced a first-magnitude personal crisis. If I could survive Amie's letter of dismissal, I could face anything else. But I dealt with the cancer deaths of my dad and mom without referencing it. And when Trish left me – it's been almost three months now – I never even considered it."

The only times I do consider it occur when my shrink spews suggestions which spark stark reminders and during my more and more infrequent nights at bars searching for a woman whose gaudy tattoo set is but a façade which hides her deep delicacy and sensitivity. I shut the coffee table drawer and take Maynard out through the park for his walk.

When we return home, the dog receives his treat and scampers out of the kitchen. He is probably repulsed by the vibrations of bitter discontent I'm still carrying. I saunter into the living room and stare in the direction of the television. "I ran into Amie five years ago and we talked. She's married with a kid. In retrospect, she feels I was basically a sympathy project, like a wounded animal she might rescue from the side of the road, and it's a credit to her that she would've entertained an attraction to someone like me." The dachshund lays a tennis ball at my feet. We head downstairs and purge our frustrations in twenty lively minutes of off-the-wall ball.

"WE PULLED UP in front of my date's house after the dance, she muttered 'Thanks, gonight' and hopped out of the car before it stopped moving." Each time I open my mouth in Dr. Rohr-Kisslinger's immersion tank, I feel as though I grow slightly smaller. "Not that I really cared about her, but it was a fitting conclusion to an appointment with catastrophe, and I'll never forget how long and lonely the final stretch of the car ride home was."

"Despite your most dire foreboding, you and your prom date didn't trip and tumble to the floor amid a chorus of ribald laughter, and you never even spilled your drink on her dress, although another girl wasn't quite so lucky." Kisslinger sighs. "We finally make significant headway against your intrinsic self-loathing. When did you recognize what a narrow margin for optimism your life holds?"

"Ironically," I offer, "I feel as though the peer group I have now respects me, whereas I never had that notion throughout my school years. Ironic because the friendships forged in childhood generally seem to be more enduring on some subliminal level. They have a dormant perpetuity about them, a purity of sorts, that can rarely be matched by relationships forged later in life that carry a political taint, or if you will, a bond of convenience, of commercial pragmatism, a cloud of social validation or even exploitation."

"Wow!" Kisslinger scoffs. "That's ass-backwards. The later in life a relationship evolves, the more sharply focused the commonality you're likely to share with the partner, the less circumstantial it is and the more control you have over its boundaries, so I disagree completely."

"That proves I'm right," I conclude.

"Does some distant little girl from algebra class still haunt you?" The counselor snickers. "Your behavioral probability cone expands to accommodate the stalker."

"It bothers me to make people who aren't toxic uncomfortable." I thoughtlessly deactivate my personal force field. "Growing up, it seemed I would develop a secret crush on each of my sister's friends. She eventually went to our mother and complained I was 'disturbing and distressing' them."

"So you feel that one or both of the female members of your immediate family shirked her responsibility as your procurement agent?" Kisslinger the scientist makes a blind stab. "Perhaps a contributory factor to your chronic underachievement in this area is your utilization of it as a feeble expression of resentment."

I hiss. "Playing on my desperation was always one of my

sister's favorite forms of recreation. A girl can commit the most awful transgressions against a boy and still consider herself a nice person. A boy conversely knows he's a detestable thing when he mistreats a girl but usually isn't all that bothered about it."

"Often," the doctor suggests, "the sister of a man with serious anger issues exhibits a rebellious streak of her own and may establish a pattern of drug abuse and promiscuity. Was she a wretched influence?"

"Far from it." I review Dinah guilelessly. "A couple of jocks tried to befriend me to get a closer shot at her. They swiftly decided it wasn't worth the effort. Hey, Doc, you know what the difference is between a four-star student-athlete and a four-star municipal bond?"

Kisslinger groans. "The bond ultimately matures?"

I snicker. "That's right, you counsel jocks, don't you? They must really consider you a nimrod. At any rate, Di was smart, poised, pretty and quite worthy of being the favored child. I'll admit I probably allowed her presence to satisfy some of my early craving for female companionship."

"At what age did you first molest her?" Kisslinger pounces.

"I never molested her," I assure him. "That's not how we rocked and rolled."

"She provoked indecent contact," the counselor perseveres.

"Try the radical therapeutic approach of paying attention," I appeal. "The closest thing we ever had to indecent contact was the time in our early teens when I barged in on her and two of her friends while they were naked. I believe trying on each other's killer clothes provided the underpinnings of their klatch. They screamed in concert and Di railed 'Get out of here, you pervert!' Always the good brother, I honored her wishes with little hesitation."

"And that's all there was," Kisslinger challenges.

"You've found a soft spot in my psyche, Sig." I expel a heavy breath. "There *was* more. Di was humiliated enough to seek me out for further revilement: 'Are you going to end up one of those creeps who goes peeping through knotholes and underneath stall doors in public restrooms?' I blithely replied, 'On the contrary, when you start working at a strip club you can now invite me down to see you without embarrassment because I've already seen you.'"

"I thought you were going to say you'd utilize your height to peep *over* the partitions," the doctor quips. "Earlier, you stated you 'craved' your sibling, so you must've felt some impulses toward her. What prevented you from acting on them?"

"Along with her other talents, Dinah was a martial artist. She'd say 'Go for me, Lisle' and have me on the ground in the wink of an eye."

"Were you paralyzed by fear of your father?" Kisslinger probes.

I snicker. "Apparently, I've said too much about my little sister because you seem to have developed some impulses of your own toward her. Is that your wife's picture on your desk? Pink is not her color. Nonetheless, let's try to redirect some untoward impulses toward *her*."

"My tolerance is not unlimited, Amonor," the doctor decrees. "I have no appreciation for wanton personal attacks on my family, even within the purview of a sick sense of humor. Do you understand?"

"Mnh," I acquiesce, "I just wonder what erratic thoughts and behaviors of your own that you sought to rationalize originally inspired you to venture into your chosen field? Is there a general form of defilement you wished to perpetrate against a particular pretty maid or vice versa?"

Kisslinger groans. "What misogynist's wormhole do you pull that one out of? I'll let you in on a secret: There's a great conspiracy of all women to deprive you of meaningful personal gratification. They get their jollies out of denying you all the pleasure that they have the power to give."

I emit a sarcastic cackle. "I can only take you in low doses, Doctor."

Kisslinger contributes a sophisticated snort. "Let's consider a more plausible explanation for why you may be your own worst saboteur in affairs of the heart." His Notemaster lights up. "When I confronted you in one of our initial exchanges about the bigotry which colors so many of your attitudes, you mentioned that your closest friend since elementary school is a gay Jewish man. I would expect this individual to exhibit a firmer command in negotiating life's quandaries than you. Does he have an athletic body, too? An endearing smile? Bedroom eyes? Perhaps your real problem lay clogged in the filter of rigid cultural taboos imposed by your professed religiosity. Could it be that you need to do a little less judging and a bit more searching for yourself?"

A moment passes before I realize the annoyed hoot that fills the room was emitted by me. "There are two kinds of romantic partners, swami, and they're both women: the ones I dream about and the ones I meet. You may maintain that if I do a more thorough job of looking for my soul mate, I'll eventually find her. And you may be uniquely on point, although when I do make contact, convincing *her* that she'd be doing herself a favor by doing *me* one will be the ticklish part."

"Are you still groping in dark romantic terms or speaking spiritually?" Kisslinger sighs. "Would you prefer to worship a god who's evil or insane?"

"Which, Doctor, is that the option?" I inadvertently rub salt in my eyes. "Shall we revisit your grim farcical analogy where God and Satan are gangsters battling for the territory of my soul? I can't imagine why Satan would bother with someone knee-high to a peon like me. What sort of disorder would you ascribe to him? Or do you believe he's female?"

Kisslinger hisses. "So we leave your unanswered prayers as something untouchable concealed beneath your security blanket. And we don't dare consider them as the main reason you don't seem to be coming out ahead. You vitiate your scant chance for success by counting on devices of no avail."

I manage a frenetic afternoon at work juggling transposons and reconditioned junk DNA. I arrive home with a throbbing headache. It's becoming a quotidian condition. I fix Maynard and myself a hearty chuck roast. I don't bother to turn on the TV. After supper I stare through my living room jumbo picture window at a nameless little girl across the street amusing herself twirling a laser toy. Multicolored lights dominated by reds and yellows enswathe her as she hops, skips and runs through a series of customized game rules. In negative space, my dearly departed heartthrob Trish Skinner rises from the ash heap of my memory and takes her reserved parking place on the pedestal of my mind's eye. She poses pertly, hands on hips, one bronze, muscular leg forward, toes pointed slightly out, head held high framed by long sandy blonde hair tossed over her shoulder in a braided ponytail. I once thought her sparkling green eyes accented by dark brows and a gleaming, ever-ready thin-lipped smile suggested an unlimited capacity for unconditional affection. I'd never given much consideration to anyone's apparel before, including my own, but I enjoyed speculating on what colors and textures she'd exhibit each night when I returned home to her. I added a few more prime numbers to her collection in order to more fully appreciate the contours of her fabulous form.

I choke on my misplaced ardor. Yet the vision deepens. Sweat glistening on her sleek arms, the flimsy yellow tank top with the blue star on the chest clings to her high, full breasts and hard, tight abs. Her movements were the raw power and sweeping grace of the dance of life. She exercised constantly, and as close as I've always held my energy and comfort, I rarely missed an opportunity to join a workout and help her squeeze my money's worth out of the bright, shiny weight room we constructed in the basement. She tabbed the renovated space "excruciation station." On the Saturday night that I recall as the beginning of our two-week-long crucible of truth, I was rambling with rare inspiration on such topics as religion and existentialism: "Let yourself love something, and you'll find to the extent that you love it, your emptiness will fade to fulfillment."

"Things slow at the lab?" She seated herself at the pec deck. "It sounds like you've been reading more of the romantic poets."

"I've been reading some of the romantic scientists," I countered. The suppression of my urge to wrap my arms around her and hold her caused me physical pain. "Trish," I challenged, "did you ever evaluate exactly why you work out?"

"If it isn't slightly obvious, I'm slightly insulted." Grunting copiously, she executed a set of heavy flyes. "I like to feel I can take care of myself."

"There's no doubt about that." I stood before her with arms akimbo. "I just wish you weren't always so eager to prove it." I considered her extensive resume as I watched her complete another set. Stints as a dance instructor and massage therapist had preceded her gig as a personal trainer at the boutique health club and yoga studio that provided the backdrop for our introduction.

"I don't believe in love," she contended. "I believe in strength."

I laughed. "I don't believe that."

Trish began her third set of flyes. I stuck my head between the opening padded bars and planted a soft, familial kiss on her forehead. In the nearly seven months she'd lived with me, kisses like this and light hugs were the extent of our physical contact. In the periodic prods where I'd convey my desire for an escalation of connectedness, she'd tout our relationship as a living model of the perfect platonic union between the sexes. I stole another quick kiss to the cheek. As I placed a third kiss on her lips, she sped up her motion and caught the tip of my not insignificant nose between the closing bars of the apparatus.

"Stop kidding around, Lisle," she demanded, springing to her feet. "We just re-established how serious I am about my workouts." She grabbed her towel and dabbed at the perspiration on her face as she moved to the super pullover station. I performed two sets of flyes and caught up with her at the squat rack. "Just another lost weekend, hmm?" she lamented.

In case my hurt feelings weren't manifest, I confessed, "I'm happy to just be here with you."

Trish grabbed a kettlebell. As she swung it, her attitude seemed to mellow. Between sets, she recalled how as a teenager she'd crashed her vehicle and called her brother for roadside assistance. Cold and bleeding, she'd waited and waited for him to come to her aid while he stopped off to smoke pot with his pals. "I would've dropped everything for you!" I swore. She handed me the kettlebell and I dropped that for emphasis. She laughed and we embraced. She ended the hold much sooner than I would've liked. She strapped on the gravity boots and asked me to boost her to the chin bar. I squeezed her hips and situated her in position for inverted twisting situps. She mechanically performed more repetitions than I could count. She rested and executed another marathon set. I assisted her return to the floor and requested that she stabilize my hips for hanging leg raises.

"Sure, Lisle?" Her eyes revealed no less concern than amusement. "This is your first workout in how many days? You don't want to overtrain."

I leapt and caught the chin bar. "It's time for a bolder approach." I clenched my teeth and summoned the wherewithal to repeatedly bring my knees up to my chest without bringing my dinner back into my throat.

"Try to keep your legs straighter," she admonished, "and get the negative on the way down!" I paused and performed another set with better form until she pronounced it finished. I dropped from the bar and clung to her greedily. "Great job!" she proclaimed. Gasping and unsteady, I released her and stumbled backward. I dropped to my knees and transferred the gravity boots to my own feet. "You're dead serious, Lisle?" she kept repeating.

I inverted myself beneath the chin bar and somehow convinced my tortured abdominal muscles to roughly mimic the movements she'd executed. The pain was as intense as anything I'd experienced outside of a dentist's chair. I disengaged from the chin bar and landed on my feet. Lightheaded, I held Trish for support. "I am so impressed, Lisle," she cooed. I gazed at her as intently as I ever had. I pressed my lips forward, and she offered me her cheek. I took her chin between my thumb and forefinger and gently turned her face back to me. Parted slightly, my lips smoothly glided onto hers. Our kiss was penetrating, and we held it for one count longer than any friendly union could've endured. "Too many endorphins," she gushed, backing away and retrieving her towel.

"I needed to kiss you," I asserted.

"I need a shower," she murmured.

"Why don't we take our showers together?" I weakly snapped at opportunity.

Her smile disappeared. "With, ah, what in mind?"

"Getting clean," I playfully ventured.

"Stay tuned for our next episode," she resisted the invitation. She left me in excruciation station with a broad grin on my face. I had more than enough discipline not to risk the spiritual spoil of a closely guarded dream for several moments of instant sublime physical gratification. The momentum of tonight's events would bring a tomorrow that belonged completely to me. I needed this woman. I needed to hold her, our limbs symbolic of our lives, firmly and hopelessly entangled. I needed to possess her, for this was the food and drink of my forlorn soul. The flush I'd been drawing toward for over eight months had finally arrived. The dawn of my winning season was at hand.

A mutual sciatica and conflict of work schedules kept Trish and me inactive for the next few days, but Thursday evening arrived wide open with potential. I left work a little early to prepare an epic culinary masterpiece of stuffed chicken Valentino, Caesar salad and vanilla crème brulee in anticipation of the evolution of our relationship. No sooner had Trish walked in the door and remarked on the pleasant aroma wafting from the kitchen than Maynard barked and the doorbell rang. A man delivered a box of flowers. The one time I'd sent her flowers six months ago she'd been irritated by my frivolity. This time she voraciously shed the wrapping and withdrew a dozen long-stemmed pink roses sent by Bruce Neichi. "Oh," she exclaimed, "aren't they gorgeous?"

More than a mere mortal chiropractor, Bruce Neichi fashioned himself a fair amateur hypnotist and magician. He'd floated the idea of staging an act and taking it on the road with Trish as his comely assistant. She caressed the flowers, admiring them for several minutes. "I'm a bit surprised," I finally uttered, "that you don't consider such a gift a little trite and cliché."

"Ordinarily I might, but context is everything." Her resplendent smile didn't lose a lumen. "And how often does your doctor send you anything but a bill?"

I nodded. "I can't help but wonder how often your doctor sends anything besides a bill to any of his clients besides you?"

Trish eyed me with fresh irritation. "Bruce was concerned he hurt me yesterday. He really got my attention, but it feels good now. You sure do know how to smother a tender moment, don't you?"

"They're lovely flowers," I conceded. "I'll fetch you a vase and get back to our dinner." I returned to the kitchen. "Just remember if he wants to saw you in half how heavy his sleight of hand is." I wonder if she heard me.

With a bit of prodding, Trish politely commended me on my foray into the epicurean zone. But she added that the effort was completely unnecessary. The massive rainbow vase supporting twelve pink roses that obscured our view of each other significantly reduced our conversation. "Let's work this off to the classics tonight" was the best banter I could manage. "Beatles, Stones, Pistols?"

"A little too much Pinot Grigio for that." She raised her glass. "You know, I think I might try painting again. I'd love to capture these flowers. If you don't mind, I'd like to drive over to the crafts shop tonight to stock up on some watercolors."

"Better draw quick before they change back into a cane."

Trish left a considerable portion of her dinner untouched and carried the vase into her bedroom. An hour later, she took the Charger to the crafts shop and purchased art supplies. I took Maynard for another walk, and after we returned, I overwatered my goodly collection of quirky houseplants and entered a state of suspended animation in front of the television. I retired early.

A day and a half later, I took Trish to the D.M.V. and we transferred the title of the Charger to her. I received a big hug on the spot for the surprise gift. Later, however, she again thwarted my plan for a joint workout by informing me she'd embarked on a strict "every third day" exercise schedule to accommodate her newfound interest in the graphic arts. Consequently, she wouldn't be ready for further training action until Monday.

Shuffled and reconfigured, our work schedules the next week proved hopelessly incompatible, and I only enjoyed her company in snippets. She drove to La Crosse on Thursday to visit her brother and didn't return until late Sunday afternoon. I cobbled together an impromptu shrimp scampi supper with tiramisu dessert, and we agreed to meet again beneath the bright lights of the workout chamber.

Trish had begun exercising while I finished cleaning up the kitchen, and her body glistened with sweat when I entered excruciation station. Breathing hard, she looked nothing less than spectacular in a black headband and new two-piece red-and-black-pinstripe exercise outfit. We traded uneasy gazes. We'd run painfully short of conversation at the dinner table and the residue of reticence remained. "I really admire your work," I repeated my first words to her at hot yoga after she caught me ogling her.

She forced a smile. "I just did 100 inverted twisties to keep your dinner from sticking to my hips." She seated herself at the preacher bench and began performing barbell curls.

I stood behind her. "I think *I'll* start tonight with a little prayer for some big biceps."

She relinquished the bench. "No more holy wars here, please."

I added a pair of paltry plates and grabbed the cambered bar. We alternated for several sets of curls, grunting and groaning over the soft rock seeping out of our audio system. She strode over to her mat sucking heavy oxygen. She lay on her back, hands behind her head with chest heaving. The clean lines of her jaw and shins glowed as she performed leg extensions. Transfixed by her magnificence, I fought to finish my final set of curls. She returned to the arms department. "Through with the easy curl?" She flashed a winsome smile. "I want to do some skull-crushers."

"I'll hand you the bar." An adrenaline rush crystallized my adoring demeanor.

She nodded and lay on the flat bench. I handed her the bar and kissed her on the forehead. "What are you doing?" she challenged.

"Offering you raw encouragement." I ached to wrap my pumped arms around her.

"I don't need it." Trish isolated her triceps in three sets of lying French press and handed the bar back to me. She sat up on the bench as I placed the bar on the floor. I nimbly plunked myself beside her, even though the bench stub was only long enough to accommodate one of my buttocks. I rubbed her triceps and back, clamped my hand on her hip and kissed the corner of her mouth. She fixed me with a wary pout.

My heart raced furiously as I stared into her emerald eyes. "Trish, let's relive what happened between us in our last workout together." I moved my hand to her shoulder. "Saturday night two weeks ago."

She grimaced. "Fortunately for us both, nothing happened." She patted my hand. "Saturday night two weeks ago." She flashed an annoyed smile. "Inversion flooded our brains with too much blood."

My hand glided gently down her arm. "Blood flow fuels attraction, and exercise fuels blood flow." The full weight of the pressure point alighted on us. "It's the vicious exercycle of life." I felt the dread of a climber who loses his nerve to the height. "Of all the muscles, my heart aches most, that I don't yet possess your tender embrace."

"Lisle, save it," she growled.

I pressed onward. "Let's hear more from your dorphs." I guided my fingertips gently over her abdomen and my lips engaged hers.

"*No way!!*" She launched herself to her feet, knocking me to the floor. "I'm out of here!" She marched to the chamber exit.

"Trish, come back!" I scrambled to my knees. "I pledge to never again mix personal feelings with our workouts!"

She backtracked to excruciation station. "There are no personal feelings! It's high time I moved on." Her footsteps resounded heavily on the stairs.

I scurried after her. "Stupid of me to try to take advantage of you that way!" I followed her into her bedroom and protested while she packed. "Trish, please," I repeated, "this is crazy!" I ultimately abandoned any pretense that I wasn't pleading. "You mean so much to me! I love you!"

"I may not know what love is, but I sure know what it isn't." She gathered her bags and faced me squarely. "If you really loved me, you'd champion my quest to find contentment, whether that includes you or not." She cast a blank sideways glance at Maynard and proceeded to the garage.

"Would you cast off even a friend so discourteously?" I hustled after her. "Give yourself a real chance with me!"

She shoved her bags into the back seat of the Charger. "I'm trying very hard to make you understand this without being cruel." She climbed behind the wheel. "We were just housemates, passing acquaintances. We're nothing anymore." She shut the door and started the engine.

"I'd devote my life to pleasing you!" I pressed my palms against the driver's door but left no tear streaks. "Doesn't that mean anything?"

She lowered the window slightly. "Would it satisfy you if I'd temporarily suffer you in order to take your house and half of everything you own?" She kept her eyes in the mirror. "Please cooperate when I send for my tanning equipment and the rest of my stuff." She shot down the driveway in reverse and paused in the street. I believe she extended me the courtesy of a subtle wave before she roared into the night.

I recall staring into the empty space for a while before staggering back into the house and plunking myself into the fashionable low-rider chair. I'd fought progressively heavier resistance until I'd achieved failure. I'd gotten all the negative on the way down and had no place lower left to sink.

I return to the low-rider chair once more. Maynard stands before me with pleading eyes. I lift him onto my lap. He licks my face and rests his head on my arm. "That's the trouble with people, boy." I scratch his neck with my free hand. "You don't keep them on a leash, and they leave you." I stroke his back. I always try to pet him at least 15 times as a ritual invocation for a long, full life. "I wonder if Trish has totaled the Charger yet. Maybe she's been reduced to sleeping on the street in her tanning bed. More likely, she's comfortably nestled in the capable arms of a real man like Bruce Neichi." The dog eyes me quizzically as I expel a bitter cackle. "My heart rejoices at the lifting of the burden of her love. It freed me to appreciate the value of the real love I receive."

I ENTER THE King Kryczek & Rohr-Kisslinger office for my seventh sensitivity training session, and Ivan greets me with "Bowwow rarf rarf."

"Is that a tracking transmitter around his neck?" I ask the receptionist about the thick black collar that the bird always sports.

"It's supposed to make his speech more distinct." She fixes me with a moue. "Dr. Rohr-Kisslinger may not be in the best mood today."

"As opposed to?" I am more intrigued that the parrot wears an audio processor to auto-correct his diction.

"He considered canceling you." Her hair has been rearranged in dreadlocks. "Dr. Kryczek was almost killed in a motorcycle accident last night and is in a coma."

I foolishly reject the opportunity to cancel myself, and minutes later I'm in the immersion tank fielding an onslaught of Kisslinger's affronts as an applied reaction to his standard deductions. "You seem to be on a hypercritical mission today, swami," I chuckle.

"That's because you view every interaction as somehow threatening." The counselor tosses a zinc lozenge wrapper into the tank. "Were you bullied more in school than you've been willing to admit?"

Circumstances compel me to submit. "I was continually assaulted by the postmodernist culture and politically correct agenda."

"Yet another deflection," Kisslinger snarls. "I envision you slinking home at the end of each school day with your nose practically down to your knees, curling into a fetal position on your family's vibrating couch in the basement, clutching your Mighty Mouse pillow to your belly and sobbing."

"Did you say 'fatal position'?" I flip the wrapper back at the doctor. "How are we going to replace Dr. Kryczek if he doesn't snap out of his herbaceous funk? The most important qual for the newbie must be a surname that starts with 'K.' I favor a recherche, polysyllabic name like 'Kwatinetz' or 'Kobradanz.' Or even something more *kosmopolitan* like 'Kapudnik.' We can bump you up in the shrinking order too, so it's King Kisslinger & Kapudnik. Otherwise, I had a high school classmate named Kiki Kuecherer, who was a total space case and would fit in here like a setscrew. If she doesn't have a degree-"

"Shut your ass!" Kisslinger rises. "Shut your antagonistic, refractory ass! I'd declare your case unsalvageable and dismiss you as a client except for the optimism and skill I believe I possess as a clinician."

I gasp. "It might interest you to know that the other day at work I gave you a recommendation. My associate Skinny Jean said she knows someone who needs professional counseling, so I began describing how we drown our sorrows in these troubled waters. The concept of the immersion tank fascinated her. I told her it rendered what we do in therapy meaningful if not reasonable." I let Kisslinger twist in the wind for several moments awaiting further accolades.

"I keep searching for something to connect you to your humanity," Kisslinger crabs, "and coming up empty." He reseats himself. "I feel an urgency to attenuate your self-destructive tendencies and by extension your desire to harm others. Because if you have a masculine bone in your body, sooner or later you'll turn the aggression of your self-loathing outward."

"Last night I had an encounter with a huge house centipede," I report. "The sight of it running across my bedroom floor startled me. It was the size of a toy panzer, the largest I'd ever seen! And I made a mental note to bring up a trap from the basement to capture the myriapod and release it outside. This morning I stepped into the shower, turned on the water, and the beast emerged in the backwash from the drain, swirling around in the whirlpool. I propelled it out of its death spiral with my washcloth and gently conveyed it out of the shower and onto dry floor tile. Too late, I lamented, as I surveyed its twisted, motionless body on the washcloth. But when I emerged from behind the curtain at the end of my attenuated shower, the centipede had disappeared."

"So you're a domestic hero, a veritable lifesaver!" The doctor's animus hasn't been defused. "These self-justifying accounts of light wildlife rescue that you're fond of citing don't demonstrate any heightened sensitivity, compassion or overall respect for life. By showing undue regard for the welfare of beasts, you take the opportunity to passively devalue human life." He offers a punctuating grunt.

"The consensus of the ids, egos and superegos of all my personalities, scullion, is that you talk out of your ass even more than the average expert." I force diplomatic guffaws. "But then we're an orgulous mob completely devoid of altruism and good works."

Kisslinger's Notemaster lights up. "Many of us grow calluses to protect us from the pokes and pricks of reality, but you erect weatherproof barriers to connecting with other people." The counselor rises again. "In our society, a man is not allowed to lose control over the hopelessness of his situation. In order to better position you to achieve transference from moping to coping, we need to resolve the underlying emotional trauma fueling your inherent undesirability. I think it would be productive if you submitted to a brain scan. It wouldn't flabbergast me if your anterior cingulate cortex is freakishly hypertrophied. That might help explain why you're habitually overwhelmed by life's basic challenges."

I nod. "I'm sure such a scan would be profitable for at least one of us."

"To take it a step further," Kisslinger persists, "you'd be a prime candidate for transcranial magnetic stimulation. By inducing electrical currents in your A.C.C., we might effectively improve your temperament."

"Happy currents make happy capillaries?" I surmise. "Mighty technological advances enter the abstruse realm of progressive mind maintenance."

"It's astounding that someone who works in a lab could be so unacquainted with basic scientific methodology," Kisslinger snaps. "Consult the peer-reviewed literature. Your inability to withstand the tension of conflict should force you to recognize your vulnerability and insufficiency. People generally want to believe that they're good custodial citizens of their world and that their acts will ultimately serve the highest of ideals. Most people really want to be like most other people."

"Life is a giant banana peel," I contribute. "We all slip and fall time and again, but as long as we keep getting up, we can't be defined as losers."

"Apologists who practice self-deception are the greatest losers of all." The counselor tosses another zinc lozenge wrapper into the tank. "If you're a walking collage of flaws and inadequacies mired in a putrid cesspool at the bottom of the dominance hierarchy, you'll likely be oblivious to precisely that set of properties necessary to take the first step toward climbing upward. Every sticky nisus you make will be in vain, so you can only watch powerlessly as your irrelevant life grows in purposelessness and abject worthlessness. You may have a transition metal deficiency."

I return home from my sensitivity training session feeling unbearably itchy, so I grab a quick shower before heading back to work. I lose my comb in the toilet, rinse it and leave it soaking in the sink. I emerge from the bathroom naked and flip on the track lights. Napping on the living room davenport beneath the picture window, Maynard opens his eyes. Clutching a tube of corticosteroid cream, I approach and offer my customary two-forefinger, big, friendly wave. A woman passing in front of the house pushing a stroller with another toddler beside her happens to be peering into the window. Her features contorted with horror, she returns my wave.

I arrive at work to find my associate Kelly pulling a cart down the hallway. The cart is loaded with apothecary jars containing human brains in formalin. She is engaged in a woolly study of rogue proteins and GABA receptors designed to compare the neurogenesis of individuals as affected by environmental factors such as exercise, injury and exposure to pollutants. "Kelly Shelley," I cast a teasing reference to Mary Wollstonecraft.

She chuckles politely. "The monster's in each of us." She points toward the stairwell. "Did you see that the huddle has been revived for three?"

"Today?" Last Friday, Sandee postponed our monthly team meeting scheduled for today. She regularly postpones these bashes or cancels them outright.

"Nancy is conducting it," Kelly affirms. "Some policy change in the works, Lisle, so look sharp." She pulls her wagon onward. "Look alive."

I leave Kelly at the cold vacuum chamber and proceed into the main wet lab. I discover two mysterious toaster-size white boxes on my desk along with a long-nose tongs, a pair of purple gloves and a penetrometer with an 8 mm tip.

"Lisle, you've arrived." Senior Research Associate Gene Napolitano appears beside me. "New project to test daily stool samples in order to tailor probiotic supplements to the individual." He taps one of the boxes. "I brought up your first two boxes from the first three skids of these down in H-4." He snickers. "Sorry for sticking you with the shit job, chief, but somebody has to do the dirty work."

"Sandee's orders?" I rub my churning gut.

"I forwarded her instructions to your inbox." Sleepy Gene touches my computer screen. "You can bitch in today's huddle. I was extended some latitude on who to assign it to." He eyes me intently. "If you really don't think you're up to it, I'll let you pull rank. On your say-so, I'll reassign it to Leah."

"I'm not vile enough to dump it on anyone else." I force a smile of absolution.

I tackle my new duty with a vengeance, and I'm grateful when the hour of three lends me relief in the refuge of the windowless conference room on the second floor. Mercifully, the huddle is to consist only of my Healthspan team. The meetings that Nancy conducts often combine Sandee's nutrition-oriented Healthspan team with Logan Dondorp's slightly larger ten-associate Healthpath team, which concerns itself with treatments targeting specific allergies and pathological conditions. A few pursuits involve overlap, but there is generally little interaction or lateral movement between the two groups. If my formal education taught me anything, it's that lab productivity is inversely proportional to the number of people directly involved in any exercise. Before the meeting begins, the topic of conversation turns to my new project. "It's about finding the ideal U.L.," I verify, "daily nutrient intake limits."

"Last year we did that genetic analysis of cow gut biome to help breed low-methane livestock," Kelly recalls. "The food diaries were undoubtedly far more reliable."

I rub my neck. "I'm sure the moo cows themselves could've kept more diligent records than what I'm up against now. Then, too, good nutritionists and climatologists are every bit as talented as anthropologists and psychologists in finding ways to fill in the problematic gaps in their research."

"Study participants wore audit apps," Nancy assures us. "There is no ideology in science."

I nod. "It's not as if a fundamental obstacle to scientific progress today is confirmation bias."

Sleepy Gene stretches. "Isn't confirmation bias what people who cling to the Catholic Church have?"

Sandee initiates the proceedings by remarking that there's no cause to be alarmed by Nancy's presence and promptly cedes control to her. "Our original fundamental mission never changes," the Duchess reminds us, "to advance life-enhancing innovation and life-extending structural refinements, and to continuously broaden our focus to make a meaningful impact in those endeavors. But we're always looking for additional revenue streams to help justify our investment in our state-of-the-art resources. So our business model evolves. One of the prime changes that might affect the Healthspan team is in the area of animal research. Our policy that we do not conduct vivisections of vertebrates is under review. Some of our researchers have requested the liberty to design live-animal studies on more sophisticated organisms. That might include the task of performing euthanasia ourselves."

A collective groan suffuses the table like a mushroom cloud. "I flatly refuse to even kill a frog," Leah decrees.

"Amen," Skinny Jean contributes. "No mice to slice is the tech spec that attracted me to this company."

"Then you better keep on my good side," Sleepy Gene quips.

"I feel your resistance," Nancy responds. "Let's hope it's a non-issue. We're also considering soliciting contract research and performing medical tests." Rumbles of objection flow around the table. "I admit some of the tasks involved in that wouldn't exactly be glamorous." She flashes a smile at me. "As Lisle was reminded today, a number of the projects we already engage in aren't always sexy. But we need to maintain a steady cashflow in this fragile funding environment to support our hard research, and we need the full commitment of the entire team to achieve our company goals. We have engineers working on efficient workflow systems that reduce repetitive-motion activities with expanded capacity. This change will probably affect the Healthpath team more."

"We could just automatically assign the more disagreeable tasks to Lisle," Sleepy Gene suggests.

"This is all a ruse to make us volunteer ourselves as experiment subjects." I smirk at Napolitano. "To start, we'll follow Gene around and corner the market in food coma studies." I elicit a few titters.

Sleepy Gene scowls. "Postprandial hypotension," he utters, "is as real as any external condition and no more appropriate to joke about." Nancy strains to refrain from fomenting further discord.

"I must've been a wicked thing in a past life," I submit. "Nearly as wicked as I am in this one." I get zero laughs but several curious stares. The moment leaves me strangely struck by how much I miss Delmar.

I stop at a Mexican restaurant after work for some takeout. I arrive home and place burrito segments in Maynard's dish. The dachshund consumes them voraciously along with the dry dog food I'd left him earlier. In the bathroom, I find the house centipede floating dead in the sink.

I sit in my secure low-rider chair and pat Maynard's head as I eat a burrito and balance a plate of rice and beans on my lap. "I'll be 34 in November, boy. It gets harder each year to make new friends. Not that I really recall the last time I felt any human companion was perfectly content to just be with me. To count on a human is to set yourself up for a disappointment." I gently scratch the dog's ear, avoid looking into his penetrating brown eyes and finish the burrito without giving him another piece. "See? Yet you'll never abandon me, will you?" He wags his tail magnanimously.

"I DREAMED AS a young man of having the world at my feet," I explore goals and objectives in response to Dr. Rohr-Kisslinger's prodding. "Now older, wiser and wearier, I mostly want the world out of my face."

Kisslinger grunts like a Russian weightlifter. "Do you have any idea of how manque that sounds? How pathetic?"

"And it's accomplished without a degree!" I slap myself on the back. "I don't mind the company I keep when I'm alone. I like the uncluttered space and the stillness. No one to groan or gripe, no one to impress, no competing demands for my attention." I fish a chunk of something like charcoal out of the tank. "My age of innocence extended into early adulthood. We all still believed in dreams, miracles and things bigger than ourselves. I could motivate myself with the vision of a distant day when I'd encounter the human subspecies who'd not only accept me but actually value me. The search for a group of superior intellects able to see through a red patch of skin and look past a modest manner continues."

"The superficial excuses continue." Kisslinger scratches his scraggly beard with disturbing gusto. "You are the center of your own universe. Yet here's an insight that you should be able to appreciate. You're aberrantly labile, a tool as such, a microbe greedily awaiting the particular phage which will lyse it. You pamper oppressions of your own device."

"I've always been easily humiliated," I concede. "Once upon a time, in fact, it seemed as though the driving passion of my existence was to prevent myself from being humiliated."

"And you're still very much like that on the subconscious level," the counselor croaks. "As we interact now, I can practically smell your overactive adrenal glands. You reek of cortisol, of hormones associated with stress. Animals, it is believed, know it as the stench of fear." He snorts. "Is it confronting what you perceive as wasted potential or squandered opportunities that terrifies you more?"

"Perhaps it's confronting how insignificant the incidents that I let affect me so deeply seem now." I rub my neck. "I recall taking a few friends I made shortly after high school into a restaurant where a former classmate of mine turned out to be working as a waitress. Let's call her Jacquie because that was her name."

"Have you tried culminating your showers," Kisslinger interrupts, "with the confidence-building, sustained cold burst I've recommended? Stoutly remaining stationary for the duration required to consume two raw eggs?"

"In retrospect," I persevere, "the people who joined all the clubs and lingered on the fringe of the in-crowd in high school seem to be the most terminally noxious. Jacquie was that sort of self-starter, kind of a maundering, high-maintenance gadabout. I interacted with her some in school, but I must've brushed too close because her attitude toward my affable initiatives grew dark and resistant." I press my fists together. "I spotted her as the hostess led my group to be seated at our table. She eyed me blankly, and I genially offered, 'So this is where all the cool kids hang out?' When she didn't respond, one of my companions suggested, 'That sounds like a definite affirmative.' Jacquie came over to wait on our table, and I repeated myself: 'This is where the cool kids hang out?' She muttered, 'It used to be.' As she drew a couple of yuks at my expense, I said, 'They hired you to chase them off?' She pointed straight at me, looked back at the hostess and stated loud and clear enough for everyone four tables over to hear: 'I am not serving this dweeb!' And indeed the waitress working the other side of the room soon egregiously expanded her territory to include my party."

The doctor emits a woebegone chuckle at my expense. "The plow doesn't stop to bury the dead. Now older and wiser, you can probably empathize with the frustration of a live wire who devoted copious energy to self-promotion when faced with a situation which would render her ostensibly subservient to a nudnik who took zero trouble to gain social status. But don't allow the affable initiative to wither as your viable deterrent against overt hostility or open scorn. You'll be amazed by how few people resent you for it."

"I believe you'd be amazed by how many do. I should've leaned into Jacquie's progressive mental cruelty with my own."

I wince. "Relationships have always drained me. I always feel as though I put far more into them than I get back from the other person. I see everyone to whom I wish to remain connected as a raw egg that I'm juggling, and the more eggs I have in the air, the more psychic energy I have to expend to keep the relationships from going splat."

Kisslinger's Notemaster lights up. "At some point during your counseling program, a stress analysis will be required. Introducing a subject to mild physical discomfort is often an effective preliminary step in behavior modification. With your approval, I'd like to consign you to a focused slow drip protocol or expose you to a reduced temperature bath in an upcoming session to provide you with additional motivational stimulus for improved cognitive function."

"I should think that the key to inducing an urgency to unburden oneself here in the overflow basin, Doc, is to keep the heat *up*." I press my lips beneath the water surface and blow. "Most of your clientele must urinate or worse in this tank, don't they? Bodies dump wind, even capsize and retch? Hey, is Dr. Kryczek still inanimate?"

Kisslinger hisses. "Is your brain putting out another vacancy announcement?"

I interpret the counselor's unresponsiveness as an affirmation. "Kryczek is likely in a thoroughly contented state of being within the transcendental womb of his own misery possessed with the weakest of wills to return to the self-destructive daily squabbles of petty office politics."

"Are daily petty squabbles actually an apt description of your own work environment?" the doctor pounces with panache.

"Mondays arrive with no mercy." I retain the urge to be candid. "Every day my job sucks a little more of my life through a straw. It seems that the ever-deafening solitude that falls on my ever-frailer shoulders finds its epicenter in the drudgery of my duties."

"That's bad," Kisslinger commits.

"That's brilliant," I commend him.

"Would you like me to refer you to someone else for a fresh start on your sensitivity training? Maybe a sparring partner? If you want my help, don't be such an irritable wart." The doctor is left groping for patience. "What keeps you in the game? What do you find quintessentially rewarding?"

"I have no desire to jump out of an airplane or drive fast," I admit. "My thrills come a little more elegantly, like observing an ant repel a much larger wasp in a territorial dispute on a rotten apple."

"Why are you afraid to operate a car again?" the counselor challenges. "Are there short-term memory problems you can recall? Trying to function under the influence of alcohol or drugs?"

"My wallet has a secret compartment for a syringe, but I wouldn't say I have a drug problem." I sigh. "I have stimulus sensitive myoclonus, so I probably wouldn't be a good candidate for water drop torture, and it might not be the best idea to suspend me in a snow cone either. My primary care physician has prescribed apomorphine. She originally thought I had an overactive dive reflex, but now she believes I'm the only known human poikilotherm. Whatever the real reason, you can believe I'm extremely special."

"It has always been your burning desire to stand apart," Kisslinger concludes. "You hoped for it in the worst way. So now you do stand apart, and in the worst way. You not only find yourself unable to fill the role of the hero in your own life but you serve as the default object of ridicule for any personality with an insecurity issue. When the lack of support you've cultivated ultimately causes you to completely implode, you better hope I'm still standing by with shovel ready to pick up the pieces."

As I reach the door to exit the King Kryczek & Rohr-Kisslinger office, Ivan screeches "Why can't birds talk? *Ayaak!* Nothing to say."

Gayle Spaatz has expressed a desire for my company several times since last weekend. He picks me up at work, and a heavy metallic clunk emanates from the rear of his Honda. "The car got messed up when I was nearly involved in a road rage event," he explains. "I'll fill you in on the deets later."

"Please tell me," I implore him, "it didn't involve a motorcycle."

"No, but you won't believe who it did involve," he snarls. "Who it *does* involve."

"Not Trish in my Charger?" I exhaust my complimentary cornucopia of guesses, and Gayle digresses through trivial problems he's recently encountered in his day job as a bill collector. He returns to his report of road rage only after we're securely seated at Pfixx's and we've been served our customary drinks and meister burgers. "I'm traveling from New Berlin into the city, and this carload of young punks is tailgating me all the way up Beloit Road. They pass me on the right in West Allis, and that's fine. But when we get to the light at 92nd to turn left, I'm directly behind them. They strike up a conversation with the guy in the car beside them. The light turns green, and the car they were talking to takes off, but they hardly move. There's an incline there, so I can't tell if they're waiting for oncoming traffic, and I wait patiently behind them. They finally turn left – there was no oncoming traffic – and I get stopped by the red light. I catch up to them again, and traffic is packed tight when we arrive at the Greenfield Avenue stoplight. The punks are behind two other cars in the left lane and I'm right behind them. The light turns green, and the first two cars pull away, but the punks just sit there. Traffic is flowing in the right lane, so I can't pull around them, but I refuse to sit there again."

"That's 92nd?" I verify. "Trish's old yoga studio is just south of there. It's a long light."

"Very." Gayle's hand trembles as he lifts his glass to his lips. "So I honk my horn, just a light touch, nothing heavy-handed. But he doesn't move. He finally pulls ahead, and I pull ahead right behind him. And he stops again. He pulls ahead again, and he stops again, with the rear bumper of his car in the crosswalk. The light turns red, and he zips through the intersection. I'm not going to let him strand me there, so I follow, but east-west traffic is already moving forward, and I almost collide with the first two cars heading west. The guy in the right lane and I both have to spin out and stop. He lays on his horn screaming at me while the guy in the left lane leaves me with the finger. We finally untangle with nary a fender bent, but the punks are gone and a few blocks up the road my car starts making the banging noise you heard."

"Gayle." I emit a vexed sigh. "You're lucky you didn't catch up with them again. They sound like quintessential assholes, seasoned and dangerous. You might not be here to tell the tale."

Spaatz nods. "'The practice of evil makes the perfect scoundrel' is the way I believe old Sol would phrase it. But I did get something else out of the experience. Lest my dyslexia betray me, I clicked pics of the punk's plate so there should be no mistake. I got it privately traced, and it came back registered to one John E. Bustelich."

"Not that John E. Bustelich." I chuckle but the mere name of our most accomplished childhood tormentor still unnerves me. "The state is likely blessed with a few varied strains of life-forms bearing that name."

Gayle hisses. "Yeah, and this strain was the infamous one's kid. It makes perfect sense."

"Nothing done by the Bustelich family we knew made perfect sense." I find my appetite suddenly spotty and I quaff some alcohol. "We're not old enough, that is, he wouldn't have a son old enough to be driving around terrorizing the streets yet, would he?"

"Hell yes he would." Gayle drains his glass. "Remember our class only inherited Johnny after he flunked fourth grade, so he's a year more mature than us. He knocked up that squirrely Megan chick while we were still in high school."

I force a snicker. "I recall my first close encounter with Bustelich on the playground. 'Hey, kid, want to see a rope trick?' He produced a coil of twine and wrapped it tight around my neck."

"I heard that Megan skank ultimately overdosed on

heroin." Gayle wipes his eyes. "First, I have the old man making me miserable as a kid and now the offspring comes after me to make me miserable as an adult."

"Think of how low the chances are that you'll ever run into either of them again." I rub my hands together and become thoroughly steeped in a world where those like Gayle: small in stature, hypersensitive and easily flustered, with rosy cheeks, a prominent nose and thick glasses; and those like myself: introverted and rail-thin, with wild curls, crooked teeth and eczema; served as prime fodder for blustery bullies extraordinaire like Johnny Bustelich. If I were Dr. Rohr-Kisslinger, I'd interpret Gayle's existential tears as a manifestation of loss. Not only would he never reproduce but he would have to watch the world fall to the wretched rabble progeny of the detestable Bustelich dynasty.

I arrive home to find that Maynard has left a rare mess in the kitchen. In the bitter throes of immoderate dejection, I admonish the dachshund to be more considerate. "I took you out at noon before I went back to work." His tail thumps tentatively against the table leg. "I try to arrange my social schedule so you're never cooped up for long hours on end. Have you no excuse?" I punish the dog by limiting his off-the-wall ball session to ten minutes and feeding him the inferior brand of vanilla custard.

"I HURT, THEREFORE I am." My ninth stop on the Rohr-Kisslinger fast track to heightened sensitivity finds me waxing philosophical. "Animals, I'm convinced, not only humans, possess a self-consciousness and social awareness."

"So Descartes had it wrong," Kisslinger scoffs.

"Do you think?" I pose.

"Do you still believe in God?" Kisslinger challenges.

"I still don't believe in man," I assure him. "It doesn't surprise me that people sell their souls; it does surprise me that they sell so cheap."

The doctor snickers sardonically. "I believe that people who speak in riddles or try to employ glib repartee are attempting to cloak a basic ignorance or phoniness."

"And you can't stand the phoniness, Doc, or just the competition?" I discharge a guffaw.

The counselor's Notemaster lights up. "In a typical work-day, how much time do you waste on wordplay?"

"Wordplay is a useful mechanism for toying with the obtuse, the obstinate and the obnoxious," I contend. "Read 'toy' to mean 'manage.' You should acquire the enthusiasm that I have for word puzzles. They'll broaden your perspective and sharpen your focus."

"Really?" Kisslinger exudes skepticism. "You're so easily distracted that I would guess they exert the opposite effect."

"Quirks of language intrigue me," I persevere. "I can kill an idle moment contemplating roughly homophonic pairs that have no surface relationship but hold some deep ironic connection. Take 'solace' and 'soulless' or 'impregnate' and 'imprecate.' You're not roughly homophobic, are you, swami? How about 'therapist' and 'the rapist'? Or 'mosquito' and 'mosque kiddo.' You're Muslim, aren't you, Dr. Kisslinger?"

"How delusional are you?" Kisslinger snarls.

"You're not Jewish," I charge. "You're certainly not observant."

The counselor hisses. "Your brainfood is intellectual bubblegum. Social activities which are intricate enough to be cognitively stimulating and which generate a sense of belong-ing, such as studying a new language or learning a structured dance, are what keep minds sharp and offer protection against neurodegenerative disease. Waste time on these, and you'll find as a by-product you're also able to connect the dots between 'irrelevant' and 'impertinent.'"

I snicker archly. "Fair enough, Doc, but when I come out

of the torture cell today, can I tug on your prickly beard to make sure it's real?"

Kisslinger sighs. "Is that supposed to make sense?"

I sigh. "If you don't believe we live in a violent society, it only goes to show how thick your insulation is. Wasn't it psychology icon Otto Rank who maintained that cave drawings demonstrate primal man was more bothered by killing animals than other humans? You must have the capacity to appreciate that, don't you? Animals for the most part are just trying to find comfort in the moment and make it through the day. Humans constantly try to inflate their own value and exert their influence over others to satisfy their ego."

"Must've been some good acid you got into this morning, hmm?" the doctor jabs. "Or are you able to do that on weed alone?"

"Loosen up, swami." I grab the float-pillow rack and begin propelling myself from side to side of the tank. "Let's take advantage of our time together. Got any idle gossip about other clients?"

Kisslinger rises. "You indicate you're miserable being here, you're miserable in your lousy job, you have no love interest in your life. I'd say Lisle Amonor is a pretty all-around miserable individual. What would you say?"

"What sort of sorry excuse for tankside manner is that, Doc?" I suppress the impulse to splash. "I thought your job here was to peddle positive bullshit."

"My professional objective," he snaps, "is to extinguish your desire to remain the deleterious nuisance to your fellow employees that you've become and rehabilitate you into a productive clinical functionary to the full extent of your limited potential!"

I award the counselor the raspberries. "You're just a fine, decent humanitarian in service to mammon."

Kisslinger discharges a heavy breath. "You approach the world through a contrariety and contentiousness, but when challenged, you wilt like a plucked prairie flower. You exhibit the classic indicators of dependence-related behavior. Do you have the courage and honesty to admit that's what we're really dealing with here?"

I laugh. "I religiously reject painkillers, flibbertigibbet, so your life is not in danger."

The doctor reseats himself. "How much sleep do you get each night?"

I decide to reply honestly. "I have the bad habit of falling asleep in front of the TV several times most evenings. I probably average a solid six and a half to seven hours of unsound sleep each night."

The counselor groans. "That's embarrassing for a man your age."

"You're saying it's a little too much or much too little?"

Kisslinger's Notemaster lights up. "For a man who by his own admission gets plenty of rest during the workday, it's disturbing that you spend so much of your life in a numb, unconscious stupor."

I snort rhythmically. "Recent history at my place of business would indicate that the strategy of hibernation is the best practice to facilitate a promotion. Don't make beta waves. Try it in your next client's session; I'd expect it to be an even more effective gateway to the top in *your* industry."

"What other bad habits trouble you?" Kisslinger rises again. "Do you have the stones to develop a gambling problem?" He exhales with condemnation. "It's role-playing, isn't it? Virtual-reality games? How bad? I'd take you for more of a dragons and dragoons aficionado than a tracers, chases, crashes and thrashers enthusiast. What's this week's most popular selection: 'The Executioner's Son'?"

"'Daddy showed me the ropes, but I stretch the definition of capital punishment,'" I facetiously confess. "I really find most video games disturbingly tedious. I've never been motivated to devote more than a passing nod to the subculture."

Kisslinger pauses knowingly. "You're hooked on porn, aren't you? Hard core? How long?"

"I'm a flawed individual, Doctor." I splash his empty chair. "I'm a stunted, primitive man with a regressive, repressive attitude toward women. The pleasure centers of my brain are nearly fried and demand more and more bizarre novelty. My only hope is a learning association scenario where I'm forced to correlate sex with physical misery. Since you've already sprung for the parrot, perhaps you could bring in your girl and set me up in a sordid pirate fantasy." I execute an imaginary cutlass thrust. "The porn angle is a grand theory, my Lord Privateer Kisslinger, but I'm afraid your crystal ship has a paper anchor!"

The doctor discharges a groan of bewildered disgust. "You could use a high, hard dose of reality. You have apparently determined that no matter how hard you try, you can never fit in, so now you'll willfully try to fit out." He reseats himself. "You lean on a rubber crutch and wonder why you can't move forward. You are incapable of managing your day-to-day stress."

I arrive at work three minutes behind schedule and find two unknown latex-ensconced techs busily unpacking urine samples and analyzing them at a temporary table in the anterior hallway. Two refrigerated skids sit beside the table. Nancy waylays me before I reach my desk. "Lisle, finally." She beckons me back to the hallway. "I need you to supervise the temps here, so put everything else on hold." My enthusiasm must be evident. "You shouldn't have to handle any of the merchandise yourself." She conducts me to the table and introduces me to the laborers. "This is Betty Liu-Huang." The female lifts her mask and smiles politely. "And Jun-Seo Shim." The male nods. "They're doing a fabulous job."

"Is the coke machine broke again?" I reference the Specitrak 500 automated urinalysis machine in the lab which resembles an old-fashioned soda pop dispenser when a rack of test tubes is inserted on its conveyor tray.

"It's otherwise engaged. This is an overflow operation." Nancy turns back to the temps. "The Specitrak conducts large-scale toxicology tests." She smiles graciously. "Temps, you can get back to work." She turns back to me and points to the laptop on the edge of the table. "The protocol is spelled out on the project tab if you have any questions. Just make sure the process is respected, no shortcuts are taken and everything gets put away." She sighs. "I have to pick up my brother's kids at the airport and I'm running late. I'm taking the rest of the week off. Keep Gene advised of your progress."

I smile dutifully. "Antsy Nancy."

She fixes me with a perplexed sneer. "Uh, yeah?" We observe the temps perform their tasks for a few minutes.

Jun-Seo unpacks the samples, transfers them to tubes, affixes labels and operates the centrifuge while Betty analyzes the sedimentary contents under a microscope and enters results on a spreadsheet. The Duchess turns to me again. "Sensitivity training going okay?"

I rub my brow. "He tells me I'm too agreeable, and I tell him to piss off."

Nancy expels an annoyed breath. "There's an acute shortage of mental health professionals in the state. Consider yourself fortunate that you have easy access to the resource."

I nod. "Today we tapped into tapping therapy. Suspension bridge EFT. I'd like to show my shrink my appreciation for his global optimization by tapping 'Yankee Doodle' into his prime meridian."

Nancy leaves me with the temps. Jun-Seo bumps the microscope twice as he prepares slides. "It's commendable to work with alacrity," I exhort him, "but when you adopt the mindset in the lab that you have to bust your hump, you generally start to lose your quality control."

Betty backs away from the microscope. "Want to watch your language?"

"Why don't you pitch in and do some real work, captain?" Jun-Seo challenges me.

"Because there's barely enough room for two people to work at this table," I assert, "let alone three. I don't know why she didn't set you up with the bake-sale table."

"Why don't you set it up?" Shim suggests.

"Carry on, cadets; I'll be right back with it." I readily trade the ambiance of the high morale area in the hallway for the dank atmosphere of the basement. I finally find the long table in the control room behind compact storage. I add a power strip and extension cord to my load and return upstairs to the overflow operation.

"Here he is!" Jun-Seo celebrates my reappearance. "We told Nancy you'd gone fishin'."

Shim and I unfold the legs of the long table and flip it over. We move it into place beside the original table and he dives beneath it with the power strip and extension cord. Betty and I transfer items to the higher, more spacious new platform as Jun-Seo reconfigures electrical connections on the floor. As he emerges from beneath the table, he jars it and nearly spills the contents of several open cups of urine. "Careful there, buckaroo," I admonish. "If we have a spill, I'm not going to clean it up."

"Who will?" he presses. "I can walk away from this job."

Kelly strolls down the hallway pulling a wagonload of apothecary jars containing brains. "You're moving up in the world, Lisle," she teases as she passes, "from number two to number one."

Jun-Seo stains a slide and adds it to the queue awaiting Betty's analysis. "You're outpacing her again," I advise him. "Workflow optimization allows you time to reseal each container as soon as you extract your portion."

Betty steps away from the microscope. "This scut work is not what I expected," she huffs. "I'm a smart person. I'm one semester and a half away from my nutrigenomics degree."

"Toiling in the obscure trenches of scientific inquiry builds character and perspective," I assure her.

Betty snickers. "I'll get the perspective of a woman witnessing a man take credit for her work."

I force a thin-lipped grin. "I guess that worked for Rosalind Franklin. At least well enough that we know who she was."

Jun-Seo submits another slide. "Get your yellow tail in gear, China doll."

Betty gasps. "Are you going to let him get away with talking to me like that?" She eyes me indignantly. "I don't have to tolerate it. I want to file a formal complaint."

I groan. "Aw, naw, wait-"

"Good, there she is!" Betty spots Nancy and summons her with a vehement wave. "I've been subjected to verbal abuse here," she informs the Duchess, "demeaning to my gender and ethnicity."

"Lisle!" Agape, Nancy fixes me with a look best reserved for encountering a berserk paranormal entity. "Of all people, how could you?"

"It wasn't me." I gesture to Jun-Seo. "I'm sure he didn't intend any harm." I smile with empathy. "Did you, Jun?" He shrugs.

Betty points at me. "He used a sexually charged reference, and I even warned him that it was offensive. Then when Jun-Seo made an even more overt slur, he denied me the opportunity to file a complaint."

"What's the matter with you?" Nancy chides me. "Don't you recognize how serious this is?"

"Unfortunately for me," I grumble, "I realize how serious it isn't."

"I have to leave!" Nancy snaps. "Take her to see Lillian immediately!"

I nod to Jun-Seo. "As a fellow Asian, doesn't he have privilege?"

"Now I want to file a claim," Shim asserts.

The Duchess glares at me. "Are you daring me to take further disciplinary action against you? Take over the operation here!" She turns to the temps. "I'm so sorry. I will personally escort you to H.R. and I'll see to it that you each have an opportunity to file a full incident report."

Jun-Seo points at me. "I'll settle for his job." He snickers and stumbles backward onto the long table. I lunge in a valiant effort to keep the table from collapsing. I fail and find myself at the base of a heap beneath lab equipment and decanted urine.

"That's lovely, Lisle!" Nancy stands with arms akimbo. "You have a real knack for ruin."

Shim springs to his feet and surveys the wreckage. "I quit!" He scurries up the hallway.

I rise to all fours. "I guess I'm the only one left who's not a victim."

"You were in charge," Nancy castigates me. "If those specimens were here for medical testing, you'd be up to your neck in trouble." She hisses. "We don't use that table because its legs are unstable!"

I hoard filter papers and blot urine from my brow. "Overflow operation."

I eventually arrive home from work to find a lethargic Maynard. He exhibits compulsive licking, his stomach keeps rumbling and he's indifferent to his supper. I monitor his condition as I tend my houseplants. We settle among the twilight shadows in the living room, and I stroke his back lightly as I recline in my low-rider chair. "Is today's dog world as full of tragic divas as the human world?" I sigh. "A stage packed with wailers way too full of themselves strutting around crooning 'Me, me, me, always me, poor me'? Harried, maligned me. If Nancy wasn't pressed for time, she would've slapped me with a reprimand if not a suspension. Maybe she couldn't resist making me sweat until she comes back, hmm?"

I tap the top of my head and the cleft of my chin. "I deeply and completely accept myself." I tap the top of Maynard's head. "You're open to feeling calm and profoundly relaxed." The dachshund gets up and relocates to a spot beside the davenport. After an hour, I sit beside him on the floor and pet him gently. He is susceptible to mild stomach disorders. In about another hour, I'll return to the kitchen and cook him a special meal of shredded chicken and rice. When I'm ill, he hangs close to me and doesn't demand his regular play or walk time. Caring for a sick companion is the quintessential opportunity to demonstrate genuine loyalty and affection. Sirach said that a real friend can only be identified in times of adversity. Sacrifice, even of a modest proportion, is the main ingredient of true friendship.

I ENTER THE King Kryczek & Rohr-Kisslinger office to find the corner that previously held the cage of Ivan the Terrible empty. "Where's the vulture?" I query the receptionist. "Not Kisslinger; I mean the grey crow, the tropical rooster."

She fixes her gaze on the corner. "They removed the bird over the weekend." She offers nothing further.

I seat myself with a decided sense of loss. The absurdity of my presence at sensitivity training becomes more patently profound. "I recall how foolish I felt the first time I submitted to therapy here," I volunteer. "About as foolish as I feel now."

Minutes later, Kisslinger has me horizontal in the tank undergoing a constructive third-person nitpick. "Weak-kneed with drooping hands, he thinks of himself in the collective singular," the counselor croaks. "He refuses all real calls to action. He won't take a chance. He pursues a class of unobtainable lovers as a means of escaping the risk of real intimacy."

I rub my neck. "What's the matter, Doc, is it a difficult operation to plug a low coefficient into my expectation maximization algorithm?" I force a chuckle. "In the words of the ancient comedians, 'Where there's cause to laugh, there's cause for hope,' right?"

Kisslinger sighs. "You're acquiring quite a pile of personal losses, aren't you? Accruing a rather long string of zeroes?" He snickers. "Don't you grow weary of living in a stuffy, stultifying atmosphere where the chronic sting of rejection hangs thick in the air?"

I splash the counselor. "What evil psychologism are you trying to pull from the dark netherworld of your subculture now, swami? Steaming me to the desired tenderness?"

Kisslinger's Notemaster lights up. "Can you honestly believe that coping with your rank unhappiness by trying to thrust misery in the lives of all those whose paths cross yours is your best survival strategy? People who thrive on ripping others lack a basic self-esteem. Don't let your fear and arrogance cheat you out of your life."

"Care to share some juicy morsels on what's happening around the office?" I toss my head back and sustain saltwater in the ear. "Has the inevitable forbidden intimate relationship developed with any of your clients? How about your receptionist? Do you have a good word to say about her? Hey, what happened to your avian warmup act?"

Kisslinger exhales heavily. "The overall feedback we received from clients was that the grey's presence here served as a distraction and it ultimately felt inappropriate, so we eliminated him. We threw a little office party. We had a chicken fricassee with meatballs, and Ivanhoe provided the meat." He titters. "Shall we turn the spotlight back on you?"

I never want to get into a physical altercation with my doctor, but if I have the slightest concern that Kisslinger isn't employing his quaint brand of sarcasm, I drag him into the tank with the cordiality of an alligator. "You're slick, cunning and ruthless, Dr. Dave, and I mean that in the most flattering possible sense. Why don't you speak to Dr. Artie about surreptitiously modifying the receptionist's personality in the best interest of your practice or as a practical joke?"

Kisslinger scoffs. "Deirdre is a diligent worker, a highly efficient professional."

I'm certain that her desk nameplate advises visitors she's *DeRae*. "You don't think she could be a bit perkier?"

"Perky," the counselor snarls, "is a valley-girl puppet with a rotating head."

I cackle. "I think I can speak for all of your clients in assuring you that it would be a special delight to be greeted here by a puppet. How familiar are you with the Companion Piece line of cheap imitation people?"

"Obviously not intimately familiar with them as you seem to be." Kisslinger emits a groan of disgust. "Your life is a giant, swirling suck hole. If sex without love is the working definition of the ultimate personal vacuum, how much less satisfying is sex without a fully engaged adult human partner? Your only hope is to achieve a catharsis in order to inaugurate your healing process and get in front of your impaired emotional dynamic."

"Oh, Doctor," I moan. "Pretending to care in exchange for pay has always been a robust industry far more diversified than the sex trade, but who would know that better than a trained professional clinician?"

Kisslinger pauses to scratch his scraggly beard. "Journeys back to sunny days that never existed and never really could no longer soothe you, do they?" He snickers. "How the despair of your static isolation must weigh upon you. How frustrating that those whom you'd run to for comfort are the ones who've most contributed to your grief. Take care that the haunting agony of your loneliness doesn't cut through you until only the cool refuge of suicide beckons on the horizon."

I gurgle with irritation. "I struggle to overcome my disappointment that people aren't better than they are."

The doctor drops his Notemaster. "You lack attachment by design. You fail to take action that might lead others to accept you, and you deliberately choke your potential to cultivate a sense of belonging, all as justification to despise people in general." He crouches to retrieve his device. "You require the introduction of additional physical stress to shock you into an elevated consciousness, such drastic measures as often yield dramatic progress in developing a subject's adaptive capacities."

I survey a break in the cloud loop overhead. "I have a history distinguished by trying to adapt."

The swami reseats himself. "No one is more attuned or sympathetic toward those who suffer from childhood trauma than I am, but yours has always been self-inflicted, a mockery of the trauma that is genuine. You cling to an envious helplessness. Instead of resenting the social prosperity of someone else, try resenting your own social poverty."

I return to work and receive a message from the Duchess to report to her office. We've deftly avoided each other for the past two days, and I expect to suffer discipline in proportion to the abuse she endured over the weekend at the hands of her relatives. Nancy is jabbering into her phone when I enter, and she gestures that I should take a seat. "The steering committee needs to understand the bottom-up process," she continues her palaver, "feel the burn of vision and responsibility." She disconnects, and we exchange polite, probing smiles. "How was your sensitivity counseling session this morning?"

"I cut my finger on the door of the office building when I left." I display my bandaged pinkie. "How was the family weekend?"

"Couldn't have gone better." The Duchess eyes me intently. "They got in a little late so I arrived just in time. Aaron came in, and we took them to the zoo on Friday. The weather was perfect. On Sunday, we brought them here and gave them the deluxe lab tour before taking them back to the airport. I don't think they understood much of Aaron's exposition, but they seemed quite impressed, especially by the 'nearly renovated' biocontainment area." The banter decays. "Lisle, our little personnel incident of last week requires reflection." She sighs. "I'll admit that if the aggrieved party hopes to flourish in the business-of-science world, it wouldn't hurt her to harden herself off."

I avoid eye contact. "Let's invite her back and toughen her up by exposing her to resistant strains of flesh-eating bacteria."

Nancy runs her hands across the underside of her desk, and I wonder whether she's training a camera or a taser on me. "Lillian expressed her extreme displeasure, and I don't appreciate being put in a defensive position where I have to protect my people."

I purse my lips and nod. "Let's expose Lillian to a nasty probiotic. The rumor leaking around the office is that Betty Liu settled for two months' worth of compensation for the two hours she worked."

"I'll neither confirm nor deny." Nancy knits her brow. "Gene Napolitano had no problem completing the project with the pair of replacement temps." She looks askance. "Lisle, isn't it reasonable to expect that you'll utilize all tools available to develop and demonstrate a greater maturity in the way you handle workplace interactions? That doesn't mean we have to maintain a gulag atmosphere around here, but if you talk to everyone like they're your grandma, you have less chance of landing all parties concerned in hot water."

I strive to boost our rapport. "The entire matter reminds me of the time last winter when that hemp-head temp – Gage? – claimed he slipped and suffered an injury in the parking lot."

"I can't reason with the blacktop," Nancy counters. "But won't you please presume it's counterproductive to use any sort of pejorative term like 'hemp-head' to describe anyone."

"'Hemp-head' is another term my grandmother had for a 'druggie.'" I leave Nancy's office and spend a fair portion of the afternoon hiding behind the fermenters, concerned that the Duchess might reconsider her lenient attitude. I take the opportunity as environmental committee chairman to clean the cafeteria refrigerator and discover new, developing strains of bacteria in abandoned food items.

I have arranged to meet Delmar Vecsey after work, and I hire a ride to convey me to Pfixx's Inn. I occupy our corner table for only a few minutes before Del joins me. I spare him details of my recent adventures in feces and urine, but I'm quick to recap the harassment crossfire into which I've been thrust.

Vecsey is impressed. "You should've told your hissy missy, 'It sounds like someone who shall remain nameless could use a good foot-binding.' Then when Nancy clomped over to fan the sparks, you could've spouted, 'Leave it to the Duchess to sandbag an underbuilt dike,' and you would've hit the racist sexist homophobic trifecta."

I'm reminded what I miss most about Delmar is that he boldly ventures where virtue-signalers dare not tread. "I confess I'm paranoid enough to have considered the possibility that Nancy set me up for a canned harassment infraction with the temps." I raise my glass. "Oh, my permanent record!"

Del nods. "Nancy is at her most dangerous when she appears to be at her most simpatico. No sooner did she reassure me that she had my back than she lowered the boom on me. You better keep her at arm's length by hitting on her." He takes a swig of whiskey. "Anyway, her marriage merits it."

"Speculation on the strength of the Detweilers' conjugal bond continues." I snicker. "Nancy mentioned that Aaron came in for the weekend as if it was a rare event. Maybe she just meant that she usually hooks up with him at the Madison mansion."

"How many times do I have to explain this, Amonor?" Vecsey eyes the space over my shoulder blankly enough to conceal his sincerity level. "A marriage with parallel residential dimensions has an X factor. Aaron located his startup in Milwaukee and put Nancy in charge of it to keep her sequestered from his personal business. Even with that, they could've established a residence in Jefferson County that allowed a tolerable commute distance for both."

I sip my sludgehammer. "At any rate, I took the opportunity provided by my indelicate incident to further prejudice Nancy against temporary workers. So hang on while I grow that germ a little more mass, and we'll reel you back in yet."

"You will not," he states flatly. "I got a new job."

"What?" I manage. "Really?"

Del raises his glass. "I spent my weekend outside Houston looking over the place and finalizing the deal. They call it The Ases."

"Texas?" I'm embarrassed by how much disappointment can ooze from two syllables.

"They produce custom compounds: bioidentical and synthetic hormones." Vecsey grins. "Synthetic proteins. They tout the manufacture of the molecules used in chemical castration."

"You mean, like for livestock?" I tap my mug against his wagging glass.

"For whatever needs castratin', I reckon." Delmar empties his glass.

"Texas," I repeat. "How long has that been in the works?"

A smug smile flickers across his lips. "I started making inquiries the day after my dismissal became official. Even before, actually, when it became evident how things were going at Anele. This opportunity popped up two months ago. I'll be a quality control coordinator. The slight pay increase is nice, but the main draw is that the work seems fairly interesting. The environment is a little different."

"Yeah, it's Texas," I establish. "It's a huge place. It's a different culture. Do you know anyone else down there? Your father is going to be okay with it?"

"Pop has been talking about moving to an assisted care facility." Del offers a grin. "This might give him the final push down the stairs he needs. Anyway, it's past time for me to test my wings, leave lovely, languid Wisconsin and explore the wild, wide-open world. I'm leaving in two weeks plus, the Friday four days after Labor Day."

I emit a series of grunts. "I'm sorry, I'm a little shell-shocked. I guess I thought we were a little tighter, that our friendship was bigger than our Allele connection." I force a chuckle. "Your departure is going to punch a gaping hole in my social calendar."

"Kelly's husband might be open to being cucked," Del offers. "Prosecute that prospect. And between you and me, there's always telecommunications."

"You're the closest thing I've ever had at Allele to a kindred spirit, Del." I take a hearty swig of my drink. "The guy without empathy is the only one who's ever really gotten my wry commentary." I rub my neck. "I mean, I don't want to resort to emotional blackmail, but have you checked whether any other enticing opportunities might exist around here?"

"I feel like I'm being emotionally blackmailed." Del's decision is irrevocable.

I buy Delmar a scotch on the rocks to celebrate change. I maintain a buoyant gleam in my eye as we speculate on his imminent quest for biotech glory, but a decided hollowness churns behind my ready smile. I fetch us a final round. Del drives me home, and the conversation grows strained and stressed, almost as a preparation for separation.

"My skeleton crew is down another skull," I advise Maynard as soon as I walk in the door. "Delmar is moving away from us, far, far away. You saw him here a couple of times. Sentimentality was never going to be his downfall, and he was never an animal guy. But he generally had a saner, more acuminous perspective than anyone else I know, and it's not going to be the same without him."

MY PENULTIMATE SENSITIVITY training session is interrupted before it begins by a knock on the float room door. "Pardon in there," the receptionist calls. "Are you down in the float?"

I hastily don my therapy thong and hop to the water's edge. "I'm your tubman!" She opens the door as I plunge a leg in the tank. "*Ayaaah!!*" I withdraw my violated limb. "It's freezing!"

"That's what the doctor ordered." She cradles an open bag of ice in her arms.

I check the tank thermometer. "It's only 12 degrees! It's horrible!"

She empties her bag in the tank. "He wants it to be 10 degrees at the start. He says your body heat will drive up the temp. I can add a top blanket of crushed ice once you're down."

"You can tell Kisslinger to spring for the standard 25 degrees plus, or this session don't float." I snatch the emergency robe from the rack. "Never mind; allow me." I stride into the swami's office and accost him at his desk. "What's with the deep freeze, Doc? How about if you man the wet end today?"

"It sounds like someone isn't doing his homework." Dr. Rohr-Kisslinger fixes me with a sardonic smile. "Have you been diligent with your cold showers?" He groans. "We've discussed the motivational benefits of an antidepressant ice bath in your previous sessions. It boosts your immune system, burns fat and lifts your mood."

I wait for 10 minutes as the alternative float room with a tank temperature of 26 degrees is prepared. "You teeter on the tipping point of an epic depression," Kisslinger claims when I'm finally flat and receptive. "A bitter terminal dysthymia. Life without living."

"Living is punishment," I incite him further.

"Depressive disorders disrupt sound cognitive functioning," the swami charges. "The gross anxiety and irritability you habitually exhibit are shallow symptoms, but the conclusive evidence is in your chronic rumination. You wrap yourself in a tangled cocoon of brooding which renders you oblivious to your inept coping mechanisms."

I spit saltwater. "I'm only too aware of what's usually going on within myself."

"Are you introspective enough to deconstruct your suffering?" The doctor's Notemaster lights up. "What torments you? That the community finds you not to be a good person? That the community finds you not to be a useful person?"

"I, the community," I riposte. "In the final analysis, my

opinion of myself is what's relevant. I reward myself every time I deny myself the pleasure of my impulses."

"Do you subscribe to a moral relativism?" He hisses when I pause to ponder. "In simpler terms, do you believe in situational ethics?"

"To a certain extent," I reason. "As I mature, I become a more rabid fan of plain truth and raw candor. In retrospect, I respect the woman at the heart of my last ill-fated romantic entanglement for finally coming out and notifying me that she didn't want to have anything more to do with me."

"She was more flesh than fantasy?" The counselor gasps with astonishment. "Comment on the factors that led to the disintegration of the relationship and their effect on your subsequent morbidity."

I resent the intrusion but comply nonetheless. "Whimsical and then stubborn, this fabulous creature whom I'd crowned queen of my dreams, light of my fading youth and preferred power source of my beleaguered spirit proved in the end to be too different from me." I relive the sting of her desertion. "She would conquer a receptive universe through the body, and I would conquer a hostile universe through the mind."

"You couldn't overcome the age difference," Kisslinger infers.

"A decade doesn't seem like much anymore," I submit, "and Trish and I were less than eight years apart."

Kisslinger forces an astringent chuckle. "There ought to be a ceremony for recognizing one's own coming of age as a dirty, old man."

"I loathe the idea that the buzz of lustful feelings should transcend the kinship of minds," I insist. "It seems logical that intellectual love should lead to physical, not the opposite, but bitter reinforcement has assured me the world doesn't operate that way, so I gave up hoping it could work that way for Trish and me. At some point, a man has to declare the audition over and make his move, doesn't he?" I sigh. "Of course, I was willing to take Trish any way she'd have me."

"I'm sure," the counselor croaks. "You describe a young woman with a constant craving for a full symphonic neural firing. She must've had a robust sex drive. Were you really able to satisfy her physical needs?"

"Are we still on the right side of therapeutic relevance, Doctor," I wonder, "or have you again crossed over the line to indulge your natural voyeuristic inclination?"

"You're here because your superior charged you with sexual harassment," Kisslinger snaps. "Any history of the expression, suppression or misdirection of the amorous feelings you experience is most relevant to your case. So far, flip-flopping and slip-sliding through a presumed quagmire of questioning seems to find you at your most potent."

"Nancy charged me with being a party in association with sexual harassment, swami," I remind him. "And I've already explained it's the magnum opus of bum raps. But to finish with Trish, I remained optimistic about our relationship to the very end because she'd been a dance instructor, and you know they're trained like sharks and shrinks: Once they get ahold of you, they never want to let you go."

"You failed to engage in any sexual activity with your Trish, didn't you?" He doesn't allow me the opportunity to equivocate. "And she lodged with you for how long? Such a pity."

"Love is a misery voyage that visits infrequent pleasure islands." I snicker awkwardly. "You won't be too disappointed to see me dash out your door for the last time, will you, Dr. Dave?" I splash him. "I surmise you can hardly wait another week to fix your high-beams on me for one last heat signature."

"You wouldn't find suspending therapy disorienting?" The doctor emits an exasperated breath. "Do you still spend your Sunday mornings on bended knee beneath the numbing din of church bells?"

"It's been suggested that religion got booted out of the schools because there's no autographed photo of Jesus and Mary at the Smithsonian," I exploit the opportunity to kibitz. "The job of our educators, it seems to me, extends beyond conducting their charges through a maze of mental calisthenics. They have a responsibility to stoke a student's enthusiasm, confidence and intellect. The school system dampened my enthusiasm, destroyed my confidence and barely grazed my intellect."

"The source of all your failures lies somewhere beyond your doorstep, doesn't it?" the doctor scoffs. "You can never own your own mess. You don't conveniently load any blame for your failed romance on your skin condition?"

"How dare you insinuate that the eruption of red, scaly patches of skin isn't a condition to be welcomed and admired?"

"Is there anything in your life that you've ever done right, Amonor?" he challenges. "Anybody?"

"You tell me, Doc, have I successfully refined your disdain to a state of the most perfect possible purity?" I clutch the float-pillow rack and propel myself from side to side of the tank. "No one takes a back seat to you when it comes to missing accomplishments. You have baby-faced-man-with-a-beard syndrome."

"Why do I have the apprehension," Kisslinger snarls, "that when I'm finally able to peel away the thin, marred outer layer of sophistry that clouds your judgement, I'll find another thin, marred layer of sophistry beneath it?"

"The receptionist told me that Dr. Kryczek is still a drooling invalid," I lie. "Do you talk shop within earshot of her? Off the record, do you and Bright Art the Brain Fart ever leave professional rumblings in the hallway?"

Kisslinger hisses. "We may generally lament how many men refuse to grow up enough to help themselves." He drops his Notemaster. "Your bizarre attitude makes you a difficult read, but I would stake my professional reputation, such as it is, that you're a conspiracy theorist. You live in a pit of despair for which delusion is the prime analgesic and you filter the outside world through a childish mind which requires the idea that a greater unknowable force such as a secret society or deep state, a god figure or man behind the curtain, maintains ultimate control over all things. You rely on a cognitive bubble which functions as a buffer against the devastating effects of reality."

I arrange to meet Gayle Spaatz after work. He picks me up and the metallic clank in the rear of his Toyota is worse than before. He assures me he is going to engage a mechanic to check the car.

"I conducted a surveillance on him," Gayle announces when we settle at our table in the darkest corner of Pfixx's Inn.

"You violated Vito?" I sip my Irish sludgehammer.

"On Johnny Bustelich." A wry grin flickers across Gayle's face. "I drove past the address on the punk's car registration a few times and I spotted Johnny out in the yard: shirt off, hairy chest, huge gut, blond hair thinning but the head still shaped like a square basketball. I recognized him instantly." The menacing ghost of John Bustelich suddenly takes flesh and carries weight. "I staked out his house the last two Saturdays. It looks as though he has two younger kids – a boy and a girl both about ten years old – and they accompany their mother to the grocery store every Saturday morning."

"A pattern." I take a heftier swig of my cocktail. "Does his wife appear to be a beast?"

"No such justice." Gayle appears preoccupied, his demeanor almost trancelike. "You'd probably think she's *cute*."

I nod with resignation. "Did you see the punk?"

"Neither punk nor car." Gayle's gaze carries an unsettling intensity. "You remember that's one of the things he used to call us: the cute guys."

"Yeah, as in 'Here's Handsome.'" A bit of Bustelich's old middle school sarcasm shakes loose in my craw. "I recall he applied some of his Spanish lessons. 'Peculiar *pequadas*,' he'd call us, or '*los peculiar pescados*,' or '*las mequetrefe mariquitas*.'" I chuckle. "You used to regularly give it back to him. I wish I'd had the balls to do that."

Gayle sips his mojito pensively. "Things I said that he seemed most insulted by sort of slipped out inadvertently. I once called him 'John Barleycorn Distillich' because I expected he'd think it was cool. He said, 'Are you trying to make fun of my name?' I said, 'No, Johnny, would you like me to?'"

"Rich." I laugh heartily. "I remember in class you once shouted, 'What's the matter, Johnny, was your mother's milk sour this morning?'"

Spaatz chuckles. "He'd ask me if I still used baby oil. I said, 'Why, Johnny, are you running low?' He'd say, 'Are you calling me a fag like you?' I'd say, 'No, Johnny, I'd never deny you the privilege of making the announcement yourself.'" Gayle begins twitching. "He never actually beat the shit out of you, did he?"

"Mostly it was just attitude and threats." I flash my version of a reassuring smile. "He'd say, 'How would you like that gap between your teeth widened?' I recall him knocking me down a couple of times, tripping me as I tried to get up, and once he punched me in the leg to give me a charley horse. 'They're going to find your head in a ditch, Amonor.'" I force a chuckle.

"Things like that-" Gayle curls his lip downward. "Things like that stay with a person. When you had your teeth fixed, you should've told your butcher-boy dentist to send the bill to Big Bad John Bustelich."

I compulsively run my forefinger over my teeth. "Let's just be grateful we don't have to deal with him anymore."

Gayle takes a sloppy sip of his mojito. "Can I tell you my Johnny fantasy?"

I take a stiff swig of my orangeman. "Can I avoid it?"

A malevolent element creeps into Gayle's grin. "I wait for Johnny's wife and kids to go grocery shopping some Saturday morning and ring his doorbell. He doesn't recognize me at first and I get the drop on him. I strip him naked and tie him up with a leather harness in leapfrog position on his kitchen table."

"'Hey, kid, you could change the pope's mind about birth

control,'" I revisit another fond meaningful encounter with Johnny Bustelich.

"I gag him," Gayle continues, "and remind him of the nasty things he did to people, beginning with the two times he pounded the living hell out of me and ending with his running predictions that I'd end up a 'spread-eagled street degenerate.' I hear the wife's car pull into the driveway and I log into Johnny. The wife and kids come in the back door, see us on the table, drop their grocery bags and scream. I withdraw and hop down. I wail 'Johnny, you swore to me you got rid of this bitch!' I grab my clothes and let myself out."

"Gayle." I rub my neck. "Fortunately, it's just a fantasy, so it won't cost you any quality time in prison or bring Johnny and his half-wit brothers around for retaliation."

Spaatz snorts. "How stupid was the Bustelich family? Johnny was the smartest of them."

As Gayle drops me at home, I invite him to the farewell soiree I'm planning for Delmar Vecsey next week, where we'll also celebrate my release from sensitivity training. He reluctantly agrees to attend.

A cool late-August air mass has settled over the area, and one of my first chores after I get inside is to toss a couple of logs into the fireplace. "Speaking with the privilege of one who remained towheaded till I hit puberty, the Busteliches were extraordinary lunkheads even by dumb blond standards." I stroke Maynard's back as I recline in my low-rider easy chair. "Twenty years ago-" I sigh heavily. "I wonder if Gayle remembers what a disgusting chickenshit I was. Bustelich knocked the absolute snot out of him the summer after ninth grade."

I gently pat the dog's neck. "I stood there frightened and did nothing. Bustelich confronted us in the park. 'Look who's together again. I'm confused; am I allowed to call you guys "queer"? If not, am I allowed to call you guys "guys"?' He starts dropping his assorted f-bombs, and Gayle says, 'Johnny, did you just come up with those off the top of your square head?' Bustelich took him down, gave him two black eyes, a bloody nose, a cut lip. In the grip of a colossal cowardice, all I could do was watch. I think I mumbled 'Leave him alone, Bustelich, you big ape.' I knew he wouldn't hear me. Gayle wound up writhing, holding his ribs, crying. He was publicly humiliated. I abandoned him by default. I should've punched Johnny Bullshitish, should've jumped on his back, should've intervened *somehow*. I should've taken the same beating Gayle got to prove I wasn't a totally pathetic excuse for a friend. That's the sort of thing that stays with a person."

AS I WAIT in the King Kryczek & Rohr-Kisslinger Counseling Solutions LLP anteroom for my twelfth sensitivity training session, I receive a message from Gayle Spaatz that his car will be in the shop for at least another day so he has no viable mode of transportation to attend Delmar Vecsey's farewell gala. I suggest that Del could pick him up.

Dr. Rohr-Kisslinger informs me that we will eschew the immersion tank and conduct our final business in his office. I sit arrow-straight in his unpadded visitor's chair and notice that the photo of his wife is face-down on his desk. "With little more than an earnest heart, I search amid the wreckage-scape of my rancid existence for a life." I mean to fully cooperate with Kisslinger on this occasion; I need a satisfactory sensitivity grade, and I can't rely on his fear of having to endure me for another twelve sessions. "I always felt somehow removed from others, as if they all sensed a malevolent element in me to which I was oblivious. When I smiled, it seemed they didn't smile back. When I extended my hand, they slapped it away or bit it. Soon I tried to smile but could not, wanted to reach out but dared not."

The doctor nods. "Are some of us genetically cursed or preprogrammed in such a manner from the beginning? Perhaps the nobility of being a monster resides in its stark alienation." He thrums his decorative plastic skull. "If that's what you've been trying to tell me all this time, we'd seem to have a classic case of paranoia working here. I've suggested as much previously, but you've ridiculed the idea and made no effort to improve. You might finally abdicate your myth that you're some misunderstood genius and strive for a deeper understanding which accepts the idea that interdependency creates successful relationships, even when that means you may serve as no more than a weak tool."

"When the rest of the human tribe leaves little doubt that they find one fit only for sweeping up their crumbs, he must decide whether that's satisfactory or he moves on." I parlay my personal animosity for the counselor into a more panoramic indignation. "I have a recurring nightmare. I'm surrounded by throngs of faceless people, and I keep screaming 'Where the hell is everybody?' Where the hell *is* everybody?"

"Would you say your grip on reality is solid?" Kisslinger fixes me with a wry squint. "Does it give you a feeling of power to lie?"

"You never know which end is up." I exhale heavily. "It would give me a feeling of powerlessness to have to lie. Hook me up to your pocket truth detector. I'll double your money from today's session if I'm rated insincere."

Kisslinger removes his glasses. "I'm trained to tell the difference between oral diarrhea that's real and the shit that sells."

I decide to toss the doctor a final bone. "When I consider the friends I've known throughout my life, my dogs are the only ones who've ultimately seemed as though they didn't have something they'd rather be doing or someplace they'd rather be than with me."

"It's a pity they couldn't talk, hmm?" Kisslinger checks his Notemaster. "You still have your same pooch, right? What's his name: Helmut?"

The counselor's question trips a sense of alarm. "Garland," I provide the canine's middle name.

"Is your little dog friendly?" Kisslinger inquires.

I grab the picture of the doctor's wife. "Probably as friendly as your little woman." I examine her image. "I know – she's not a nag, just a motivational clotheshorse."

Kisslinger snatches his wife's picture. "As a closet Christian, you must ultimately expect to be rewarded with a luxury condo in the kingdom of heaven. Do you believe there'll be a luxury kennel unit out back there for Garland?" He plunks down his wife's photo face-up. "You're aware, aren't you, that the principal Catholic theologian Aquinas explicitly denies the existence of a doggy heaven." He snickers. "Nothing without a rational soul can be immortal. Animals serve their purpose on this earth and have no place in the hereafter. So you'd better bond with a rational soul here, or you'll find yourself having an even lonelier afterlife."

"I trust more in God than in a mad monk," I submit. "A lot of clerics confer preferred status on humanity by virtue of the fact that we're created in God's likeness and image." I again grasp the picture of the doctor's wife. "But if God is Love, as clerics are also fond of asserting, then the being most ready to give and receive love merits the highest status. There's no doubt that my dogs have loved me more than any human. They've sure as hell been most loyal, and loyalty is the purest marker of love there is. Loyalty is the backbone of devotion. Personal sacrifice is a function of service in loyalty."

"Feel free to create God in your own likeness and image." Kisslinger takes his wife's picture and tosses it in a drawer. "Loyalty is loyalty, love is love and truth is truth."

"To my salt-of-the-earth taste," I spout, "Thomas botched the mechanisms that underpin the sacraments. Read his account of transubstantiation and you have to conclude that *he's* not a rational soul. His celebrated brilliance is punctuated with episodes of sheer folly in much the same manner as is the career of Stephen Hawking." I smile archly. "I believe there's a reason why 'priest' is the second most discredited occupation in the Bible, no modern-day professional offshoots excepted."

The doctor scoffs. "I've never encountered a case quite as dismal as yours, where an individual was so desperate on the subconscious level to be accepted and so devoid of skills on the conscious level to net that result. It's a disturbing recipe for frustration, resentment and requital." He consults his Notemaster. "Treading carefully so as not to violate your confidentiality, I've alerted the authorities that I am professionally acquainted with a person who spews anarchist rants. You're aware that the form you signed upon commencement of this treatment authorizes your therapist to arrange for the institutional commitment of any client who exhibits dangerous sociopathic tendencies, and I've initiated these proceedings this morning."

I lock my eyes on the counselor. "Would you care to repeat that offer, Dr. Dave?"

Kisslinger leans back. "Of course, the transition may be difficult, but you'll be amazed at how swiftly you adjust." He erupts with raucous laughter. "I thought I'd interject a bit of humor on this dour occasion."

"How many clinicians does it take to change a light bulb." I chortle graciously. "There's not a neurosis that you can't quickly eliminate, swami, but by flipping it into a psychosis."

The doctor leans forward. "Our fundamental problem here, Lisle, has been to determine how you've developed into the most cynical, narcissistic and surly of men. How can someone so self-involved manifest so little self-awareness? If the fatuous defense mechanisms you cling to aren't an attempt to evade some dark, haunting secrets of your past, they must represent your effort to outrun the shadow of dread you anticipate overtaking you in the future. Your treatment has witnessed no significant breakthrough, and I *am* concerned about what nefarious design you might entertain should you ever marshal the thimble of boldness you possess. I must rate your outcome here as unsatisfactory."

"A lame shot from a lame duck, Doc." I tap on the desktop. "We're still doing your comedy routine, right?"

"I'm afraid not, Lisle." The counselor shakes his head solemnly. "A mitigating factor in the clinician's final report will be that you have a limited IQ, but I cannot in good conscience advise your employer that you pose a low security threat." He recovers his optimistic smile. "I hope you still welcome raw candor. Whether you believe it or not, Lisle, I stand concerned about your well-being."

I slap myself. "Oh, don't shatter my complete lack of faith in humanity, swami."

"I don't view you as a contemptible figure, Lisle." Kisslinger returns his glasses to his face. "But you need help. Dr. King at our clinic has enjoyed remarkable success in the past with seemingly hopeless cases, and I would encourage you to petition him to accept you as a client."

"I'd rather sort buttons and blow up balloons with Dr. Kryczek." I rise. "Just what insanely ignominious equation for a few more bucks lies at the root of your bloodsucking practice, meterman?"

"I'm an overcharging, shekel-pinching tightwad, Lisle." Kisslinger leans back and titters. "If it makes you feel better, spew any vile slur you're struggling to suppress."

I stride to the door and turn to face him. "What's the difference between a bird and a shrink? The bird is smart enough to realize he has nothing to say."

I stop at the receptionist's partition on my way out. "You should hear Dr. Kisslinger in the interrogation room," I advise her. "He has not a good word to say about you." I exit the office.

I shuffle through a radically unproductive afternoon at work behind the fermenters, and I await Vecsey and Spaatz at the curb in front of Ideal Allele doubting the advisability of arranging for Delmar to pick up Gayle first. Del's Chevy SUV arrives several minutes late, and Gayle voluntarily vacates the front passenger seat for me. "We're discussing cities we'd most like to live in," Gayle chirps in my ear. "We decided if New York is the city that never sleeps, Milwaukee is the city that never wakes up."

"But when it does finally wake up," Del contributes, "it rolls over and smothers Waukesha."

"Anyone who says you can make it anywhere if you can make it in New York," Gayle adds, "never tried to break through as an artist in Milwaukee."

We arrive at Pfixx's and man our customary table. "I would've gone out and got a massage earlier," Delmar remarks, "but I had nothing to wear." I'm pleased that the mood breaks light and cheery because it distracts me from the realization that tonight is the last time I'm likely to see my friend for months or years. And our tentative reunion in the distant future will probably find that the courses of our lives have drifted so far apart he'll seem like a Delmar Vecsey impostor. "Don't keep us in suspenders," Del chides me in between sips of Irish whiskey. "How did sensitivity training turn out?"

Gayle raises his mojito. "Are you a proud graduate patient ready to take your place among the pantheon of feeling, thinking human beings?" He takes a long gulp. "Did your trainer soften you up?"

"My final parley with my counselor Kisslinger was far less than the victorious sigh of relief I'd anticipated." I drink to the doctor. "In fact, for several anxious moments I thought I might jeopardize the prospect of my freedom from the man's influence by murdering him." I drink again. "Our journey together was a transformation. He started out ragging on me for displaying dysmorphia, which he explained as a condition in which a person sees himself as smaller than he actually is, and progressed to accusing me of cultivating delusions of grandeur. He got in his last licks insulting my entire family."

"Shrink, shrank, shrunk," Del snarls. "All those lobe-thumpers do is lob obscure labels at you. They've been telling me I have spectrum disorder since I was in grade school. My dad said 'What's that, like mild Asperger's syndrome?' The school shrink said 'Oh, we would never use such an inimical term.'"

"In ninth grade, the nurse practitioner told my mother I needed my allostatic load lowered," Gayle reports.

I nod. "Kisslinger dumped me back onto society with the admonition to imbibe the spirit of cooperation, but he's refusing to certify me as a low potential security risk to my employer." I laugh. "He awaits my return with open palms. We'll see if Nancy forces me to undergo another round of this skulduggery."

"I'm living proof that the Duchess is into the death penalty. But you can look for her to subject you to a situation likely to inflict further heavy psychological carnage before she takes steps to eliminate you." Delmar rises. "I have to visit the men's room."

"How old is Delmar?" Spaatz inquires as we watch Vecsey cross the floor.

"Three years older than us." I recognize to my amusement that Del could pass for a teenager.

Gayle turns to me. "How'd he hurt his leg?"

"I can't believe you can detect that slight hitch." I swirl my lager in my mug. "One of Del's legs is a little longer than the other so sometimes his gait gets gimpy."

"I don't miss the deets." Gayle smiles knowingly. "That's what separates scientists like you and artists like me from the rest of the working peasants, and why we need to control their destiny." He loses his smirk. "I have to admit I concur with your shrink's original opinion. You know what's the difference between you and the common slug? Most guys think they're ten times tougher than they are; you're ten times tougher than you think you are." His demeanor grows even more somber. "Admit it. In school, you were always the guy who stepped aside in the hall to let others pass."

I emit a self-conscious snicker. "I remember a couple of teeth-rattling collisions when I didn't."

Gayle sips his mojito. "I staked out Johnny's house again. The punk kid showed up in the menacemobile." His contempt is palpable. "They were standing in the driveway together, and I was overcome with the urge to pull in and run them down. I started my engine – and drove off." He emits a heavy breath. "You recall my last personal encounter with Johnny?"

I take a full minute to exercise my keen memory. "You told me it was at Druthers bowling alley, didn't you?"

"Yeah, Dibb's right before ownership changed and it became Druthers." He grimaces and clears his throat. "I must've been 19, and I'd arranged to meet someone there. I walk in, and there's Johnny standing at the bar. He looks at me and suddenly recognizes me. 'Gaylord!' He comes over, puts his arm around me, and for an instant I idiotically anticipate he's matured and wants to apologize for the ornery cuss he was when we were younger. He swings me around, takes me back to the door and gives me a token shove outside. 'You're not wanted here.' I stood frozen with my hand on the door poised to barge back in until some other people came. I stepped aside so they could enter and I left."

"Johnny was just lucky you don't bowl," I offer.

"Luckier I don't shoot," Spaatz snarls.

"Don't elevate Bustelich to worth-the-worry status," I insist.

"Talking about your old buddy again?" Delmar returns. "Can't you jazz your position as a collection agent to ruin his credit?"

"There you go," I expand the theme. "Arrange to have the punk's car repossessed."

"That beater." Gayle finishes his mojito. "Johnny's credit is already horrible. But his affronts were always so personal that any legitimate response would need to be in kind."

I've invited the entire Ideal Allele Healthspan lab team to the "self-catered black-tie-optional farewell affair at Pfixx's Inn," and Kelly stops by. So does Skinny Jean. Delmar swallows shots and confesses he's harbored romantic feelings for both women. He further reveals a scheme he hatched to leave provocative messages for each that appeared to originate from the husband of the other in the hope that the spouses might fight a duel and he might inherit the loser's widow. Kelly leaves after one drink. But Skinny Jean knocks down some shots, plies Del with questions about his new job and nicknames him "Downstream Diva." She is quickly in no condition to make an informed decision about how willing she is to risk being stopped for D.U.I. She lives a short distance from my neighborhood in Elm Grove, and I protectively volunteer to drive her car and take her home.

Delmar and Gayle follow us to Jean's residence with the intent of subsequently locating an alternate party site but we ultimately decide to curtail the festivities, and they drop me off at my house. Del and I exchange sincere smiles, a firm handshake and a few trite words of encouragement. I hope that my good name doesn't sustain too bad a battering in the space it takes for Del to convey Gayle home.

Maynard greets me inside the back door, and I pat his head affectionately. "I often lament how barren my social life is, pal, but whenever it picks up, I seem to end up wishing it hadn't." I let the dachshund outside, and when he returns, we head for the smart low-rider chair in the living room. "In a way, it's almost a relief to see Del go." I stroke the dog's back as he shakes his stuffed skunk. "Those ridiculous tiffs he'd have with people, especially nasty Nancy. I hope he and Gayle don't get into an argument. My best friend of convenience and my best friend of circumstance both burn so much impotent energy. The world will always be full of people like Johnny Bustelich. The best coping strategy will always be to hang in places far above their stomping grounds."

I COLLECT MY next memo to report to Nancy Buetow-Detweiler's office on the Friday afternoon two weeks and two days after Delmar Vecsey's going-away celebration. She manages to display a tranquil smile as I seat myself on the receiving-end of her desk. "I've read the final assessment from your sensitivity counselor. It's hard to believe you're through with him already."

"Already?" I strain to keep my feet motionless beneath my chair. "I feel 15 years older than when I started with him."

"Of course, he's unable to relate specifics which would violate the privacy of your medical information, but to understate the case, he indicates that he wasn't overly impressed with you." The Duchess furrows her brow. "I'm pleased that you feel you benefited at least a little from seeing him."

I chortle. "My smarmy swami can sort your oppositional defiant disorder from your occupational reliant dishonor without breaking a sweat. He's well-positioned among the looming legends of talking medicine to be rated as a blooming bludgeon."

"You selected him." Nancy eyes me intently. "He remarks that your obstinate resistance to change was an insurmountable barrier to a positive outcome in counseling." She rises. "He states that he confronted an attitude of chronic overall dissatisfaction and denial that you have a problem, and he concludes that he cannot certify you aren't a festering security risk."

I nod. "That Kisslinger will go out on a limb for you."

The Duchess places her hands on her hips. "You tell me what your attitude is."

"I don't entertain any notion of setting out to cause trouble here." I stand. "Should I become disenchanted, it'd be far easier and more elegant to simply leave. I can't truthfully state that there's anybody on the team that I really dislike. I even consider the shovers and makers in H.R., sales and legal more comical than they are contemptible."

"It's interesting that you'd use a double negative there, because your counselor strongly hints that you carry an overload of negative energy." Nancy reseats herself, and I follow her lead. "Aaron believes that our company will gain a reputation as a 'stress shop' if employees feel they need to tiptoe around one another and that such a reputation will make it more difficult for us to attract and retain talent. The prof also advises us that such an atmosphere is not conducive to robust inquiry. I don't know that I necessarily agree that we benefit when employees can't count on being shielded from personal indignities and disrespect, but your 'smarmy swami' recommends you be given another chance to succeed with another therapist before further action is considered." She turns her attention to her computer screen. "So I'll expect you to work out that business on your own and trust you to follow through because Sandee and I have better things to do than run after you and check up on it." She looks up. "We have a lot of interesting projects in the pipeline: bioprinting; cryo-electron tomography; optogenetic systems; nanoparticles; improved resolution; increased separation efficiency; optimal linear velocities. Obscure processes and fancy toys."

"I don't like to think I wouldn't be here for it." I leave her office and return to my mutant fat cell cultures.

It is apparently the time of the season for social messaging. Before the evening turns to night, I receive a warning from my sister Dinah that she will call me early tomorrow. Next, I receive an invitation from Gayle Spaatz to accompany him tomorrow on a Saturday morning stakeout of the John E. Bustelich residence. I politely decline. Lastly, I receive a message from Delmar Vecsey in Pasadena, Texas extolling the sweeping grandeur of the area, the extraordinary cordiality of the locals and the exquisite beauty of the women. In a rambling narrative, Del further indicates that he feels lonesome, lost and concerned that he committed the biggest blunder of his life by leaving Wisconsin. I reply that I stand ever-ready to throw him a welcome-back bash.

Exchanges of real-time voice communication with my only sibling have become progressively less frequent since our mother's death two and a half years ago. It isn't so much that our relationship is strained as it bears the stretchmarks of her transglobal wanderlust. Dinah was drawn across the state line to attend college in magnetic Minnesota, where she met her husband Fitsal Malonazo, a native of the Philippines. Di continued distancing herself from home-cooking following graduation, settling with her spouse in British Columbia and then migrating with Fitz and their infant son to Zamboanga City. My sister would pretty much have to leave the planet to lay any more metric degrees of separation between us. Knowing Di, she could very well be working on it.

I believe I've overcome my petty feelings of resentment that Dinah left me to be the caretaker for our parents in the final years of their lives. Logistics would dictate that the child who remains local shoulder the load, especially when the one who performed the disappearing act moved a half-day away. I once tried to introduce the topic in therapy but Kisslinger was more interested in exploring the "here and now" trauma of a bad haircut. Di has returned once since our mother's funeral. We took the car tour of Door County and other forested regions in northern Wisconsin that we enjoyed almost every year with the folks when we were kids. And we admired the bright autumn colors that had somehow seemed much more vivid in times past.

The call pops into the computer at nine A.M. sharp Saturday morning. The transmission is crisp and clear. Dinah's cocoa brown hair appears longer with more blonde highlights than in recent sightings. "I really don't know why we don't do this more often." Her opening line is as welcome as it is stale.

"You look great, Di." My offering is as trite as hers but it's probably more sincere. "The tropics do agree with you."

"Yeah, life is a beach." Dinah rises from her couch, and the camera tracks her. "In other words, you have sunburn, blisters, abrasions, delirium, nausea, dehydration, diarrhea, vomiting and insomnia."

"I guess you choose either to dodge typhoons or suffer snowstorms." My surprise at the vigor of her complaint lingers, and I can't resist referring to Fitsal by my preferred term of endearment. "Sal Manila treating my favorite sister okay?"

She exhibits a lackluster smile. "One of the prime discussions we're having now is whether we view the Philippines as our permanent home."

"Considering giving winsome Wisconsin another shot?" I'm disgusted by how solicitous I sound.

"Perish the thought," she scoffs.

"I worry about you each day, Di," I confess. "I keep close track of news from the Mindanao area, and it seems there's always some political unrest, some upheaval underfoot."

She expels a heavy breath. "We live in the best part of town. Most large American cities are much more dangerous."

"Are you sure?" I look askance at the screen. "The other day in therapy I recalled the time in our early teens when you confided your fantasy about being abducted by revolutionaries."

"I believe that was *your* fantasy." A sly grin crosses Dinah's lips. "The main reason we'd move is for Angelo. The multicultural base we're trying to provide for him abhors thick roots and extended stagnation."

"I hear Mongolia is nice this time of year." I chuckle at Di's perpetual restlessness. "I trust my favorite nephew is still doing great in school?"

"His interests seem to have outgrown math and science," she laments. "He turned ten since the last time we talked."

"He wasn't much more than a toddler the last time I actually saw him." I believe I've interjected this observation into every conversation I've had with Di since.

"How's sensitivity training progressing?" she inquires. "It must be comforting to be able to count on someone to always be in your corner."

"Once upon a time, you handled that duty." I'd mentioned I was starting therapy in a note with the birthday card I sent in June, but I don't burden my sister with news that my adventure in ennobling self-discovery is over. "And you charged a more reasonable rate. If you want the job back, it's yours."

"I have enough problems back here to fill every moment." Dinah reseats herself. "Although I do have some business in the Midwest coming up at the end of next month. I'm considering taking the opportunity to pay you a visit and show my son the spectacular fall colors of Wisconsin. Would that work?"

I chortle with zeal. "As I told my shrink, I live for pleasant surprises. And anytime anything good happens, it's a pleasant surprise. Can you specify a date?"

"How about the first weekend in November?" She checks her crystal planner. "Six weeks from today."

"Super!" I offer my most agreeable smile. "Amboy Fitz coming along?"

Something akin to sentimentality pools in Dinah's azure eyes. "Fitz doesn't go on vacation any better than you." I've previously disclosed that I spend most of my time when I travel wishing I was in my backyard playing with the dog.

"He'll have previous obligations. And speaking of that, Lisle, there's a related favor I need to ask of you. While I take care of some personal business, I'd really appreciate it if you could host Angelo for a day and a night. It'd be off-the-charts great if you would because he has so many relatives on his father's side, and on my side there's only you. I'd love for him to have the chance to become familiar with his Uncle Lisle. But if you have other plans or you don't-"

"Your presumptuousness," I interrupt, "is adorable. I'm sure that such an arrangement will help cement an essential pillar of fulfillment in both our lives."

"Okay, I'll get right to work on travel arrangements-" Her voice is smothered by frenetic barking, as Maynard spots a man walking a large, shaggy dog past our house. "I'd nearly forgotten to ask if you still have your wiener dog."

"He's a great little guy," I insist. "Give him a chance, and you'll learn to love him like Gus."

"Argus was always *your* dog, Lisle." Our old Weimaraner was probably the only creature under the sun who ever preferred me to her, although he might've given her more consideration if she'd taken more regular care of him.

"Hearing from you this weekend, Di, really was a pleasant surprise." I purse my fond lips and straighten my posture. "I'm eagerly looking forward to your visit."

She spreads her thumb and pinkie. "You know *you* can always call *me*."

I nod. "I did call you twice this summer, and you never replied."

Her features adopt a wry, pensive cast. "I remember one

call that came at a hopelessly busy time for us. I'm sorry, opportunity slipped away."

"It happens to the best of us." My sister and I trade goodbyes, and she pledges to send me a verification message as soon as her itinerary is finalized. I sit in my stylish low-profile chair with guarded optimism, even as a smorgasbord of occasions where my parents favored Dinah over me pops into my consciousness. She was probably disappointed to receive only half of the estate. My younger sister was always the more accomplished child. I don't believe that my parents ever fully appreciated the extent of the physical and emotional suffering that life inflicted on me. It's amazing what a few red bumps can do for your social outlook. Nevertheless, I was proud of Di too. And I know that our father and mother tried hard to be good parents, and they succeeded a lot more often than they failed. So in the final analysis, I consider myself blessed to have been a member of the Amonor family. Providence could've just as easily made me a Bustelich.

Maynard sits beside me, and I stroke his back tenderly. "You're going to have to be on your best behavior, boy. But if Nancy can orchestrate a successful visit from the relatives, so can we."

THREE DAYS AFTER our chat, Dinah sends a message to inform me that she and Angelo are set to arrive in Milwaukee on Saturday morning October 25th with an option to return any day the following week. I leave work early and celebrate my impending family reunion by purchasing a clean, preowned stealth grey GMC Yukon XL SUV. The four-wheel drive Yukon sports four new snow tires, which I'm frugal and lazy enough to leave in place. I send Gayle Spaatz an announcement that I'm weaponized with another motor vehicle and invite him to join me on the upcoming Saturday for a slightly squishy joyride. Gayle extends his congratulations on my addition and his regrets that he'll be busy over the weekend. I obsessively commence removing spent flowers and gnarled leaves from my African violets and embrace the project of otherwise sprucing up the house.

Four and a half weeks later right on schedule, my sister Dinah roars into my driveway in her red Tesla Model X rental car. She opens the falcon-wing doors, extracts my nephew from the back seat and tugs him along the walkway. Angelo is wearing shiny black shoes that will probably leave skid marks. Di smiles and waves. Barricaded in the kitchen, Maynard barks sharply. I open the door to receive my guests. "Step out on the porch, Lisle," Dinah directs me. "The last time I visited, it took me two weeks to remove all the hair from my clothes." The last time she visited, Maynard nipped her. "We'll have enough to do to clean up Angelo." I shut the door behind me and step forward. "I don't know why you can't just have a miniature poodle."

"Wirehaired dachshunds are quieter." I kiss the air in the proximity of Di's cheek, and she reciprocates. I bend slightly and extend my hand. "Hello, Angelo Vesuvius, I haven't seen you in person since the week before you turned three."

"This is your Uncle Lisle." My sister presses firmly on her boy's back. "Do you remember him?"

"Hell no." Angelo grasps my hand weakly for a moment and flicks it away. "But seeing your face again explains one of my nightmares."

Dinah grimaces with mild irritation, and I force a chuckle. "You've indicated he's as precocious as he is precious."

"He doesn't approve of his middle name," Di apologizes.

"Oh, 'Vesuvius' is a proud, majestic name," I assert. "It connotes danger."

"You like my middle name?" Angelo challenges. "How about my middle finger?"

"Angelo!" Di snaps. "Sometimes he's too dangerous for his own good."

I nod. "It sounds like he watches too many sitcoms."

"He earns his recreational media time," Dinah counters. "He's already fluent in four languages just like Mom. Say something to Uncle Lisle in German, honey."

"*Leck mich im Arsch*," Angelo articulates.

I speak barely enough German to ballpark the apt retort. "*Mit einem Stiefel.*" Di sighs, and I smile at the boy. "Who's not looking forward to touring the great Wisconsin north woods? With vibrant scenery to rival the Black Forest?" He mutters something beneath his breath and hangs his head.

"I think you reminded him that he recently received his first pair of glasses," Dinah discloses. "He's still a little upset about it, so now he may brood for a while."

I pat Angelo on the shoulder. "I clearly recall my own emotional distress at the onset of flat eyeballs. But the really smart people all wear glasses."

"Geeks and nerds wear glasses," he corrects me.

"Geeks and nerds rule the world," I observe.

"My dad doesn't wear glasses," the boy huffs.

I contort my mouth. "Just think how even more awesome he'd be if he did."

"It's your family's defective genes," he gripes. "The ass-munch Amonor curse."

I wonder if Angelo's perspective would improve upside down in the shrubs. "In a few years, you can have a corrective procedure like I did so you rarely rely on your specs."

The boy stands silenced, and a smile creeps across Di's lips. "It sounds as though you two could actually become friends."

"We already are, right, A.V.?" I extend a friendly fist but Angelo ignores the fellowship gesture.

Dinah remotely opens the trunk of her Tesla. "Angelo, please retrieve your luggage." The boy scowls and trudges to the rental car. Di turns back to me. "So the chick you had here flew the coop before I even had a chance to meet her."

"Before you even had a chance to fustigate her." I watch Angelo climb into the Model X. "She blew off the best opportunity she'll ever have to do something productive with her life, or at least reproductive. So it's just me and Maynard again."

"It sounds like it's going to be just you and the dog forever." Di probes my festering emotional wound with spiritual rock salt. "You're running out of time, Lisle, till you're officially certified as a hermit." My nephew remains in the car. "You recall my old friend Amanda Bogzaran, don't you? I've made arrangements to have dinner with her on Monday."

"Commanda Amanda." I awkwardly shuffle in place as I recall Di's bonny schoolmate. "One of those sneaky beauties whose neotenous features could change in an instant from sweet to lethal."

Dinah snickers. "Yeah, she's Amanda Hastings now with four kids. But she mentioned that she's still good friends with Belinda Shukel from your class. And Belinda is freshly divorced."

"Ah, Belinda." I smack my lips. "Known better as Dusty. Busty Dusty, crusty but lusty, with thick brows beneath loud bangs. So Amanda will invite Belinda to join the party if you invite me. So sorry, Snake-Oil Sally, no sale."

My sister hisses. "You're so predictable, it's disgusting. Why not?"

"Because I picture Dusty Shukel, who didn't speak three words to me through high school, at age 34 sans husband, saying grace with some militant feminist mantra and explaining she's reconciled with the fact that her life has reached the 'settling stage.'" I imagine Kisslinger's clueless input on why I feel threatened by this opportunity. "I'm not broken; I don't need to be fixed up."

"Give her a chance." Di's gaze radiates with condescension. "Most people eventually get over themselves enough to develop some sophistication in their social interactions."

"Whatever," I riposte. "I'll keep searching for another reason to get up in the morning."

"Angelo!" Dinah turns away from me. "Where are you?" The boy emerges from the Model X holding his Megalophone. He stuffs the device in his shirt pocket, snatches two modest grey suitcases from the trunk and waddles back to the porch. Di plucks the Megalophone out of the boy's pocket and hands the item to me. "He was supposed to leave this back at the hotel. Hide it. Don't let him have it until I come to pick him up tomorrow."

Angelo drops his bags heavily, and Maynard begins barking vigorously again. "Shut up, mutt!" the boy shouts.

"He generally loves animals." Dinah runs her fingers through her son's hair. "So are you two going to do the zoo?"

"That seems like a perfect way to spend a perfect afternoon." I look for a glimmer of glee in my nephew's eyes and find none. "Sure you won't come in for a bit, Di?"

"If we wear grunge on Tuesday, maybe I'll come in then." Her eagerness to leave is palpable. "I'll be back to pick up Angelo tomorrow after lunch." A rough 28-hour countdown unofficially begins. "Be a perfect little gentleman for Uncle Lisle, Angelo, and Mom will see you soon." My only two close blood relatives embrace. "I'm a resource to call if you run into a problem, Lisle, but I'm positive you'll do just fine with him." I stand beside Angelo and wave as his mother drives off like a madwoman.

Angelo holds out his hand. "Give me my MP, boob."

"Maybe if you ask me nicely," I admonish him. "After our field trip." I pick up his luggage. "I'll follow you inside."

Angelo enters my living room like a condemned little gentleman, and Maynard barks sharply. The boy points at the dog. "I sure as hell don't need this." He makes assorted hand gestures, guttural sounds and jerky movements. The canine barks ferociously.

"Don't let him bite you," I instruct the boy. "I'll have to dump your body in some abandoned well so your mother never finds out." I step over the barricade and calm the dog. "He doesn't readily suffer strangers in his house, so he'll be spending most of your visit in his cozy corner of the basement. Maybe when we get home from the zoo, we can all take a short walk together, and you and he can develop some rapport."

"I don't want to be seen with him." Angelo edges a step closer. "He's goofy-looking. His head is too small, and his body is too long."

"He thinks your head is too big and your body is too short," I playfully reply. "His full name is Maynard Garland Amonor."

"How stupid," the boy snarls. "How surprising."

"You don't have any pets?" I verify. "No rat, spider or viper with whom to share your moods?"

Angelo scoffs, and Maynard growls softly. "Get the bowwow out of here, will you, *Uncle Lisle*?" The boy retreats to the davenport.

"All right, I'll let him run around the backyard for a few minutes before we leave." I let Maynard out the back door. When I return to the living room, Angelo's pockets are stuffed with candy from the jumbo glass party bowl on the coffee table. "Help yourself to some Halloween treats."

Angelo seats himself in my low-rider chair. "In my American Culture class, the educator says referring to the Harvest Festival as anything else is uninclusive, ignorant and rude."

"You say Halloween is just for suckers, Pops?" I pat the thick mat of professionally styled hair atop my nephew's head. "Let me show you where the bathroom and your bedroom are. I imagine you'd like to slip into some more comfortable clothes before we go out, wouldn't you?"

Angelo eyes me coldly. "My dad warned me that you're a pervert."

"Too bad no one could warn you about your dad." I smile with exasperation. "Look, kid, let's try a little harder to get along and not drive each other crazy, okay? I'm sorry if you're upset about being forced to go cold turkey without your electronic pacifier for a whole day-"

"Maybe if you didn't try so hard, you wouldn't be so sorry," the boy snarls. "My button-down and slacks are fine. Maybe if you dressed up some, you'd be more presentable and earn a little respect."

I bring Maynard back inside the house, lock everything and usher Angelo into my GMC Yukon XL for our excursion to the zoo. "How do you like my wicked new wheels? It's a little up in years, so it doesn't have an entertainment center or navigator to link your MP to, but it's clean for a classic, hmm?"

"My dad would call this a jackwagon." Angelo slaps the dashboard. "He calls *you* a jackwagon."

"He drives a tricycle, doesn't he?" We take the scenic route, and I attempt to fan the boy's bestial enthusiasm. "Do you have a favorite animal?"

My nephew frowns. "I don't know." He produces a choco-late bar. "I don't care. Unicorn?"

I grope for another avenue of amity. "So, Angelo, is there a preferred nickname that you go by?"

The boy hisses. "Here we go with the name-calling again. What's *your* middle name, twit?"

"Daniel," I divulge. "I'm L.D. Amonor, just as your mom was D.L. Amonor."

"Oh, *Danny boyyy*," Angelo warbles. "Why don't you go by 'Danny'? That's a good name for a bendy man who tap-dances in tight pants." My nephew rubs his hand over the window and door interior. "You tap-dance in tight pants, don't you?"

"Only across the faces of people who really irritate me." I inhale deeply. "'Daniel' is an extremely *venerable* name, if you know what that means. There's a Biblical prophet named Daniel. The Persians put him in a lions' den so he'd be eaten alive, but the emotional and intellectual strength that he derived from his faith enabled him to stare the lions down, and they left him alone."

"No shit?" Angelo seems genuinely impressed. "We're taught that those stories in the Bible are just myths for weak-minded people. My dad says religion is a way of escaping mortal reality the same as drugs or booze, just without the pleasure. Do you really believe in God?"

"I believe!" I expel the words so forcefully that it almost scares me. "Is Dinah tickled pink that you're down with popular atheism?"

"The thing is, Danno, we have perspective in my family." Angelo sticks a candy cigarette between his lips. "Someone like you would be incapable of understanding why an enlightened person would never develop an interest in religion."

I nod. "Right before your mother slipped into her Che Guevara phase, she was fascinated with Rasputin, the inscrutable cleric of the Russian court. Count your blessings your name isn't 'Rasputin Guevara.'"

The boy hisses. "You must really believe you rattle me when you trash my name, huh, dork?"

"Your parents attempted to capture in your name the romantic climate of their trip through Italy during which you were conceived." We reach Bluemound Road and draw to within several blocks of the zoo. "Or else your mother just had an agonizing labor." I snicker. "If you were to be renamed now, your middle name might more appropriately be 'Erebus.'"

Angelo sneers. "Danny, Danny, diaper man – his car's a turd; his bed's the can."

We park in the east lot of the zoo. Angelo and I begin

exploring the grounds. "If you don't promise to return my MP the minute we get back to your house," the boy snarls, "I'm going to take off, and you're going to have to tell my mom you lost me at the zoo."

"How about if I just tell her you achieved a release when we visited the cathouse?" I lead Angelo to the feline exhibit in the heart of the zoo. We stand at the rail and observe a male and female lion basking in the sun. "Quite the magnificent beasts, hmm?"

"Think what they'd do to your dumb, little dog." My nephew discharges ripping and crunching noises. "I wish we'd brought him along so I could throw him into the cage, because what I really want is to see you jump in there and stare the lions down, just like your old prophet Daniel did, because I don't believe anything like that ever happened."

I expel an exasperated breath. "Don't talk like a little imbecile."

Three middle-aged women stand a short distance from us. Angelo backhands the closest one in the hip and points to me. "Watch! Daniel here is jumping in there with them!" He points at the lions. The women scrutinize me through horrified expressions.

I emit a chagrined chuckle. "Don't talk like a little idiot."

Angelo and I venture inside the big cat center. "Do you remember coming to this zoo with my mom when you were kids?"

"Many times," I acknowledge. "Those are some treasured memories."

"Your memories are part of you," he verifies. "And you believe in heaven, and in eternal life?"

"Yezzz," I warily concede.

Angelo rubs his chin reflectively. "So if you live forever, you'd have lived billions and billions of years and you'd just be getting started. How would your little pea-brain have the space to remember the things you did in all that time?"

I consider the problem. "Maybe your brain is the hard drive that preserves your most precious memories along with pointers to various locations in the cloud that hold your semi-precious ones."

Angelo shakes his head slowly. "And he calls *me* an idiot."

A man with three children stands at the glass partition of the tiger cage as the striped beast paces back and forth in front of them. The man roars, raps on the glass and gesticulates threateningly to elicit a rise from the cat. Angelo roars and waves likewise. I rap the boy lightly in the back of the head. "Animals are here to be admired, not harassed."

Angelo points at the tiger teaser. "Tell him." My nephew approaches the man, raps him in the hip and points at me. "That guy says you're a jerk for harassing animals."

The man is stocky with a beard. He approaches and stands directly in front of me so I can process the stale scent of one of his toiletries. "What's your problem?" he challenges me.

"I never called you anything." I shrug. "The boy's a mind reader."

The tiger teaser glares at me for a long, cold moment. "Come on, kids." He turns to his charges and bumps my shoulder as he brushes past. "Wuss-pipe."

Angelo and I exit the big cat exhibit. "My dad likes to tease my mom," the boy volunteers, "that I'm an only-child just like her." We visit the bears and moose. "Why don't you ever send me presents, Danny Boy, like my dad's brothers do?"

I rub my neck. "I think I'll wait until your visit is over to decide if you merit a gift."

We proceed to the reptile house and arrive at the cage of the boa constrictor. "Do you have any boas, anacondas, or similar paunch-pinchers in the 'Pines?" My innocent query elicits an ardent gasp of scorn, and I try to disengage with glib deference. "No giant nest of pythons out in the backyard?"

"You know what I'd really like to do?" Angelo asserts.

I nod. "Bring a rubber snake in here and deposit it somewhere not readily conspicuous?"

"I'd like to get one like that." My nephew sticks out his tongue at the serpent. "I'd bring it over to your house and watch it devour your dumb, little mutt. The moment Mange-ard realized he was about to be annihilated would be the best. The long bulge would slowly slide through the snake's tubular body as it got digested." He claps his hands together. "Let's ask if we could rent this one."

I discharge a petulant breath. "I'm glad you're sensitive enough to appreciate the pleasure that animals can bring to a person's life."

"Don't judge me!" the boy snaps. "Really, why don't you virtue-signal someone your own size, wuss-pipe?"

"I'm content to improve the value of the few vessels over whom I'm granted stewardship," I advise him, "especially those who suffer from overexposure to gross leniency."

Angelo fronts me with arms akimbo. "Is that how a chick-enshit validates himself?"

I suppress the impulse to present my nephew for adoption at the cobra cage. "Civilization has evolved in a manner which renders avoiding trouble the paramount mark of intelligence."

Angelo sighs. "Whatever it takes to make you feel good about yourself, wanky."

I treat my nephew to a burger, fries and ice cream at the concession parlor. He chides me afterward for subjecting him to an unhealthy diet.

We return to my home, get Angelo settled and take Maynard for a walk. The boy and the dog reach a tenuous truce. "Uncle Lisle, my mom says you can't even keep a kept woman. Why did the house tart you had leave you? Because you have a lousy job? Why do you have to work in a germ gallery?"

"My lady friend snored like a wildebeest." I hop to keep my feet from tangling in the dog's leash. "I had to dismiss her because the neighbors were getting restless."

Angelo nods. "She got a better offer. I'm sorry you're a loser who has to live alone."

I gesture to Maynard. "I don't live alone."

The boy rolls his eyes. "My dad calls you a 'super lightweight.' Having a dumb name like 'Lisle' doesn't help, but if you went by 'Daniel,' it'd be even worse. You should change your name to 'Lilac.'"

"Do your parents get after each other every once in a while, or is it all the time?" I trot to the next tree as the dog spies a squirrel.

Angelo snorts with contempt. "We all coexist just fine!" He remains several steps behind us until Maynard twirls at the curb and defecates. I produce my scoop and bag. My nephew dashes to the house we're in front of, rings the doorbell repeatedly and pounds on the door. The boy hops off the porch as an elderly woman appears. "Our dog," he announces, "just crapped all over your lawn!"

"I'm taking care of it!" I display the scoop and bag. "Please pardon the boy, ma'am! He has a mental defect!"

Agape, the woman opens the door a crack. "Whatever it is, I'm not interested! Get out of here, weirdos!" She slams the door shut. I growl at my nephew.

Angelo chuckles raucously. "Yeah, I have a mental defect." He picks up a stick and whacks each tree that we pass. "What do the putzes around these parts mostly do for excitement?"

"We putzes are mostly looking for peace, not excitement."

"Is that what you told your floozy right before she took off?" The boy snickers. "Or couldn't she take a punch?" He hurls his stick over a passing car. "I'll bet she *looked* like she could take a punch."

"What do you do for excitement in Zamboanga?" I counter. "Stage a coup?"

Angelo shakes his head. "I'll have to give my mom more credit for getting her sorry ass out of this shithole."

We walk another block in silence. Maynard adopts an alert posture. A man approaches on the other side of the street escorting a large, white dog with the features of a Siberian husky. My dog and his dog pull on their respective leashes and snarl menacingly at each other. My nephew rushes into the middle of the street. "Our dog can rip your dog to shreds!" he taunts the husky handler.

"*No, no!!*" I wave and point at Angelo. "Please excuse the

boy, sir! He has behavioral issues! You have a beautiful dog." The man fixes me with an indignant glare as he and his dog pass.

Angelo discharges a series of harsh guffaws. "None of you dinks around here have any sense of humor."

"You crazy, little bastard, do you really think you're cute?" I jettison any pretense of charm. "We're lucky that guy kept his dog under control! Giving someone a split second to guess whether they're faced with a real threat isn't cool!" I take a deep breath. "Too many dinks around here are out with their dogs off-leash. They don't clean up after them, and they let them get in Maynard's face. When there's a skirmish, it's somehow our fault for being there."

The boy frowns. "You don't like me, Uncle Lisle." He sniffles. "I could tell you didn't like me right away."

"Save the woebegone bit, kid." I lead my contingent across the street to avoid another dog and walker. "I'll give you your Megalophone as soon as we leave the restaurant following supper tonight — if you can be civil until then."

We complete the neighborhood circuit and return home. Angelo seats himself on the living room davenport like a little prince, and I gamble that my nephew and my dog can peacefully coexist. The boy leaps to his feet and grabs more candy; the canine barks and nips him in the hand. With Angelo moaning, I banish Maynard to the basement. I take the boy into the bathroom and examine the wound. Skin of his middle finger is broken but there's no blood. "Rotten, damn dog!" Angelo snarls. "I hate dogs!" I run warm water over his finger and wash it with disinfectant soap. "He's vicious! He needs to be put down!"

"Chill." I pat Angelo on the head and attempt to calm him with the soft deportment of a grief counselor. "If we ever come to snuffing out everyone who demonstrates vicious tendencies, son, we'll drop you into an active volcano — a double benefit because then you can't testify against Maynard."

Relations between my nephew and me improve as I treat him to an elegant dining experience at the Crystal Kettle Supper Club. He drops his mixed vegetable plate on the floor, emits a few resounding burps and performs a crude impression of a dog licking the bottom of his salad bowl, but his behavior is satisfactory. "You wouldn't have so much trouble in life," he advises me, "if you were better-looking."

We return home and I present him with his Megalophone. He complains of travel fatigue and retires to his bedroom. I check on him three hours later and he's lying on the bed engaged with his electronic device. "Don't disturb me," he carps, "I'm monitoring world news reports."

I smirk. "Anything going on that I should know about?"

"In San Francisco, 25 to 30 armed men broke into a home and killed the owner in what police are calling a botched burglary." The boy sighs. "How about a late snack?"

I repair to the kitchen, trust to popular Filipino gourmand sources and prepare the garlic fried rice dish of sinangag along with a batch of loaded fries. I also take the opportunity to marinate tilapia fillets for tomorrow's breakfast. I add a mild sedative to the loaded fries. I coax Angelo out of his room, and we eat our snacks while watching iconic cartoons such as *Popeye* and *Bullwinkle* on TV. The boy complains that the cartoons contain "disturbing stereotypes." I finally escort my drowsy nephew back to his guest room and lock him inside. After taking Maynard outside, I proceed with the dog to my bedroom and lock the door behind us with a tremendous sense of relief. I sleep with one ear open, and we somehow make it through the night without incident.

I rise early and prepare fried fish steaks along with rye muffins, poached pears and the highly touted chocolate rice porridge called champorado. Angelo complains that the food is too "sweetly slimy" but consumes it voraciously. I inform my nephew that he will accompany me to church.

"Get real," he scoffs. "I don't twerk to that tune."

I sidle behind the boy and clamp my hands on his shoulders. "Even if you don't believe in a deity per se, it doesn't hurt to humbly drop your important tasks and weighty responsibilities for an hour each week to formally recognize that you're not the center of the universe."

"Time is finite," he grumbles. "You don't want to waste it."

"I don't want to leave you and Maynard alone here," I submit, "even for an hour. If you humor me, I'll tell your mother that you were indeed a perfect little gentleman for the duration of your visit." I smile affirmatively. "If you refuse, I'll confiscate your Megalophone again."

Angelo sighs. "All right, Dandy, if you promise to send me a fabulous gift for my next birthday."

On the ride to church, I attempt to further develop my nephew's sense of decency. "Take the opportunity to give thanks that your life is more comfortable than that of 99 percent of other hominids that have ever walked the Earth."

"Let me give thanks that I'm not you!" Angelo guffaws.

"People thought our natural world was of secondary importance for a thousand years so they didn't study it. Religion is the reason our scientific progress is a thousand years behind a reasonable timetable."

I look askance at the boy and see a 10-year-old David Rohr-Kisslinger. "Don't throw the movement out with the movers. Religion is what gave men like Newton and Mendel an opportunity to make their discoveries. Sir Isaac even calculated a date for the second coming of Christ."

Angelo snickers sardonically. "Is there an expiration date on this second-coming business?"

"The theme of the resurrection on the third day is recurrent in the New Testament." I'm pleased that my nephew is engaged by the topic. "A letter of Peter states that a day is to God as a thousand years and a thousand years are as a day. Combine those clues, and I'd expect the Lord's reappearance to occur in the dawn of the third millennium of the so-called common era."

"That sounds straightforward and simple-minded enough." The boy stares pensively into space. "If we hit the midpoint of the millennium with no god to show for it, would you give it up and concede you've been living in a tangled web of irrational fantasy?"

"My spirits would be dampened," I confess. "Every generation must believe that the final days are at hand, but I sincerely don't know how the world can continue much longer in its progressive moral decline."

Angelo shakes his head. "Then you better step on it."

We arrive at church in good sodality, but no sooner do we

populate our pew than my nephew produces his Megalophone. "Good morning and welcome, All Saints Francis parishioners and guests," the lector commences. "At this time, please holster your weapons."

I tap on the boy's electronic device. "That means that."

Angelo and I lock antagonistic miens. "Aw, all right." He deactivates the Megalophone and returns it to his pocket.

We stand and sing the opening hymn. A sideways glance finds Angelo interacting with his Megalophone again. "Let me have the toy." I grab the device but he refuses to release it. He flops onto the pew. "Give it to me." He stands up on the pew maintaining his hold. I catch a glimpse of the dismayed faces of fellow parishioners and guests. I lunge at Angelo and win the possession battle but he tumbles off the pew into the aisle. I hear a collective gasp. The boy holds his head and moans. "You're not hurt; stand up."

"Aw, all right." Angelo staggers to his feet, and we return to our positions in the pew.

Angelo begins kicking me in the ankle. "Give me back my MP," he demands. I ignore him. He rubs his head, totters and tumbles into the aisle. Another collective gasp rises behind us.

I squat beside the boy. "Get up, Angelo." He feigns unconsciousness. I pat his head and shoulder. "Don't do this to me."

"He's a little slow to respond." An usher appears at my side. "Would you like to carry him out to the vestibule? Call the paramedics?"

"He just has a conversion disorder." I pat Angelo on the cheeks with increasing intensity. "Get upright, you worm." I clutch his belt and yank him to his feet. "Stand up, Vesuvius."

"Sir, please," the usher whispers. "A more understanding attitude might be in order."

The priest appears to be scowling at me. I take Angelo by the arm and conduct him up the aisle toward the rear of the building. "Please don't hurt me anymore, Uncle Lisle!" he wails. "Don't bend me over again!"

I lug my nephew outside the church and he shakes out of my grasp. "Get in the car!" I steer him toward the Yukon.

The boy sneers. "Apparently, Lisle, you're still laboring under the misconception that you're in charge. You should've had more consideration for your guest's feelings." He extends his hand. "Give me my MP and go back inside. I'll wander around and call you to pick me up later, beta."

"Your visit is over." I'm too livid to call Dinah and discuss the situation. I deliver Angelo to the SUV door.

"God, you're full of yourself." The boy hops inside the vehicle. "You're a miserable host." He shakes his head. "You have a lot to learn about treating people right."

I ignore a string of multilingual invectives as we head for downtown Milwaukee. "Why don't you like me, Uncle Lisle?" my nephew gibes.

I can't resist stating the obvious. "Because you accentuate your ornery disposition by making a special point of repaying generosity with obnoxiousness."

He folds his arms dismissively. "So what are you getting me for my birthday?"

"Whatever it is," I pledge, "you can be sure it'll explode or attack you."

"A little short on Christian charity, aren't you, marble-mouth?"

Angelo snickers. "I have friends back home who attend Catholic school. They hate it. All the intolerance."

"As someone privy to the new world order," I observe, "you should recognize that militant secularists are generally about as tolerant as a firing squad."

Several blocks from Dinah's hotel, Angelo unbuckles his seat belt. "Watch out for that car!" He jerks the steering wheel so the Yukon nearly swerves into an oncoming vehicle. "Imbecile," he cackles.

I pull over and park illegally. I produce my handkerchief and fill it with a full nasal load. The boy groans. I thrust the handkerchief in his face. "Cause me the slightest trouble from this point on and I'll gag you with this!"

I escort Angelo around the corner, up the street and into the heavily upholstered lobby of the Fulton Baroque luxury hotel. My prayer for the day is answered when I threaten the front desk clerk and she furnishes his room number. "You're insufficiently compassionate," the boy advises me, as I drag him into the elevator. "Christian hypocrite." I drop his Megalophone and he pounces on it. As we complete our ascent, the awful thought occurs to me that Dinah might not be in her room. I promise myself that under such a circumstance I'll message her my regrets and leave her son hogtied outside her door.

We march down the hallway and reach Dinah's room. I knock. There is no answer, and I knock once more. The door opens and a large blond man wearing nothing but a pair of tight, black pants stands facing us. "I'm sorry," I haltingly offer, "I thought Dinah, ah, this was Dinah's-"

"Who is it?" Dinah's voice bleats in the background.

"Who are you?" The blond man strokes his chest hair.

Dinah emerges wearing a plum silk bathrobe. She beholds the boy and me with something akin to overwrought alarm. "What are you doing here?" she snaps.

"I can't take your pubescent tormentor for another second!" I give Angelo a token shove forward. "I'll have his baggage sent." I fix Di with a glare, turn and stride back down the hallway to the elevator. "Discipline," I repeatedly grumble all the way home, "discipline."

I receive a call from my sister at four in the afternoon. "Where do you get off," she skips any greeting, "mistreating and disrespecting my son?"

"At the point where he gets force-fed his just deserts," I estimate.

"I trusted you!" she screeches. "And you took the opportunity to browbeat him! You actually struck him! You allowed him to be bitten by that awful dog!"

"Did he tell you I molested him?" I agitate. "That's the sick impression he left my church congregation with."

"What was he doing at church?" she demands. "You know Fitsal and I don't want him exposed to that indoctrination mill at such an impressionable age!"

"Angelo," I submit, "is an overindulged, unruly, jaded postmodern snowflake, who needs to be introduced to the primitive concepts of discipline, humility and piety."

"Humility and piety," Dinah scoffs. "Are those the keys to your success? My boy is gentle. He can be a hyperactive prankster, but he's highly sensitized to the mistreatment of others. He was disturbed by seeing animals locked in cages. The problem here is you, Lisle! You finally got ahold of someone *you* could bully, and you tried to take full advantage! You better convince me he's exaggerating when he says you threatened to hurl him into a pit and send him a bomb!"

"I was speaking facetiously." I force a chuckle. "The former allusion was a payback joke for the times he wished my dog dead. If he's highly intelligent, he couldn't have believed I was sincere."

"I'm tempted to contact the police," she fumes, "and file a formal complaint that you're harboring a dangerous animal that has attacked at least two people I'm aware of."

I emit an exasperated breath. "You're slightly overreacting, Di."

"I'm overreacting to your threats to murder my son?" Her voice quivers. "You're out of control! He doesn't know you! He doesn't know how inept you are. He doesn't know how warped and depraved your sense of humor is. And it seems to have grown more warped and depraved every time I see you. Frankly, I don't know if I ever want to have anything more to do with you."

I scratch my neck. "Does that mean our trip to Door County on Tuesday is endangered?" She terminates the connection. "I'll keep the date open, mood-swinger."

"How do you guys manage it?" I sink to the floor and put my arm around Maynard. "How do you endure human beings?" His tail fans the air and I pet him gently. "Did I bully, gaslight or otherwise mistreat my nephew? Am I the reason our time together turned into some kind of disaster? Did I discount his fear of you or *me* or disregard his anxiety about being in an unfamiliar place? I'm ashamed to admit that I let the old familiar fear of being humiliated in public supplant my concern about providing the boy with a kind, protective environment."

I pat the dog on the head and return to my feet. "Am I a monster to you, too? I might find it intolerable to live with myself if I weren't a little more layered than the fellow who meets the eye. But then, it would seem that all the kids in my family are more complicated than you'd think. Di was once more religious than me." I catch a glimpse of myself in the mirror. "Please don't judge me too harshly." I'm not certain whether I'm still speaking exclusively with my dog.

MONDAY MORNING ARRIVES. I pack Angelo's bags but reconsider my commitment to send them to the hotel. I send Dinah a message directing her to come to the house and retrieve them. I'm not in a humor to do her any favors, but I also provide her with an excuse to reconnect. Monday passes. Tuesday morning passes. I've had no further contact with my sister. I consider taking the trip to assess the kaleidoscopic splashes of arboreal color throughout points north by myself but decide it's not worth the effort. Maynard and I find ample domestic amusements around the house and yard, including the seasonal indoor relocation of my two containers of Brazilian fireworks plants with their vibrant magenta flower spikes. I spend Tuesday evening in excruciation station. I finish assembling the inversion board and proceed to execute my most rigorous workout since Trish left me. Wednesday arrives, and there's still no word from Di. I'm tempted to call her and apologize, but I theorize that such a weak gesture would only infuriate her further. I must accept the reality that my sister's irked embarrassment will require months to dissipate, and I spend the day nursing my overall soreness. Thursday at dawn I send Dinah a message that Angelo's luggage awaits pickup on my front porch. I remit two vacation days and return to work.

Late in the afternoon, the telephone on Delmar Vecsey's vacated desk rings. This infrequent occurrence generally indicates that some business contact hasn't been effectively advised of Del's ouster. Skinny Jean jumps up and answers it. "Lisle," she summons me. "She wants to talk to you."

I meander to the phone and prepare to deliver the regrettable tidings. "Hello?"

"Don't mention names," a sexy female voice dictates. "Costume party at the Inn Friday night for Harvest Moon Fest."

"You mean Halloween," I admonish her. "How did you get this number?"

"Be there shortly before midnight." She disconnects.

"Who was that?" Kelly inquires.

"Private number," I submit. "Probably one of Dr. Aaron's charges at the U. treating herself to a little Halloween prank hacking his directory. She babbled something about costumes and hung up." I have little doubt that Delmar sponsored the call. It was either his idea of a trick or his way of announcing his return.

"Wild women are out there, Lisle." Sleepy Gene joins the conversation. "They consider you their diamond stud, and they're out to get you."

I nod. "They heard I'm a working mad scientist instead of

a mad working scientist, and it gives me major cachet around this time of year."

I return to my desk buoyed by the hope that the ghost of Delmar Vecsey will actually appear at our old designated haunt. I wonder if his presence will be permanent; he could've returned to visit his father. To debar potentially overwhelming disappointment, I entreat Gayle Spaatz to accompany me. Gayle has always exhibited a keen flair for Halloween parties. I recall the year he dressed as a peg-legged pirate. The only thing he was missing was Kisslinger's parrot. When he withdrew his sword from its scabbard, it proved to be a scimitar-size phallus. Since I haven't seen him in nearly two months, I send him my message marked urgent.

I spend two hours on Friday evening dispensing holiday vibe and candy to an unsteady stream of costumed neighborhood trick-or-treaters. Per usual, Maynard is spooked by the intermittent incursions. I wistfully expect Dinah and Angelo to be counted among my frightful visitors, but neither appears. I resign myself to the likelihood that my kinfolk has left the country, but I leave the luggage on the porch nonetheless.

Friday night at 11:45 finds me at the Pfixx's Inn bar in the company of the only remaining confidante I have that's allowed in the establishment: my stout Irish sludgehammer. Spaatz ignored three messages, and I drink to the absolute sucker I'll turn into at midnight if it turns out that Vecsey chased me out here as a prank.

A man in a grey sweater and khaki pants pauses beside me to order drinks. He scrutinizes my costume. "What are you supposed to be?"

"A chimera." Before he can inquire further, I expound, "It's a genetic hybrid mythological monster."

"Not as scary as mine." He taps his chest. "I'm a climate scientist." He produces a large melted thermometer. He gets his drinks and walks away.

A short person attired in a burnt orange hoodie, horns and hoofs holding a cardboard pitchfork approaches me and smiles. The gaze through the demonic mask is somewhat unsettling. A sequined scarlet bikini top protrudes from his breast pocket. "I cracked a wisdom fang," he declares in a familiar voice. "When devil-worshippers curse, do they say 'Satan save it!'?"

"Gayle!" I can barely contain my jubilation as I leap to my feet. "What rabbit hole did you fall through?"

He holds his forefinger against his lips. "Recall the protocol, slow jinn: Use no names."

"How did you identify me?" I pop my goat shirt. "You've been harder to track than a Sasquatch."

"The class you exude betrays you." Spaatz looks around warily. "I called you at work through my pro Voice Changa-Ranga. I have to be careful I'm not being targeted. Pick up your drink. Let's go somewhere we can catch up."

Clutching my orangeman and tucking my serpentine tail into my pants, I follow Gail to the empty alcove beneath a suit of armor. "I've gone underground," he informs me. "I've taken a personal leave of absence from commercial collections. I can't believe I was intended to spend my best days being cussed out and threatened by deadbeats." He eyes me intently. "I'm an artist, and I'm going to function as one until some cold, hard circumstances like destitution and starvation prevent me from doing so." He leers. "You're familiar with performance art. I'm pushing it beyond the limit to invent transformance art."

"You're making my head spin, Old Scratch." I take a swig of my sludgehammer. "Slow down and tell me exactly-"

"I'll show you!" Spaatz thrusts his Megalophone into my face. A video plays. Strapped to some sort of grill or metal frame, a naked, potbellied individual tugs at the restraints. The man's skin glows. He appears bereft of body hair. He discharges a running commentary of mumbled expletives. "We're recording, Johnny," Gayle's off-camera voice announces. "So turn up the charisma for social media."

"You son of a bitch!" the square-headed man snarls. "You son of a bitch!"

"Now now, Johnny." His back to the camera, Spaatz struts into the frame naked. "Clean it up for posterity."

"You goddamn son of a bitch!" Bustelich roars. "Let me out of here right now or I'll kill you! I'll make you feel what real pain is, puke-head, and *I'll kill you!!*"

"Talk tough!" Gayle exhorts. "Talk tough, Johnny! I love it when you talk tough."

The video cuts to a high-angle shot of a supine Bustelich bound on the grate. With a handheld or head-mounted camera, Spaatz climbs aboard so a potbellied torso fills the screen. "Johnny has naturally big, beefy nipples like a woman's," Gayle observes in a voice-over. The camera zooms in on Bustelich's plump pecs. "So we have a working head start."

The video cuts to Spaatz straddling Bustelich. Gayle curls forward and buries his face in Johnny's chest. Bustelich grimaces, twists his head back and forth violently and squeals.

"You fucking freak, you motherfucker!" He emits an agonized howl. "You son of a bitch!"

The video cuts back to a close-up of Bustelich's chest. Trickles of blood issue from each of his nipples. "Johnny's ready now to nurse vampire babies," Spaatz remarks in a voice-over.

"Meme me in the mammaries." I take a belt of my sludgehammer. "It looks almost too real." Spaatz shakes his head. I laugh exuberantly enough to attract the attention of several people in our proximity, and Gayle closes the video. "I get it!" I muss my leonine mane. "The moaning threw me, but the swearing should've given it away. Calling in on Delmar's line, it all fits." I reduce my voice to a whisper. "A Johnny Bustelich Companion Piece. It's a fabulous likeness, an excellent, excellent gag."

"What would that accomplish?" Gayle challenges. "Hold me up as the pathetic, frustrated loser Bustelich always said I was?" He rubs his jaw. "I let Johnny get inside my head, and it began to dominate my fantasy time. He was always ripping my manhood, so I decided to return the favor with interest."

"Gayle." My throat goes so dry I can barely speak. "You really, ah, compromised him?"

"Chance opportunities keep the rolling snowball growing." Spaatz snickers. "You remember big Curt Wolczukowski from high school, don't you? He wasn't really a bad guy, but he hung around with Johnny some after we graduated. Curt owes one of our medical group clients some money, and I had the occasion to give him a call. He was delighted to talk about anything but his debt, so we touched on some of the old guard, and he divulged that the Bustelich brothers own a seasonal cabin together on Pleasant Lake up in Waushara County. So I ramble past Johnny's house several Saturday mornings ago and spot him and another of the numpty brothers hitching up a trailer to their electric blue pickup truck. I can guess where they're headed, so I fill up my tank and challenge myself to happen back upon them on the highway somewhere in central Wisconsin. Sho'nuf, an electric blue pickup pulling a trailer blows by me as I travel west on 21, and I don't lose visual contact until they turn onto this little twisting road. I proceed to cruise around Pleasant Lake until I spot the vehicles of interest in a gravel driveway on Pleasant Road. I take note of my location and head back for the first tavern I can find in the nearest town." Gayle's eyes open wide. "Hey, didn't you text me your sister was coming in? How's Dinah?"

I remove my muzzle, wipe the perspiration from my face and struggle to speak. "Never better."

Spaatz nods approbatively. "I always liked Di. I haven't spoken with *my* sister in seven years. Anyway, I wander into this small-town public house – it's called Horsepower – and seat myself at the far end of the nearly empty horseshoe bar. My grand intention is to have one drink to purge the country dust cleaving to my sinuses, and I order a 'spot of sherry with some finesse.' The *nixologist* advises me that he can only sell me an entire bottle, but the price isn't out of this world, so I purchase the bottle." Gayle eyes me intently. "I could use an ice wine mojito right about now."

I thrust my sludgehammer into Spaatz's hand and hustle to the bar on his behalf. The notion of leaving the Inn and refusing any future contact with my old friend occurs to me but it feels like the ultimate wuss-pipe move. He had to drop that poignant factoid about his estranged sister. I reject the opportunity to abandon Gayle and order an ice wine mojito. I return to him and we exchange drinks.

"Much obliged, Lisle." Spaatz toasts me. "You're a friend to the end, worthy of the title." He savors a sip. "Back at the horseshoe bar, I work on the bottle of amontillado and expeditiously empty it. I decide to have a tall ice tea before I exit to chase the influence of the alcohol from my system, and no sooner do I order it than who should swagger into the pub but the four-strong square-headed Bustelich bunch, including – I'm inferring – the bastard who tried to get my car wrecked in West Allis."

"Him and his father and his two uncles?" I take a hard gulp of my orangeman.

Gayle nods. "The brothers order beers all around, but the bartender questions the punk's age and flatly states he can't serve him his flat brew. They argue, and the nixologist gestures to me like he suspects I might be some inspector. 'That twerp can't be a cop,' one of the brood brays. Johnny gives me the fisheye, and for an instant I think he recognizes me. 'Aren't you about to vamoose, pal?' he goads me. The bartender announces my ice tea as he sets the tumbler in front of me. The brothers titter."

Spaatz sips his mojito. "The Bustelich buzzards start blathering among themselves about how much nicer their neighbor's cabin is than theirs and what a waste it is that the neighbor has already closed it up for the winter and fled to Florida. One of them suggests they should keep it warm for him while he's away." Gayle snorts. "All of the sudden, Douggie the youngest brother – I always thought they were calling him 'Duckie' – glares at me and says, 'What's the matter with you?' I point to myself interrogatively. 'Every time I glance over there,' Douggie complains, 'he's staring at us.' Markie the oldest brother says, 'Maybe he'd like to buy us a couple rounds.' Johnny waves his fists and says, 'Maybe he'd like to go a couple rounds.' I nod and mutter, 'Maybe I'd like to pump a couple rounds into you.' They go, 'Say what?' Through my smooth sherry smile, I reply, 'A true nobleman trifles only with other noblemen.' They stare at me blankly and I hop off my seat with the intention of making an overdue stop in the men's room and taking off. 'You're not really in the army,' the punk challenges me. 'Then why you wearin' an army jacket?' Markie pipes up, 'Yeah, dwarf, take off the jacket.' I ask the punk, 'Why don't you wear your shirt and pants backwards to match your baseball beanie, binky? Buttoned up behind, that's some swag.' I can't locate a latrine sign so I reseat myself and ask the bartender for directions. 'Better take him by the hand,' Johnny advises the publican, 'he'll need to get it up to reach the urinal.' Douggie says to me, 'Hey, Sweaty Betty, is that peach-yellow big wheels out front your peewee peepee machine?' Markie pokes him. 'Think that's the armored vehicle of a snake-eater, Douggie?'"

"So none of them ever recognized you." I drain my mug.

"Shit no." Spaatz pats his chin with his pitchfork. "Beard is in, nose is reduced, glasses are gone. Little fuller around the middle. My British accent alone would've been enough to blind them." He takes a swig of his drink. "But back at the pub, I sneer at Markie, point at Douggie and say, 'What do you call him: 'Duckie'? What does that make the rest of you: Goosey, Batty and Buggy? Or perhaps it's the other kind of Duckie, and the rest of you are: Dippie, Dodgy and Jumpy.' The Bustelich baboons all stand erect. 'It's getting a little mean, guys,' the bartender says, stepping to center-shoe. 'Let's not have any trouble.' I wave my hands in palliation. 'Just teasing, chaps. I'm a courtier, not a warrior.' The big, bad Bustelich bangers reseat themselves, pucker their lips and blow me kisses."

"They can't hold a grudge any longer than any other thought," I attempt to nudge the narrative in the direction of Johnny's predicament.

Spaatz finishes his mojito. "My bladder was about to burst so I started for the restroom. A pair of them popped up and followed right on my heels. I just walked the length of the bar, circled around some tables and returned to my seat."

My empathy is shaky. "What did you suppose they were going to do to you?"

"Maybe nothing." Gayle takes a deep breath. "But even an embarrassing photo sent to social media was more of a violation than I felt like submitting to." He hangs his empty glass on a pitchfork prong. "The publican started pressuring me to leave."

I nod. "That's shrewd advice worthy of an overpriced shrink, isn't it?"

"He's shrewd enough to recognize that a homicide is rarely a business-friendly event." Spaatz bares his teeth. "To conclude, I really wanna go cuz I really gotta go, but I'm sure the mule team is going to follow me outside and amp up the bash in the street. When Markie and Duckie get up to play darts, I start to leak on my stool. I jump up and race to the front door.

Two darts hit me in the back. I get outside and run down the street to my car pissing liberally in my pants all the way. I look back and see two hooting square-brows at the Hummer they thought was mine outside the tavern. I leap into my car and take off straining to stem the raging drip." He wipes his eyes. "And I drive all the way home practically gagging on the reek of urine even with all the windows open, my nose running and my teeth chattering."

"Aw, Gayle." I pluck his glass from his pitchfork. "I'll fetch another round. When I return, you can explain how you were able to *recruit* Johnny."

Spaatz declines another potable with a wave. "We need to be more security-conscious." He tugs me farther away from the prying ears of bystanders. "You recall Stephanie Recktenwald, of course," he cites one of the girls at the apex of our high school pulchritude pyramid. "As someone who walked down the hallway behind them while his hyperactive fingers explored her curvilinear ass, I can vouch for the fact that Johnny was fond of her too." Gayle puckers his lips. "She called him 'Stelly.' She aspired to be a nurse practitioner, another blast which occurred to me several weeks ago when I encountered a picture of a hottie in nurse garb on social media who looked just like her. It turned out not to be her, but it sent me searching for the real Stephanie, and I couldn't find a trace of her. She's not listed among our precocious decedents on the alum site, so I presume she still walks among us, just somewhere in the cracks of the grid. And if I couldn't find the genuine Stephanie, then I trusted neither could Johnny."

I force a smile. "I would've expected her to maintain a prodigious body of contacts."

Gayle removes his mask. "We'd been attempting to collect a debt on behalf of a vitamin supplier from a failing business called Team T Squared. Familiar with them?"

"Team T Squared." I shake my head.

He wipes his forehead. "They marketed themselves as a proactive testosterone-boosting clinic. They stopped answering our calls, so we paid a personal visit to their office in Wauwatosa. They'd absconded, and they didn't even take their crummy office furniture. They even left their brochures." He snickers. "So I suddenly had a temporary office, and I didn't even need to change the sign on the door."

"Team T Squared," I echo.

"Softer." Spaatz places his forefinger against his lips and rubs it over his lower teeth. "I whipped up a flyer that tricked Johnny into believing that Stephanie Recktenwald was the nurse practitioner at the Team T Squared clinic in Wauwatosa, and I lured him to make an appointment with the promise of a $200 coupon for spa services at a popular Wisconsin Dells resort and an insulated travel bag just for submitting to a brief evaluation."

I can't resist. "An insulated travel bag?"

"Why would an offer that wasn't completely legit bother to include such a cheesy gift?" A smug smile crosses Gayle's lips. "So Johnny wanders in two Saturday mornings past, and I'm there in my blonde Shirley Temple wig, fake cast on my hand, playing the receptionist. 'Nurse Stephie will be with you shortly.' I talk him into taking some pinhead gunpowder tea that happens to be laced with GHB, and we prattle away. 'What happened there?' He points to my cast. 'Vicious car door,' I reply. 'You look familiar,' he says. Beaming, I exclaim, 'Been to Ontario?' He grunts. 'You don't send out blanket solicitations. How did you pull up my name?' I fess up, 'This is a sideline for me; I work in state government.' I smirk. 'I can compile more info on anyone I target than they know about themselves. For example, I know where you work, Johnny, and how deep in the toilet your credit rating is. I have deets on your wife and kids, including the unscheduled one you had by the late Megan Borsak.' He gasps. 'Take care who you try to tread on in Waushara County taverns, bitch.' The scales drop from his eyes. 'You're that creepy little prick from Horsepower!' he roars. 'How the hell are you connected to Steph?' I shrug. 'Packing your school history, I plucked her out of the yearbook.' His jaw nearly drops, he hurls his teacup at me, and I have to subdue him with the handy taser I have concealed beneath my cast."

"The gunpowder tea probably invigorated him." I muss my mane. "He never recognized you as his old classmate?"

"As brilliant as he was when we knew him, Lisle, he's been knee-deep in weed ever since." Gayle chuckles. "My blonde curls and platform shoes proved too much for the man. Immediately upon tasing, I grabbed the rag I had soaking in chloroform from the tub in the desk drawer, hopped on Johnny and turned his lights out. With the help of a large box and my insulated travel bag, I shackled him and bundled him up, and with the help of the convertible hand cart and cargo van I borrowed from Vito, I whisked him away through the back alley with no witnesses and no one the wiser."

"You abducted him?" I drop my sludgehammer mug. "Which leaves Johnny where now?"

"That's the truly delicious part." Gayle dons his mask again. "I kept Johnny blindfolded in transit, so he has no idea where he is. He's up at Pleasant Lake in the vacant cottage next to his own." He cackles. "I could tell it was the shack the brothers paid tribute to in the bar by the funky little windmill in the front yard." He taps his pitchfork against me. "But I have to quibble with something you said, goombah. 'Abduct' is too harsh a word; I *arrested* my attacker."

"Soooo-" I pause to fully process the situation. "What are your plans for him?"

"Transformance." Spaatz rubs his jaw. "Johnny gonna swing like a pendulum do." I expel a horrified gasp, and he slides his hand to his throat. "Not by the neck, you mythical brute, hormonally. I've begun him on a six-week cycle of steroids to engender preliminary aromatization. I'm running him on testosterone propionate stacked with trenbolone acetate." He giggles. "We're adhering to a strict parenteral approach, and I administer the blend with a real hippo harpoon of a needle. When this cycle is complete, we'll run him in the opposite direction, with anti-androgens like diethylstilbestrol and leuprolide, so we can see what sticks and affirm what he's really made of."

"You can't, ah, you're going to pickle, ah-" I strain to react coherently. "You could damage his liver and kidneys."

"We're not doing his heart any favor either, are we?" Spaatz lifts his mask and smirks. "All gain carries risk, snollygoster, and I did technically promise to boost his testosterone, didn't I?"

I wince. "You're risking giving him cancer." I lower my voice. "Gayle, you can't hold someone against his will like this. What's going to happen when you release him? What the hell are you thinking?"

"Cancer." Spaatz narrows his eyes. "Oh, don't you recall the incident the summer we were 15 where I ran into Johnny at Mayfair? My mother took me and we split up to shop. My father had just been diagnosed with leukemia, and I was wearing my *F&@K CANCER* T-shirt. Johnny and his pack of roving wing goons come up to me, and Johnny says, 'Hey, Spitz, there's kids around.' He plants his finger in my chest. 'People find that language objectionable. You take that shirt off right now and turn it inside out, and if I see you wearing it the offensive way again, I swear I'll tear it right off your back!' I stand frozen, and he shoves me. 'Take it off!' I don't know why, but I punched him in the gut and darted down a side corridor. They caught me. 'What a weak, pussy swing!' Johnny taunted me. 'Did your mom teach you how to throw a punch?' All the laughing goons surrounded us so no one else could see while Johnny worked me over. 'Here's how you put a swing on somebody!' He didn't do as much physical damage as that time in the park when I was with you, but it hurt more. I was so scared that my mother would see what they were doing to me. They left me sitting on the floor in tears with my torn T-shirt turned inside out on my lap."

I sigh deeply. "Yeah, I remember you telling me." I pat his shoulder. "I'd never argue that Johnny doesn't deserve a world of shit. But let him bring it on himself naturally; I'm sure he'll manage. Don't go down the road that could cast you as the same model of thug that he is."

Gayle sneers. "What are you saying, Lisle, that you're going to report me to the police?"

"If anyone takes this to the cops, it needs to be you." I eye him sternly through my mask. "But why don't you first blindfold him again, drive him back down here to a spot close to his house and just let him go? Even if he infers your identity, the whole mess is bizarre enough to be completely deniable."

"You have the wrong attitude." Spaatz replaces his mask and adjusts his horns. "You, more than anyone, Lisle, should understand. I'll bet you're secretly pleased." He nods at his empty glass in my hand. "You want to grab me another?"

I pick up my mug. "Just destroy the video."

He waves his Megalophone. "The device is going into cold storage before I go back up north." I start toward the bar. "Don't be a detractor because you're squeamish!" he calls after me.

I shuffle to the bar and order another ice wine mojito. When I return to our niche in the back, Gayle is not to be found. I somehow expected that he would be gone. I scour Pfixx's and linger for a while. I drink the mojito. I don't particularly like it.

I return home in a state of mild shock. Maynard and I sit up and watch television for three hours. I go to bed with no idea of what programs I viewed.

I roll out of bed in a cold sweat. In the three hours I lay tossing on my mattress, I probably got twenty minutes of sleep. Breakfast consists of half a doughnut, a cup of coffee and a joint. I generally refuse to take an aspirin, and I hadn't consumed a nonalcoholic intoxicant in my nearly seven years of employment at Anele. I can still hardly believe Gayle Spaatz's revelation from the previous night, and the cannabis provides little relief. I cling to a faint hope that the crisis will prove to be a practical joke.

I take Maynard for a long walk. We return home, and I try to settle into my domestic routine. I have no desire for lunch. I return to my pot stash behind the false back of my cupboard and withdraw another joint. I grab my pair of suction cups from my dedicated junk drawer, proceed to the bathroom and detach the covert panel from the midst of the wall tiles. I retrieve my processed comfort kit and spread the contents across the kitchen table: amphetamines, barbiturates, hash bars, cocaine, meth, MDMA, DMT. Recreational substances have never held much allure for me because I'm loath to surrender my will to any outside influence. My assortment was a thirtieth birthday present from Delmar Vecsey, who won the supply in a poker game. Del was never a consumer either. I showed Trish my secret pillbox, and she expressed an ardent lack of interest. I sit down and occupy myself pondering whether to light up again.

Maynard barks sharply. The doorbell rings. I presume that Dinah and Angelo have finally returned. I deplore my unhinged condition and scoop my entire comfort kit into the wastebasket. I look out the front window and see a black SUV in front of my house. I view a large man in sunglasses and a brown blazer on my front porch. The doorbell rings again. I barricade Maynard in the kitchen. I don't believe that my visitor is the man who was in Di's hotel room last weekend, but he might've gotten a butch clip, and I've never seen him in shades or a shirt, so I can't be positive.

I open the door. The man displays a badge. "Mr. Lisle Amonor," he verifies, "I'm Detective Cybyske of the Waukesha Sheriff's Department. I'm investigating the disappearance of John Bustelich."

"John Bustelich," I echo. "The John Bustelich I went to school with?"

"Yes, sir, I believe so." Cybyske smiles authoritatively. "John has gone missing, and I'm here to check whether you might have any information about it." I laugh with some gusto, and the detective removes his eyewear. "Did I say something amusing?"

"No, sorry." I rub and pat my face. "The only information I can give you about John Bustelich disappearing is it happened 25 years too late to suit me. He was, to put it nicely, a nasty ass and then some, and I'm quite pleased to be able to report that I've had absolutely no contact with him since we graduated from high school." The cop remains silent. "As I recall, he knocked up at least one girl. If your next question is who might want Johnny harmed, my answer would be probably everyone who ever interacted with him."

"I'm surprised to hear you say so." Cybyske edges closer. "Because everyone interviewed about it so far has spoken highly of him. What makes you suspect he's been harmed?"

I shrug. "It's quite a reach to seek out one of his old schoolmates. I trust you wouldn't go to that length unless you suspected foul play."

Cybyske pauses for an unsettling moment. "Would you want him harmed?"

I expel an irritated breath. "I really hadn't thought about it in ages. What current connection to Johnny could you possibly believe I have?"

"I'm surprised you didn't ask that question initially." The detective eyes me menacingly. "It's a bit cool out here. Could we continue this conversation inside your house?"

I hesitate. "I suppose we can jabber in the front room. But my dog isn't very welcoming to strangers, and he'll make a fuss."

Cybyske furrows his brow. "Can't you confine him in a side room?"

"Will do." I leave the officer on the front porch, pet Maynard briefly and banish the canine to the bathroom. I return to the front door and open it.

The detective points to Angelo's two suitcases on the porch. "Heading off somewhere?"

"I'm surprised that's not the first question *you* asked." I snicker. "Those belong to my nephew. I don't know what happened to my sister. They were supposed to pick them up a few days ago. We're lucky nobody's stolen them, or you'd have to investigate *that* disappearance, hmm?"

Cybyske steps into the living room. "Why don't you call your sister and ask her about it?"

"She and I had a little disagreement about the way she's raising the boy and aren't exactly on speaking terms." I point to the candy bowl. "Peppermint cigarette? Evil eye sucker? Wax lips?"

"No, thank you." The detective surveys the living room. "How familiar are you with Gaylord Spaatz?"

"Gayle?" I exclaim. "We grew up a block and a half away from each other and kept close through school. I still see him periodically and consider him a friend. Ask *him* what a pleasure Johnny was to be around."

The cop smiles. "We'd love to do that, but he's no longer at his last known residence. Neither of you seems to maintain a presence on social media. Would you happen to have his contact information?"

I sigh. "That tends to be a problem. Gayle's a gypsy."

"Literally?" Cybyske's demeanor is solemn.

"I'm sorry, is that offensive?" I shrug. "I can't keep up. I won't hear from Gayle for months, and then he calls me from a new number." I head off the detective at the pass. "That may not sound like much of a friend, but he moves about within the community, so there's going to be gaps. He spends a lot of time with a favorite of his. I think it's 'Guido'?"

"The community?" Cybyske challenges.

"The gay community," I utter defensively. "That's not what this is really about, is it? Rousting gays?" I'm pleased with my strategic placement of the preference card. "Did Johnny come out now too?"

Cybyske scowls. "I wouldn't think so. He has a wife and kids."

I scoff. "That doesn't necessarily mean diddly."

"It means there's a woman and a couple of kids worried sick about him," the detective snaps. "I must admit, Mr. Amonor,

I sense a bit of resistance on your part to cooperate with this investigation."

I shake my head. "I just can't fathom why you'd suspect Gayle might have a connection to Johnny. By the way, who linked me to Gayle?"

"That's not your concern." Cybyske fixes me with a cold stare. "A suspicious vehicle registered to Gaylord Spaatz was observed near the Bustelich residence. Are you aware that he recently purchased a firearm?"

"Gayle did?" I exclaim. "I can't imagine Gayle as a gun guy."

"It doesn't sound as though you're inclined to consider a number of possibilities." The detective produces his cell phone. "What's the last number you have for him?"

I turn my palms upward. "I don't enter contact numbers. We might check the call log, but as it happens, I can't find my phone. I first noticed it missing after returning home from a walk with my dog late yesterday afternoon. That was probably the absolute worst time of the year to lose it, huh, right before trick-or-treat? We jogged along the stream, so it could even be underwater. But it's been weeks since Gayle has called, and I doubt that I'd recognize his number anyway. I took the dog out through the park again this morning and retraced our steps from yesterday, but I didn't find it."

The detective keeps an eyebrow raised. "Most people would be a little freaked out. Give me your number. I'll call it, and we'll try to locate it."

"I disabled all of those location accuracy and emergency features." I blurt out the number with transposed digits, and

Cybyske calls it. "In all honesty, sir, you're not really here on behalf of my spiteful sister or ex-shrink, are you?"

"Should I be aware of other complaints against you?" The officer reaches generic voicemail. "As I previously stated, I'm investigating the disappearance of one John Bustelich."

"Please don't trouble yourself." I emit a self-conscious chuckle. "This isn't the first time I've lost the slippery thing. I try to proactively keep any personal information from floating around, so I habitually erase coveted nuggets like my call numbers history."

"Who's your cell phone provider?" Cybyske eyes me intently. "They should be able to produce the list."

I expel a beleaguered breath. "I try to generally support the police, trooper, but as a good libertarian, I resent the presumption of anyone that they can rummage through my personal records. If you want to do that, I believe you'll need to arrange the foray through my lawyer."

"I assumed that as a good citizen and a decent human being, you'd want to voluntarily provide any helpful information you could." The officer plucks a card out of his pocket and hands it to me. "Mr. Bustelich was last seen at his Milwaukee residence supposedly headed for his Waukesha workplace, and I'm working in conjunction with Lieutenant Cripesdale of the Milwaukee Police. He's going to want to talk to you, so please call him." He flashes another authoritative smile. "One more question about Mr. Spaatz. Where does he work?"

"He's a freelance artist." I sigh. "He may do portraits and caricatures, but I think he mainly adds design flourishes to clothing, tableware and bric-a-brac. I recall he once created a shower curtain."

Cybyske grimaces. "Does he make a good living at that?"

"He complains about what a tough market this area is, so I doubt it." I snicker. "That's probably the prime reason why he has to keep moving around."

"No family ties?"

"Parents are long dead. His only sibling is his sister Tammy. She was a dippy hippie girl, who took off for parts unknown, and I have no idea of what became of her or what name she might be using."

The detective proceeds to the front door. "It's been my experience, Mr. Amonor, that people who are generally a bit uncooperative generally have a bit to hide."

I offer an arch smile. "Frankly, constable, I'm not interested in being inconvenienced one bit because old bugbear Bustelich is probably out tomcatting somewhere."

Cybyske nods. "You said you were seeing a psychiatrist about anger issues?"

I exhale heavily. "Am I some sort of suspect here?"

"You're some sort of person of interest." The detective opens the door. "Please call Lieutenant Cripesdale at your earliest opportunity. Good luck finding your phone and reconciling with your sister." He closes the door behind him and strides down the driveway to the street. He climbs into his vehicle.

I release Maynard from the bathroom. The canine charges into the living room, sniffs the air, jumps onto the davenport and peers out the window. My phone rings on the kitchen counter. My relief that it didn't ring while Cybyske was in the house turns to dread with the expectation that the call has been placed by some representative of law enforcement. I shamble to the kitchen like cornered prey and note that the area code and number are unfamiliar. I answer "It was here all the time!"

"Hey, hey, L.A.," the whimsical monotone staccato of Delmar Vecsey assails me, "it's your very own Lone Star soy boy. Sorry I've been so scarce, but I've been busy keeping busy in order to slide through my adjustment period here with minimal stress."

My thoughts tangle in a vortex. "Del," I muster.

"I've been just about living in the lab," Vecsey continues, "coming in extra early every day and aggressively seeking more work, so I'm considered an outright dynamo around here. I feel a solid bond developing with some of my coworkers, and I think I'll stay for a while." I jam my Megalophone inside my shorts and saunter back to the front window. Cybyske is still sitting in his vehicle. Maynard keeps him under a soft growl scrutiny. I retreat to the bathroom and produce the phone. Delmar is still rambling: "Texas driver's license, the works. Yes, sir, I think the great southern migration is going to pan out. How's the Duchess?"

I'm paranoid enough to believe that Cybyske might've bugged my house, but the restraint necessary to skirt the issue of the day eludes me nonetheless. "How's the hormone surplus side biz?"

"How's that?" Vecsey challenges.

"When someone who shall remain nameless having no known acquaintance with the metabolic molecule mosaic suddenly possesses a savvy bio-jock familiarity, there has to be a beacon."

"This is a riddle?" Delmar groans, eliciting my counter groan. "Oh, you've been chitting with your pack rat Spaatz. We started joking after my party about slipping your old nemesis – Bullspinach? – hormone highballs, and before I knew it, he was ordering product."

"So you casually agreed to become his bio-arms dealer?" I half-expect to hear Maynard warn of Cybyske's rapid return. "Even you could plainly see how suggestible he is. He's always overreacted to crazy ideas!"

"I thought that's what you always said about me," Vecsey scoffs. "If a batch or two down here get mucked up beyond commercial viability, I might make hay out of my access and rescue them from the compost bin."

I snicker with exasperation. "You're giving him a contaminated supply besides?"

"Not giving," Del objects. "Please remind your bill-collecting bud to pay off the rest of his tab promptly. Our discards are probably better quality than most labs' pure-grade stuff." I groan, and he hisses. "You're the one who would always rail against gratuitous experiments that torture animals, so unregulated therapies and unvetted treatments are what we rely upon for advancement."

"Advancement!" I hoot. "Advancement crashing and burning?"

"That's your problem, Amonor," Vecsey reasons. "You always ask questions you don't want to know the answers to." A female voice in the background makes an unintelligible comment. "People are coming in, so I'll get back to you, Lisle. Later."

I jam my Megalophone back inside my shorts. I replace my covert bathroom wall panel and return to the living room. Cybyske is still sitting in his SUV. Maynard jumps off the davenport, proceeds to the kitchen and stands at the back door. I toss my suction cups and phone into my junk drawer and venture into the backyard with the dog.

Mired in thought, I drift along the fence and wind up behind the garage. I hear a car door slam in front of the house. I let Maynard in the back door and wander around the house to the front yard. Cybyske remains in his vehicle. I consider approaching and offering to fix him a sandwich. Angelo's luggage is gone. I return inside through the front door. I snatch Lieutenant B. Glen Cripesdale's card from the coffee table. As a decent human being indisposed to landing in jail as some sort of accessory, I can't stand by idly as Gayle Spaatz commits heinous crimes against Johnny Bustelich. I have to call Cripesdale and inform him of the situation.

But not today.

I lie down on the davenport and fall asleep. I'm awakened by Maynard warbling. I stagger to my feet and look out the window. Cybyske has finally gone. The dog asks to go outside again and I let him out the back door. I sit down in my low-rider chair and fall asleep again.

I wake up to a house that's completely dark. I fling myself out of the chair confused about the time and the day. I flip on the track lights. The clock displays ten minutes before six. I've slept for nearly three hours. I look for Maynard. I recall letting him outside and realize I never brought him back in. I rush to the back door. I hope he hasn't been howling and disturbing the neighbors. I turn on the porch light. He isn't waiting outside the door. I call but he doesn't respond. I take my tactical flashlight and comb the backyard calling him. I find the gate open. Maynard is gone.

I SNATCH MAYNARD'S collar, short leash and some jerky treats, and I range a block and a half north. I sweep two blocks west and comb two more south. Every few strides, I bellow "Maynard!" With each utterance, more desperation escapes from the back of my throat. I swing my flashlight from side to side as I strain to discern movement in the night. The cloudy sky improves the overall visibility on the dark streets of my neighborhood.

I arrive back in front of my house. I cross the street. Maynard strayed once previously about four years ago. He was two years old, much livelier and more rambunctious. In that instance, the dachshund had dug his way under the fence and ventured into the backyard of the house next door to the one across the street to visit the miniature white dog who resided there. I haven't seen that dog in months. "Maynard!" I search the yard. "Maynard, come!"

I spot window activity shadowing my movements so I ring the front doorbell. No one answers, and I ring twice more, knock and step back. The front porch becomes bathed in brilliant light, the inside door swings open and the middle-aged woman who I believe to be the sole occupant appears.

"Hello, ma'am." I gesture over my shoulder to my house and stumble off her porch. "I'm your neighbor Lisle from across the street. I'm looking for my dog, my dachshund. I recall he ran off a few years ago and wound up over here." She doesn't reply. "I was checking your yard, and I thought I'd check with you, especially since it's after dark." I display my flashlight. "I don't know if you still have your dog; I haven't seen him in a while." She says nothing. "My dog's name is Maynard. I hoped maybe you'd seen him or if you should see him, could you please alert me? You might even try to herd him into my backyard yourself and shut the gate?" She doesn't respond. "Thank you." I turn to leave.

"I lost Tonya over a year ago," the woman offers.

I turn back to face her. "I'm sorry. I wondered-"

She points to the lavender house three doors down from mine. "You might want to ask them. A couple hours ago, I saw them pick up a roadkill and put it in a box."

I nod and start toward the lavender house. My unsteady legs grow progressively weaker as I hustle the short distance and ring the front doorbell. My heart pounds. The young man who opens the door appears to recognize me. "What's going on? It's a little late."

"I'm sorry to disturb you." I point in the direction of my house. "I'm your neighbor Lisle Amonor from down the street.

My dog, ah, my dachshund is missing. My gate was open, and-"
My words stick in my throat.

The man flashes a wry smile. "I thought it seemed a little quiet." The volume of the college football game on his television is earsplitting. "So sorry."

"The woman across the way," I muster, "told me you, ah, removed an animal from the street this afternoon." I strain to keep a tear from escaping out of the corner of my eye. "Was, what was it-"

The man narrows his eyes. "You think I got your dog?"

"I only know that my dachshund is gone," I appeal, "and I'm trying to find him!"

"That was a possum we hit." The man shakes his head. "Learn to know the difference."

My relief crystallizes as a deferential smile. "I needed to check. You haven't seen him at all?"

"I have nothing I can tell you." He starts to shut the door.

I raise my hand to delay my dismissal. "His name is Maynard. Would you please contact me if you do?" I point toward my home. "You know I'm three houses down, with the red burning bush out front and the picture window."

"Who was that, honey?" A woman's voice in the background rises over the sports din.

The man turns his head and rubs his thinning hair. "Our neighbor Lisle from down the street!"

"That weird, gawky guy?" she replies. "I think there's something seriously wrong with him!"

"Seriously?" The man faces me and titters. "She thinks you're already gone."

"Oh!" A young woman wearing red-framed glasses arrives at the man's side. "Hello."

"He can't find his dog." The man casts a longing glance toward his television. "He seems to have the idea that because we picked up a dead possum, we might've picked off his dog, too."

"Aw, your wiener dog is lost?" The woman raises her eyebrows. "He'll turn up. Do you know, Mr. Lisle, if there's a special government department you're supposed to call for dead wildlife in front of your house? We just threw it in the garbage. It's unusual for them to be out before evening, isn't it? Maybe your dog flushed it out of its nest, or I suppose coyotes could have."

"No clue." I regret the dismissive note in my voice. "I'm just asking that you kindly contact me should you spot my dog running loose."

"We wouldn't intentionally harm an animal," the woman asserts. "Growing up, I had cats. We're practically vegans, for God's sake."

"Thank you," I utter guilelessly. "Sorry if I seem a bit unstrung; he's just, ah-" I hop off the stoop with renewed hope and head back into the night as the door slams shut behind me.

"Maynard!" I retrace the steps of our three most popular walk routes, each of which take me over several city blocks and into the park to the west. I move slowly through the wooded areas calling him repeatedly and shining my light in all directions. My dog is nowhere to be found. I proceed back to concrete. I call his name every ten steps. My light fails. I embark on a mission to tramp up and down every street in the neighborhood if necessary. "*Maynard!!*"

Lights sporadically switch on as I pass houses. A man steps onto his front porch. "Shut up!" he requests.

"I'm looking for my dog!" I advise him. "You haven't seen a dachshund running loose?"

The man returns inside and slams his door. It's not quite eleven o'clock. Lowering my voice two decibels, I call Maynard every twelve steps. I arrive back at my house and comb my backyard again. Exhausted, I stagger inside, charge my flashlight, collapse in the low-profile chair and sip an energy drink. I try not to contemplate my abject desolation. I pray.

I return outside shortly after midnight. I move more deliberately. I call more softly. I patrol in haphazard patterns directed by whim. I range all the way down to busy Bluemound. I head back in the general direction of home. I experience the sensation of drifting aimlessly and impotently.

Like exercise repetitions, my steps seem to require more and more conscious effort. My physical discomfort registers as added emotional lading. How could Maynard have wandered away? I consider how the gate came to be open and proceed to play the blame game. I review my steps yesterday afternoon. After letting the dog in the back door, I opened the gate to walk around the house and check whether the detective remained out front. Was his protracted presence designed to serve as some intimidation ploy? Could Cybyske have opened the gate to prowl around the premises? Did he expect to spot Johnny Bustelich's severed head in the cabbage patch portion of the garden? I don't recall closing the gate before entering the house again through the front door. Could I really be guilty of such a terrible omission?

My agitation accelerates my pace. If Jean Zagieboylo hadn't gotten drunk on a couple of shots of amaretto, I wouldn't have had to chauffeur her home, and Spaatz and Vecsey probably wouldn't have struck on the idea for their program of depravity, and Cybyske would never have appeared at my door. Why doesn't Skinny Jean eat some prime rib with a baked potato and buttered roll and bulk up her wispy body so it can metabolize a little alcohol? Of course, if Nancy wasn't too full of herself to take a joke, she might've let Delmar off with a three-day suspension and sensitivity conditioning, and there wouldn't have been a farewell party that brought the co-conspirators together. Why did Del flee to Texas with such eagerness anyway? Is distance supposed to impress the dreary stiffs back home? Was that the impetus that drove Dinah halfway around the globe to shack up in some exotic mud flat? My estrangement from Trish had left me distracted and diminished by itself, but then to be derogated, abandoned and boycotted by my dear sister and her demon-spawn child left me borderline functional. Yet my negligence was inexcusable, and I could hardly be a more complete loser.

I find no trace of Maynard and return home after three. Shortly before dawn, I jump into the Yukon and roll through the streets I just scoured on foot. I arrive home empty, stumble around the backyard and head into the house to try to rest.

It's a bit before seven when I set out to pound the pavement again. At about this time on a typical Sunday morning, Maynard and I would squeeze in a brisk walk around the block. I search for hope in the daylight that transforms the visible landscape. Might someone have taken my faithful friend into their home to protect him? With each pass, I aspire to become more identifiable as a search party.

I round a corner eight blocks from my home and spot a stuffed black plastic bag resting against the curb. I must've passed it unknowingly at least a couple of times in the dark. As I approach, I discern a cleft of the contents into two unequal segments, with the smaller one at the top shaped like the head of an animal. The flaps of the bag flutter in the breeze, and though I feel my grief rise I take a grain of consolation in the fact that I'll have the means to carry his body home. I peel the plastic back to reveal a smashed pumpkin and a dead wintergreen boxwood shrub with dried root ball.

I continue onward calling the dog in a louder voice. It occurs to me that since I returned to church five years ago, I have not willfully missed Sunday Mass. My parents raised my sister and me in a strict religious environment, and I prayed fervently when I was a kid. Rising above the quotidian palaver with which I troubled the Deity, the most profound prayers of substance that I recall were for our family dog Argus, who survived two strokes before his eventual death when I was age 22. I believe that the stranger who possesses too little faith to show up and worship until he desperately needs help has little right to request a favor, but I will not attend Mass today. It's hard to give glory and praise when you feel as though you want to cry and vomit. God's presence has seemed to grow progressively more distant for many weeks now, and I've been struggling mightily with my faith. There's nothing I want more than to humbly return to church next Sunday and give honor and thanks for Maynard's recovery.

I return home at about noon exhausted. At least I have no reason to believe that Maynard isn't still alive. I post a Lost Dog notice with Maynard's photo on my neighborhood watch website. Starting with my local animal shelter, I call the Elmbrook Humane Society. The woman who answers checks the shelter database. No dog matching Maynard's description has been picked up, but she advises me to keep monitoring the shelter website, where I complete and submit a Lost Animal Report Form, including microchip information and attached photo. I next call the Waukesha County Animal Control Center. The person who answers informs me that no dog like Maynard is currently being held, but I am directed to monitor their website and file a Lost Pet Form, which I do. I call the Wisconsin Humane Society in Milwaukee, from which I adopted Maynard when he was four months old. I reach a recording that refers me to the Milwaukee pound. I accordingly call the Milwaukee Area Animal Control Center, and the contact person suggests that I physically visit the shelter. She further refers me to their website, from which I ascertain that no dog matching Maynard's description is in custody. I further ascertain that by Wisconsin state law, a shelter need only hold dogs for four days following capture day before they can put them up for adoption or dispose of them. I backtrack and check the Wisconsin Humane Society website, but I find no trace of my best friend.

I fix a sandwich and nibble about half of it as I peruse the fair outpouring of support I've gleaned from my surrounding cyber-community. One person contributes "He's cute. Very sorry." Another posts "Time is of the essence; leave no stone unturned." Three women root for the return of my "fur baby." I can hardly express how irksome I find that term. A man suggests that I contact the Department of Public Works to check whether any deceased dogs were collected from the streets. I wonder if he's related to the football fan in the lavender house. I post a Lost Pet Report through the Lost Dogs of Wisconsin website. I nap briefly and return outside shortly after three.

My next-door neighbor to the south is on his front lawn raking leaves. "Mr. Lancaster." I wave and approach him. "My dog Maynard is missing. You haven't seen him by any chance, have you?"

"He took off on you, did he?" Lancaster is the only neighbor whose surname I know.

I nod. "I must've left the gate open. Yesterday was crazy."

"I noticed a guy sitting in his car in front of your house for a while yesterday morning." My neighbor ceases his labor. "Then while the wife and I were observing him, a woman drove up and grabbed some suitcases off your porch. Rhonda insisted she'd seen her over at your place before. She looked like she belonged. She used to be blonde, didn't she?"

"She used to be my sister." I return to my search mission. "If Maynard should turn up, please hold him if you can, or entice him back into my yard – and shut the gate."

I tramp through the streets. I periodically call my dachshund's name. I hadn't conversed with Russ or Rhonda Lancaster in several weeks. The only other neighbor with whom I maintain a more substantial connection than a wave or a nod is "Chet," the avid gardener on the property behind mine. In late August, I remarked with admiration on his onions.

I keep moving until dark. I return home demoralized but not defeated. I spend the evening producing *LOST DOG* handbills which offer a generous reward of unspecified magnitude for the return of my best friend.

At ten I climb back in the SUV and slowly cruise around the area. I realize that I have no effective means of attaching handbills to objects where they might be effectively displayed. I return home a little after midnight as alone as I've ever been. After some expletives fly and a few tears flow, I'm totally drained.

I wake up Monday morning at dawn. It takes me a few moments to process the reality of my nightmare. I take another determined march around the neighborhood, return home and try to eat some breakfast. I'm the first customer at the hardware store, where I purchase two spools of baling wire. I start at the maple tree across the street from my house, and I affix a handbill to a tree or light pole every twenty meters beneath plastic wrap and wire. I don't suppose that my postings are strictly legal and I don't strictly care. Let Detective Cybyske cite me for arrogating public property. Let him discover my real phone number. In three hours, I've worked my way back home and distributed nearly all of the handbills I printed.

I call Anele to excuse my absence and arrange for additional days off. I'm not interested in justifying my lost dog as a valid excuse to miss work time, so I submit the muddy generality that I'm dealing with a close friend's personal crisis. Gene Napolitano naturally requests minutiae. Gazing at my backyard through the kitchen window, I begin pushing the alibi that my sister in the Philippines is threatening to commit suicide.

Maynard suddenly emerges from the bee balm bushes behind the vegetable garden. I drop the phone and charge outside. The animal I saw proves to be a large cat that I infrequently spot around the neighborhood. I feel as though scavengers are already trying to claim vacated territory. I snatch a pear from the ground and hurl it minatorily. The cat scurries out of my yard. I return inside and retrieve my phone. Sleepy Gene is no longer on the line, so I presume he's enough of a human being to have documented and processed the disturbing articles of my improvised pretext.

I review the websites of the Waukesha and Milwaukee County animal shelters for updates. I drive into Milwaukee and visit the Animal Control Center holding tank. I don't find Maynard. I drive around the streets and parks of Wauwatosa and Brookfield on my way home and post my remaining handbills. I take another walking tour of my neighborhood, pause to force-feed myself some lukewarm soup and expand the scope of the search area again in the Yukon. I experience a few more Maynard sightings and promptly recognize each as a phantasm. I head back to my house to rest and wait for notification that some exceptional person has come to our aid. I keep monitoring all concerned websites, including local marketplace postings that might be offering a dachshund for sale. I take intermittent walks and rides throughout the rest of the day and night. The piercing quiet inside my house and the shadow prospect of looming detachment amplifies the crushing pain inside my head.

I thrust myself out of bed on Tuesday morning with some difficulty. My hope is fading. I'm heartsick. I go out and patrol the surrounding areas on foot and in the Yukon. I repeat virtually all of my activities from the previous afternoon.

I check recent replies to my posting on the neighborhood watch website. A man comments "The first 48 hours are critical. If he's not found in that time, chances are poor you'll recover him." I find a picture of a dog, but it looks more like a springer spaniel than a wirehaired dachshund. The contributor writes "Hope you find your dog. This is our dog Boots. We have a tracker on his collar, so if he ever got loose, we could follow him on a GPS map. We love our dog." As optimism becomes a dot in my rearview mirror, I reflect on the life and times of my pup. I struggle to maintain a functional outward composure, and I double down on the exclamation points that punctuate my prayers.

I decide between search efforts to clean my house. I discard an old cabinet and some lamps. I empty my closets of superfluous financial documents, books, clothes and holiday decorations. I remove expired foodstuffs and nonessential cookware from my cupboards. I dispose of my remaining stash of cannabis and obsolete drug paraphernalia. I toss out an old rug and some worn blankets.

On Wednesday morning, I find the escalating pain in my heart and stomach leaving little room for faith. This is the fourth day after the day Maynard went missing. My unyielding agony drives me to call the Elm Grove Department of Public Works for information on whether a deceased dog had recently been removed from the streets. The woman answering and the one to whom she transfers me both seem flabbergasted by the inquiry and have no such incident to report. I continue perusing the online found dogs files of all concerned databases.

The photo of a dog at the Waukesha County Animal Control Center catches my eye. He's listed as "Punky," a "Wirehair Terrier Mix" but the face sure resembles the one that's greeted me every morning for the last six years. My trembling fingers struggle to hold the phone as I call the shelter. "I believe you have my dachshund!" I exclaim deliriously. "I'm looking at his picture on your website. 'Punky'? He's mislabeled as a mix, but I'm almost positive that's my boy!"

"Okay." She sounds skeptical. I refer her to my Lost Pet Form, and she checks her data. "Punky was picked up last weekend. He's just been listed because he was receiving veterinary care. Punky has a microchip, and unfortunately, sir, it doesn't match your dog's. You're looking for a dachshund?"

"What kind of care?" I gasp. "I want to come out there immediately and claim him!"

"He's expected to recover." She sounds vexed. "Come out for in-person identification, but you might want to temper your expectations."

I jump into the Yukon and roar up busy Bluemound Road. "Punky has to be Maynard! I couldn't be seeing an illusion again!" I refuse to doubt myself. I know my dog.

I take the wrong lane and wind up lost for ten minutes in the labyrinthine city of Waukesha. I finally reach the shelter. I grab Maynard's paperwork, collar and leash and race into the building. "I'm expected!" I inform the young woman at the front desk. "I just talked to someone here; I believe you're holding my dog!"

"Oh, yes." She frowns. "You're under the impression we have your Dalmatian?"

"Dachshund!" I assert. "You have my dachshund! I was told he's receiving some sort of medical treatment?"

"Please calm down." She eyes me indignantly. "Nell will guide you momentarily."

An enormous person approaches from the periphery. "I'm Nell. You are-"

"Lisle Amonor." I display a photo of Maynard on my Megalophone. "I believe the dog you have listed on your database as 'Punky' is my dog Maynard."

She steps behind the desk and takes control of the computer terminal. "When did the dog go missing?"

"Saturday afternoon or evening." I hand her the health record including rabies vaccination certificate and a microchip barcode sticker that I received from the Wisconsin Humane Society when I adopted Maynard.

"And there was no license or other tag or identification?"

"The moment I bring Maynard home from a walk, I discard his whole yoke."

Nell eyes me indignantly. "Punky was picked up early Sunday with no collar by the rescue team. She had some injuries, presenting with a laceration to her right withers and ataxia in the hind limbs. The injuries aren't necessarily related. Punky was examined by a veterinarian and assessed with spinal shock or possible F.C.E." She looks up. "Fibrocartilaginous embolism, which is spinal disc rupture leading to blockage of blood supply to the spinal cord. It's very rare for a purebred dachshund. I.V.D.D. was initially suspected, but a myelogram identified no pressure on the spinal cord. Initial lameness in her right hind leg has improved to a slight limp." She pauses.

"Punky has a microchip but the number scanned doesn't match the one you've provided."

"Then somehow they scanned the wrong dog or they gave me the wrong chip number. I have a hundred pictures of Maynard, ma'am, not a few with me."

"Please don't call me 'ma'am.'"

I feel like I'm negotiating the delicate release of a political prisoner. "Agreed, if you stop calling Maynard 'Punky' and stop calling him 'her.'"

Nell sighs. "We want to restrict the movement of the dog in question, so I'll take you back to its cage. But the sort of mistake you suggest is highly improbable, so keep your obstinacy curbed." She returns my tight-lipped grin. "I'm texting my associate Clare to scan the dog once more so there's no question."

Nell finishes some cyberspace business, comes out from behind the desk and leads me back through the inner sanctum of dog cages. A cell with brick walls up to my clavicles on the end of an aisle displays a *DO NOT DISTURB* sign on the door advising traffic that the occupant has just had surgery. Nell stops at the door and I take a peek over the wall. "*Maynard!!*" I shriek. Several neighboring dogs start barking and I thrust my body atop the wall like it's an obstacle course barrier.

"Excuse me, slugger?" Nell snaps. "Get off of there and enter properly through the door!"

Maynard struggles to his feet as I slide down the inner wall and wind up in a handstand. He whimpers, warbles and licks my face. "Oh, my boy, my very best pal, I've been going nuts!" I carefully lower my entire body to the floor, upset the water dish and hug the dachshund for all I'm worth. "I've been soooo worried! Where did you take off to?" I glance up at Nell peering at us through the door. "Any further question — besides who's in charge of who?"

"I'm afraid so," Nell utters. "This dog's microchip does not match your dog's."

Another woman almost as husky as Nell appears. "That dog has two microchips." She points at Maynard. "And one is a match for the Amonor dog."

"Two?" Nell scowls at me. "Care to explain why there are two microchips?"

I shrug. "Before he was transferred to Wisconsin, he was in another shelter in Kentucky. They must've tagged him in both places."

I slip Maynard's collar over his head and attach his leash. Nell opens the cell door and we proceed back to the front desk. The dachshund has a slight limp and a bandage over his shoulder. "We have to do a much better job of taking care of each other, partner."

At the front desk, Nell concedes that no doubt remains about whether I'm the dog's guardian. "He's walking much better than yesterday. The vet believes in time he'll make a complete recovery."

I wait impatiently for Nell to complete her litany of fees: shelter pick-up and intake; boarding; veterinary care, featuring wound suture and full neuromuscular exam with spinal radiographs; pain, anti-inflammatory and sedation medications; and overlooked municipal licensing. I pay a small fortune to effect Maynard's release but I'm too overjoyed to care about the exact sum. She completes our transaction with stern home management instructions of strict activity restriction for at least two weeks, and she presents me with our paperwork and home meds.

"You're watching closely for worsening neurological signs, so have him rechecked by your own veterinarian in three days or immediately if he regresses." She takes a final glance. "He *is* cute."

I nod. "Uncanny how dogs take on the characteristics of their guardians."

RUNNING ON VIRTUALLY no sleep, I return to work on Thursday morning with the hope that I can arrange to take off early and tend to Maynard all afternoon. Nancy is gone on a vacation day. Gene Napolitano has taken a personal day, and Jean Zagieboylo informs me that no more excused absence time is available for the rest of the week.

Sandee calls me into her office for true confessions. "You still work here? You sure?" She contends that I was away without authorization the last two days and reminds me that a sequence of three consecutive unexcused absences qualifies as job abandonment.

I insist that I cleared a request to miss time with Sleepy Gene. "He must've slumped off during our conversation." I repeat the canard about my sister's mental instability. Sandee doesn't seem quite convinced, but when I recite some corporate gibberish about protected health information and the universal right to confidentiality, she declines to pursue the matter and assigns me a project to analyze tau protein level in blood samples.

I struggle mightily to concentrate on my task. I have lunch with Kelly and relate the unvarnished account of Maynard's stray spree. She exhibits empathy and recalls the time her papillon got loose. The instant I return home, I give Maynard a prolonged hug and pet him 15 times. Later, I finish a roll of paper towels and tease the snoozing dachshund in our customary manner by placing an end of the cardboard horn beside his ear: "*Give it up for Maynard!!*" The canine flails at the horn with his front paws, commandeers the intrusive instrument and chews it into smithereens. I can hardly imagine how devastated I would've been if I'd lost him.

Subsequent time away from my dog moves with a painfully high resistance to flow. Nancy returns on Friday and calls me into her office. "I hope your sister is getting along okay."

I resist the Duchess's transparent skepticism. "She's still out on the ledge, but she's back on her heels." I force a chuckle. "In all sincerity, she's a hot mess, but it doesn't appear to be terminal." I pat my head. "I'd prevail on my old sensitivity counselor Kisslinger to take a therapeutic whack at her standoffishness, but when one moves to a distant corner of the globe, she forfeits her prime support group."

Nancy grimaces. "You're exhibiting a rather cavalier attitude for someone who just dealt with an emotional trauma, aren't you?"

I nod. "You order everything well-done, and Sandee already grilled the tenderness out of me."

"We *would* appreciate a little more conscientiousness in your attitude toward your job." She exhales with mild annoyance. "We all endure personal misfortune, and the world keeps turning. You'll recall that last year I buried my father."

I feel that she's trivializing my private ordeal. "Well, he was already dead, wasn't he?"

She scrunches her nose. "Life is tough all over, Lisle, so I'll disregard that gauche remark."

I offer my most congenial smile. "Really, I'm sorry for your loss."

She stiffens her neck. "I'm reminded that you never even signed the office sympathy card, did you?"

"Uh, I believe I was on vacation that week." I strain to retain a fair degree of compassion.

"How convenient." Nancy fixes me with punctilious eyes. "It's also convenient that you happened to mention your sensitivity therapist. Didn't you make me a promise, Lisle?"

I nod. "To love, honor and obey." I raise my eyebrows. "In which of those am I lacking?"

The Duchess appears imposingly roiled. "You agreed to seek the services of another professional counselor. I promised I wouldn't audit you, but your behavior warrants it."

Her attitude indicates knowledge beyond that which she has disclosed. Did Kelly betray my confidence? "I've been in a holding pattern with that project. I'm awaiting an opening with the ideal therapist." I rise to indicate my profound hope that my visit is complete. "I'll expedite." I proceed to the door, and she doesn't emasculate me by calling me back.

I return to my desk and arrange to undergo a series of

weekly sensitivity training sessions with Dr. Arthur King of King Kryczek & Rohr-Kisslinger Counseling Solutions LLP. My first appointment is set for the second Wednesday in February. I spend the rest of the afternoon pondering a simple question: What is wrong with human beings? The common folk in my dreams and fantasies are vastly superior to the rabble I encounter in real life. I imagine individuals who really care about me. We're genuinely willing to devote quality time to each other. Flesh-and-blood people are so petty, crude and shallow. Even when they make a gracious gesture, it seems to be more for the purpose of puffing themselves up with good feelings than the actual desire to do something nice for someone else.

The weekend is dedicated to the dachshund. Saturday brings three sessions of confined at'im ball. I devise a series of puzzles that require little movement but pay off big in treats. I leave my socks on the coffee table. Maynard snatches them and we play gentle tug. We toss around his pink fluffy bone. I give him a new cultured rawhide chew. I remove his ottoman and revoke his davenport privileges but present him with a new foam mat. He steals my slippers. I trade him a piece of soda bread for the slippers, and he promptly buries it beneath the foam mat.

Sunday afternoon brings a break in an unanticipated call from Pasadena, Texas. "Are we feeling a level more pro-social today, Lisle?"

I pull no punches. "Meditations on the value of friendship have invaded my troubled thoughts recently, Del. Our lives are filtered through those we choose to spend time with. Aristotle called cultivating an appreciation of another party's virtue a fundamental latchkey to a life well-lived. I've determined it's life-affirming as well as laugh-affirming, and I'm ready to reinforce trust and loyalty."

"I'd say I have a renewed respect for caring myself," Vecsey chirps. "I'm really starting to feel like I belong here. Some of my lab cronies have been taking me out mountain biking. I never even knew Texas had hills. The rear wheel came off the bike I was riding two weeks ago, so I bought myself a Trekster. You should see this super marvel of deviant engineering; I swear the tires are fat enough to be on a quarry truck. I used it for the first time yesterday, and I took some radical spills. This time though, I couldn't fault the machine. In more ways than you'd imagine, it was a bad-ass experience."

I suspend my disbelief. "It sounds like a whole new direction for you."

"Nearly straight down." He snorts. "I've also taken a cue from you and delved into the world of pets. I'm now the proud possessor of a pygmy rattlesnake."

"Not really," I challenge with the audacity of guarded optimism.

"My buddy Bob found it while we were biking," Vecsey verifies.

I'm stricken with a touch of nausea. "That's not a pet; it's a threat."

"A lot less trouble than a dog."

"Until the first time it nips you." I hiss. "You can't bond with it. You can't share joy. If you have the desire to keep something like that, you get yourself a rattlesnake Companion Piece."

Vecsey gurgles. "That's a fabulous idea. I'll take a huge Companion Piece serpent into work in a few months and tell Bob this is what became of his pygmy rattlesnake!" He discharges a laughing jag and struggles to catch his breath. "You've inspired me in another broad sector as well, Lisle, that being the Oriental. Your little social justice melee put the yen for a Malaysian mama in me. There's a real cutie down here named Maitai, a Chang Gung alum. She's spoiling to fast-forward to hardcore exploratory research on human subjects. So I was noodling around and I hit her with a proposition: I would let her do anything she wants to my body if she lets me do anything I want with hers."

I smack my phone against my head. "You don't think, Cap'n Vecsey, you might be navigating hazardous waters there? You were lucky to land a decent job without a recent reference."

"Mai is stable," he asserts, "a good egg. And I hate to tell you but the Duchess gave me a glowing reference."

"Seriously." I'm more than a bit flummoxed.

"Nancy knew that living at home paying discretionary rent I had some money to invest," Del explains. "So we helped each other out."

"She sold you a job reference," I verify.

"Lisle," Delmar coos, "the riffraff who start startups aren't the brand-conscious, white-knuckled wonders that run established companies into the ground. They take chances. Nancy's a shrewd shrew. The company burns loads of cash, and she's not going to squander an easy opportunity to make some of it back." He snorts. "Any self-respecting scientist with a healthy survival instinct these days is adept at cherry-picking data, so she might've simply chosen her descriptive adjectives carefully and neglected to mention an incident or two that could blunt the positive thrust of the presentation."

"I should give her a little credit," I concede. "May I request the price of her integrity?"

"You may not, but giving credit reminds me of a festering sore point." Vecsey interjects a purposeful pause. "Will you please prod your pal the bill collector to cough up the remainder of my money for his custom biochemicals? The contact information I have for him is no longer valid."

I emit a wary breath. "May I inquire how much he still owes?"

"You may not, unless you must be insufferably nosy." Del emits a nasal tone. "I suppose you are indirectly responsible though for the transaction, so I will volunteer the information: 24 thousand dollars total. That's what the company would charge retail. So with the insider discount I'm giving him, there's only 12 thousand outstanding. And that includes the free special delivery I arranged by uncommon carrier."

I'm determined to dismantle the Bustelich gender nullification operation from the bottom up, and that begins by removing all loose ends. "It sounds rather steep, but *I'll* pay now on his behalf and settle with him later if you pledge not to supply him with any more product."

"That's quite white of you, Amonor," Vecsey approves the transaction.

"I believe I have all of your vitals. I'll ship you about half in cash, and the rest will be in your crypto wallet by next weekend. But remember, Gayle is as of now cut off."

"If Spaatz contacts me, I'll insist that he obtain a notarized prescription from you before I consider accommodating him further."

"That works, but there's one more condition attached." I feel my paranoia rise. "You need to promise you'll never disclose to anyone else that you gave him these substances. Not even the cops."

"Especially not the bustards." He uses his byword for overzealous peace officers. "Anything else new with you?"

"There's really nothing going on here to report." I rub my neck. "Except that the dog got out of the yard and I nearly went out of my mind trying to find him."

Vecsey wheezes. "Nothing new at the office either?"

I magnanimously dismiss his indifference to my personal ordeal. "Napolitano continues to learn the ropes as lead cockroach. Nancy and Sandee keep busy making excuses for him."

"Skinny Jean and Kelly and the rest of the zomboids still functioning with synergistic cheer?"

"They're good. I'll give them a big 'Bless your heart' from you."

"Hook 'em, horns. And thanks again for playing pay pal. When I have my molecule money, I'll be able to wine and dine Maitai Texas-style. I suspect we'll talk to you again soon."

"Yeah, okay, goodbye." I terminate the connection and turn to Maynard. "Who was that guy? All that's left of the Delmar I used to know is his lack of social graces." I shake my throbbing head. "He exaggerated for effect! And he now has a mountain bike? When he lived up here, he was the first recreation snob to ridicule playtime activities like that. We once encountered some kayakers, and he remarked 'Why do I bother to come out of the house?' He even criticized my motor skateboard. I thought he might lose some of the finer points of his perspective over the course of a few years, but he seems to be in a race to erase his entire old self." I water my plants. Even the moonstones and the jade plant are hurting for moisture. When I've finished, I stop to visit with Maynard again. I slide my hand up the dog's spine. "Please pledge to remain true to your higher-minded canid nature so *you'll* never go turncoat, okay?" He rests his chin on my free hand and licks my face affirmatively.

PART TWO
DOG DAYS

A TEENAGE BOY with fire-engine red hair zips out of his driveway on his bicycle and wipes out in the middle of the street. Maynard and I witness the mid-morning miscarriage of equipoise as we shuffle along the roadside. A greater than normal amount of precipitation throughout the month of December in a mix of rain and snow has left inconvenient icy patches. The chagrined youth springs to his feet and climbs back on his ride. The spill reinforces my overprotective instinct. The dachshund is romping around again with only a slight hitch in his gait, but we take extra care to tread lightly.

A bioassay at Allele changes my work schedule for the shortened holiday week. From noon to midnight, I am to run a continuous processing operation for intervention of bioactive compounds in nutritional factors such as biotin and hydroxytyrosol to alter the fatty acid composition of cellular membranes in aged mammalian tissues under high-glucose conditions and strengthen the resistance of cellular components to oxidative damage by free radicals with an overview to establishing whether extra supplemental antioxidants have beneficial effects on the anti-aging process.

I park myself at a table in the cafeteria with a few of the Healthspan team members to eat a snack as I wait for the bioreactor sterilization cycle to complete. "The execs want to harvest some hyperaccumulators," Kelly advises me. "You know, plants able to absorb high amounts of metals from the soil. I suppose it could lead to a more economical strategy for manufacture of more digestible minerals."

"Or horizontal gene transfer to code for proteins that mediate bodily toxins," Spencer reasons. On TV, onlookers gasp as the 15-year-old daughter of a glamorous Hollywood actress appears to be her mother's doppelganger.

"Or just make crops more suitable for poor-arability soils," Skinny Jean weighs in. "Botanicals hold so many layers of hidden potential, I can't believe we don't have a greenhouse."

"It's in the planning stage," Sleepy Gene submits, "if they can find the cash."

Kelly turns back to me. "One variety is rattlepods, which have pretty, bright yellow flowers."

I shrug. "Probably an indication they're sitting on a gold mine."

"As things stand now, they'll stage them in back within the containment suite," Zagieboylo speculates, "where they have the grow-lights and fan humidifiers set up for the dangerous plants."

"How poisonous are they?" Leah picks at her mesclun.

"They're dangerous to the touch," Napolitano asserts. "Those stinging bushes are in the vestibule corner in their own Plexiglas enclosure. To service them, they wear Tyvek suits with gloves duct-taped to the sleeves and full-face respirators."

"One nasty neurotoxin," Kelly concurs. "Even casual contact with the dried trichomes is supposed to be as excruciating as a battery acid burn. They call it the suicide plant because you just want the unbearable pain to stop."

"I believe the pain-inducing peptide is moroidin," Spencer contributes. "It's similar to spider or scorpion venom."

"They really think that neurotoxin is going to shrink malignant tumors?" I agitate. "Better than a trained virus?"

"Seems to be the prevailing idea at this point," Napolitano affirms.

"The cure will probably be worse than the condition," Kelly gibes.

"I miss that applemint and those herbs they used to have growing down in the holding area," Leah muses. "So aromatic. I'd sometimes go down on my break just for a little whiff."

Our collective attention is directed to a TV news report of a mystery illness, which seems to be highly transmissible and potentially lethal. The outbreak has occurred in a cluster around St. Cloud, Minnesota, afflicting victims with flulike symptoms such as vomiting, fever and delirium. Persons infected experience severe limb pain, suffer muscle control trouble and talk gibberish. The pathogenic agent appears to enter the bloodstream and induce organ failure. Hospitals report that patients turn blue and suffer sepsis. Four related cases have already resulted in death, ten more have required amputation and nine others are being treated with medically induced comas.

"It'll probably just turn out to be tainted health food," Sleepy Gene theorizes. "Bad chard. Or stinging bush leaves got mixed into the salad."

"If talking gibberish is the main symptom," I pose, "carriers could be almost everyone."

"Everyone except you, scatman," Spencer retorts.

Gayle Spaatz calls me again at work on Delmar Vecsey's vacated line and extends holiday greetings. I caution him that Ideal Allele is liable to deactivate Del's line any time, and I proceed to disclose that the company is encouraging nonexempt salaried employees to enjoy a four-day weekend by taking a nonpaid holiday the day after New Year's. Gayle counters with a cordial invitation to visit him at Pleasant Lake and provides directions. He sounds a bit forlorn. I tell him I'll consider the trip, but I decline to commit. I eat my New Year's Eve dinner filtering broth and evaluating the best guilt-skirting excuses.

Early Friday morning finds me driving up to Pleasant Lake in Waushara County. I have disabled the location tracking function of my Megalophone. I hope to convince Gayle to release Johnny Bustelich and end the depravity of his transformance escapade. Otherwise, I'll take a more proactive approach toward Johnny's liberation, either through corporal force or by appealing to the authorities. Exactly two months after Maynard's AWOL episode, I'm still anxious about being separated from him, so the dachshund comes along for the ride.

I spend a good portion of my two hours plus on the road

reviewing my personal history with Bustelich. His attacks on me generally rated as more boorish than brutish, even if egregiously cruel and abusive. "Hey, Amonor, you familiar with hoarfrost?" Assuming a collegial timbre, I explained, "It's twisted crystals posing as a feathery inflammation." He countered, "It's what a poor boy gets when he tries to make it with your sister." If he ever bothered Dinah, she didn't mention it. "Hey, Anomor, you know what an anagram is? Yeah, you're Amoron." He would spot me in the corridor, survey me up and down, shake his head and remark, "Life just ain't fair, is it, Lloyd?" When we reached high school age, Johnny would accost me in the parking lot of any popular hangout. "Hey, Anomor, you feel like a pizza? You look like one." He liked to play me for giggles to gaggles of girls: "What lucky lady is going to end up schtupping him? Can't you imagine a whole houseful of little brats running around that look like that?" But each succeeding semester seemed to offer less occasion to reboot hostilities. Near the end of our senior year, I approached a table in the student union at which Spaatz sat as Bustelich stood over him trying to entice him to bet against a card trick. Formally recognizing my arrival, Johnny gibed, "Whoa, here's Lionel the man. Watch out!" Gayle and I both refused to contribute to his scam. "If you geeks were really smart," Johnny grumbled, "you'd mutilate your ugly mugs. When you look like hell, why not at least look dangerous, too, and get some respect for it?" In the clear analysis of calm hindsight, perhaps the worst thing about brushes with Bustelich were the ominous potential they always harbored to shift swiftly into physical combat mode.

I reach Pleasant Road and locate the maroon cottage with

the decorative lawn windmill and the crippled utility trailer in the driveway. Per Spaatz's instructions, I carefully maneuver around the trailer and park. I don my hooded clean-room frock, tinted goggles and textured exam gloves. I take Maynard out of the Yukon on his leash for a relief break. It's damp and chilly but unseasonably warm for the day after New Year's in central Wisconsin. I place the dachshund back in the SUV, lower the windows slightly and leave him to burrow beneath his quilt and blanket in the cargo area. I walk around the cottage and tap on the side door. I find it locked, raise my goggles to my hairline and rap with more vigor. Gayle finally appears and opens the door. "Don't be so impatient, Lisle. I had my doubts that you'd show."

"Identity protection protocol!" I place a finger over my mouth. "You're sure he can't hear us?"

"From the wine cellar, I doubt it." Spaatz snickers. "Anyway, faithful friend, welcome. You come alone?"

The question disturbs me. "I have the dog in the car. Who else would I bring?" I step inside. "I'm basically here to try to talk some sanity into you."

"Able to squeeze past the trailer okay?" He closes the door behind me.

"I'm glad you directed me, because I would've guessed that's the neighbor's driveway." It doesn't feel much warmer inside the cottage. "The Bustelich cabin is the one on that side?"

Gayle nods. "That *is* their driveway. The beastly boys seem to have busted the axle jumping on their trailer the day before Thanksgiving. I don't believe they've been back since."

I stare at him agape. "Why am I parked in the Bustelich driveway?"

"I spy a midnight blue SUV buzzing around." His lips form a sly grin. "I suspect it's a cop. He may be aware that the owner of this place is in Florida, and I worry that his curiosity could be piqued if he saw a random vehicle in the driveway here. An auto in front of a trailer looks less conspicuous."

I'm overwhelmed with worry about Maynard and the Yukon, but I suppress the sensible impulse to turn around and return them safely home. "This predicament can't be worth the stress."

"The project is progressing promisingly," he responds. "Ready to see for yourself?"

"Gayle," I plead, "Johnny's treatment of us over the years was inexcusable. The abuse you suffered at his hands was particularly abhorrent. He's an asshole which nobody can deny. But by simply moving on, you can move him out of your world – him and all the rest of his blood relatards. Bullying is a plague by which a defective, toxic personality seeks to score dominance points through a dismissive exploitation of the disadvantaged other. So you take it upon yourself to defeat Bustelich not by hating him but by finding the wherewithal to ignore and thereby void his influence. Leave Johnny to wallow in the misery of his own device. Release him in a field halfway between here and Milwaukee and be done with the whole bitter affair."

Gayle grimaces. "It sounds like you rehearsed a perfectly wonderful harangue all the way up here, gubbins, but you really have no idea of what you're talking about."

"I've always been perfectly content to operate in a fashion that validates the Dunning-Kruger effect." I smile graciously. "I know it's freakin' frustrating. Society seems to have mechanisms in place to advance and protect the interests of everyone except single guys like you and me. But you're hanging on the hollow tenets of the two-wrongs-make-a-right school of philosophy."

"The last time you started to preach at me, altar-ego," Spaatz snips, "I thought we reached an understanding. When I'm interested in converting to Christianity or heterosexuality or any of the other mainstream cultural institutions that seem to have panned out so well for you, I'll let you know. Until then, I again request that the secretary-general of Amonor International kindly respect my boundaries."

I emit a heavy breath. "I can't stand idly by as your friend and watch you mess up people's lives, especially your own. You've descended into a seriously dark place here."

"Yes, Lisle, it's a wine cave." Gayle snickers sardonically. "You've never had an appetite for art, but maybe if you come on down and see for yourself what I'm doing with him, you'll be in a better position to judge and appreciate the good work yet to come." He offers a sweeping arm gesture, and I reluctantly start down the stairs.

I pause midway and turn to him. "What code names are we establishing for each other?" I pull my collar up over my nose and position my goggles over my eyes.

Spaatz nods. "Now you're getting into the program. How would it be if I call you 'Cyclops'?"

"Refer to me exclusively as 'Doctor,'" I demand. "I'll call you, uhm, 'Plumber.'"

"*Plumber?*" Gayle protests. "Why Plumber? If it must be a profession, how about 'Undertaker'?" He is amused that I'm annoyed. "I've always had a desire to be called 'Catcher,' for Holden Caulfield."

"How about if we call you 'Left Field'?" I continue to the basement floor. Stacks of bottled water and toilet paper interspersed with sundry junk objects such as lamps, broken chairs, pottery, a snorkel and fins, rods, paint cans, a cracked solar panel and a pair of crutches line the wall of what appears to be an enclosed room which occupies the rest of the basement except for a narrow space at the rear.

Spaatz points at the solid redwood door to the enclosed room. "If this rec room weren't here, the owner might've shut off the electricity for the winter, so it's a double bonanza. The sinks and toilet don't work, so he must've shut off the water. Or maybe they never worked. The well with the hand pump in the back works, and most conveniently so does the outhouse."

I snicker anxiously. "How did you gain entry?"

"The lock on the door upstairs yielded easier than the one at the Team T Squared office." He smirks. "There's a bogus alarm sign in back, so I drove off and returned in a couple of hours. There were no badges swarming the premises, so I brought Johnny inside, and we've lived cozily ever after. Since then, I've found the spare keys."

I scratch my head. "Where's your vehicle?"

"Vito's drywall van?" Gayle drums on an overturned bench. "I drove it into Coloma, called Vito and told him where to come pick it up. He and Rudy the slut drove up in my car and retrieved it. Vito then dropped me off here with some of my personal belongings and some supplies before heading back.

Rudy is a dedicated biker and beater miser. My car is being stored in his garage in West Allis."

"For how long?" I groan. "Someone is bound to see suspicious lights here or spot you out back at the hand pump-"

"The owner has various lights programmed to switch on randomly." He snorts. "The first night, I worried that he might actually have some remote monitoring or the place may be haunted. A spruce tree in back and the outhouse obscure the pump from view pretty well, and it doesn't make much noise. There isn't much activity around. I don't think many of the local yucks winter here."

"I can't quell my concern about running into Johnny's bereft brothers."

"Tell them you're up here looking over this place for potential purchase, and the realtor simply directed you to park in the wrong driveway."

"What if they should come up to their cabin to do some ice fishing or something?"

"Enough stalling, Lisle." Gayle smiles wryly. "Doctor. Let's alleviate your stress over reconnecting with Johnny by reconnecting with Johnny." He strides to the redwood door and opens it. "Come on, Doc." He slips inside.

I inhale like a cliff diver and follow him. I discover a spacious finished wine cellar complete with oak flooring and diamond-pattern redwood racking that covers three of the four walls. About an eighth of the compartments hold wine bottles. Dim recessed LED lights illuminate the room. In one corner of the space is a makeshift bed of iron bars in the form of a giant spider web bearing a thin foam pad at the hub. Reclined on the web in a gaudy black, white and green floral frock is a large human form I recognize with considerable difficulty as John Bustelich. A cable fastened to the top of the web passes through two screw eyes extending from the oak ceiling and is attached to a hand-crank winch anchored to a barrel a short distance from the foot of the frame.

Spaatz conducts me webside. Bustelich's limbs are splayed. Both of his wrists and his right ankle are cuffed to the thick bars which constitute the second outermost spiral of the structure. Johnny turns his head slightly to assess us through dull blue eyes. The last 15 years have thinned his blond hair and left it with streaks of grey. His widow's peak with shaggy locks on the sides renders his head strikingly bulbous. But he is clean-shaven, and he displays a pouty sneer. I can't recall the Bustelich boys ever exhibiting any idle expression besides a smirk or a pouty sneer. When acting aggressively, they tended to display the same expression that Maynard makes the instant before he devours a chunk of meat.

"Here's the patient, Doctor." Gayle grins proudly. "His attitude has become relatively civil. He'd kick me early on but we've now come to an understanding that good behavior results in coveted privileges: He can keep one limb unbonded, his shock collar gets removed, and at the end of the day, he gets a spot of wine. You see there's some choice Rieslings in here." The catcher pats his captive on the secured leg. "We had a little trouble with potty training, but Johnny quickly came to appreciate that if he fouls his environment, he's the one who'll be most adversely affected. He claims the urge comes upon him suddenly, so every once in a while we still miss our paint-can break, but I'll grant the drugs may have something to do with that. His appetite is great now. He attempted a brief hunger strike shortly after we arrived – I think he had the ulterior idea that his wrists might grow thin enough to slip out of his cuffs – but he only had enough discipline to last a few days. He should have no complaint about the menu here. I feed him a super-rich diet of fruity soy-based pastries and edamame with flax seeds. I believe Johnny eats better now than ever, and that's saying a lot."

"Doctor?" Johnny fixes his glassy gaze on me. "What kind of doctor?"

"Shrub doctor," Gayle crows. "His collection of pruning shears is sick."

"Sick." Bustelich's eyes evince a combination of rage and dread. "You're sick, so sick."

"No, no." I wave my arms dismissively. "Chill."

Johnny scrutinizes me. "Is that you, Amonro?" I'm struck speechless. "Uh, Anomor, Loyal, er, Lisle, enough is enough. Talk to this lunatic! *Spaatz is out of control!*"

"I'm out of control!" Gayle scoffs. "Have *I* battered *you?*"

"He's been coming slowly unglued since grade school," Bustelich perseveres. "You could watch it happening."

"Let's take five, J.D." I grab Spaatz by the arm and haul him outside the wine cellar. I slam the door behind us. "When did he discover your identity? How?"

"I admitted it as soon as I determined this was the perfect staging area for his transformation." Gayle beams. "Half the drama would be drained from the exercise if Johnny wasn't aware of who his transformer is, wouldn't it?"

I gasp. "If he didn't recognize you, he could simply be released and you'd be done with this nightmare!" I tear off my goggles and hurl them to the floor. "You could've denied it all! I'd assumed you were able to keep your identity concealed!" I tuck my collar under my chin. "Now I'm implicated too!"

"Chill," Spaatz snarls. "Your crony Delmar included a supply of propranolol with my shipment." My expression apparently conveys utter bewilderment. "It's the drug that wipes out the memory of a recent traumatic episode. Del explained that it blocks the functioning of stress hormones which stamp memories on the brain and it keeps them from forming. When I no longer desire to keep Johnny, I'll slip him some propranolol, and he'll never remember who altered him or how. He'll just find himself on some desolate roadside in an evening gown." Gayle chortles. "He still has no idea *where* he is. I had him convinced for a while we were on a Mississippi River houseboat. 'Feel the waves rocking us, Johnny?'"

I want to slap Spaatz silly and Vecsey sillier. "Gayle, a cop came to my house two months ago investigating Johnny's disappearance. He asked me some questions about you."

Gayle eyes me warily. "He brought up my name, or you did?"

I glare. "I'm not your Judas! One of Johnny's neighbors apparently recorded your car license when you were staking him out. I told the cop you move around a lot and I'd lost touch with you."

Spaatz furrows his brow. "I'll tell Vito to have Rudy strip my car, if he hasn't done as much already."

"Gayle, I won't turn you in." I exhale heavily. "You need

to turn yourself in. Let them find you wandering along some desolate stretch of highway repeating 'Johnny, oh, Johnny.' I'll testify how Bustelich tormented you. We'll pound the word 'bully.' These days there's nothing that doesn't qualify as a mental disorder. With a woke judge and jury, the most you can expect to get for this snafu is two years to simmer in a mental health institution." I snicker anxiously. "You may actually like the facility. With the exception of the clinical practitioners themselves, the people there won't be as phony as the ones you find on the outside. You'll probably have all the taxpayer-provided art supplies you want, and you'll be able to create with minimal distractions."

"Maybe I should move Johnny to Dane County and surrender him there, because there's no place on Earth where they value wackadoodles more." Spaatz transforms his weak smile into a strong scowl. "Did you check to make sure you weren't followed coming up here?"

I pull the hood off my head and wipe the perspiration from my brow. "Please appreciate that I have your welfare at heart."

"You barely spoke to Johnny." Gayle nods to the wine cellar. "Let's finish your visit." He opens the door, and I grudgingly follow him back inside. He proceeds to the decorative barrel opposite the web. "Time to get up and dance for Dr. Lisle, Johnny." He cranks the winch and suspends the web in a position nearly perpendicular to the floor. "I found this boat winch right down here in the basement. I call it my wench winch. The heavy-duty web is from Vito's discarded kinky dungeon collection. A lot of disassembly required, but he was happy to get rid of it. This barrel was part of the base of a table in here.

Johnny had to spend our first few days and nights on the floor, but by and large, I couldn't have custom-designed a timeshare any more perfect than this place."

"Free up my other foot." Bustelich supports his substantial weight on his unfettered foot.

Spaatz clutches his throat. "Johnny, focus on projecting your voice from a higher place in your larynx, and interject a little more breathiness to help yourself be heard." Gayle smiles at me. "You haven't commented on Johnny's wardrobe. His buttons fasten on the side for easy changes. The fit is loose around the middle because he's not getting any skimpier. Color options are limited, but there's a swank set of coral drapes upstairs, and I'm going to make Johnny a jumper."

I remove my uncomfortable suit. Bustelich fixes his indignant eyes on me. "Your skin is less of a mess, Amonor. At least it don't look like you're scratching your brains out anymore. Is being clearer a relief, or does it direct more attention to your hooked nose and other hideous flaws?"

"Step up, Lisle," Gayle prods. "Get in touch with your innermost feelings and vocalize them."

"Can I speak with Johnny privately?" I reply. "We have a personal issue to settle."

Spaatz raises his eyebrows. "Can I trust you not to take advantage of the situation, Doctor?" He shrugs and giggles. "Don't get too close." He leaves the wine cellar and slams the door behind him.

"Aughh, Lowell, er, Lisle," Johnny sighs. "Spazz is out of his mind. He's a psychotic son of a bitch. I think he keeps the cuff keys in the top drawer of the cabinet by the door, or else we can try to tear this frame apart."

I expel an irritated breath. "What's the matter, Bustelich, don't you think the crack under the door is wide enough to allow you to ooze out?"

The fury in his features becomes tinged with shock. "You're not up for this shit, numb-nuts! Spaatz has no impulse control. He doesn't think things through, but you do!"

I move directly in front of him. "Do you think things through, Johnny? When you were harassing kids unequipped to stand up to you, did you ever figure you could be made to regret it?"

Bustelich scoffs. "You guys should thank me for toughening up your sorry, pampered asses and giving you the opportunity to develop some street smarts. Being messed with by guys like me at least must've been better than being ignored by everyone else."

I hiss. "Why yes, you do deserve credit for showing us we might have personal worth serving as objects of ridicule."

He grimaces. "Whatever, you know this ain't right, Amonor." He tugs at his restraints. "You hold me prisoner, torture me, you know you'll ultimately have to kill me! What did I ever do to you that comes close to warranting murder?" He groans. "Are you really up for murder, Amonor? *Murder!!?*"

I smack Johnny in the middle of the forehead with the heel of my palm, and Gayle re-enters the wine cellar. "Nobody here," I assert, "is talking about murder, Bustelich."

"No, not close," Spaatz affirms, "not yet." He stands beside me. "You made a career out of putting others down, Johnny, but we won't put you down. We have better things to do with you."

Bustelich spits in my face and kicks me in the knee. I stagger backward, and he tries to kick me again. "If you were in my position here, Anomor, you'd be crying like a tea kettle!"

I rub my knee. "Life just ain't fair, is it, Johnny."

Spaatz places his hand on my shoulder. "I'm sorry to have interrupted so soon, Lisle, but you should know your pit bull is barking and howling up a storm out in your car. That can't be in our best interest if we're trying to avoid drawing attention." Gayle is wearing a bulging fanny pack.

I wipe my face. "We're finished here anyway."

"You have a pit bull, Lloyd?" Bustelich shakes his head. "You were always more of the *toy* pit bull type, weren't you?"

"It's actually a dachshund, isn't it?" Gayle offers too much information.

"A wiener dog?" Johnny chortles.

"Don't worry, Bustelich, I won't introduce you." I retrieve my suit and head for the cellar door. "I wouldn't want him to pick up any of your bad manners."

"Make this little psycho release me right now, Amonor!" Bustelich tugs vehemently on his restraints. "Or one way or another when this story comes out, you and everything you care about will get caught in it and crushed!"

"Do you really think that's the way to influence people, Johnny?" Spaatz grabs a bottle of Shiraz, a corkscrew and two flutes. "We work to earn wine points here." He follows me out the cellar door.

"*If either of you two losers had kids,*" Johnny's bellow chases us up the stairs, *"you'd realize how rotten, weak, wretched, wicked, immoral this is!!"*

I hold the side door open and Spaatz joins me outside. "Your first viewing of the new Johnny might've worked out better." He accompanies me to my vehicle.

"I came up to see *you*, not him." I coo and wave at the mewling Maynard as I circle the Yukon. "My preference would be to never see Johnny again." I climb into the SUV and enjoy moderate success calming the dog.

"It hurts my feelings when you talk like that," Gayle protests. "Johnny remains a piece of work in progress."

"I hope you'll reconsider what we talked about when I arrived, Gayle." I lower the window farther and accept the glass of Shiraz he offers me.

Spaatz and I raise our flutes. "To the new era of the New Year." He drains his glass, sets it on the hood of the vehicle and leans against the door. "You'll come back inside and set awhile, won't you?" I smile politely and shake my head. "You really think I'm crazy, don't you?" Maynard snarls softly.

I empty my flute and emit a cynical sigh of disillusionment. "We're both crazy for expecting this cruel world to give guys like us any breaks." I hand him the glass and start the engine.

Gayle peers at me intently. "We all lash back at outrageous fortune in our own way. You treat your dog ten times better than any woman who ever shunned you could honestly hope to be treated by the man she chose over you. It's your way of saying: 'I found a worthier being, honey. No man would've ever been more devoted to you and treated you better than I would've, and see how all of that energy goes into caring for a dog instead. You missed bad on me!'"

"I never worry that my love and affection are misplaced." I shift the Yukon into reverse, slowly maneuver around the utility trailer and plant my foot on the brake. "Gayle, the cop looking for Johnny told me you recently bought a gun, and I'm really concerned about it."

"The cop is a scaremonger." Spaatz reaches into his fanny pack. "Just like me." I'm a fraction of a second from jamming the accelerator to the floor. He produces a note, makes a small tear in the center of the paper and slides it over the neck of the wine bottle. "The handgun is a prop dedicated to the proposition of gaining a little respect and a lot of discipline. It's what I might employ should the other Bustelich bastards ever wander over here, but it's never been loaded, and I don't even remember where I put the ammo box." He passes the bottle of Shiraz with attached note through the window opening, and Maynard growls. "Please accept the Shiraz as my gift. That's nobody's will attached to it, but a wish list of provisions that Johnny and I could use." He collects his flutes and steps away from the vehicle. "Can I pester you to do me a favor, Lisle? If you could see your way to coming back up in a week or two with some of the requested items, your holiday spirit would be much appreciated."

A cursory examination of the list suggests that the cabin is in need of a boxcar-load of groceries. "Possibly," I gamely resist commitment, "if the weather doesn't get too frightful."

"I'll call you at work anon." Gayle and I exchange waves as I back out of the driveway. "I hope I can count on you,

Doctor!" He withdraws a huge syringe from his fanny pack and brandishes it.

I drive cautiously up Pleasant Road. The last thing I need is to be stopped for some minor traffic violation that creates a record connecting me with the vicinity. I'd expected my compassion to escalate at the sight of Johnny the internee, but I'd felt it evaporate instead, even before he insulted or assaulted me. If Gayle genuinely expects to change Johnny internally, I trust he's going to be sorely disappointed.

"Johnny Bustelich has now officially become our problem, too," I advise Maynard. "I know you were thinking like me that what we could really use is a new problem."

By the time we arrive home, I have no intention of returning to Pleasant Lake. Regardless of my personal history with Gayle Spaatz or what I promised or may owe him, I recognize that I have to report him to the authorities. I stash the Shiraz on the bottom shelf of the fridge and fix myself and the dog sloppy joes and rice. I sit down with my phone after supper to contact the police, but I'm drained from the journey and I presume nobody will be working on the long holiday weekend anyway, so I fall asleep watching television instead.

AN ODD ATMOSPHERE of intellectual curiosity and visceral tension pervades the Ideal Allele cafeteria. According to the news at noon, the mystery turbocharged superbug in St. Cloud was now being referred to as the dog zoonosis. The Minnesota Department of Health had traced the source of the infection to bacteria in dog saliva and identified *Capnocytophaga canimorsus* as the responsible organism. "State health officials in conjunction with the CDC have identified the index case and are taking every necessary measure to contain the spillover. The CDC confirms that patient zero has been linked to a kennel and transmission appears to require sustained contact with the dog reservoir. A natural constituent of the canine and feline biome, *C. canimorsus* is present in 74 percent of dogs and normally arrested by human immune cells." However, the mutated variant responsible for the outbreak has apparently evolved an enzymatic mechanism or exchanged genetic material with another microbe enabling it to enter the bloodstream, evade immune responses and inhibit antibacterial drugs. "The WHO states it has no evidence of infections from this pathogen reported anywhere else in the world."

"Hey, WHO," Gene Napolitano crows from the next table, "go back and check China again! Not like they don't have the creds as an incubation source and worldwide exporter of this sort of gift; admit into evidence at least two of the bubonic plague pandemics plus cholera spread by contaminated bilge water dumps, not to mention the more memorable SARS family outbreaks."

"If you or I suggested that," I whisper to Kelly, "he'd be the first to accuse us of ethno-baiting."

"No," she disagrees, "the second."

"It's too early to conclude it's not altered," Leah submits, "isn't it?"

"Absolutely." Kelly stops eating her soup and stirs it.

"MERSy me," I comment. "If it's a biohacked bug, I'd expect it to have originated somewhere in the Middle East, perhaps Saudi Arabia, where dogs are considered dirty. I believe one has to be on the sultan's crony list to be able to own any pet."

"I guess that means you're not an Arab," Spencer chides me.

I trade subtle smiles with Kelly. "I'm advised I do have some Sumerian DNA."

"I don't deny that the source could be closer to home," Sleepy Gene perseveres. "Maybe they'll find patient sub-zero in the anomaly zone between Plum Island and Lyme, Connecticut, or retrace it back to Fort Detrick, where they *used to* conduct germ warfare research. I won't believe that's a done deal until I can have a look in the sub-subbasement. The smart money says you'd find some holdover activity."

"It's all outsourced to foreign entities now," Kelly ventures.

The idealist in me hopes that American strategic biological weapons research is no longer being conducted but the pragmatist fears we're lambs on the world stage if it's not. "There's a reason why the CDC keeps a pitcher of smallpox on ice," I suggest.

Napolitano stands up. "Come on, you people, you work in a biotech lab! Find a cure for this thing! Nobody leaves tonight until your solution is on my desk!" He laughs, and a strain of titters ripple throughout the room.

Gayle Spaatz calls me on Delmar Vecsey's vacated line late Monday afternoon to observe the passage of the tenth day since my visit. He advises me that his food situation is dire. I reply that it would be impossible for me to miss work the next day and an absence the day after that would be only slightly less difficult to arrange. But I agree to make an effort.

The instant the radio traffic reporter notes an ebb in Wednesday morning rush hour volume, Maynard and I leave for Pleasant Lake. It's an ideal opportunity to end the transformance tribulation by demonstrating how finite its resources are. Thirty minutes into the journey, I inattentively take the wrong exit and end up in West Bend. I stop at an upscale strip mall and purchase more pantry supplies than my vehicle can comfortably haul. I hope Gayle appreciates the bulk lot because I intend to emphatically drive home the point that this load is to be the extent of my provisioning.

I spend most of my time on the road racking my brain for the key to solving the unbalanced equation set before me. The gentle extrication of all parties involved might require extraordinary measures to ensure my own safety, such as hiding behind an identity change and moving far away. Maynard and I could relocate to a densely populated college town and open a Thaw'n'Go stand, providing biohacker clientele with exotic cell cultures and yogurt treats. Perhaps I could ask Sandee to suggest an Indian name that defies pronunciation like Sooriyabandara Gupti-Vaithilingaraja. I wonder if Delmar Vecsey could assist me in securing low-profile employment with his emerging hormone company in Texas. Otherwise, I may have to reconcile with Dinah and coerce her to board us above her garage in Zamboanga.

We arrive at the cottage and park in front of the crippled utility trailer. I step out of the vehicle. The ground is frosted with a dusting of snow. Spaatz promptly slips outside to greet me. "Lisle, always walk around the back way! We don't want to leave any tracks in the snow out front!" Gayle's coat is unzipped, and I notice the handgun tucked beneath his waistband. "Did Vito catch you?" he inquires. "I called him Monday from the pub. He has my footlocker full of personal side effects, and he promised he'd drop it off at your house this morning so you could bring it up with you." I shake my head. He admires the groceries and exhibits the firearm. "I still can't find the ammo. I should've put shells on the shopping list, hmm?"

I force a smile. "Unfortunately, I didn't go to a high-end

store where they carry silver bullets." I scrutinize the weapon. "That *is* a bit of a cannon, isn't it?"

"Just nine mil." Gayle replaces the gun in his pants. "The head honcho at Horsepower is an expert on firearms. I like to keep the Colt close as a talisman for Johnny, and even closer for Markie and Duckie. Last time I think I told you I spotted them casting longing glances at this shack over Thanksgiving." He points his trigger finger at the Bustelich cabin. "I feared they might try to force entry."

"You think they spotted activity?" I open the rear liftgate and usher Maynard from the vehicle on his leash.

"No chance." Spaatz grabs two grocery bags. "They were probably up here for deer-hunt season. I thought they might try to break in on general unprinciple." He snickers. "If they knew about the wine cellar, they'd have come to call before the cold wave that chased out the owner lifted. I've never had the stuff for a bluff; I wonder if I could've deterred any malice in the palace with my empty piece."

I shudder at the prospect and the cold. "You originally took down Johnny with a taser, didn't you, Gayle? Why don't you just carry that around instead, so any malice in the palace would be less likely to cause permanent damage."

"I passed the stun gun back to Vito." Spaatz smacks his lips. "It actually belongs to Rudy. I didn't have any more darts for it anyway." He eyes me intently. "There have been a few times when I've really had the desire to shoot Johnny. Best to be aware that blasting away would lead to slaughter."

Gayle conveys all of the supplies into the cottage as I attend to Maynard. We remove our coats and turn to inside matters.

"It's not toasty in here, but it's comfortable, eh, padrone?" I rub my hands together glad I'm wearing a heavy sweater. "Thanks so much for this. It takes a lot of wine to get my minimum daily requirement of minerals." We stock the bare shelves, situate the dachshund in the parlor and proceed downstairs to the wine cellar.

"Hey, look who's riding to my rescue," Bustelich acknowledges me the instant I enter his crib, "again." He's attired in a yellow gown festooned with abstract tondi. "We expected next time, Doctor, you'd show up in your full bunny suit." Gayle cranks the web perpendicular to the floor. Both of Johnny's ankles are bound but one of his arms swings freely. "What's shakin', Amonro? Besides you."

"Johnny." Spaatz taps his throat. "Mezzo-soprano?" He turns to me. "I've been reading to him from Bernie Shaw's *Pygmalion*, and I swear I gain more and more empathy for Higgins as we go." He smiles at Bustelich. "Is *Pyg* still your favorite classic, Johnny, or have you acquired a preference for some of the juvie lit that I've scared up? I'd like to expose you to some chick lit."

"I should've taken care of you when I had the opportunity," Bustelich grumbles. "Both of you."

"How does a peaceable guy like you make so many enemies, Amonor?" Spaatz teases. "One of the juvie-lit page-turners we've delved into employs transhumanism as a backdrop. I wonder if you might be scientist enough, if necessary, to ultimately upload Johnny's mind to a tree or a household appliance. I would think a pussy willow or a refrigerator would be most appropriate."

I'm troubled by the sincere tone of his sentiment. "Re-arranging the basic order of the universe might be a tall order, even for me."

"You see, Amonor, you ass-wipe," Bustelich snarls, "Spazz has gone absolute batshit; he's off his nut; he's over the deep edge! Are you co-loco?"

"After cancer took my dad," Gayle asserts, "I would feel a connection to him beneath the wind chimes of the loblolly pine that he and I planted. That tree isn't even supposed to be hardy in our horticultural zone, but it thrives!"

"Gayle, I've had almost nothing to eat today. Would you please sponsor a cholesterol-raising event for us while Johnny and I dig a little deeper into an effort to bury the hatchet?"

Spaatz raises an eyebrow. "All right, I'll rustle up some cottage fries." He opens the column of buttons on the side of Bustelich's garment. "But first I want to show off what fabulous genetics Johnny has." He adroitly removes the tush pad and denudes his captive. "Look how smooth his skin is. There's not a trace of acne or any other rash, despite the harsh biochemicals he has exposure to." He slaps Johnny's buttocks. "Just a few knots where he receives his injections." Gayle tosses the dress over the barrel and heads for the exit. "Don't forget that Johnny has a free hand." He leaves the door open and marches upstairs.

Bustelich and I trade glares. "Really enjoying the spectacle, Roscoe?" His mien crystallizes as a pugnacious smirk. "Your life sure must be worthless to throw it away for the sake of messing me up like this. I had totally forgotten you even exist. You're so damned forgettable, so fucking pathetic."

"Guys like me," I utter, "always want to know just what makes guys like you."

"Guys like you, Amonor?" Johnny scoffs. "You mean weird, warped wussies, fiends, freaks, kidnappers, torturers? Fucking murderers?"

"What was the real reason behind it all, gobshite?" I retrieve his dress and flip it to him. "Was Daddy too friendly with too many of the ladies at work or up the street? So Mommy coped by making the whole family suffer, and the Bustelich boys brought all that misery to school and passed it on like vectors transmit an infection?"

"What the flying fuck?" Bustelich positions his garment over his groin.

"Or was it all on you, Johnny?" I persist. "The harassment, intimidation, beatings? Have you always been so twisted you just can't take pleasure in anything except someone else's misery?"

"You guys deserved everything you got!" Johnny snaps. "More! You were a pair of pustules always begging to be popped! You and Spaatz acted like you were entitled to special consideration, and the rest of us were expected to handle you with extra care because you were so delicate and sensitive. And all the while, you both had nasty mouths and stuck-up attitudes." He tugs on his handcuff. "The real divide between us, Amonor, is power, strength, toughness. The tribe or village or what-have-you has always crushed the weak and contrary. The resisters either get strong and conform or they're driven out. Anything less, and the village struggles to stand. That's just the raw way of the world."

"So you see yourself as performing a service for society by bullying us," I infer, "doing your Darwinian duty as a natural selector of who's fit to survive." Maynard enters the wine cellar and scampers across the oak floor to me.

Bustelich fixes his gaze on the dachshund. "Ho, little doggie! My brother Doug had a dog for a while. It bit him, so he kicked it right out of his yard! Your foot-long fur-ball will end up with a heavy foot planted in the middle of its back and its throat and tail pulled up until its yelps end with a *snap!*" He slams his elbow against his frame. "If you don't want that mutt mangled, this may be your last chance to save him by saving me."

I kneel beside Maynard. He sniffs at Johnny and takes a step forward. I hold him in place and pet him. I'm overwhelmed by a feeling from long ago of the fear and loathing induced by the presence of an unavoidable menace. I expel the dog from the wine cellar and shut the door. I return to Bustelich and emit an embittered breath. "All right, Johnny, it's time to get real. I can feel Gayle losing his passion for this project. He realizes he's made his point, so now the problem becomes how we dispose of you in an eco-friendly manner." I begin pacing. "You're too tubby to stuff in a recycling bin, so let's deal. How much compensation will it take to make you agree to walk away from this indignity without a word to the authorities and without pursuing any other sort of personal reprisal?"

"*Indignity?*" Bustelich drops his dress. "My balls are raisins! The whole works is shut down! That may be your normal condition, Lowell, but it'd take a hell of a lot more money than you've got to make me whole again!" He shakes his head.

"You've really got to be out of your fuckin' mind! I'd need a ton of money — instant retirement, seven figures – to even consider anything so warped, and that's assuming I can bounce back and make a full recovery!"

"My parents were good at managing money," I disclose. "I inherited more than most people suspect. I live a modest life and I don't have a lot of upkeep, so I could probably cobble together one hundred thousand dollars for you." I smirk and move directly in front of Johnny. "It's yours if you can guarantee that the cops will never learn about your little misadventure with Gayle. Plus you guarantee that no harm will come to Gayle or me or our property or interests, such as my house or my dog or even my reputation, in retaliation for the inconvenient displacement you've suffered here."

"Inconvenient displacement." He snickers sardonically. "A hundred thousand. For real? If you free me right now, it's a deal!"

"Your release needs to be accomplished downstream of Gayle's initiative," I explain, "so it'll probably take a few more days, maybe even a few weeks. I'll keep sowing the seeds of detachment; successful diplomacy is the product of patience."

"Just as long as my money is payable in a lump sum upon my release!" Johnny extends his hand. "Shake on it."

I extend my hand and he grabs it belligerently. He twists it sharply and drives me to my knees. I grind the knuckles of my free hand into the back of his hand, and he clasps my neck. I liberate myself by delivering a punch to his groin. I slide back, stagger to my feet, and we both discharge coughing jags. "You can still feel that," I gasp, "so you're not gone down there yet." He holds his genitals and moans. "Your prime problem, Bustelich, is you've always assumed everyone else is as stupid and treacherous as you." I rub my eyes. "I made my offer in good faith, but you just proved that as soon as you had my money, you and your bottom-feeder brothers would've come around and expressed the full range of your destructive talents, wouldn't you?"

Johnny grits his teeth and squelches a cough. "How about we're allowed one good thumping upon payoff, if we promise to leave you and Spazz alive and alone afterward."

I take a couple of deep breaths. "The offer still stands, but your cut is down to eighty thousand. I'm passing the other twenty to an insurance agent. He's a special kind of insurance agent with whom I'm acquainted from my professional descent into the field of microbes and germs. Should some mishap befall Spaatz or myself, he'll slaughter your family with a pathogenic agent like brain-eating amoeba."

Bustelich exhibits anguish, and I'm tempted to take a snapshot. "Have some compassion," he blubbers, "please show some mercy, some decency!" Tears run down his cheeks. "I miss my wife. I want to see my kids. *They must be emotionally devastated, distraught!!* You've punished the shit out of me! I want to go home! Please, stop this madness! Please!"

"I miss my wife and kids too, Johnny," I confide. "And I haven't met them yet." The wine cellar door opens, and Maynard returns with Gayle. "Because I'm still in the process of locating the girl lucky enough to end up with me and waiting to beget the children lucky enough to look like me."

"You let me loose," Bustelich bellows, "and we can settle

any old score you like man-to-man! Let's go, you wimp!" I consider the agony I endured throughout the short period that Maynard was lost, and I'm not without pity for Johnny and his family. "You want to see a hater, Amonor, a real bad guy, a truly spiteful son of a bitch, take a long, hard look in the mirror! That image should be rougher than ever for you to endure now because you're just plain deranged by bitterness! You're worse than Spazz!"

"What have you done, Lisle?" Spaatz assesses his internee. "You've perturbed Johnny. He waxes moody and emotional, so you have to handle him as you would a figurine." Gayle smiles primly. "And moving forward when we refer to him, let's replace traditional gender pronouns with denatured ones, so adding a Milwaukee twist: 'he' becomes 'they' becomes 'dey'; 'him' becomes 'them' becomes 'dem'; and 'his' becomes 'their' becomes 'deir.' I believe we've reached a point where it's appropriate."

I hiss. "We're not going to recalibrate the language for him. The fact is that Johnny and I just had a breakthrough. He's ready to admit that he's predominantly responsible for his present predicament because it was his mistreatment that made us into monsters bent on subjecting him to a personal reign of terror. I hereby declare the mission of our vengeance accomplished."

"I hereby declare this your dinner warning bell," Gayle retorts. "You can instruct Maynard to start salivating. We're having roast chicken and saffron noodle gratin. A special thank you for picking up the saffron. We'll let Johnny break deir diet for the day and sample it. Anyway, it'll be ready in a jiff, so why don't you pick out a nice bottle of light white, and I'll meet you in the parlor in a few minutes?" He titters. "Johnny's a little overdue for a bowel movement."

"Why don't you two turds," Bustelich snarls, "pitch yourselves some prison-style meatloaf in preparation for what you'll soon be eating for dinner every night for the rest of your shitty lives?"

"If we're tossed into a shithole teeming with Johnny Bustelich sorts," I submit, "weathering the particulars like meatloaf every meal will be the least of our woes." I grab a bottle of Jose Rose and conduct Maynard upstairs.

Gayle has already set the oak table. I seat myself and decant blush wine into flutes. I take a swig and contemplate the open concept of the ground floor. The taupe rug isn't thick but it's soft. A small bathroom stands in the corner and two doors apparently lead to compact bedrooms in the rear. The kitchen counter, cabinets and major appliances stand toward the side door while three battered easy chairs are clustered around a flat-screen TV on the other side of the room. I wonder how minimal the interior of the Bustelich cabin must be.

Spaatz returns upstairs after two full flutes of Jose Rose have graced my gullet. "I shamed Johnny for being insolent," he reports. "I forced him to recite his pledge to always show respect and never bully." Gayle swipes a sip of Jose and revisits his business around the range. I retrieve Maynard's food packs and hollowware from the SUV and set him a place beside the refrigerator.

Spaatz puts the finishing touches on the simmering cottage fries and roast chicken, and we savor a sumptuous meal. I attempt to subtly apply all known principles of persuasion to induce Gayle to terminate the transformance enterprise. He ultimately eyes me peevishly. "Let's be completely candid, Lisle." He sighs. "You're falling in love with Johnny, aren't you?"

I discharge a spot of wine from my nose. "I could laugh all the way home at that suggestion as long as I know it's not a projection of your own feelings."

Spaatz scowls. "Lisle, if I harbored desire like that, would I be turning Johnny female? Will you please suspend your Free-Johnny campaign for the rest of your goddamn visit?" He gets up and grabs the carving knife. He cuts us generous slices of the blueberry pie I provided for dessert and pours us cups of coffee. "Maybe if you were a little more inclined to reminisce, you'd be a little less ready to moralize."

I slip Maynard the chicken I've saved for him. Gayle sits down again and emits a heavy breath. "Seeking relief from the authorities in the form of protection from the Busteliches has already been tried and failed. I wonder if you recall a series of events from the end of sixth grade. I believe you were absent most of the week in question with some debilitating mystery malady, but I certainly apprised you of it when you returned." He drains his flute and rubs his face vigorously. "It followed from an incident where Johnny and I simultaneously kicked at a rolling soccer ball. He struck the ball and I struck his shin. Of course, he made a big stink about it and stayed hopping mad for a couple of days, really giving me shit wherever possible." Gayle's breathing becomes agitated. "So Ms. Fessler-Shlissel calls on him to work a math problem in front of the class, and as he walks up the aisle, he clips me in the back of the head. I've had it with him, so I jump up and grab his arm.

He pulls me and my desk over into the aisle and hops on top of me. Once Ms. Fessler-Shlissel recovers enough from hyperventilating with horror to direct our disentanglement, she sends Johnny and me down to see the principal together. Staggeringly enough, Johnny threatens me, stomps my feet and keeps trying to trip me all the way to Mr. Truax's office."

"Mr. Truax." I'm not sure whether to wince or chuckle but I attempt to exude palpable empathy.

"Truax is on a conference call when we arrive," Spaatz continues. "Sounds like the league of principals reassuring each other they're always the smartest person in their own domain. Johnny immediately starts grousing that people keep messing with him and he only tries to stick up for himself but he gets in trouble for retaliating. He whines that I've been taunting him about flunking fourth grade for three years. Truax will have none of it. 'We won't tolerate brawling in the school regardless of what triggered it,' he admonishes us. I say, 'There's no imbroglio that you can't charm your way out of, is there, Bustelich?' Truax gives me the evil eye and incorporates processing us for discipline into his multitasking. He demands our student I.D. tags but neither one of us is carrying them. 'Then state your full name,' he directs me. 'Spaatz,' I reply, 'Gaylord Myron.' Johnny snorts, and I notice a mean, little smirk cross Truax's lips. 'Bustelich, Mark,' he prompts Johnny. 'I'm John Edward,' Johnny corrects him, 'Mark Anthony is my brother.' 'You said "John Edward"?' Truax reloads. 'He said "John N-word,"' I volunteer. Truax has a conniption. He disconnects from his conference call, exchanges messages with Ms. Fessler-Shlissel, dismisses Johnny and slams me with a three-day suspension for using hate-speech and bullying Johnny."

I nod. "That makes perfect nonsense. You should've said, 'Sorry, sir, I didn't understand that Johnny was given "E-D."'"

"I understood at that moment that Johnny could bully with impunity." Gayle rubs his face. "Truax told my mother that insensitive microaggressions thoughtlessly tossed out by people like me are exactly what's sustained an atmosphere that leaves marginalized groups behind. My mother pointed out to Truax that no marginalized group member, except maybe me, was involved in the incident. Truax explained that social justice is a constant, regardless of the identities of the individuals involved in any particular incident. My mother suggested that Truax pass his own purity test before he lecture her by ceding his job to a deserving member of a marginalized group."

I raise my flute to salute Gayle's mother. "At any rate, I'll never again question your ability to subvert the spirit of hate-speech by using it with a filter."

"While you're at it, don't ever question my veracity again either." Spaatz glares. "My mother was so furious she contacted a lawyer about suing the school district. I had to throw the biggest tantrum of my life to prevent her from thoroughly humiliating me by proceeding with it." He gobbles up his pie. "Ask Johnny right now: I'm sure he'll concur with the official school record that he was the one being bullied." Gayle rises. "I'm going to take a plate down to him. And I like to give Johnny his shots right after food. He has another date today with Big Leu. Come on, Doc, you can assist me."

I feed Maynard my last two bites of blueberry pie. "We really need to head out if we're going to make it home before dark."

We exchange a little more idle chatter before I collect Maynard's gear and grab my coat. Spaatz accompanies us outside. "Put the grub on my tab. Thanks for delivering." We exchange solemn nods. "I'll take another invigorating five-mile walk into town tomorrow and call Vito from the pub to see what's going on with my footlocker. Maybe you could bring it up next time and spend the night here. A sleepover like when we were kids."

"I don't know." I force a congenial smile. "Can't Vito bring it up himself?"

Gayle eyes me intently. "You're the only other person who knows what's going on with Johnny. Vito has a big mouth. He thinks I'm here on a nature-sketching retreat. I really don't want anyone else hanging around. You're the only one I trust."

I can't bring myself to decline outright. "I imagine something might be worked out."

Spaatz nods. "If you think of it while you're out shopping, Lisle, pick up something pretty for Johnny."

As I drive home, my neck and the wrist I strained in my scuffle hurt more and more. I consider Bustelich's desperate contention that his influence had inadvertently served to toughen me up. An emotional callus develops from being deprived of basic human needs; Trish, Amie and the cavalcade of evanescent heartthrobs who rejected me instilled strength, not Johnny. An unsinkable rugged quality results from being denied a break; the educators and employers who dismissed me with prejudice hardened my mettle, not Johnny. It's the struggle, with extended periods of being denied one's way, which builds character. As he never had anything I wanted, Johnny couldn't have contributed.

I realize that I'm dabbling in serious legal jeopardy. My first responsibility is to Maynard. There'd be nobody to take care of him if I got removed from polite society. I could probably avoid any sort of life-ravaging crisis by reporting Gayle to the authorities. It's undeniably the right thing to do, and it might ultimately benefit everyone involved.

Maynard and I share a family-size deli pizza for supper. The moment we've finished, I gather Milwaukee Police Lieutenant Cripesdale's card and my phone. I need to be shrewd about how I release information. I must carefully gauge how it's being received and protect my own interests. The parley could easily go bad. I'm distracted as the dog starts whipping around his fuzzy bowtie pillow. I decide to play tug and postpone my call.

"NEW GIRLFRIEND?" FROM across the lunch table, Jean Zagieboylo references the four fingerprint bruises on my neck. "Isn't that a cluster of hickeys?"

I feel my face glow red with embarrassment. "I don't think you'd classify the perpetrator as generic girlfriend material yet. And that's all I want to say about it." I bite voraciously into my gooey banana protein bar.

A news report on the cafeteria TV teases a significant development in the dog zoonosis spillover. Serge Kenower, deputy director of the Division of High-Consequence Pathogens & Pathology with the U.S. Centers for Disease Control & Prevention, has been designated as point person of the government effort to combat the Capnocytophaga epidemic. The new official face of the enterprise steps to the microphone for his first official press conference. "So now 'Capno' enters the popular lexicon," Kenower begins, once he's thanked other "great and small" members of the eradication team.

"He's kind of cute for an old bureaucrat," Leah remarks.

"Too bad he's not taller," I stunt the attraction.

"We have the utmost confidence that the pathogen is being contained," Kenower continues, "and there will be no spread beyond the hot zone." He cites a hodgepodge of statistics on suspected and confirmed cases. "We do not find signs in the sequenced genome of inserted sequences, indicating it is unlikely that variant CCSC-01 had been artificially altered. The sudden increase in serious infections caused by the pathogen and its heightened virulence would indicate a single nucleotide polymorphism."

"It's too early to make that assumption," Sleepy Gene asserts.

"It may have been manufactured in a research facility just like ours," Skinny Jean suggests. "Exactly what again was that special project you were working on two weeks ago, Lisle?"

"The never-ending quest to isolate health effects of individual nutrients in the interest of developing biobetters," I rehash the specs, "mainly targeting biomolecules that induce or delay a cellular senescence response, as found in such natural compounds as oleuropein and flavones."

"Whenever these bioterror episodes turn out to be the doing of some lone degenerate," Napolitano contributes, "the perp always seems to be someone like you, Lisle."

"The evidence is strong in support of horizontal gene transfer with another microorganism," Kenower answers a reporter's question. "If the *Capnocytophaga canimorsus* bacterium has experienced a natural recombination event with a cyanobacteria plasmid, it may have been equipped with an injector protein that allows the pathogen a more viable entry way into human cells."

"Wouldn't it be easier to modify the rabies virus so vaccines didn't work?" Leah wonders.

"Lyssavirus neurotropic pathogens would be less transmissible," I maintain, "with longer incubation periods that would militate against an epidemic."

Skinny Jean gestures to me. "See, he's an expert on the whole situation already."

"The dogs appear to remain nonsymptomatic," Kenower responds to another reporter's inquiry, "although a possible subtle decline in motor skills has been observed in a few hosts. We're setting up holding centers for dogs that may have been exposed. We realize it can be difficult for people to surrender their animals, but tests need to be conducted to determine the health status of any animal that is potentially a carrier. The tests are getting better all the time, and it's likely that a healthy dog can be returned to its owner."

"That's bullshit!" Sleepy Gene contends. "They're sending tissue samples to the national veterinary lab in Iowa. I have a friend there who says the supercharged Capno causes tiny brain lesions in the host animal, and the gold standard test requires a postmortem."

"Distance your dogs from other dogs and people when possible," Kenower provides the appropriate public response. "Veterinarians might make house calls where relevant. Watch closely for signs of illness. There's no reason to panic, but this disease can strike fast and hard."

I return home from work Thursday evening to find an olive drab crate tethered to my gate with a bicycle chain. An accompanying note reveals that the smart padlock anchoring the chain can be opened by entering *GMS 8NO BDAY*. I truncate my work week at lunchtime on Friday. I retrieve the footlocker and the dachshund from home and head north for Pleasant Lake. It is my intention to spend the night with Gayle and Johnny and return home early Saturday morning. The first major snowstorm of the season is forecast to strike southeastern Wisconsin on Saturday afternoon.

We reach Pleasant Road and follow a UPS truck through the sinuous dips. We spot Spaatz waddling up the Bustelich driveway and pull in behind him. Startled by our presence, he produces a bicycle pump from beneath his coat. He recognizes us, and his concern dissolves into a puzzled smile. I park in front of the crippled utility trailer and step out of the Yukon. "I got your special package." I rub my neck. "I hope it contains some tranquility balloons to blow up Johnny's irascibility."

Spaatz tucks what appears to actually be some sort of pipe back inside his waistband. "Johnny has been feisty the last couple of days. I believe your visit Wednesday upset him, er, dem. I feel like we've regressed a bit."

I rub my brow. "Those gender-neutral pronouns are a corruption of the language and a bit discommodious." I open the liftgate and hold Maynard in place. "Frankly, I find such fluidity fitting only for an era when everyone was a prokaryote." I take the jumbo footlocker, turn and hand it to Gayle.

"You're right, dey give me a headache too." Spaatz chuckles. "Let's drop dem." He swings the footlocker onto his shoulder. "Vito brought this by your house late Wednesday morning. You would've already been on the road. He was going to just leave it then, but he said there were guys walking around your yard looking inside your windows, so he didn't stop but instead came back yesterday."

"I have some nosy neighbors." The streets of Waukesha County tend to meander and can be confusing to the uninitiated, and I surmise that Vito had the wrong working address on his Wednesday morning foray.

Maynard and I escort Gayle to the cottage, and I hold the door open. He carries the footlocker inside and sets it on the oak table. We remove our coats and sit as if to conduct business. I appreciate the extra insulation of my thermal fleece Henley. Gayle presents the pipe again and shows that it's really a gun. "This is a Welrod Mark IIA, a vintage Second World War British Special Ops assassination pistol. You caught me coming back from town, where I just acquired it. You see, the magazine is the grip. Isn't that cool?" He attaches the magazine and demonstrates the odd grip safety and trigger action. "Shooting it is a little tricky. We took it outside and tested it. Shot noise is soft as a cap gun. I traded my Colt Combat Commander for it." He grins. "Off the books, of course."

I chafe. "So the handgun registered to you is now out of your control? What if it's used in a crime?"

Spaatz shrugs. "What difference would it make, Lisle? I'm underground."

I suppress the impulse to commandeer the Welrod and pistol-whip him. "Are you planning to remain underground forever?"

He offers a wry smile. "If pressed on the issue once I resurface, I'll say it must've been discarded in the process of moving and somehow landed in the hands of shady figures unknown." He purses his lips. "I traded it to the proprietor of the pub. He's a decent guy – homey and pleasant to chat with."

I hear myself hiss. "You were supposedly keeping a low profile. It sounds like you're becoming a little too conspicuous around town."

"You're not jealous, are you?" He detaches the Welrod magazine and sets the firearm aside.

"I'm concerned that you're going to soon find yourself in deep, deep trouble, and I'm liable to find myself being dragged down with you."

Spaatz rolls his eyes. "Your best survival strategy in prison, Lisle, would be to get yourself isolated in solitary." He rises. "I need more social contact than that. Variety is my spice rack."

I nod. "It's your relish tray."

The tension between us deflates. "On the strength of those analogies, can you stay for chow?"

I offer a deferential smile. "I was actually thinking I might take you up on your recent suggestion that we stay overnight."

"Fabulous!" Gayle opens the refrigerator door and surveys the contents. "Johnny had a bit of a bad reaction to his last date with Big Leu. He got a headache, along with some puffiness around his eyes and armpits. He's complaining that he still has some numbness and tingling in his hands and feet." He removes a package of pasta from the cupboard. "We'll give him a little while longer to recover and see if he's up for another shot after supper."

I am concerned about Bustelich's overall health condition. "What sort of dosage is he getting?"

Spaatz squints into space. "Two milligrams twice a week or so." He eyes me keenly. "I believe that's what your colleague Delmar recommended."

"Del is a walking wild-ass-guess." I consult my Megalophone. "He made some monumental messes in our lab. It looks as though you wouldn't want to exceed eight milligrams every four weeks, but I'm only a mock doc, so for all I know even that's a dangerously high level."

We begin sorting through objects in the footlocker. Spaatz extracts an airbrush kit and acrylic paint tubes. He withdraws various other art supplies such as pens and ink cartridges, pastel sticks and Bristol board tablets. He produces a two-fingered smudge-guard glove and a blaze artist's beret. I wonder if Trish is still painting. Gayle displays a leather neckerchief. He withdraws a blue suede flogger and a long, braided nylon rope. "Got a jeweled saddle in there too?" I anticipate the spectacle of a disassembled mechanical bull. He produces his prized collection of caricatures of our former classmates and teachers, which he began generating in high school. Covering the name, he displays a drawing of a girl with chipmunk cheeks and a wide, toothy smile. "Ah, Liz Finn," I guess correctly. "Remember we used to call her Lynn Fizz." Gayle shows me a drawing of a boy with pinprick eyes and prominent gums. "Dylan Spangler. Those were sure some thick glasses he wore, hmm?" He shows off his enhanced nude portrait of the lovely Stephanie Recktenwald. "That's what you call an exposition." I scowl playfully. "You always swore you'd never do me; I better not be concealed in there somewhere."

"No, you're too elaborate." Gayle displays an incomplete picture of a woman with a square superhero jaw. "This is Jeff Hurst. I started drawing some people as I'd expect them to appear if they had a sex change." He sets aside the caricatures and removes another blue suede flogger from the footlocker. "I was never into dungeon kink like Vito used to be." He produces a *Pro Beach Badminton* set. "This is more my kind of toy." He sets a thin stack of books on the table and holds up the top one: *The Art of the Tattoo*. "I'm going to study this manual, and then I'll lend it to you. If you can get us a cheap used tattoo gun kit, we can cover Johnny with tats. We can use his legs for the 'self-tattorial' and work our way upwards once we've mastered the craft. I envision a Blowing North Wind icon surrounding his navel or more appropriate orifice."

"Gayle," I object, "this thing cannot careen further in the direction of gratuitous physical abuse."

"Then I won't suggest we color half his face tribal indigo." Spaatz starts tentatively petting Maynard. "Hey, pooch, do you find the term 'sausage dog' demeaning?" He sticks his hand inside the dog's mouth and shakes his snout. The dachshund shows admirable forbearance. "I've never had any pets. Never been much of an animals aficionado. I'd fancy cats, if anything. You might recall my sister had a little tabby for a while."

Gayle and I reminisce over coffee. I take the opportunity to see if I can frame Bustelich more favorably. "Overall, that Marty Ulvog was a worse s.o.b. to me than Johnny. Tom Crotty as well. In tenth grade, Crotty snatched my brand-new basketball, ran over to the court and heaved it into the middle of a pickup game some college guys were playing. I summoned all the courage I had to ask for it back, and they laughed and threatened to beat my ass. I waited till the end of the game and asked for it again. This guy pulls out a knife, shreds the hell out of the ball and hands it to me. I had to go home and tell my parents I lost it and take a load of crap from them for being so irresponsible."

"But they eventually bought you another one." Spaatz titters. "In tenth grade, I had my only conversation with Stephanie Recktenwald." He raises an eyebrow. "One more than you had? I was wearing my rainbow sweater beneath my coat of many colors. She ogled me and exclaimed, 'You look positively divine!' I said, 'Really?' She giggled and said, 'You are so feminized.'"

I flash an empathetic scowl. "You should've said, 'Too bad you're not.'"

"I should've said, 'Suck my titties.'" He wiggles his tongue. "Think of the heaps of trouble I could've gotten into for that."

"I don't recall you ever mentioning that little brush." We continue trawling memory lane, and I intensify my wheedling to secure Johnny's release. When our nerves are mutually frayed, we declare a truce. We head down to the wine cellar with the braided nylon rope garnered from the footlocker. Bustelich is wearing a gingham smock and his shock collar. A swelling appears to engulf his face and extremities, and Spaatz applies a cold compress to the most prominently inflamed areas. The treatment replenishes Johnny's vigor, and Gayle deftly rebinds him independent of the web with dragonfly sleeves and a leash tail. We take turns walking him around the room. He pauses to rest every few minutes but the entire exercise lasts almost two hours. We decide to forgo Johnny's leuprorelin injection and reattach him to his web frame. Gayle grabs a Riesling, and we return upstairs.

Our late supper is worth the wait. Gayle fixes a delicious garlic shrimp spaghetti plus carrot cake bars. Over dessert, we achieve what I interpret as a rough breakthrough. Gayle proposes that we conduct an overnight mind experiment. At bedtime, he and I will haze Johnny, slip him a light dose of propranolol and with a binaural beat induce a deep theta wave sleep. In the morning, we will investigate whether the subject recalls the humiliating incident.

I'm able to slip downstairs while Gayle finishes the business of kitchen clean-up. Bustelich and I exchange cold, silent gazes. His right foot is unbound. I crank him nearly upright and get in his face. "You thought any more about the deal we discussed?" I edge closer to transmit the full aromatic pleasure of my garlic breath. "Persuade me you're sincere about settling this matter for eighty thousand dollars."

Johnny remains silent for about a minute. He finally grunts. "You said a hundred thousand, and I'm thinking that's nowhere near enough." He displays a pouty sneer. "As previously stated, honey, I'll need a gunny of money."

I nod. "My enforcer will keep you honest for ten thousand,

so I'll raise your total to ninety, but that's the final offer. I can arrange a silent green disposal for you far more cheaply than that."

Bustelich scowls. "What are you suddenly, Amonor? Trying to play some mob boss?"

I make no effort to conceal my spite. "I'm sure you have a lot of packages delivered to your house, Johnny. How easy it would be to take one that's on your porch while pretending to deliver another one, taint whatever is inside with some infectious agent and replace it. You want to live in fear that taking a bite of food or touching your doorknob is liable to set you bleeding from every orifice? Want to watch the brains and intestines of your wife and kids melt into oozing gelatinous globs?"

Spaatz enters the wine cellar shortly after eight o'clock. "No more private consultations with Johnny, Lisle. I'm going to start worrying that you're talking about me." He sets several cherry-scented candles around the room and lights them. He binds Bustelich's unfettered foot. "Before you bed down, Johnny, we want to get to the root of more of the hell you subjected us to in school." He deftly removes Johnny's smock, collar and diaper. In the eerie light, the man's obesity is striking.

Spaatz opens the badminton set, withdraws two rackets and flings one to me. He removes a shuttlecock and discards the rest of the equipment. "You've always grown listless easily, Johnny, so we're going to liven things up with a simple game. Remember in phys ed how we'd compete in badminton? We're going to play the derivative game of bad-Johnny." Gayle flips me the birdie. "To review the rules, we take turns serving, and the server bats the shuttlecock off the ceiling. When it comes down, the servee tries to trap it against Johnny's belly. If you succeed, you score a point. If you leave a mark on his body in so doing, you score three extra points! First to eleven wins."

I toss the shuttlecock back to him. "Why don't you show me?"

Spaatz pats Bustelich's gut. "Freaks first, eh, Johnny?" He strikes the shuttlecock upward but it hits the winch line. "Fault." He snatches the birdie and shovels it to me. "Damn, I'm rusty. You show *me*, Lisle." I reluctantly smack the shuttlecock against the ceiling. Gayle winds up and strikes the birdie on its descent, but it ticks off the frame of his racket head, which he slams flush into Johnny's massive paunch.

"Ouughhh!" Bustelich moans. "You twisted, little mother!"

Spaatz retrieves the shuttlecock. "Ready, Lisle?" He pops the birdie against the ceiling. I catch it on my racket and flip it onto Johnny's belly. "You can't carry the birdie!" Gayle protests. "When it comes back, you have to spike it in one motion!" I pick up the shuttlecock and pop it against the ceiling. Spaatz takes a more controlled swing but shanks the shot. He smacks his lips. "I left a nice mark." He rubs Bustelich's gut. "But no birdie, no points." He redistributes Johnny's paunch with his racket. "You observe, Doctor, that the anticipated atrophy continues to progress, although periodic occurrences of arousal are still documented."

Johnny fixes his indignant eyes on me. "Why don't you lean in closer, Amonro? Get a stronger taste." He smirks. "You look like you sleep with your mug pressed into that racket." He squints. "Have you had some touch-up work done, waffle-face?"

He shakes his head. "You'd have been better off to stick with your scabies."

"Careful, Johnny." Spaatz pats Bustelich's belly rhythmically. "Or Lisle will carve your pizzle into a tassel. He's been lobbying me all day to finish you off."

Bustelich holds me in an even more lethal glare. "You lying piece of sheep shit."

Gayle giggles. "Did Lisle offer to carry you away from all this drudgery, Johnny?" He retrieves the shuttlecock and smacks it against the ceiling. When it comes down, my racket buries it in Bustelich's belly, drawing his expletive-riddled howl of disapproval.

"Stellar form, Doctor!" Spaatz examines the aftermath. "That was an ace. You're up four-love." I bat the shuttle off the ceiling, but Gayle again smacks it wildly, finishing with his racket in Johnny's boobs.

"Your turn again, waffle-face," Bustelich chides me. "I bet when Mummy calls you for breakfast, she yells 'Waffle-face! Ooh, where's my awful waffle-face?'" Spaatz pops the shuttlecock off the ceiling, and I belt it into Johnny's gut. "Ouww, you fucking bitch!" His eyes fill with immoderate fury. "When Mummy calls you for dinner, she wails 'Pizza-face! Where's my zitty pizza-face?' You had a shitload of acne and eczema at the same time, Anomor? That's making a real statement you're a two-time loser."

Spaatz tickles Bustelich's lips with the shuttlecock. "You can give Johnny his next leuprorelin injection tomorrow, Lisle." Gayle flips me the birdie, I bat it off the ceiling, and he smacks it into Johnny's paunch. "Not much of a belly spank."

He thrums the target area. "But at least I'm on the board. Eight-one."

"Pizza-face," Bustelich taunts me. "The doctor who delivered you probably drove weekends for Gianpietro's."

Spaatz smacks the shuttlecock off the ceiling, and I slam it into Bustelich's gut with a ferocity that startles even me. "If I'm the pizza face, doughboy, does that make you the thick crust?"

"Game over," Gayle snickers. "Did you enjoy that, Johnny, as much as elbowing me in the groin during seventh-grade basketball? We'll play again soon." He reaches into his pocket and produces two grey tablets. "For the time being, please take these two pills for sweet dreams."

"Sure," Johnny scoffs. "Fuck you."

Spaatz holds the two tablets at Bustelich's lips. "Take your meds, Johnny, and I'll give you a tall tumbler of Riesling to wash them down."

Johnny reluctantly opens his mouth, and Gayle drops the tablets onto the tongue. Johnny spits them both into Gayle's face. "Game on, you fucking twerp! Two points for me."

"No problem." Spaatz saunters to the counter beside the door and opens a drawer. He prepares a syringe and returns. He displays the large needle. "It comes in an injectable form too." He jabs the needle into Bustelich's lower abdomen and winks at me. "Sixty milligrams the express way!" Johnny winces slightly as Gayle delivers the medication. "Doctor, if you'd set your Megalophone on speaker and select an eight-hour isochronic symphony, you may step outside the exhibition hall while I tuck Johnny in for the night." I leave my Megalophone on the barrel beside the winch crank to project an isochronic symphony suggestive of lying in a hammock on a breezy afternoon while a lawn mower runs in the distance. As I reach the door, Gayle coos, "If you find your spirit guide, Johnny, give him a kiss from the lost party at ninth-module lunch." I proceed upstairs and pet Maynard until Gayle returns. We reminisce further, play word games and drink more wine.

"Naturally, I rule the master bedroom on the queen-size mattress," Spaatz advises, when we decide to end the evening. "I'm willing to share, or else there's a cot in the guestroom if you prize your privacy."

Gayle removes assorted clothing and towels, a blaze orange backpack and a camouflage duffel bag from the cot to provide us with unlimited access. He throws them over a black leather travel trolley suitcase in the corner of the room. Maynard and I squeeze onto the cot, and I'm able to sleep soundly through the night with my vigilant canine friend stretched across me. My nightmares and blood pressure are both less intense than they were when I entertained Angelo.

Early Saturday morning, Spaatz and I eagerly storm the wine cellar to investigate how the overnight therapy affected Bustelich's brain. He groans and wheezes as we approach, and I turn off the isochronic soundtrack. "Leg cramp," he gasps.

"I'll trade you my tension headache," I reply.

Spaatz frees Bustelich's ailing limb and massages it. "Johnny, this is important. Do you recall the general theme of the interaction the three of us had last night right before you went beddy-bye?"

Johnny eyes me rancorously. "Waffle-head."

"Think, Johnny," Gayle insists. "If you can tell me exactly what game we played, I'll fix you bacon and eggs for breakfast."

Bustelich emits a flustered breath. "You cock-mittens paddled me."

Gayle and I retreat to the parlor, and he prepares a breakfast of bacon and eggs. "Kosher bacon?" I tease. "The cultured variety we're growing in the lab would probably qualify, hmm?" Maynard receives a heaping portion and so does Johnny. Gayle discloses that he found a document cache which provides the name of the cottage owner: Cory Ryscavage. "Could be male or female," I remark. "Seems appropriate." I stretch. "Does each day seem to pass a little more slowly than the last?"

"Glad I brought my game player." Spaatz follows my gaze across the room. "Ryscavage must've shut off their premium TV. There's a couple of over-the-air stations that come in all right, but I don't watch much. Really, I have plenty to read, and I listen to music on the radio sometimes, but I try to avoid the news. Is there anything I should know about happening in the world?"

"Wildfires laying waste to Antarctica. Closer to home, the United Nations welcomed its first extraterrestrial extratranssexual aliens." I cackle. "As you hinted, it's mostly 'different day, same shit.'"

I help Spaatz fetch water, and we wash dishes and tablewear in buckets. He plays briefly with Maynard. "I've kind of taken a liking to him," he grants.

We decide to survey the lakeshore. I gather Maynard in my arms, and his silent snarl reminds me of how disagreeable he finds the arrangement. Gayle leads us down the weathered wooden steps behind the Bustelich property. The slope behind the cottages on the south side of the lake is steep and sylvan, and one long flight of stairs leads to a landing and then a second long flight of stairs. I set Maynard down at the bottom, let go of his leash and he scampers a short distance down the beach. No other activity is discernible in either direction along the shore or on the other side of the lake. I don't even spot any birds, although Gayle assures me that crows, gulls and ducks maintain a robust presence in the vicinity.

"I've been coming down here to do laundry," Spaatz volunteers. Several red caution flags stand intermittently spaced about thirty meters out on the lake ice. "They say it freezes over completely more years than not, but you see now it's thin and a little dangerous." I regain control of the dog, and the three of us venture a short distance over the lake ice. We hear cracking beneath our feet, and the surface grows discernibly slushier. We return to the shore. "They're waiting for an overdue cold snap to thicken the plot before ice fishing and snowmobiling can commence in earnest."

The western sky is darker than the grey haze directly overhead, and the wind gusts suggest that flurries are imminent. "It *would* be a trip to walk across," I venture.

"It's about 500 meters to the little public access beach." He points to a sliver of turf on the opposite shore. "It's supposed to be about seven meters deep for most of that stretch. I understand that the natives get kind of pissy about intruders on their private property, but I don't know how many are around to object at this time of year."

"Where are you picking up these slices of the local culture?"

"Guy at Horsepower named Gil," Gayle chirps. "I take pains not to overexpose myself." He is amused that I'm alarmed. "There's an annual fishing jamboree the second Saturday of February, and we're counting on you to come up for it."

"What if-" The plethora of troubling possibilities prevents me from completing my thought. I pick up Maynard, and we trudge back up the steps to the top.

I agree to play video games, and Spaatz thrashes me several times at "The Executioner's Son". I rehash my fundamental arguments to effect Bustelich's release, and we break for a hearty lunch of franks and beans. We return to the wine cellar for one more exercise session. Gayle reconstitutes the rope into a body harness, and he walks Johnny around the room ahead of Maynard and me. We lose track of the time, and we return upstairs to observe that a light snow has begun falling.

Weather predictions continue increasing the expected snowfall totals of the fast-moving storm poised to impact southeastern Wisconsin. Gayle urges me to extend our stay another day rather than race the storm home, but I sense that our mutual patience is growing as thin as the lake ice, so I politely decline the invitation.

I place Maynard and our gear in the rear of the Yukon. I climb behind the wheel and start the engine. Spaatz shivers as he leans against the driver's door. "You can get a tattoo kit with ink that fades in a matter of months. It's a diversion to consider bringing along next time so we can enjoy the pleasure of marking up Johnny's body without causing any permanent deterioration in value. And we'd have the opportunity to re-mark areas once the previous styling fades. I'd really like to lay a diamond pattern up his spine. I'll call you at work next week and tell you exactly what to procure at the craft store."

I expel a protracted breath. "Gayle, I really don't expect to come back up here. You refuse to listen to reason, and my presence doesn't seem to benefit anyone. Please don't call me again until you've thought long and hard about what you're doing and you're ready to end this grisly business."

Spaatz winces. "Thank you for coming up this weekend, Lisle." A sad smile graces his lips. "I do appreciate the logistical support you've given me as well as the moral support, even if that's a little more lukewarm than I believe I have a right to expect." He snickers. "Someday if society compensates me for my handiwork, I'll compensate you for all the materiel support you've delivered here." He chortles. "I'll also compensate Cory for rental of this gallery along with the house wine and crackers."

"Work on your racquet skills." I offer a sympathetic smile. "And please initiate the process of winding this project down to a conclusion. Give me a call when you've resolved to do that."

"I'm going to try jacking up Johnny's propranolol dosage." Spaatz raps twice on the vehicle door, and Maynard emits an excited yip. "I'll be in touch soon."

I wave, and the journey home begins a bit before three. Presuming all relevant roads have been plowed at least twice for good measure, we should arrive home shortly after dark. As I drive, I consider how Kisslinger would negotiate the Spaatz situation. The good doctor would undoubtedly counsel me to hire high-powered legal counsel to cut an arrangement with the authorities to shield me from significant punishment in exchange for giving up Gayle. The swami will always have a place in my personal toolbox as a handy reverse barometer.

I struggle to stay alert behind the wheel. The snowfall becomes heavier as we travel east. I stop to fill the tank in Oshkosh in case we encounter a delay. We struggle with something close to blizzard conditions as we head south, but the roads are barely passable all the way to the house, and I'm able to pound far enough through the snow to park in the driveway. Powdery evidence of snowdrifts cling to the picture window and front door. I tread through shin-deep snow to conduct Maynard from the rear of the vehicle, and he follows in my tracks as we head around to the back door.

Maynard and I enjoy greasy chuck steaks for supper, and by the time we finish washing a few days' worth of dishes, the snow has stopped falling. I return outside to clear the driveway. I make three passes through knee-deep snow with my snowblower, and my neighbor Mr. Lancaster confronts me. "Did your G-men catch hold of you?" he queries. I kill the snowblower engine and stand aghast. "They showed up yesterday afternoon, and more came back at sunrise this morning and hung around your house all day. My wife nearly crapped her britches when the guy came over and said he was a federal agent. He wanted to know all about you: When are you usually home? When did we last see you?"

I never doubted that the authorities would return to advance their investigation of Spaatz. "What did he say exactly?" I force a chuckle as I dread hearing something along the lines of "Kidnapping is a federal offense."

"He was pretty evasive about specifics," Lancaster remarks.

I offer a wry grin. "The problem is likely that I was too." Russ waits for an explanation. "I did some freelance lab work, and I may not have reported my full income. May not have administered the sales tax." I expel a beleaguered breath. "I've been delinquent in submitting all of the proper forms." I see no alternative to fully cooperating with the authorities from this point onward.

Lancaster nods. "We figured it couldn't be too serious. They spent a lot of time looking in your windows. We told them you're a churchgoer. You don't appear capable of being anything too dangerous." He points to my front door. "They left their calling card." I discern a red document on my door handle beneath the curtain of snow crystals.

"Thank you for the tip, Mr. Lancaster." I restart my snowblower and finish clearing my driveway. I chuckle to myself that revenuers would probably be the only government agents dogged enough to endure through a blizzard. I've given Gayle multiple opportunities to abort his overreaching vendetta. I pray I'm not too late to save myself from significant penalty. I drag the snowblower back into the garage and park the Yukon beside it. I grab the red card on the front door and return inside the house.

I boil water to make tea and read the card. "Order for Surrender and Quarantine. The Secretary of the US Department of Health and Human Services has declared that CCSC-01 constitutes a public health emergency. Under the Public Health Services Act (42 Code of Federal Regulations Part 70) individuals exposed to others infected with this disease constitute a probable source of infection, and the Wisconsin Department of

Health Services reasonably believes that subject dog belonging to subject person Lisle D. Amonor has been exposed to subject animal R-10 confirmed to be infected with Capnocytophaga variant SC01. The Centers for Disease Control and Prevention supports the conclusion that quarantine and isolation are appropriate. By order of the CDC and Wisconsin D.H.S., subject animal must be surrendered immediately for isolation in authorized quarantine facility. Please keep animal in voluntary home quarantine until surrender. This notice may also serve as a warrant for official entry of dwelling for involuntary seizure of animal. When examination of subject animal has been conducted and negative result is confirmed, animal will be returned, if possible."

The order continues with D.H.S. convenient contact information for subject animal surrender and helpful instructions for subject person during voluntary home self-quarantine for a period of no less than seven days. It ends "You must cooperate with the efforts of federal, state and local health authorities to contact other exposed individuals to prevent the possible spread of a quarantinable communicable disease, or face appropriate fines and imprisonment. This includes providing information regarding anyone you had contact with, places you visited or traveled to in the past 90 days and your medical history."

I SIT CAMPED with my dachshund in our SUV on the fourth floor of the parking garage at the casino. I hadn't expected to be handed a full-blown existential crisis tonight, and I'm not prepared on short notice to confirm the value system which colors my ultimate reality. Despite his blankets and chew toys, the dog paces skittishly, aware that something is fundamentally wrong. I intermittently start the engine to heat the vehicle, and I worry about having to make an extra stop in the aftermath of the storm to replace the depleted fuel. We've taken refuge here because I'm anxious we're being watched by one order of the authorities or another. I wonder if the cops have already tapped into my cell phone. Even though I maintain a privacy setting that purports to block location tracking, I'm paranoid enough to believe that the government has a working surveillance backdoor for every occasion.

I have to chuckle when I consider the celerity with which

we packed and got out of the house. It rivaled the whirlwind in which Trish left. "I wonder if we'll ever cross trajectories with her again," I burden Maynard with blather. "Not if Bruce Neichi turned out to be the high-quality action-man she couldn't find in me, hmm?" I recall how I dangled the prospect of the project to build a luxury sauna adjacent to the gym in the basement. "That would've been just about two weeks before she deserted us." I thought she responded rather dubiously, so a week later I showed her the physical plans and advised her that I'd made an appointment for an electrician to install the requisite wiring. I rub the dog's neck and shoulders. "How castles come tumbling down." I didn't cancel the electrical work in the wake of her departure, but I never bought the construction kit, and the space sits empty. I resolve on the spot to complete the project shortly. "See if Neichi gives you a private sauna, love."

Reflections of Trish rarely fade without first broadening. We'd declared excruciation station officially finished with the installation of a big-ticket sound system, and I reminisce about our first joint workout listening to the clear, crisp contemporary mix flowing from the soundbars. "This music is doing great things for my workout," she commented.

I couldn't fill the approval-seeking sneakers of the eternal simp eagerly enough. "It's inspiring, isn't it? I believe the artist is Rap Sheet. I'll take that plucky bass line. And the bold tribal drumming is stimulating enough to keep a hungover student alert through an economics lecture!"

"I hate rap and hip-hop," she clarified. "I work harder because I grunt louder to drown it out." She grabbed a pair of dumbbells. "We're being generous by calling it music."

"Generosity is admirable." I parked myself on the bench facing her. "Your plans fail too easily in the shade of obstacles. Did you ever notice that?"

"Did you say 'Earplugs fall out as easily as monocles'?" I wasn't sure whether she was trying to be a smart-ass, so when I took the dumbbells from her, I kissed her on the corner of the mouth. I didn't receive an elbow in the throat, but I didn't get a pass either. "Not the goal for our relationship," she reprimanded me.

I started performing side lateral raises. "I've been giving you extra space, and I thought I could feel an attitude change, a thaw."

"That's probably because you were just outside with the dog." She performed another set, dropped the dumbbells and sat up. "You know, Lisle, I don't think even most true believers feel that they can really trust in God." She grimaced, and it seemed to come more from her speculation than her exertion. "When you look at who thrives and who suffers in the world, it's not fair and it's just a shame. It seems like the only beneficiaries of miracles are people who don't believe in them. To love something is to set yourself up for a bed of pain. The real sin is to care. You have to understand that you're just here to use people and things. If you can be satisfied with that, you can be satisfied with this life."

"That's why some of us can't be satisfied with this life." I wondered if she was testing me or trying to prove that she wasn't quite as shallow as she may have feared she appeared.

I often tried to coax her to accompany me to church but never succeeded. She claimed to be "spiritual but not religious."

I'd respond, "That's like saying you laugh all the time but you have no sense of humor."

The phone rings. I instantly imagine that the authorities have cornered us, but the call originates from Pasadena, Texas. I remove my Alpine Avalanche hat with the ear and mouth flaps and answer. "Just having a miserable Saturday night," Vecsey opens. "Thought there'd be a strong chance you're having one too, and we could share the despair."

"You know me too well, Del," I extend him idoneous courtesy.

"Needless to say, the raging romance has fizzled." He sounds slightly intoxicated. "I finagled a coffee lounge date with Maitai, the Malaysian babe I might've mentioned, and it appeared to go like gangbangers. We talk a little shop and I smartly segue to the topic of what restaurant to make the site of our first formal dinner date. She tells me she's on the paleolithic diet, you know, where they limit themselves to foods eaten by our pre-farming hunter-gatherer ancestors, like wild nuts, wild cherries and wild oats."

"Wild pumpkin spice cappuccinos." In some warped way, I'm grateful for the momentary relief of trading my consummate burden for someone else's petty adversity.

"Yeah, wild." He pauses. "I tell her, 'It's always wise to adopt the sustenance habits of people whose life expectancy was about thirty-seven and a half years.' She laughs and says, 'I'll be honest with you. I find rich, savory food sensually stimulating. It gives me the desire to get passionate with who's ever at hand.' I say, 'I know this fabulous Italian restaurant where they serve up lasagna in a bucket.' So last Saturday night I pick her up for dinner in a teal limousine, because her hair is dyed teal. She comes in with a new nose piercing. I think, 'All right, if that's her misguided way of trying to impress me, then it's adorable.' And we head up to this French bistro."

"Named Plaster of Paris, Texas?" I expect.

"However you say Napoleon's Revenge in French." Vecsey emits a protracted gurgle. "Things test positive enough at the start. I tell her I prefer Asian girls because they don't make me sweat the details like I have to with American girls. I don't feel that I need to play social director and keep plying them with amusing little insights to round them into an agreeable mood. Well, damn if she doesn't proceed to make me eat my words as the main course of the meal."

It's frustrating to be reminded that the guy has such a hard time keeping his Machiavellian thoughts to himself, and I'm sure much of his trouble with Nancy stemmed from this fault. "Strive never to give away your process."

"She stands her MP on the table and brings up her balanced nutrient tabulator." He pauses with irritation. "She says her default mode is protein-rich, and I mention a study at Allele – maybe you know if it's ongoing – that indicated a protein-rich diet accelerates the aging process."

I snicker at the awkwardness of the romantic exchange. "Sounds like a study that Van Leskosek might be wasting time on."

"I suggested that she might quickly catch up to me age-wise and overtake me." He snorts. "Maitai says she doesn't believe in menus, and asks the waitress to recommend a low-nitrate superfood. When we've finally ordered, I take her hand for the pleasure of holding it and the purpose of diverting her from playing with her electronic pacifier. She compares the size of our hands, and shit if the little lady's hand isn't just about as big as mine."

"It sounds like a good excuse for a critical comparison of other body parts." The strife in my own life limits my sensitivity. "I hope you were at least quick enough to initiate a titillating boot exchange beneath the table."

"She pitches a stink," Del grumbles, "because the flaxseed sourdough bread made with almond flour and wild yeast doesn't have enough 'tang.' She goes on to complain that the celery is soggy. Have you ever interrupted a free meal to fret over soggy celery? And the critiques keep on rolling: the plantain wedges are bitter, the oysters are over-rinsed, the ratatouille is perceptibly low in guanosine."

I laugh. "You should've brought up an app on her MP that compiles complaints. 'Was the wild salmon too tame? Were the pine-needles not sharp enough, babe? Was there not enough gilding on the walls for a room with a chandelier, countess?'"

Delmar groans. "For dessert, she lets on that she wouldn't be attracted to a guy like me because she mostly likes the bad boys."

"Dammit," I sympathize, "you shouldn't have brought along your macrame."

"I should've arranged to bring *you* along," he retorts. "I could've introduced you as my parole officer. I told her I used to be into some bad shit and I'd get charged with one or two counts of sexual assault every year, but I've evolved out of it."

"You shouldn't have kept popping tongkat tabs in front of her," I suggest.

"She liked the fact that I defied her," he contends. "Some tense, adversarial bottlenecks remain, but I sensed I was able to rekindle a little interest. I figure I still have a shot to salvage some squeeze play, but I recognize that the probability is low, and I'm disgusted by the exorbitant sum I've already spent on the car and the meal. We can't go back to her apartment because her roommates are hosting some women's empowerment event, and I don't want to take her back to my place because Tobaccy is missing."

"Tobaccy," I echo.

"Tobaccy the pygmy rattlesnake I was keeping. I came home from work the Wednesday before last, and it wasn't in its cage."

"The krait split the crate. I trust you weren't holding him in a maze?"

Vecsey grunts. "I'm pretty sure it's a she, which figures. I couldn't find her anywhere. I thought I heard her when I was in bed the other night, but I might have just been dreaming. Anyway, I don't want to take the chance that the snake will emerge from beneath the couch when I'm with Maitai."

"That," I concur, "would be a severe case of a reptile dysfunction."

"Peculiar way to put it," he responds.

"Like losing your snake can have devastating limplications," I persevere. "Although it would serve as additional incentive to keep her feet off the floor."

"Do I savvy?" Vecsey's periodic flashes of opacity notwithstanding, he probably deduces I'm being ribald. "Well, with the night slipping away-"

"Let me guess," I insist. "After dinner, you stopped at a box store for a carton of beer and a carton of prophylactics, and you took her to a hassle-free mattress store."

"You should be a dating coach." He hisses. "She introduces the concept of clubbing, and I feel I could really impress her with my creativity in offering endless excuses for not dancing. But it'd be even more money pissed on pie in the sky, and I've never seen one of those places worth the admittance charge."

I nod with empathy. "They could probably make more money if they charged you to leave."

"Instead, I took her to a cheap laid-back bar. She spent more time talking to another guy we met there than me, although he did buy me a drink when he bought her one. On Tuesday, I prevailed on her to have lunch with me alone in the cafeteria, and she agreed to lend me a few minutes of her precious time. So we're sitting there, with her munching flakes of hake and hunks of hemp and seaweed crackers. I try some hemp, and it tastes like a clod of dirt sprinkled with xylitol. So I decide it's time to roll out the decisive big gun and I present her with a jar of my own superfood-"

"Not the vaunted manuka honey?"

"Raw raw raw." Del emits a protracted grunt. "I recite a short litany of its virtues: 'It's great for the gums and throat, it has awesome anti-bacterial and anti-inflammatory proper-ties, and it works wonders for the digestion,' which I think should be extraordinarily useful when you're consuming dirt and seaweed. And she pitches an absolute fit that those on a genuine paleo diet do not eat honey. I should think honey would be one of their staples. I tried to shrug off her insolent ignorance, and I told her she was a 'colorful panda.' I believe one of her roommates interpreted that for her as a racial slur." He moans. "We barely acknowledged each other the last couple days; it's been very strained."

I rub my neck. "I'm sorry your Malaysian heat petered to a malaise." A pause ensues. "If you're racking your brain for a better approach, heed the evidence that oscillation breeds isolation."

"I don't want to remind you of any personal traumas, but I knew you could relate." He smacks his lips with resignation. "You got anything else?"

"Just another gentle reminder about how important it is that we keep our extraneous personal business transactions completely confidential." I sense his blank stare. "Snoops with credentials and the wherewithal to apply pressure may show up to try to pry."

"Affirmative," Vecsey ventures. "Thanks for squaring my accounts receivables with Spaatz." He either terminates the connection or is cut off. He doesn't call back, so I delete the vestiges of his communication from my phone. I exercise an app that purports to disguise my device in "spoof status," and I reflect on my own misery again.

I nap sparingly. A messy flashback of the only serious romantic relationship I had in the span of 13 years between Amie and Trish presents itself. Donna had a child and seemed to believe that she'd done me a real favor by performing the onerous task of procreation without me. "Are there any real men left?" she wondered. "I'm seeking someone strong enough to accept my son." I decided in due time that I was both. She decided shortly thereafter that she and the boy would be better off with no man. At least that's the incontrovertible message her ghost left by refusing to return my calls or answer my messages. I refuse to believe that she could've found another man who would've been more devoted to her or would've tried harder to be a fabulous father to young Derek than I would've. A few months after that relationship ended, I did myself a real favor and acquired Maynard.

I finally sleep for an extended period before I'm reawakened by the cold. I start the engine and let it run. "Electric vehicles are just a conspiracy to force those contemplating suicide to have to prove they really want it," I advise the dachshund. I open a window, doff my Avalanche hat and we listen to the snowplows clear the streets below. We start out shortly after daybreak.

As I drive north, I consider the immediate ramifications of my action. I am potentially placing the welfare of many people in jeopardy. I resolve that my deep bonds are few, and I would do virtually anything to protect a genuine love. Ultimately, the decision is not a difficult one.

It's apparent as we head west out of Oshkosh that the snow total is much lower than in southeastern Wisconsin. Highway 21 is in prime condition, and the traffic volume is particularly light. We arrive at the cabin and claim our regular parking spot in front of the utility trailer.

It's still early enough that I fear we'll wake him. After waiting an hour, I go to the door and knock softly. There is no answer, and I check for fresh footprints in the snow that would indicate he ventured down to the lake or into town. I return to the vehicle and sleep fitfully.

I'm awakened by growling and rapping. Spaatz stands at the driver's window of the Yukon waving his Welrod. "What did you forget?"

I lower the window. "The value of preventive landscaping. Morning, Holden." I step out of the vehicle with my tactical flashlight. "A couple hours after we got home last night, part of that big bur oak in my backyard crashed into my house," I lie. "Right into the kitchen."

"It was really that windy there?" He tucks his side arm beneath his belt.

"Windy enough, I guess." I sigh. "I didn't see many other branches down or hear of any power outages. I noticed a little crack in the trunk a few months ago. The tree must've just been too weak to support the weight of the snow, and we did get plenty of that. If my brain hadn't been so scrambled this morning, I would've taken some pictures. One limb didn't spare my basement window either, and I'm concerned it did some foundation damage. So I have a big favor to ask you."

"A *tree-mendous* favor?" Gayle appears amused by my trepidation. "You could probably make a good argument that I owe you a little reciprocal altruism." He gestures to the cottage. "Shall we remove ourselves from the cold, and see if I can warm up to it?"

I shiver. "I really appreciate it." I switch off my flashlight and hand it to Spaatz. "You can find a use for this up here; consider it a bribe." I take Maynard out of the SUV, and we head inside the cabin. I remove my hat and coat and sit down at the parlor table.

Spaatz serves coffee. He seats himself beside me and assesses my Henley. "Same shirt?"

"Different day, same shirt." I take a soul-deep breath. "The favor I need is close to outrageous in its magnitude, Gayle. I can hardly begin to unpack all the insurance and craft people I'm going to soon have traipsing over my property, so it would really help me out if you could keep Maynard up here with you for two or three weeks until the dust settles."

"Is that all?" He reaches out to pet Maynard, and the dachshund moves to dodge his hand but then sniffs it and allows the contact. "I'll enjoy the company."

"For real?" I rub my neck. "If you're not aware, there's a superstrain of Capnocytophaga bacteria infecting the dog population. Most kennels and a lot of veterinary clinics are closed. And even if I could find a receptive one, I'd be fearful for Maynard's safety."

"Yeah, Capno." Gayle grimaces. "I've heard some alarm bells, but I haven't paid close attention. A guy on the radio was saying it's like mad cow disease so it should be called mad dog disease. The infection lends itself to high presymptomatic transmissibility from dogs to people? I'm sure it's being overhyped."

"You're sure you're fine with this, Gayle?" I press my luck. "There are a lot of considerations for dog-sitting. He'll have to go out four, maybe five times a day, even in the bitter cold. And he has to stay on a leash, or he'll run off. And he needs two square meals a day. He's claustrophobic, so you don't want to have any real close contact with him, but most of all, you have to protect him from Johnny." I eye him intently. "Johnny wants to hurt him. He bluntly told me so. You have to make sure he doesn't get a chance. You need to employ extreme safety measures."

"I've got it, Lisle." Spaatz snickers. "The shock collar provides a fail-safe system for keeping Johnny restrained. I've seen a tutorial by a death-row guard. Consider it all under control. You're not sure for how long?"

"All I can do is estimate it'll be at least a couple of weeks." I pat him on the forearm. "Gayle, you're a lifesaver. I hardly slept last night. I don't know what I'd do if I couldn't count you as a resource."

He flashes a demure smile. "Do you have to get right back, or can you stay for some good eats?"

"I was able to bandage my wall damage with some tarps, and there's more snow cover on top of them, so the shanty shouldn't be hurting for a lack of insulation that would need immediate attention." I pet Maynard briskly. "It's going to be weird going back alone." I rub my neck. "I'd be delighted to partake in any excuse you'd offer to put it off for a while."

"You seem a little lightheaded." He rises. "Feel undernourished? I'll make us some shakshuka, the brunch of Jewish champions. It's fancy eggs with tomato sauce, which should keep your vital signs jagged." He places a bowl of apples on the table. "In the meantime, gobble one of these nice, juicy Blushing Lady pomes you bought. Maybe a little too tart for my taste, but they sure are big and crisp."

"And good keepers, aren't they?" I pet Maynard and devour a Blushing Lady as Gayle occupies himself at the counter and stove. I offer the dachshund the core. He takes it and tosses it on the floor. I return to the Yukon and fetch his supplies and accessories, including a giant bag of dogfood, hard and soft treats, bowls, sleeping pad, his stuffed skunk, the little stuffed bull we call the Blue Dozer and a can of fresh tennis balls. I arrange an all-inclusive canine corner and write memos with feeding instructions and play recommendations.

The shakshuka is a culinary triumph. We give Maynard a sample, he gobbles it up and wheedles another portion. Spaatz and I each grab a Blushing Lady to complete the meal. "I'm going to toss some trail mix into Johnny's feed bag and take it down to him." Gayle rises. "Come along?" He proceeds to the counter and pours granola into a Rex Wrex Towing tote bag. He hands the bag to me and withdraws his pair of blue suede floggers from the cabinet. Leaving the dog tethered to the table, we shuffle down the stairs carrying our respective materiel and munching our apples.

Bustelich lifts his head slightly when we enter the wine cellar. His web is parked at a 45-degree angle, and his left arm is unbound. "Super!" He hisses. "Here's the jism twins again. You going to finally do something about how cold it is in here, bitch?"

"Johnny sings the blues," Gayle responds. "Maybe if you use the proper tone of voice." He turns to me. "Would you like to help bathe Johnny, Lisle? A little soap and a big sponge. We'll make his crotch and armpits smell like pansy pistils."

"You moving in, Amonor?" Johnny wears a shabby grey dress with purple pinstripes. "You look like *you* take *meteor* showers, you scary-ass mofo. Pukefest can use your smiley crater-face as its logo."

"Bow your head, Johnny, and extend your free arm behind

the grate." Spaatz turns to me. "Loop one of the bag straps over his natural mullet, Lisle, so it catches on his dowager's hump."

The feed bag fits tightly over Bustelich's bulbous scalp, and the strap scrapes his ears. "Sod!" He reaches into the sack and hurls a fistful of rolled oats, bean pods and dried figs into my face. "Gash!" He chomps some gorp. "One of you fucktards fetch me some wine!"

Spaatz retreats to the winch crank and suspends the web perpendicular to the floor. I finish my apple and deposit the core in Johnny's feed bag. Gayle has only taken a few bites out of his apple, and he sets it on Johnny's head. "Dominant hand beneath dress and hold still," he instructs his internee. "Sing the finale of the William Tell Overture or face the consequences." Johnny shakes the apple off his head and it rolls across the floor. Gayle flips me one of the floggers, retrieves the apple and holds it in place atop Johnny's head with his forefinger. "A lash apiece, Doctor?" Johnny spews a tirade of jumbled expletives.

I shake my head. "Let's just leave him to his elevated hormone levels and find me a cheerier excuse not to go home." I head toward the door, and Spaatz knocks the apple to the floor with a crisp flogger strike. I place my flogger on the counter and wait as Gayle retrieves three bottles from the racks. He opens one, instructs Bustelich to tilt his head back and decants wine into his internee's open mouth. After a few gulps, Bustelich spits a mouthful into Spaatz's face and tries unsuccessfully to grab the bottle. Gayle brings all three bottles to the counter, extracts a towel from the drawer and wipes his face. He hands me the half-empty bottle of Ningaloo Reef Sticky, snatches his other bottles, and we march back upstairs.

We seat ourselves at the table. I untether Maynard and give him a rawhide chew. Gayle pours me a flute of tawny port and himself a flute of sherry. "L'chaim." We clink vessels and knock back opening swigs.

I smile with profound gratitude. "I recall us as teenagers standing together on a corner talking or waiting for the bus and you'd start dancing. When was the last time you did that?"

"I'd get into the groove and start waving at passing cars." He nods. "I haven't had oodles of opportunities recently." He swallows more sherry. "But a little more manzanilla could put me back on the boogie track."

I sigh. "We used to laugh our asses off when we were younger. Even while dealing with loads of devastating problems. What the hell happened?"

He takes another swig. "Social awareness? Pressure? Ego?"

"Maturity," I translate. "Responsibility. Heartbreak. Losing someone to whom you've given a piece of your soul, through death, circumstance or worst of all, plain, old rejection. It catches up to all of us, and I don't think we ever fully recover."

Spaatz rubs his face. "If you had your life to do all over again, and you made good on all the things you swore you'd do differently, the second result would probably be worse than the first." He empties his flute. "For some of us, youth must simply be recognized as a no-win proposition."

"If I strain hard enough, I can force myself to miss some of those lean times." I take a hard swig of port. "Remember we must've been fifteen. That big house in hoity-toity Tosa where they used to scrawl ultra-liberal slogans in chalk on the sidewalk? It had that sign on the front lawn: *HATE HAS NO*

HOME HERE. And you whipped up an 'N' and an 'H' of the same size and color and pasted your 'N' over the first 'H' and your 'H' over the 'N' so it read *NATE HAS HO HOME HERE.*" We both laugh boisterously. "You claimed you actually called the Wauwatosa police and complained?"

"I called from a pay phone in the park." Gayle refills our flutes. "I said, 'Excuse me, but over on Mary Ellen Court, you have an openly operating sluttery.' Dispatch said, 'A what?' I said, 'A house of ill repute. This guy Nathan is advertising his bordello.' I don't know if the cops ever investigated, but the sign got removed in short order."

We consume more of our potables. "Tell me the truth, Gayle. Did you really slip that packet of betel nut extract I gave you into Mr. Ormerud's lunch?"

Spaatz eyes me quizzically. "I recall Ormerud our chemistry teacher, but-"

"Yeah, you had him in the morning, and I had him in the afternoon." I take another swig of port. "He used lab equipment to prepare his lunch, and he'd eat while we were doing our experiments."

Gayle nods. "That's right, he wouldn't eat in the faculty lounge with the rest of the pedagogs." He takes a swig of sherry. "He must've been peer-reviewed to be peerless."

"Just too illiberal." I sip wine. "Remember he was making our lives miserable, and I bought some betel nut extract from an ad in a science magazine. The stuff was guaranteed to turn people's teeth black and make them froth at the mouth with red sputum." I snicker and gulp more wine. "I volunteered you to put it in Ormerud's lunch, and you claimed you did, but come afternoon, he didn't exhibit any of the desired effects."

"Are you sure it was me?" Spaatz refills his flute with manzanilla. "Oh, you're right, snollygoster, I'm guilty." He takes a long drink. "I snuck over near his food supply while I thought he was occupied, but he spied me and chased me out of the area. So when Keith Ramstead tried to borrow money from me, I gave him a few bucks on the condition that he plant the poison. He told me he did, so I told you *I* did."

"Keith Ramstead. He had that real heavy beard and his sister had those real big bazumas." I swallow more port. "I remember he stole crystals that Mr. Zlatko brought back from vacation in Arizona and had on display in his classroom."

"What did he do with them?" Gayle takes a large gulp.

"Nothing that I know of." I empty my flute. "He simply stole for bragging rights, for the hell of it. He probably didn't need the money he squeezed out of you."

"I liked those crystals." Spaatz knocks back more sherry. "I'll bet Ramstead was friends with Johnny. Let's go back downstairs and beat it out of him."

We continue reminiscing. Spaatz drains his bottle of manzanilla, and I empty my bottle of port. I begin feeling decidedly giddy, and we split the open bottle of Ningaloo Reef Sticky. We rise shortly thereafter. Gayle weaves his way past Maynard to the cupboard. He produces a yellow mug bearing the radiation hazard trefoil symbol. "You remember my indispensable traveling mug?" He withdraws several fishhooks and displays them. "Ryscavage must be an angler. I've found a half dozen of these in the drawers here. I found some more down by the lake." He returns the mug to the cupboard but retains the hooks in his hand. We each select a Blushing Lady from the bowl and stagger down the steps to the wine cellar. Maynard follows us. We retrieve our floggers from the counter and approach Johnny.

"And the big brains are back." Bustelich sneers. "The guys who really get it, along with their faithful mascot: the dingy footlong hair sandwich." Johnny holds his malevolent gaze on me as Maynard investigates the discarded feed bag on the floor. "That is one scraggly animal, Anomor. Are you sure it's a full-blooded wiener dog? I'm guessing you were schnookered. They unloaded a beast on you that's part schlong hound, part wharf rat."

Spaatz kicks the feed bag aside and grasps the empty handcuff. "Full lockdown mode, Johnny."

Bustelich spits. "Fuck off, fuck-wad."

"Do you really need to be persuaded?" Gayle retreats to the counter, removes the shock collar and remote from the drawer and proceeds behind Johnny's web. He fits the collar around his internee's neck and works the control buttons. "Low power." Johnny twitches and groans. "Care for more?"

Johnny growls and places his wrist in the cuff. "Does this calm your nerves, twerp?"

"Not as much as being drunk does." Gayle locks the cuff and staggers around the web.

Maynard yips. "What keeps you connected to that mutt, Lowell?" Bustelich wonders. "The same mutant genes you carry making *him* ugly?"

"Those with ugly eyes can't see where beauty lies." I balance my apple atop Johnny's head, and he sheds it with a bob.

Maynard takes possession of the fruit and scampers out of the cellar.

"You hold still, Johnny," Spaatz cackles, "so we can have our sport!" He plants fishhooks in the bottom of his Blushing Lady and anchors it on Bustelich's scalp. Johnny winces and utters homophobic obscenities. "Johnny, how tight were you with Keith Ramstead?"

Bustelich snorts. "What the fuck? Who?"

Spaatz dispatches the apple with a smart flogger lash. "Wrong answer!" He picks up his pome and replaces it on Bustelich's head. Johnny makes a weak effort to shake it off again but doesn't succeed. "Get a lick in, Lisle!"

I displace the Blushing Lady with a sprightly flogger strike which stings a section of Bustelich's brow. He squawks more obscenities, and we exchange glowers. I retrieve the apple and delicately resituate it on his head. "You want one more crack, whippoorwill?" I call over my shoulder.

"Step aside, Lisle!" Spaatz answers from a position near the door.

"You going to take a running start?" I skip back and turn toward Gayle to see him pointing the Welrod Mark IIA at Johnny. He fires and a crack with the intensity of breaking Styrofoam rings through the room.

"Gayle, no!" I wave my arms.

Spaatz shuffles sideways to gain a clear shot, ejects a shell casing and fires again. The bullet shatters glass in the racks. "*Stop!!*" I demand.

Gayle lowers the weapon. "Mnh, I wasted a bottle of wine. But I cored apple, didn't I?"

I look back to find Bustelich quaking. The apple sits on the floor in front of him. Maynard scoots back into the room, and I scoop up the fruit before he can. "Never treat that gun like a plaything!"

Spaatz grimaces. "Its future career is purely in self-defense, Doctor." He tosses the firearm in the counter drawer and joins me in front of Bustelich. "I figured he had a couple of sport pops coming." He examines the apple. "I didn't even graze it! Johnny flinched and spoiled my shot." He looks up. "That's how you get nicked, sluggo."

"You deranged little maggot," Johnny raves. "You're really going to fucking murder me!" He turns his livid sensibilities on me. "You were always a walking horror show, Anomor, and now your acts match your looks! You know you're the most hideous thing ever to hike down the pike, and your whole life will always be nothing but an unfixable mess!"

Spaatz and I return upstairs with Maynard and a bottle of Merlot. I really need another drink, and I end up staying for a light supper of franks and beans, during which we finish the bottle of wine. "If your root objective was to make Johnny fear you," I submit, "there's no doubt you succeeded. You've certainly noticed he's been heaping a preponderance of his frustrated animosity on me."

Gayle scrutinizes me. "You shouldn't take things that Johnny says to you personally, Lisle. Design students are taught that high-contrast patterns can be uncomfortable to look at because they produce a horrid visual signature." He scrunches his nose. "The high-contrast of some of your skin tones probably provoked an overactive physical disgust reaction in Johnny."

Since I've consumed a fair amount of alcohol and the following day is a paid holiday, we determine that I'll spend the night. Maynard and I share our familiar cot, and I caress him with special fondness. I sink into an uneasy sleep, from which I revive every twenty minutes in a queasy delirium. I can't pet Maynard enough, and he keeps crawling over me in search of a more comfortable position. My anguish stretches each waking moment and keeps the night from slipping away too quickly.

I RISE BEFORE dawn on Monday morning. It feels as though it'll be easier to leave while it's still dark. Spaatz is already active. He entreats me to have a hearty breakfast before I go, and he offers a bowl of cinnamon oatmeal, cinching the deal with an apple. I have a minor headache, and the conversation is sparse. Maynard senses something is inordinately askew and lies beneath the table with his head on my feet. I pet him continuously as I eat. "Relax, pappy," Gayle coos, "we'll be fine. It'll only be a couple of weeks, right?"

I finish my breakfast and kneel beside my dog. "You be good, Maynard, and I'll see you soon." I pet him a final 15 times and grab my winter garb. "You guys take good care of each other." I hand Gayle the dog's leash and $740 in cash I'd gathered from the nether vault of my house. "Keep him on a tight rein." I head to the door and look back. "I'll hurry the process as much as possible."

Spaatz smiles mischievously. "If you find you have a total shambles on your hands, you can always turn right around and come back again."

"I'm pretty confident the damage is mostly superficial and can be fixed in short order." I spy the Welrod in his belt. "Remember you swore there'll be no more target practice. No more William Tell."

He rolls his eyes. "You know I don't swear, Lisle, but I did give you my assurance, and I'm not a liar. The only William Tell we'll be doing will be composing lyrics for the *Overture*."

"They're well overdue." I open the door. "I really can't express how grateful I am."

The dachshund whimpers, and Gayle holds him by the collar. "I'll call you at work before the week is up."

I flash a toothy smile, step into the cold and close the door behind me. I start my journey home at 5:21. I remain vigilant for anyone taking an unnatural interest in my movements. If unimpeded by road conditions and with the cooperation of light-volume holiday traffic, I should reach Elm Grove just around sunrise.

By the time I start east on Highway 21, I'm consumed with self-loathing. I hate to lie. It makes me feel weak and inadequate. Lying to a friend is a betrayal so it's even more unbecoming. The fact that I'm lying to one friend to protect another is of small consolation when I'm exposing him to a potentially lethal health risk. But I've also been protecting Gayle at my own peril for nearly three months, and I've been diligently endeavoring to serve as official fixer to unmake his unspeakable morass. So I feel as though he owes me something.

Maynard is the one who's shown me unconditional love, so I owe him everything. His welfare merits my full industry, and I couldn't risk confiding that he's been declared an enemy of the state. On the chance that he really could be harboring the more virulent strain of Capno, I just have to stand by him to the end. So many things could go wrong that I recognize I'd be prudent to brace myself for his loss. I'm not sure what I'll do in two or three weeks if Maynard remains in the government's cross hairs. Threats far more serious than us are likely to begin emerging in waves.

Light flurries begin flying as I head south through Oshkosh, and I culminate my soliloquy with fundamental rationalization and regret. When Spaatz showed me his Bustelich Bound video at the Halloween party, I should've walked straight out of Pfixx's Inn and averted all future contact. But I felt I owed him something better. To ghost someone is a violation of the ancient concept of hospitality. That's even true on Halloween. I should've just gotten Gayle drunk and freed Johnny the first time I ventured up to Pleasant Lake.

I spend a good chunk of the last leg of my drive home trying to purge all such negativity. A thinking man should be able to stay a step ahead of a clumsy government bureaucracy. When I arrive home, I will establish distinct strategic points through which to filter the canine concealment project and avoid any criminal liability.

From a distance of two blocks, I spot the flashing lights in front of my house, and I take a quick left turn. I would've expected the state to conduct a slightly more discreet surrender operation. I stop one block over and observe a black SUV parked facing the wrong way in front of the property directly behind mine. I take another quick left and cruise farther away from my house. I'm tempted to simply drive off and postpone my showdown with the authorities, but I decide it's time to start exercising my confrontational verve, especially since a convenient parking spot looms in an evacuated snowbank two more blocks up the street. I shut off the engine and sit in the Yukon for a few minutes. I buckle my mouth flap, hop out and trudge back toward my house.

The black SUV behind my property begins crawling forward as I approach the cross street to my block. The vehicle turns left and I follow it. The driver turns left again onto my street. I proceed to my street corner and ascertain that the emergency lights I spotted belong to municipal snow removal equipment. I've long held a theory that one of my neighbors is a public works department honcho and my block gets special severe weather effects management. Occupants of the black vehicle converse with the person inside the compact track loader. The snow removal operation ceases, and the loader and truck migrate toward me. I turn and wander back to the next street over and stop in front of the house behind my property where the suspicious black SUV had previously been parked. The limited field of view through my neighbor's property reveals nothing unusual.

I receive a call from an unidentified source. "Mr. Lisle Amonor?"

In heightened defensive mode, I anticipate the trouble a simple affirmative could bring. "Who's asking?"

"Mr. Amonor, this is the Elm Grove police," the deep voice announces.

I try to project my response from a low place in my larynx. "I believe this is Amonor's cell, but this ain't Amonor."

"Please put Lisle Amonor on the line."

"He's not here. I'm house-monitoring."

"And your name is?"

"Dr. Neichi. I'm a friend of a friend, checking the place from time to time while Amonor is, I believe, traveling abroad."

"Where is he?"

"I'm under the impression that he's on a Pacific island, but whether that means Vancouver or Bora Bora, I haven't a clue."

"Who would know?"

"I don't know if I'm at liberty to say. If there's some legal issue with my presence here-"

"Where's the dog?"

"What dog? I have cynophobia. I wouldn't have agreed to this duty if there's a dog involved."

"Who's the source of your information?"

"Hey, not to be difficult, but revealing the identity of the person for whom I'm doing this favor could have some personal reper-"

"Sir, we're going to require immediate access to your home. Please place the dog on a short leash, open the front door and step back from it."

I perceive red flashing lights on my street. "Yeah, I'm going to need some kind of warrant or something. In fact, if I stumbled into the middle of some crime scene, I want legal counsel to be present when I answer any questions."

"Please," the spokesman wearily advises, "don't make it necessary for us to force entry."

"I'm closing the window. Let it be noted that you have not advised me of any rights."

He scoffs. "Your personal rights are superseded by the interest of the general public. This is a public health emergency situation. Wisconsin Department of Health Services agents attempted to serve a quarantine order 48 hours ago. Remain in the home. A team has been sent-"

"Well, can I, can I, at least use the bath-" I terminate the connection, re-encrypt and reset my data and turn off the Megalophone. I drop it on the walkway and stomp it into the salt. I pick it up and jam it into my back pocket. I start back toward the Yukon. I'm not sure if the authorities are aware that I'm not inside my house. The events of the weekend have left me feeling rather oppressed and defiant. If officers attempt to intercept me, I'm going to run. Let all concerned slip and slide and wind up in a snowy heap.

I reach the SUV without incident. I start the engine and drive away. I've calmed down. If the police pursue me, I will pull over and comport myself in a civil manner. I impulsively cruise two miles in the direction of the strip mall where Bruce Neichi's chiropractic office is located. I may have previously rambled past the mall a number of times to admire the Charger in the front lot. I reach a street behind the mall and approach the *DEAD END* sign behind the giant snow pile in the corner of the back lot. I park, climb over the chain-link fence and squeeze through a partial cleft in the snow pile. I stride across the parking lot with my elbow raised and my head lowered on what I estimate to be the periphery arc of the snow-laden surveillance camera attached to the corner of the building. I attempt to turn on the Megalophone. Lights signify that the device isn't dead but in a nonfunctional coma. I head to the nearest dumpster and pretend to toss the phone into the refuse heap. I return to the snow pile, clamber around and punch a deep hole. I dispose of the device and cover the hole. I disengage from the snow pile and get back into the Yukon. I turn my vehicle around and head straight to Ideal Allele.

The parking lot is nearly empty, and the offices, labs and storage areas are eerily devoid of human activity. I stuff my identifiable flap hat into an amalgamation of refuse. I have several projects in progress, not the least of which is excrement prep and analysis. I work a little, hit the vending machine and tour the cavernous confines gorging myself with tortilla chips and grapefruit juice. I'd hoped to enjoy a little downtime on the overstuffed periwinkle sofa outside Lillian's office but that pleasure is denied as I find the door to the personnel office suite upstairs locked. I learn that I don't have the building to myself. A maintenance worker walks across the hall and into the office of one of the operations managers.

I stroll among the benches cluttered with flasks, incubators and small centrifuges toward the back of the building and find myself among the Class I biosafety cabinets. I observe the maintenance man stop at the cabinet on the end of the aisle, remove a badge from beneath the counter and use it to enter the containment biosafety suite area. It's gratifying that he has access to the hot zone which is denied to me. I approach the door.

"Oh, hello, Amonor?" Van Leskosek, intrepid bacteriologist with whom I've had infrequent interaction, materializes behind me. "I didn't know you were essential enough to work holidays."

"I'm not." I feel my lips contort into a deferential grin. "I had nothing better going, so I thought I'd lighten my backlog a little, set myself up for a soft day tomorrow."

"Breakfast?" He gestures to my food. "Haven't you done enough work for me to know you add several years to your life by skipping that?"

"It's just a snack." I offer Leskosek a chip and he declines. His research with rapamycin, the bacterium-generated macrocyclic lactone responsible for regulation of the mTOR nutrient-sensing metabolic pathway, converges with studies that measure how other nutritional factors contribute to physiological aging. "I have a gluten deficiency."

"Try to reduce your fiber." He proceeds to the stainless-steel door to the containment suite. "Hey, you ever hear from Vecsey?"

"Yeah, you know he found a home on the range in Texas." I'm immoderately wary of speaking about Delmar. "Quality control at a Hormones R Us facility. He claims their recipes for sophisticated molecules are spicier than ours."

"Smart dude." Leskosek presents his badge to the security scanner. "Just lacking poise and personality." He strikes the keypad four times and opens the door.

"He doesn't know about the secret work that goes on here at odd hours," I tease. "Could it be that an approval for a hot zone upgrade has occurred?"

Leskosek grimaces. "You'll never see BSL-4 projects conducted anywhere outside a government agency or privileged university environment."

"You'll never *see* them." I gesture to the containment suite. "We're already holding some of the deadliest biological payloads known, aren't we? The toxins in the aquarium organisms, and several genera of plants with 'suicide' in the nickname?"

He lets the door close. "Last word I heard, Aaron was bolstering our case with NIAID for funding to expand and upgrade our BSL-3 suite facilities for work with bacteria as well as prions."

I nod vigorously. "Aaron can be pretty irresistible in a positive pressure suit. Ask Nancy. I imagine him offering agency bureaucrats flattery galore and honorariums they can't refuse."

"Don't be so cynical, Amonor." Leskosek exposes his badge to the security scanner again. "We want to build a robust antibiotics research team precisely because of the dearth of research into antibacterials throughout the country, the folly of which is underscored by the current Capno crisis."

"Super-Capno," I submit. "Hopefully, federal regulators will at least issue Aaron a liquor license for his trouble."

He snickers sardonically. "Keep up the heroic grind, Amonor." He enters the same digit into the keypad four times and opens the door. "If you'll excuse me, it's time to milk the box jellyfish."

"Skip breakfast," I repeat his mantra once the door closes. "Start your day light on your feet and more aware of your surroundings."

I retrieve my laptop and head to the staging area to prepare samples for Sandee's abstruse proteomics project. I optimize microbial protein specimens with chromatography, prepare particles with negative stain and apply them to grids and vitrify them. Mentally exhausted by midafternoon, I settle into the velvet recliner of the front reception area and catch several hours of sleep. Returning to the proteomics project, I convey the cryostat holding my grids to the imaging room and start loading them in the electron microscope. I position them and read them. I finish EM a little after eleven and return to the vending machine.

I carry a turkey sandwich, almonds and hot chocolate out to the Yukon. As I sit in the warm, dark, music-filled cocoon of my SUV, I watch the Chantilly Food Service truck pull into the loading bay. The door is raised, and the driver disappears inside the building to feed the vending machines. I consider how easy it would be for an unauthorized person to gain entry to the facility. When I've logged about three hours in my vehicle, I grab the auxiliary purple T-shirt I keep stuffed under the front passenger's seat and return inside the building.

I perform more excrement prep and analysis. Shortly before dawn, I return to the biosafety containment suite. It takes three attempts, but I gain access to the vestibule. I peer through the window of the first interior door to the right and observe a decontamination hallway with change rooms. To the left is a gallery with a plate glass window which holds the aquarium and several terrariums containing exotic plants beneath grow lights. The corals and sea sponges in the aquarium are thought to produce antibacterial compounds, and I'm fairly certain that some of the corals produce palytoxin, the most potent naturally occurring poison known. I believe that the shrubs in the Plexiglas cell on the far end are the "suicide plant" specimens that Napolitano has mentioned. I enter the same 8-8-8-8 combination into the gallery door keypad that opened the outside door, and I hear the lock release. I'm tempted to venture onward, but I turn and leave the biocontainment suite.

On the way back to my desk, I consider how problematic it could be that management has a record of my unauthorized entry into the anteroom of their secure area. As I did no harm, nobody in a position to care probably does. The company obviously saves money on security.

I review my EM images. Here low contrast is my undoing. At points, the ice is too thin, I've excluded target particles and the production is altogether too noisy. There may also be some radiation damage. Sandee will chide me for B-Factor faults. I resolve to redo some of the fungi in this series with the algae specimens I'll be running next.

I slip into my fresh purple T-shirt, and the rest of the workforce files in to find me busily engaged with processing algae for heterotrophic fermentation. I struggle valiantly with distraction and fatigue, but I hit the workday wall in the early afternoon, and I mark my 30th straight hour at Allele by falling asleep at my desk. Kelly pokes me awake before I incur the wrath of anyone in management. Sandee begins her message reviewing my EM image submissions with the statement, "Nutraceutical research is messy." And she pans my pictures for B-Factor faults. But somehow I hang on, and I'm able to make it to the end of the day.

I return home to find a red tape wrapped around my property and a yellow semitrailer parked out front blocking my driveway. It appears to be a reefer. A searchlight mounted on a stanchion points directly at my house. A jumble of my possessions is gathered on the front porch. A pile of Maynard's toys, spare leads, old collars, dogfood bags and treat packs lie beside it. A hyperactive team of space cowboys in orange Tyvek biohazard suits enter and exit through my front door and appear to be rummaging through the house. One of the commandos periodically stoops to take samples with a swab kit. The Lancasters stand shin-deep in snow in their front yard shivering and observing. I wave to them. Mr. Lancaster sheepishly returns my gesture.

A man with a shock of dark hair falling over his forehead wearing an N100 mask, earmuffs and a chartreuse jumpsuit approaches and waves a document. "Lisle Amonor?" He shows me a search warrant, opens a plastic bag and demands my identification and cell phone. I deposit my driver's license in the bag and insist that I lost my MP. "Remain outside the perimeter until the investigation is complete." He walks back toward my house.

"So hey," I shout to no one in particular, "do we know each other from Kepler-452b?" The man who showed me the search warrant captures the attention of a space cowboy on my front porch and points to me. The two of them escort me to the trailer. The man with the thick hair ushers me up the steps, through a side door and closes it behind me. A transparent partition inside divides the front section of the reefer in which I find myself from the larger rear. The intensely lighted front section contains a stool, a plastic bottle of water and a speaker through which I can clearly hear the bustle on the other side. The more softly lit rear section contains desks, stools, electronic equipment, lab equipment, a sink and cabinets along with a man in a sweater vest and a woman in a lab coat. My escorts enter through a door at the rear of the trailer.

I rap on the partition. "Is this Lexan?" I presume they can hear me. "Harder than Plexiglas?"

The woman in the white coat approaches the partition and identifies herself as a nurse. "Are you ill at present?" She runs through a list of symptoms that would be consistent with septicemia. "How's your mental health?"

"Defective," I snarl. "I feel extraordinarily violated. Does that count as a personality disorder?"

My space cowboy escort putters forward. He removes his bubble and flashes a radiant grin. He has receding grey hair. "Mr. Amonor, I'm glad we can finally meet. I'm Jarboe Hullickson, envoy to the operations director of the state D.H.S. Division of Public Health." He points over his shoulder to the man with hair to envy. "You've already connected with Officer Shirley of the Elm Grove P.D."

"Sergeant Bob Shirley," the cop elucidates.

"You know why we're here," Hullickson advises me. "Where's your dog?"

I grimace. "I don't have a dog."

"Mr. Amonor, pull up a stool and sit down." He doffs his biohazard suit with the help of the nurse and discards it along with his bubble in a plastic bag. "Are you really going to make my wife keep my supper warm tonight?" He is exceptionally scrawny. "You're putting a coalition of local, state and federal government agencies to an awful lot of unnecessary trouble."

I shrug. "It's my tax money."

Hullickson is provided with a laptop and a stool by the man in the sweater vest, and he grunts as he seats himself and puts on his glasses. "It's at least part dachshund," the envoy rehashes what he reads. "He was rescued by the Waukesha County Animal Control Center last November, and you purchased an overdue dog license to have him released. You've paid the fee for a current dog license already this year." His features exhibit a wry weariness. "Maybe you'd like to revise your answer, so we'll ask you once more. Where's the dog?"

"Promise?" I move the stool close to the partition and seat myself. "Just once more?"

Shirley sashays forward. "Are you trying to be a smart-ass, Amonor, because that's really not smart at all." He's divested himself of his jumpsuit, and he's wearing a shoulder holster and handgun.

"I'm not smart, Shirley. I can't even decipher which of you is supposed to be the nice one."

Hullickson emits a weary chuckle. "Mr. Amonor, we're here in the interest of the public, including you, to protect you from a grave health threat. The dog you had at the Waukesha County Animal Control Center last November was exposed to another animal that has since tested positive for the virulent SC01 form of *Capnocytophaga canimorsus*. Your dog needs to be evaluated before he infects you and anyone else he comes into contact with and maybe your whole bloody neighborhood. Where is he?"

I hang my head and fixate on how spindly Hullickson's legs look. "Maynard," I utter. "He's no longer around." I look up. "He's dead."

"Oh, for God's sake!" Shirley snaps. "Do you think you're protecting him? You're just putting everyone in your circle of acquaintances in jeopardy and quite possibly extending the dog's death sentence."

"If that's the best you can do, Mr. Amonor, let's just complete this transaction." Hullickson nods through a thin-lipped smile. "Your objection to surrendering him is noted. If we don't take custody of him, any subsequent outbreak could not only result in untold human misery, but you would be held criminally and financially liable. The CDC has not yet conclusively ruled out the possibility that this pathogen transmits human-to-human. Does it really serve you to risk your health and your freedom?"

"*He was killed!!*" I lunge and slam both fists against the Lexan plate like a great ape in a zoo cage. "Hit by the fucking train!" The entire reefer seems to vibrate, and even Shirley is visibly startled by my outburst. "Sunday afternoon." I reseat myself and hold my head in my hands.

A pause ensues. "Why didn't you notify the health department?" Hullickson can't quite conceal his condescension. "Did you suspect you wouldn't be believed?" I lift my head but remain silent.

"Then where's the body?" Shirley demands.

"I led him right into it." An incident occurred a little over two years ago in which Maynard and I were walking beside the railroad tracks that border the park. I decided to cross to the other side of the tracks, so I tugged the leash, took a step onto the ballast incline as I turned my head to survey the tracks behind us, and a freight train loomed right beside us. I still can't imagine how I didn't hear it coming. I just remember the illegible bubble letters and hippie sun face graffiti on the side of a silver car that must've been second or third in line behind the engine. One step more and Maynard and I would've wound up rail kill. "I just didn't hear the freight train closing in on us. Maybe street noise from North Avenue or I was engrossed in thought. I decided we should cross, and as I looked back to check the tracks, it was right there. It snatched the leash right out of my hand, took him and dragged him. He gave a short yelp and was gone." I emit a barely audible groan. "I recall a hippie sun face tagged on a silver car as I tumbled backward." Shirley snickers and covers his mouth. "I walked up the tracks calling his name. I found his hindquarters against the rail. I knelt by them and moved them off to the side of the tracks. I walked up the tracks further, repeating his name softly, but I didn't find any of the rest. Maybe mercifully. It was dark, and I turned back. I walked the center of the tracks back, reached my vehicle."

Hullickson sighs. "So you could point out to us a particular spot along the tracks where we'd find his body parts?" I don't answer. "Blood? Mr. Amonor?" I still don't respond. "Mr. Amonor, please?"

Shirley paces with an astringent impatience. "The most common mistake people tend to make when crafting an alibi is making it too elaborate and bizarre. There's no shortage out in lake country of half-frozen bodies of water. If you'd simply claimed you were walking the dog on Okauchee or Nagawicka and he broke through the ice and drowned, or you just left your gate open and he ran off again, there'd be really no way for us to tear apart your story."

"Like to amend a detail or two in your account?" Hullickson challenges.

"Why don't you just offer me a polygraph?" I counter. "Even though they're too unreliable to be admissible in court, you could come back no matter what the result is and swear that it demonstrates I'm lying." The police sergeant's sneer is more pronounced than the public health officer's. "Or have the nurse give me a brain scan, and you can claim the area of my cortex that's lighting up is precisely the part of the brain people use when they lie. Or just assert that your vast experience in these matters affords you the expertise to tell by observing my mannerisms that I'm incontrovertibly lying."

Shirley hisses. "Since you mention it, you're rubbing your hands together, you've lowered your chin in a protective gesture as if to cover up, and you keep touching your face, all behaviors displaying mental discomfort. Your blink rate has increased since you've perched on your stool, you compress your glabella every several seconds and your feet are crossed, all defensive stress managers. You frequently swallow hard, your respiration rate has increased markedly, and you're sticking the tip of your tongue out at the end of each sentence, all indicators of a flustered, fearful state of mind."

I expel an irritated breath. "Sorry you didn't get the baseline program, because then you'd be aware that I'm uneasy like this pretty much all the time."

Hullickson interlocks his fingers behind his head. "Mr. Amonor, my expertise is in infectious diseases, as certified by my master's degree in vaccinology from Oxford, so I appreciate how dangerous the issue we're dealing with is. What we will offer you is a cigarette, chocolate bar and cup of coffee, because it looks like we're all in for a long night. Let's digest these details." He refers to his laptop. "You had your dog suddenly ripped out of your grasp by his leash to be dragged and pulverized beneath the wheels of a moving locomotive – two days ago? I'd expect to find you distraught rather than defiant. We're not the enemy. We're trying to avert a health crisis here."

"I have complex bereavement disorder," I submit. "Ask my ex-shrink. My shock and despair may be expressed in a seemingly inappropriate way or not at all."

"That's psychobabble!" Shirley folds his arms authoritatively. "What did you do right after this incident occurred? Where did you go?"

"I drove aimlessly, a coping mechanism I've relied on often since starting cognitive therapy last summer to take my mind off my troubles." I trust that any official interview of Rohr-Kisslinger will only torture my profile more radically. "I guess I wound up around Fond du Lac. I couldn't face coming back to an empty house, so I went to my workplace instead."

"What part of the train did the dog's leash catch on?" Hullickson presses. "It must've struck your hand or wrist as well. What sort of injury did you sustain?"

"None that I'm aware of." I examine both of my hands. "Not a mark. I continually switch hands and grips."

Shirley props a stiff-arm against the partition. "Where do you work?"

"Ideal Allele," I confess. "It's a molecular biology research laboratory."

"Sounds impressive," the public health officer gibes. "Does the research you do have medical applications? Some gain of *flunction*?"

"We do work with leeches, and we've applied for government grants to study other parasites."

"You wouldn't have your dog stashed there?" Shirley disregards my head shake. "Do we need to rip apart your business premises? They'll appreciate that, hmm?"

"What we can do to your neighborhood is even sweeter." Hullickson rubs his face. "I have the authority to declare a public health emergency and order a full lockdown. Think of this: A word from me and your county public health officer can cordon off a two-block radius and order an evacuation of everyone within that area." He leans forward. "I assure you, Mr. Amonor, your identity as the source will not be protected. You thought you were popular around here before? Your neighbors will go from shunning you and ridiculing you behind your back to screaming in your face, throwing rocks through your windows and other acts of progressive vandalism in order to show their profound gratitude for the tremendous health risk you've exposed them to, the rigorous inconvenience you've subjected them to and the financial hardship wrought by the depressed property values of their contaminated homes."

"The neighbors will be out for you with lanterns and pitchforks," Shirley concurs.

"And I haven't even mentioned the measure that will thrill the yokels the most," Hullickson huffs. "If your dog does not provide a negative SC01 test, Mr. Amonor, the state can declare this neighborhood a hot zone and order the surrender for quarantine of every pet dog and cat within the two-block radius."

"That'll be nice, won't it?" Shirley asserts. "Little Timmy down the street loses his pup because a wacko like you was too selfish and stubborn to face a disagreeable inevitability. Are you willing to carry that guilt for the rest of your life? Or are you actually some heartless sociopath?"

I nod. "Let's study how much more atrocious P.R. you can stand. Images of you guys grabbing people's dogs isn't playing too well in some areas around here. I see some public opinion is already manifesting itself with extreme prejudice."

Hullickson and Shirley withdraw to the rear of the trailer and confer behind some cabinets. The public health officer returns to his stool while the police sergeant remains in the background. "I'm aware that a police presence can be intimidating for some people." Hullickson smiles cordially. "See, Lisle, you seem like a decent enough guy. You like animals. You just want to lead a simple, quiet life, to do your job and be a good citizen. You vote regularly, go to church on Sunday, participate in a recreational bowling league. You appreciate and honor the social contract you have with your fellow citizens, and you strive to do the responsible thing."

"I haven't bowled in several years, but I do what I can."

"Good, then you want to do what you can now. Let's go pick up the dog." Hullickson waits over a minute for a response beyond my frozen glare. He forces a disarming smile. "When you were bowling, what was your handicap?"

I purse my lips. "It's so sweet that you'd take a personal interest in me that I'm going to open up. But I'll also expect you to give me a massage while you interrogate me, you elite mealy-mouthed bureaucratic prick-ass."

Hullickson scoffs. "Okay, we're through accommodating you, Lisle. You've been selling us a story, not telling us one. You're going to reveal the whereabouts of your dog so we can prevent a potential health crisis. And until you do, you're going to sit here."

"So I'm under arrest?" I recite the magic words: "I want to lawyer up."

Hullickson hisses. "Did I indicate that you're under arrest?"

"If not, then what we have here is a false imprisonment situation."

"You're being detained as a potential health menace," he explains. "Attempting to shield your sick dog, Lisle, will only result in your own personal destruction."

"You already have the facts of the matter," I maintain. "If this show must go on, Jarboe, bring back your tufty himbo, because you're just the straight man."

I'm subjected to two more interview cycles, one less coercive and one more confrontational than the initial probe. Shirley intermittently rejoins the parley, but I reject their bids to rebuild rapport and I stick to my specifics. The only additional detail that I let them siphon is the exact location of the train impact.

Hullickson confers with the man in the sweater vest for

several minutes as Shirley hovers over them with arms akimbo. The public health officer makes a brief phone call, and the nurse joins the scrum. The police sergeant approaches the partition. "We're impounding your Yukon for further inspection. We already recovered a spare key fob in your house."

"If you'll submit to the standard test for Capno SC01," Hullickson directs me, "we'll take no more time with you tonight. If the test proves negative, you'll be required to remain in isolation in your home for a period of up to one week. We're going to investigate further, and we reserve the right to interview you again at any time. Are these terms acceptable to you?"

I'm so eager to escape from the chilly trailer that I consent without inquiring about the return of my vehicle. "Expect to be called as soon as early tomorrow morning," Shirley adds, "and prepare for a field trip up the railroad tracks."

The nurse dons a full biohazard suit with hip respirator and grabs a black bag. She follows Shirley and Hullickson out the rear door of the trailer and re-enters alone through the door on my side of the partition. She threatens to take cerebrospinal fluid but settles for three protracted blood draws and pledges to contact me with test results within 48 hours.

It's a few minutes after midnight when I return inside my domicile. A property receipt in the form of a green card sits on my coffee table. It concludes: "Investigation conducted under the auspices of the Wisconsin Department of Health Services. Any claim of property damage is to be submitted to D.H.S. for adjudication."

The commandos found the secret compartment behind

my kitchen cupboard and the pillbox behind my covert bathroom wall panel. If I still had my illicit drugs, they might've gained a little leverage for their trouble. They moved both my refrigerator and range in the kitchen and my washer and dryer downstairs. It would take quite the miniature dachshund to be able to hide among the dust bunnies in those confines. The investigative team ripped up every one of the interlocking rubber floor tiles defining excruciation station. Drawers throughout the house were upended, the contents obviously dumped and scooped haphazardly back into place. One jar of tacks burst open when it hit the kitchen floor and sharp micro-spears remain strewn about. I flip on the track lights in the hallway. My large framed photo of Maynard has been knocked off the wall, the glazing shattered with about a third of it spread on the floor in shards and bits. Some gouges now mar the picture, and the paint is cracked in a spot on the wall. Did the cowboys suspect that Maynard might be hiding behind his picture? Did they feel his eyes following them around? The act was apparently intended as a message. I stand in the hallway holding the damaged picture of Maynard removing the larger fragments of the remaining cracked glazing. The only thing worse than lying is lying poorly.

NINE DAYS AFTER the D.H.S. joint task force raided my home, I ride the familiar three-mile route to Research Drive off Innovation Drive and return to work. My Thursday morning commute is punctuated by four spills, but the all-terrain wheels on my DDbeLL XX7 electric longboard and the padding of my quilted puffer parka with faux fur hood prove that the forbidding world of bitter cold and slippery streets can't prevent me from reaching Ideal Allele in a relatively robust condition. A Health Department worker wearing an N100 particulate respirator mask and a fanny pack appeared at my house on Saturday, informed me I'd tested negative for Capno but tested me again. A woman from the CDC showed up yesterday to confirm that I'm Capno-clean but warn me to watch carefully for any basic symptoms of illness. She likewise cleared me to rejoin active society should it accept me. I called work from a public phone shortly thereafter and alerted Sandee of my situation. She disclosed that Nancy had been in contact with concerned authorities at all levels, and the company was poised to welcome me back.

I arrive at Allele an hour early as Sandee requested, and I find her waiting to receive me at the front door in a black biohazard suit. She provides me with an N100 mask and escorts me to the biosafety containment suite at the rear of the building. Sandee conducts me into the vestibule, directs me to view a biohazard suit protocol video and places me in the care of a Healthpath team member named Pushmeet. I follow Pushmeet through the external and internal change rooms and into my own surgical scrubs, flexible pressurized breathing helmet with hip respirator, black Tyvek spacesuit, rubber boots, double surgical gloves and transparent plastic head-bubble. With my ensemble complete, I wave to Sandee through the vestibule window and speak to her on the intercom. I joke that for the first time, a spacesuit will be protecting the environment from the wearer rather than vice versa. Pushmeet puts me to work at the prep table purifying and arranging intrinsically disordered protein samples.

A little before noon, Sandee calls the hot zone and orders me to decontaminate and take my N100 mask to lunch. I find Gene Napolitano holding court at the Healthspan table in the cafeteria. "In ten years," Sleepy Gene submits, "your jobs will all have been rendered obsolete by microfluidics. Sandee will enter a process key at her desk, and robotic chips will conduct every step of the operation from material preparation to final analysis." I respectfully take a seat with my gooey mango protein bar at the next table, but the entire crew jumps up to greet me. I announce that I've been officially declared sound of body by government health experts and mock my mask as a prop concession to the Allele legal team. Kelly and Leah join me at my table. "Lisle, without consulting your Megalophone," Kelly banters, "is the orientation of an organism toward or away from a light source 'phototaxis' or 'photoaxis'?"

"'Taxis,'" I confidently conjecture.

Kelly giggles as Leah shakes her head. "I thought 'axis' made more perfect sense," Leah utters. "Gene thought it was 'axis too." She turns and impugns him with her big, hazel eyes.

"That's why your MP is the critical anchor of your universal utility belt," Napolitano observes.

Kelly inquires about my dog. I reply that I no longer have the dog and indicate that I'm too upset about the situation to provide details. Gene wonders if I've viewed the governor's latest viral video.

"It's very sad," Leah warns. She sends me a link to a feature in which two little girls stoically pet their dog outside their house. A man in a brown uniform and a black mask takes the leash and walks the dog to his camper-shell-equipped pickup truck. He boosts the dog into the shell. The girls wave as the truck pulls away, and close-ups catch them shedding tears. The woman narrating the piece cites diligent contact tracing as the means by which health authorities pinpointed the dog's Capno exposure to another infected dog in a veterinarian's surgery center. The girls' mother ushers them into the house, where an elderly gentleman who happens to be their doting grandfather as well as the governor presents them with the gift of two ferrets. A short interview with the governor reiterates that the health crisis is unprecedented and demands that average citizens make difficult decisions. At the end of the video, the governor's granddaughters are seen happily playing with their new pets. Kelly and Leah watching the video in parallel with me both subtly wipe tears from the corners of their eyes.

"That takes courage," Leah contends. "At least he doesn't expect his citizenry to make sacrifices he won't make in his own personal life."

"Not when it allows him to score cheap political points." Since Vecsey's departure, I ensure that my group has sufficient exposure to political cynicism. "Opportunism runs thick in pol blood. They love to take scientific ideas to extremes in order to milk the political capital out of them."

"The ferret has been conventionally considered the ideal reservoir model for human influenza infection," Skinny Jean volunteers. "It may be something less than brilliant on a scientific level to choose it as your replacement pet."

"Ferrets would presumably make a great Capno amplifier," Kelly agrees. "A little interaction between dogs and ferrets, and the pathogen will probably come back a lot more virulent."

"It would've been more prudent to give those kids pet bats," Sleepy Gene concludes.

I return to the biosafety containment suite for the rest of the afternoon and make another contribution to the protein-folding program. I suit up under the auspices of Tyler of the Healthpath group, add a splash apron and assist him in preparing isolated protein strains with a prion-forming propensity for exposure to environmental stressors.

At the end of the workday, I decon myself and my DDbeLL

XX7 and exit the hot zone. The unplumbable biome outside the building is enduring a heavy snowfall, and Skinny Jean offers me a ride home. So I pack the motor skateboard in my locker and follow her out to the parking lot. I help her clear a few inches of wet fluff off her Toyota hybrid vehicle and give her an initial push to free the car from its snow dune. We both don N100 masks, and she safely conveys me through sloppy driving conditions to Elm Grove with windows wide open. She turns onto my street, and I spot a black SUV parked in front of my property. It's been exactly one week since the authorities removed their reefer, so if the SUV is government issue, the oppression is at least getting streamlined. Zagieboylo dutifully offers to pick me up tomorrow morning, but I respond that I'm contemplating taking some personal time and coming in late. I don't want to take advantage of her gutsy generosity, so I'll procure a commercial ride.

I step out of Skinny Jean's car and wave appreciatively as she drives away. I proceed up my driveway, but a large man in a grey suit and knit cap steps out of the black SUV before I can scramble through my front door. "Mr. Amonor!" He strolls up the driveway after me. "You'll recall I'm Detective Barry Cybyske of the Waukesha Sheriff's Department." I take a couple of steps toward him and extend my hand. He stops at a distance slightly beyond my reach.

I withdraw all of the fingers of my outstretched hand except the forefinger. "You were leading the hunt for Bust-elich." I smile politely. "So I surmise you found Johnny, hair and clothing slightly disheveled, sheepish little grin on his face, in some closet with a floozy?"

Cybyske's features harden. "To my knowledge, he has not been found. Haven't you been cooperating with the Milwaukee Police Department? Lieutenant Cripesdale, wasn't it?"

"We never connected," I report. "I wasn't getting paid to coordinate the dragnet, so when I never heard back from any of you guys, I assumed Johnny had come marching home again, hurrah hurrah, or everyone involved had basically lost interest."

"Assume the search for Mr. Bustelich remains ongoing. But I'm here on an unrelated matter." He takes a bold step forward. "You're apparently not cooperating with Health Department officers either, as they've had to request assistance from local law enforcement agencies."

I smile affably. "If there's a silver lining to these pandemics, they've apparently taught various turf-stingy government agencies to share information and coordinate their efforts." I raise a triumphant fist. "Troopers are coming together, crossing jurisdictions, and society should be the better for it."

He eyes me menacingly. "Why did you feel it was necessary to impersonate Dr. Bruce Neichi?"

"The good doctor." The more courtesy I extend at this point, the guiltier I suspect I'll appear. "I believe you have that ass-backwards. Neichi is the crack-packer who broke up my live-in relationship with my beloved Trish. I'd like to impersonate him now, since she seems to think he's the hottest thing since dripped wax." Cybyske bares his teeth, and I bare mine. "Do you know how to keep a woman from straying?"

"Like to travel?" the detective demands.

"Is that a tip, er, ha, am I to infer from your tone that you wish to ask all the questions?" I sigh. "As a solid civil libertarian,

Officer Cybyske, I'm a little more irked than flattered by the extraordinary interest you seem to have taken in me."

"It's only going to get better." He gazes at me until it's uncomfortable. "Have you recently been out of town? Out of the state?"

"Only out of my mind."

He smiles authoritatively. "Where's the dog, Lisle?"

I expel a harsh breath. "Unless you just bumped mugs with Officer Shirley at Hari-Kari Coffee, I believe you're detective enough to already have the answer to that question." I hold my head. "The dog is dead, and I'm not disposed to having that wound ripped open again!"

"I'm here at the behest of the County Health Department." Cybyske grimaces. "There isn't anyone privy to your explanation for the dog's 'disappearance' that doesn't consider it a silly evasion, and it's only a short matter of time before investigators expose it as such."

"Is it your general purpose that reps of every feathery arm of the government starfish take their turn trying to squeeze blood out of me?"

"I wouldn't waste the effort to come over here if I believed your alibi had any credibility." He chews on his lip. "Our introduction left me feeling a little sorry for you, Lisle, so when your name came up on this, I'd hoped I could give you a last recourse to resolve it the smart, easy way. The U.S. Marshals Service will get involved next. They will have zero patience with a pissant who's enabling a public health emergency." He steps to the side and surveys my home. "This is a nice house, but the fines will be substantial enough that you could lose it.

Of course, you won't need a house if you go to prison. And yes, prison time is a real possibility for refusing to surrender a biological health hazard."

I focus on the large snowflakes which have clustered on his brow. "It'll play out in the vein of an eminent domain for pathogen carrier eradication."

"The Marshals are used to dealing with the very worst thugs that society has to offer, Lisle, so you'll be a simple pushover." The detective's mien remains solemn. "And they won't stop with your process crime. Word of the threat you're fostering will get out where you work, and people will panic. The idea may leak out that the pathogen was created in your lab and released by you. Locals may protest, even burn down your lab. Your coworkers will thank you."

"If you haven't noticed, constable, there's a swelling public backlash against government crackdowns."

My Yukon pulls up behind Cybyske's SUV. The driver gets out and stands at attention between the vehicles. "The cover-up only magnifies the crime, Mr. Amonor. Society will be better for your cooperation." The detective heads down my driveway to his SUV.

"Should I consider myself under constant surveillance?" I look skyward at a figurative drone.

Cybyske opens his driver's door. "Someone knows something, has seen something, will sell you out. It's never in your interest to withhold information from the government." He and the other officer climb into his vehicle and drive away. I retrieve my driver's license and key fob from the Yukon and attain temporary refuge inside my home.

As I consume my lonely frozen chicken dinner, I peruse an online catalog searching for such exotic fare as interceptor drones, perhaps the sort that carry a rocket able to demolish any surveillance drone encountered. I don't come across anything close, but I do find a Companion Piece Nile crocodile, a life-size automaton that emits a "chillingly realistic roar" and lunges forward to expose a "mouthful of bloodthirsty teeth." It costs a few thousand dollars more than I'd ordinarily pay for a novelty item, but I can't resist a quirky monster with a security benefit. The manufacturer claims that there are only three left ready to ship, so I order one. I can't wait to see how Maynard reacts to it when he gets back home.

What's one more grandiose expenditure anyway? I didn't waste my time in quarantine last weekend. I ordered a custom-cut home infrared sauna kit, which was delivered yesterday. I also arranged with an exterior remodeler to replace all of my basement windows with frosted glass block. The job is scheduled to be undertaken on Saturday.

Work starts feeling normal again around midmorning on Friday. Sandee releases me from my prion prison in the BSL-3 suite and assigns me to sit at my desk and evaluate nucleotide sequences for an abstruse senolytic proof-of-principle study. She directs me to use personal protective equipment for infection control at my discretion.

At the lunch table in the cafeteria, I make an announcement about my missing mask. "Sandee conducted an experiment yesterday. Since none of you keeled over from exposure to me, she theorizes I'm not contagious, and she's invited me to rejoin the general population with no restrictions."

"Defective immediately?" Sleepy Gene verifies.

On the TV screen, dog zoonosis point man Serge Kenower calls for calm. "There's no reason to be discouraged," he insists. "We must simply continue to focus on getting ahead of community spread of the novel *Capnocytophaga canimorsus* pathogen. The CDC has categorized Capno as a notifiable disease, and the WHO has issued an infectious disease alert."

"You're saying there's no connection between the Minnesota and Georgia strains?" a reporter interrupts.

"Genome sequencing of the Georgia outbreak has established that the cases are closely related to those in the Midwest," Kenower concedes, "but we have no reason to suspect that we're dealing with a genetically manipulated microbe."

"You've determined that CCSC-01 isn't an artificially constructed pathogen," a reporter presses, "no lab leak, no bioterrorism bug."

"What we're seeing here," Kenower explains, "is a horizontal gene swap negotiated through the natural process of bacterial conjugation, the most common mode of prokaryote DNA transfer. In this instance, a cyanobacteria plasmid exported to the Capno recipient has expressed genes that provide the organism with a greater ability to evade white blood cells in the human body and render it extremely resistant to antibacterial drugs such as amoxicillin, extended-spectrum cephalosporin and even the carbapenems, with which we'd expect to be able to resolve this infection."

"Is that definitive," the same reporter challenges, "or science-based speculation?"

"Medical facilities are reporting case fatality rates in the range of 30 percent," another reporter asserts. "Will you confirm that?"

"It may climb that high only in the worst-case scenarios," Kenower contends. "It's so important to seek immediate medical attention at any sign of illness, especially for someone with heightened risk factors, such as a weakened immune system, and obtain a rapid diagnosis before the infection progresses to septic shock, which can lead to serious consequences like limb amputation and even claim lives. The DNA integration has also rendered the pathogen neuroinvasive, and it can amplify explosively in the human brain. It's imperative to prevent entry of the pathogen into the lungs."

"Have we now established there is human-to-human transmission?" a reporter infers.

"That's a great question, and I wish I had a great answer." The point man scratches his head. "I have no reliable data on that at this point. Some household outbreaks might suggest it, but such transmission seems to be difficult and rare. It's proven hard to determine because symptoms of infection appear so gradually, or even not at all, in the animal reservoir of the pathogen."

"What is the likelihood that the infection can be transmitted through fomites?" a reporter wonders.

"There's no evidence I'm aware of to support that," Kenower offers, "but it's best to play it safe, use disinfectant where appropriate whenever possible and always, always wash your hands after handling a dog."

"Can we detect a little change in spin?" Spencer ventures. "Last week he emphasized that the definition of a bioterrorist is rapidly broadening, but now he's trying rather hard to make the case that no microbial engineering could be involved."

"If they ever feel justified to do gain-of-function research," Kelly submits, "it should be limited by international treaty to some place a fair distance from any population center."

"How about some small corner of Antarctica," Skinny Jean recommends, "with a mandatory quarantine period before lab workers are allowed to leave the continent."

The discourse ultimately turns to attending an upcoming crafts fair with spouses, and I return to my desk a few minutes early. Delmar's vacated telephone rings. I rush to answer it. "Lisle?" Gayle rasps. "I tried calling you three times within the last week. Two different days. Those are cold hikes into town in January. They said you weren't around. Where have you been?"

"I was forced to take some vacation days." I verify that no one is within earshot. "Is everything okay?"

"I'm coping-" Spaatz sounds depressed. "Everything's fine. Maynard is doing good. I think he likes the country. I have to hold tight when we're outside because of all the wildlife he spots: foxes, coyotes, deer, wild turkey, blue heron, maybe a bobcat, and that was just this morning. Anyway, it's more diversity than he gets in Waukesha." He sighs. "Why the hell haven't you come back up here?"

"I'm busting to come up," I assert. "I had to be home for some masonry work and it's hard to get more time off." I lower my voice. "Moreover, our old friend the cop who was asking about you in November came around again. I'm pretty sure his trail has gone as cold as my average Valentine's Day, but I'm concerned they've put a tracking device on my vehicle. I'm sort of boxed in here."

"Rudy the slut has a friend Andy who's a counter-surveillance pro and specializes in finding listening and tracking devices. I'm going to talk to Vito again right after I finish with you. I'll have him have Rudy have Andy pay you a visit. Does anytime over the weekend work?"

"I'd probably sleep better." I regret the words as soon as I've uttered them. "On second thought, don't bother." The more people involved, the trickier operations become.

"No, really," Gayle insists, "Andy has spent time in jail for refusing to cooperate with the cops and is completely trustworthy, the exact opposite of Rudy. You could make your life a little more secure, and I think we'd both sleep easier."

Sleepy Gene and Skinny Jean stroll past me together and proceed to their respective desks. "Very well, if you think that's the best method," I instruct Spaatz. "Keep it all sailing smoothly, and let's talk again soon." I terminate the connection and look beyond Zagieboylo so she doesn't get inquisitive.

"That wasn't Delmar?" she agitates.

"It usually feels like his call is inadvertent," I maunder. "He's got a teal-haired Malaysian girl in his lab he's pantouming over. She revealed that she's a pescatarian, and it has him doubting his agnosticism." I'm satisfied that I've left all interloping parties stupefied enough to be unmotivated to pry further.

I cook a can of beef stew for supper, and I review my sauna construction guidelines as I consume my meal. I skip dessert, proceed downstairs and immediately start work on the project. I've thoroughly cleaned out the basement space beside excruciation station, and I meticulously arrange materials. I inherited my father's incomparable stockpile of tools, and I feel set to erect with a rotary hammer drill and designated bits, speed square, framing and finishing nailers, vice-grip clamps, laser level and everything else, including workman's stilts, that one could imagine to make a job go smooth and easy.

It all starts with the framing, and I'm working almost exclusively with brown pressure-treated lumber. I believe that 10 X 8 constitutes the perfect dimensions for a cozy heat haven to accommodate two people and occasionally an imitation Nile crocodile. The studs are cut to nuzzle my high basement ceiling, and once I form the frames, I'm able to situate them without sacrificing too much excruciation station floor space. The assembly instructions recommend that novice builders attach bottom plates to a concrete floor with removable fasteners, and the kit provides a bag of Tapcon screw anchors. I'm satisfied that the completed room skeleton is sturdy, and I suspend operations for the night.

The window replacement crew duly appears at seven o'clock Saturday morning. The sauna is situated directly between two windows, and I take care to build out of the installers' way and not burn down the house. I drill a pathway through the frame for the conduit containing the dedicated circuit line, which the electrician attached temporarily to the basement wall plasterboard. The wire from the electrical panel will attach to the digital controller of the sauna, which will feed the junction box with wires that feed the two dozen 300-watt carbon fiber heating panels to be mounted on all four walls. The sauna will have recessed LED ceiling lights like the wine cellar at Pleasant Lake, and the wires will run directly to the digital controller. I mount the junction box on the frame. The electrician left detailed follow-up instructions, and I will connect all of the electrical components as I construct the interior of the sauna. The window crew takes less than three hours to install the six new basement windows, and by the time they leave I've attached the cabinet-grade plywood outer walls.

I grab a light brunch of bacon over potato pancakes and resume construction. According to the kit guidelines, an outside-in order of operations should be followed once the framing is complete. I stuff and staple fiberglass insulation into the frame, place a plastic vapor barrier on the inside and cover that with a reflective radiant barrier. The tongue-and-groove cedar boards which constitute the sauna interior fit perfectly enough to allow for expansion and contraction.

I work late into the night and commence again early Sunday morning. I install a single-tier bench against the left wall and a double-tier bench in the back without a screw showing. I build the doorframe and hang the exquisite mahogany door, which features a nautical porthole window. I lay the molding, finish the floor, mount the digital controller on the front outside wall and complete the electrical connections.

Shortly before six o'clock on Sunday evening I declare the project complete. I flip the breaker switch, thrum the thermometer and harness 50 degrees Celsius. I intrepidly enter the sauna wearing a towel. The heat becomes oppressive in about twenty minutes, and I savor the stuffy breath of success. A sauna activates heat shock proteins, which prevent cellular damage, and they've been shown in reputable studies to increase longevity.

In a development that I deem less than shocking, Rudy's dependable friend Andy failed to show.

MY WORKWEEK AT Ideal Allele starts with two extraordinarily busy days, and I arrive home late on Tuesday. I cook a frozen meatloaf dinner in the conventional oven, boil some canned chop suey vegetables on the stove and toss some cultured bacon in the microwave. Without Maynard to serve, the convenience of highly processed food trumps high sodium and low nutritional value. The doorbell rings. I catch a glimpse of a familiar car in the driveway. The blood starts pounding in my temples so hard that I fear the woman in the tasseled knit hat and camel's-hair coat standing on my porch will detect the vibration. I open the door. "Color me paranormal," I utter. "You have a pretty tan face for a ghost."

"I've been calling and calling you." The infamous Trish Skinner displays a pouty smile. "I don't even get voicemail."

"I've moved beyond the pale, beyond the tower and even beyond the mundane satellite, to automatic telepathy." I place my fidgety fingertips against my throbbing temples.

"Why would *you* change your number?" Her cool energy is palpable. "We need to talk."

She steps into the living room and I shut the door behind her. "Stylish coat. Is it new? Let me take it." She shakes her head and plunks herself into my low-rider chair. I accede to the beanbag chair and try to nod disarmingly. "How's the Charger high-performing for you?"

She gazes out the window. "The power steering had to be repaired. My brother is interested in taking it when the weather gets a little milder."

My synapses stall. "I might be a bit more optimistic about your presence if your pointy-toe ankle boots were sandals." She forces a weak grin. "What can I get you? It just so happens I have some Shiraz chilling. It portends to be an irresistible fix for the sheila who has no partiality to sweetness."

"No, thanks." She expels a frosty breath. "I'm not thirsty."

"I'm still making dinner. Nothing fancy, but I'll share. Are you hungry?"

"I don't want any creature comforts." She stares at me in silence, her demeanor gradually evolving from annoyed to perturbed. "What garbage did you feed the cops, Lisle? Bruce was with a client. The cops burst in and hauled him out of the office in handcuffs."

"Never a dull moment with Bruce." I interlock my fingers behind my neck. "Did he provide the handcuffs? No matter. No cuffs should pose a problem for a slick D-list magician. Is he still on that kick?"

"Bruce is an *established* man with a healthy business, and he has rewarding hobbies that enrich his own life and are interesting to those with whom he cares to share them." She scowls. "What reason did you have for involving him in whatever god-awful shady business you're trying to perpetrate? Was it just to get back at me?"

I shake my head. "That's only part of it. The better part is that Neichi seems like a guy you can count on to compulsively bend the truth and play fast and loose with the facts." I can't resist a cheap digression. "Still spending a lot of time with him, are we? And he still checks all your boxes?"

She sighs. "I'm working at Bruce's office."

"So he still gives you a good discount on vitamins?"

"You're dark and twisted!" Trish springs to her feet. "You are such a liar, Lisle! What could you possibly hope to gain in the end?"

I titter with mild restraint. "So Neichi's actually sitting in the hoosegow now?"

"There was a brief scuffle, so the police held him at the station and questioned him for three hours." Trish hisses. "Lisle, where's the dog? Where's Maynard?" I remain silent, and she repeats the question.

"Maynard is no longer with us." I rise. "I'll bet it didn't take much heat to make Neichi sell you up the creek: 'This misunderstanding must be the work of some depraved fiend from the world of Trish Skinner!' What do you do at his office anyway: massage, imaging, hand-holding?"

She exhibits a thin-lipped grimace. "No longer with us how? He's dead?"

I expel a beleaguered breath. "I was walking him on the

tracks, and I don't know how, but I just didn't hear the train, and it, it caught his leash, and it took him-"

"Bullshit!" She wags her forefinger. "You'd be a basket case. Do you have him at work?" Her eyes widen with greater animosity. "Is one of your loser friends holding him?"

"I have my own way of dealing with grief." I rub my neck. "You taught me that a woman only respects a man if he's emotionally unavailable, and I've been working overtime to build up a blanket callousness."

"Maynard!" she calls. "Maynard? *Maynard!!!*"

"Why don't you check downstairs? You can admire my hobby project the deluxe sauna. I've just finished it with the other home improvements I made after the health authorities broke in and messed things up." I smile graciously. "Wouldn't you like to see excruciation station again? I've improved it, too. How about another workout down there?" The oven timer beeps. "For old time's sake? I need to take a minute in the kitchen. Wouldn't you care for some cultured bacon?"

"May I please use your bathroom?" She emits an exasperated breath. "It's not that I don't trust you, Lisle." She proceeds into the bathroom and slams the door behind her.

I march into the kitchen and turn off the oven. I add water to the sizzling vegetables, stir them briskly and lower the temperature. I stray to my dedicated junk drawer and withdraw the Charger key fob that I still possess. While Trish is in the bathroom, I decide to check whether my fob still registers. I move to the picture window and successfully flash the lights. In the middle of some workday, I'm going to remove the auto from Neichi's lot, an act that should verify whether someone is watching me.

I hear Trish calling Maynard in the basement. I hurry down the stairs and find her emerging from the sauna. "You piqued my curiosity," she explains.

"It looks nice, doesn't it?" I stand close beside her. "Completes the level? You're aware that the health benefits are numerous, from increased aerobic capacity to reduction of hypertension and stroke risk to burning fat to boosting the immune system. It sure would be fun to sit in there sipping a Shiraz."

She stares ahead blankly. "Come clean, Lisle. Where is he? Where's the dog?"

I survey her from head to toe. "I'd almost forgotten how remarkably good-looking you are." She winces and heads back to the stairway. "You've been with Neichi for ten months now? You must be bored silly." She hustles up the steps, and I follow. "Do you see yourself with Bruce permanently, assuming he doesn't get himself thrown back behind bars?"

She discharges a petulant moan. "I am so upset with you. I had all I could do to keep Bruce from pressing charges against you."

I chortle. "For impersonating an established man with flamboyant hobbies?"

"For every stripe of fraudulent misrepresentation," she snaps. "He wanted to pressure the D.A. to charge you with lying to the police and obstructing an investigation. People who work at the D.A.'s office go to Bruce for treatment."

"He labors to stiffen their spines so they don't bend to pressure to betray the public trust?"

She huffs. "You really have a way of needling people, don't you, of irritating them to the point of outrage."

"Didn't I treat you pretty well while you were here?" I slide seamlessly from flippant to sincere. "Hell, I gave you my car! I could really use a little T.L.C. right now."

"Your extravagant gift wasn't my idea," she scoffs. "Take your own friendly advice, Lisle, and stop constantly seeking the approval of women. In this age of feminism, you don't say things like, 'I stand in awe of your beauty and charm.' It makes a woman think you need a surrogate mother." I roll my eyes. "A man-child with his dog and mommy issues at the bottom of the dominance hierarchy doesn't inspire romantic tingles."

I offer a deferential smile. "And yet, how many of the real men you've found fit to fuck didn't groan to press their lips to your nips?"

"We're through here." She leads me out to the Charger, and I trail stoically. She starts the engine and lowers the driver's window. "I might've at least remembered you as someone I liked."

I tap my chest. "There's no consolation prize when you have your heart set on love and respect, kid." I watch her leave for the last time. "Goodbye, Trish."

I discard my supper. I need to get out of the house. Trish twisted me inside out emotionally, and I don't have Maynard to comfort me. I hop in the Yukon and drive around Waukesha County. I hate to admit I've always harbored a desperate hope that my nearly beloved might come roaring back into my life, and her reappearance tonight lent that sentiment one last gasp. But now the reality that she never will be my lover launches me deep into melancholia. I expect that in the coming days I'll regret waxing rude and crude, but I don't figure I'll burn immoderate guilt over it, because Trish must recognize that if she valued kindness and consideration, she could've had the mother lode in me.

I end up on Appleton Avenue in Menomonee Falls. I'm not even sure of the name of the tavern. *Coyote* imported craft beer and *BURGERS* signs grace the windows. There's one unattended woman seated at the curved, shadowy bar. She's wearing her dress off her right shoulder. I park myself with a one-stool buffer zone between us. She has a nice face, with thick, dark lashes and a chiseled chin. Her hair is dyed canary yellow, and she's sipping a margarita. She has a bloody-tipped dagger tattooed on her left biceps, which I concede I could be persuaded to find rather sexy. If I ever see Trish again, I'll suggest that she acquire one. I order my Guinness sludgehammer. I'm in no mood to be coy, so I lean close enough that the canary has to glance sideways at the looming menace impinging on her nest space. "I like your dagger; it's a conversation starter." She responds with a silent scowl. "It's edgy."

She rolls her big, brown eyes and sighs deeply. "Get real."

"I'll get to the point." I redouble my feeble attempt to hit on her. "Does the bloody tip signify we're not dealing with a virgin dagger?"

"Get lost." She emphasizes how much she resents a low-value wooer by hiking up her dress over her exposed shoulder.

I preserve a piece of my wounded dignity by employing the Kisslinger method of offering psychological insight. "I'm sorry that a man hurt you. We're not all scum." I take a long, hard swig of my drink. "It's just the awful 98 percent that ruins it for the rest of us."

"Get fucked," she thoroughly rejects my presence.

I smack my lips. "Cold cuts."

Clutching her drink and purse, she marches her short skirt and her toned, shapely legs with a tattoo on each calf around to the other side of the bar. She takes refuge beside a square-faced man and turns summarily gabby. She points at me.

"Were you bothering this lady?" Sir Galahad holds his inimical gaze on me and gestures to his windfall companion.

The man is twice as bulky as me, but I'm sure I'm twice as truculent as he is, and I'll never be more ready than I am at the moment to prove it. "She should get inked all the way up her legs!" I assert. "Then when she runs, it would look like you're flipping through the pages of a comic book!"

Galahad laughs. I take another gulp of my orangeman and return home.

I'm slouched over my bathroom sink early on Thursday morning slathering shave cream across my face when the doorbell rings. I suspect that my Nile crocodile Companion Piece has arrived. I hope little assembly is required. I head to the front door and spot a pink utility van with *STRAIGHT A's Assertive Measures* painted on the side in my driveway. A young woman in a hoodie and pink bib overalls occupies my porch. She eyeballs her tablet as I open the door. "T.S.C.M. I'm Handy Andy."

"I'm vial Lisle." I survey the porch for a package.

She grunts. "Rudy told me you need a debugger?"

I fix my surprise on her embroidered *Andrea* bib patch as I nod. "I'm concerned there's a tracking device on my SUV."

"The vehicle's where?" She instinctively starts toward the garage.

I bound out of the front door to escort her wearing my long johns, fluffy slippers and a face full of foam. I open the garage door and she struts around the Yukon. "Anyone with a motive have interior access?"

"It was actually impounded." I cross my arms across my chest as I shiver.

"Why don't you continue about your routine, and I'll conduct a thorough sweep?" Andy opens the liftgate. "Shouldn't take two hours."

I nod and dart back into the house. I wonder how expensive this exercise in paranoia will be. Through the window I watch Andy tow a mechanic's creeper loaded with tools from her van into the garage. I get primped at a leisurely pace and eat a mixed bag breakfast. I call Anele and reach Sandee. After a brief squabble and the solemn promise to return early tomorrow, I arrange to take a personal day. I return to the garage in my puffer parka. The vehicle rests on a jack and the technician labors at the undercarriage. "Anything I can do to assist?"

A modest disc rolls out from beneath the Yukon. "There's your issue, or at least one of them." A flashlight beam shines on the device as I pick it up. "Stuck to the bottom with a magnet." Andy emerges on her creeper and sits up. "Let's take a little ride and I'll check for passive reinforcement."

I chauffeur Handy Andy through the mean streets of Elm Grove in the Yukon recollecting my desperate search of the area for the missing Maynard three months before. She crawls around the cargo area with a bug detector offering technical perspectives on "sleeper mode" and "burst mode."

"What can you tell me about Rudy?" I banter. "He sounds like something of an enigma."

"He's something." She snickers. "Typical unscrupulous bastard. More goopy, I suppose." Her detection device begins beeping. "Not the attention-getter you are." She taps the floor. "There's something evil down there. Take us home, and we'll take a look."

In my garage, Andy isolates my spare tire as the source of the device. But she's unable to make visual contact. "I know a user-friendly garage on the east side of Brookfield." She rolls the tire down the driveway and out to her van in the street. "I'll be back in a bit!" She tosses the tire into her vehicle and drives off. I run to the bank and withdraw three thousand dollars in cash.

Andy returns in about an hour. She rolls my spare tire up the driveway and drops what looks like a flash drive into my hand. "They housed it inside the tire. You should be clean now."

I examine it briefly, produce the other tracking device and offer them both to her. "Can you just dispose of these?"

"Let's think about this." She squints through acerbic eyes. "Some of my clients like to repurpose found trackers. Stick them on other vehicles?"

I feel a wily smile cross my lips. "I just might get a charge out of doing that."

"Don't get caught. There've been cases with criminal charges for car owners removing police trackers." She displays her grimy hands. "Can I use your bathroom? Just to wash up quick."

"Uh, fine." I reluctantly lead her into my house and through the hallway. "First door around the corner on the right." I'm instinctively squeamish about letting strangers use my facilities.

Handy Andy freshens up and returns to the living room. I meet her beside my low-rider chair. "So what's your finder's fee going to be?"

She chews her lip. "You're aware that your bathroom is bugged, right? There's a listening device on top of your medicine cabinet."

My internal fraud detector beeps. "There sure shouldn't be." Is she planting bugs and scheming to charge me by the quantity?

Andy removes her detector from her bib pocket and holds it over the chair. "Got another one here?"

I lift the chair cushion with the stark realization of what other stranger recently occupied my bathroom and low-profile chair. Andy locates another listening device beneath the chair arm. I bid her to conduct a cursory sweep of the entire house. I open the covert wall hatch in the bathroom and the false back behind the kitchen cupboard, and I await the result in my low-rider chair. She returns to the living room in another hour and presents me with two listening devices. I toss them into the coffee table drawer with the one that had resided beneath the chair arm and usher Andy outside. "One of those was from the medicine cabinet, that I told you about, and the other I found beneath a bench in your sauna room downstairs." I hold my head, which continues to spin with denial that Trish would participate in such an ambush. "If we're done, the final cost is two thousand razoos. Since you're one of Rudy's rowdies, I should charge you more. Payment in cash, gold or silver will get you a fifty percent discount."

"I'm profoundly grateful." I hand her a generous $1300 in bills. "Want to give me your business card in case I need you again?"

Handy Andy tears a $100 bill in half, scribbles her contact information on one portion and passes it back to me. "Next time we'll jam the signals." She returns to her utility van and is gone before eleven.

I retrieve my full complement of invasive devices and my old Charger fob. I hop into the Yukon and drive to the parking lot of the supermarket down the street from the strip mall containing Bruce Neichi's chiropractic office. I stroll to the strip mall parking lot and locate Trish's Charger. I attach one tracker behind the front bumper and open the trunk. I deposit the other tracker beside the spare tire under the access cover. I close the trunk and unlock the car. I toss the three listening devices under the seats and re-lock the car. I return to the supermarket and buy a heaping cartload of groceries. I stow the groceries in the Yukon and head up to Pleasant Lake under an increasingly cloudy sky.

There is still only minimal snow accumulation in Waushara County. I park in front of the crippled trailer in the Bustelich driveway, hustle next door and knock on the cabin door. There is no answer so I pound harder and repeat. I decide to follow the most prominent set of man-and-dog footprints into the backyard. I jog toward the slope to find Maynard and Gayle arriving at the top of the Bustelich stairway to the lake. Maynard spots me first. Gayle does a double take and releases the leash. The dog plows through the shallow snow, and I get down on all fours so he won't hurt himself jumping on me. He knocks me onto my back, warbling, spinning around and licking my face exuberantly. I pet and kiss him without restraint. "Maynard, my boy, oh, my pal, I've missed you so much! How are you? Finding lake country to your liking? Is Uncle Gayle taking good care of you?" I look up at Gayle. His delight at the sight of the reunion seems more tepid than I would expect. I take the leash handle and brush the snow off my pants as I stagger to my feet.

"He's more than ready to go home," Spaatz submits.

"I'm sorry I haven't been able to get back up here sooner." I brush a few more flakes off my parka. "Handy Andy just paid me a visit and tweezed two trackers off my vehicle, so I feel like I've regained some liberty. I stopped off and bought you a glut of groceries. Things going good enough here?"

"Not so much." He rubs his forehead. "I'm afraid Johnny is really not well. His eyes are puffy, and he's very pale, very lethargic. He's sweating profusely. His ankles are swollen, and he complains of chronic joint pain. He's having trouble swallowing and defecating."

I puff out my cheeks. "He's white and not yellow?"

"It's serious, Lisle." Gayle stares intently.

"I'm enough of a play doctor to know if he's yellow, it indicates a liver problem." I let Maynard lead the way to the Yukon.

"I'm afraid we're about to the point where we have to take

some action." Spaatz runs his hands over my vehicle. "I've started constructing a pair of fake license plates. If need be, what do you say we slap them on this beast, take Johnny up to the hospital in Wild Rose and dump him outside the door to the emergency room?"

I raise my eyebrows. "Why don't we just call for a police ambulance and have them drop us off at the jail on the way to the hospital?" I open the liftgate. "Before we panic, let's take a painfully close look at him. I suspect Johnny's having no trouble at all bullshitting."

Spaatz and I convey groceries from the SUV to the cabin. A partially completed fabrication of a Wisconsin license plate lies among the pastel drawings of our former classmates on the parlor table. Before the Stephanie Recktenwald drawing is set aside, I review its glorious detail. In three trips, Gayle and I complete our commodities transfer, replenishing the bare shelves of the refrigerator and cupboards. We provide Maynard with some treats, and we head down to the wine cellar.

I enter first, and Bustelich fixes his hard gaze on me. "Here's Handsome." His tone is subdued, and he does appear pale. His dingy yellow gown embellished with abstract tondi looks sweat-soaked.

"And *heeeere's* Johnny!" I give him a mild slap on each of his cheeks. "Rusting hulk of an ogre that he is." His weak kick misses me. "I understand you're trying to score sympathy points by claiming to be sick."

He winces. "I need to go to the hospital, Amonor. I feel congested, really tight in my chest and gut." He coughs. "Having trouble taking a shit."

Biased by his record, I'm unconvinced. "Man up, Bustelich. It's just a hot flash. Focus on how the new you is going to crush it in every women's recreational sports league."

Johnny draws a labored breath. "Must be tough to be loved by nobody, Lowell, but don't use that excuse to be so damned heartless."

"Maynard just demonstrated that's not the case," Gayle trumpets.

I sigh. "How long has this bellyacher appeared to have systemic congestion?"

Spaatz studies his internee. "About a week?"

"When is the last time he got a hormone injection?"

Gayle grimaces. "Not since the last time you were here, Doctor."

"No more meds," I decree. "You're awash in vegetables and herbs now. Keep him on a light diet of functional foods, and let's see where we are in another week." I counter Bustelich's groan with a grin and turn back to Spaatz. "Speaking of food, let's arrange an early supper. How about some chili?"

Johnny spits. "Yeah, bitches, retreat upstairs for hot beef injections." He holds his malevolent eyes on me. "Nothin' says 'I love you' like mutual butt slams!"

Gayle strides to the wine racks, selects a bottle and returns. "The vino reserves are getting rather thin." He hands me the Merlot. "You can get our meal started while I finish tending to Johnny's personals."

I return upstairs, get the chili cooking, set the table and open the wine. I pet Maynard and sip Merlot until Spaatz joins us. He washes his hands in the bucket and starts chopping an onion and celery. "I trust you're spending the night?"

"I'm going to have to head back as soon as we're done eating." I offer an apologetic smile as he turns to face me. "There's a project at work I'm already in trouble for not having completed that I must absolutely get to early tomorrow morning."

Gayle casts a tender glance at Maynard. "I think I'll miss him."

"Not yet." I force a chuckle. "I have to ask you to keep him a while longer. My sister and my demented nephew are coming in for the weekend." I'm compelled to move beyond the home repair pretense because Handy Andy could speak to its lack of veracity. "I've told you that Maynard has bitten them both, so I don't want them in the house together, especially since I'm going to have to make a few quick runs to work while they're here. And I still don't want to board him commercially because of that nasty Capno dog infection going around."

"You can't just lock up the dog in your basement?" Spaatz sighs. "Nobody else can take him?"

"Please, Gayle, just a few more days. I promise I'll come and get him by Wednesday at the very latest." I pose Maynard's front paws in a gesture of supplication.

"You're aware you really *will* want to get him out of here before the *following* weekend." Spaatz turns back to the chili. "That's the Pleasant Lake ice fishing jamboree. As I understand it, the area gets pretty busy. A fellow is going to have to squat extra low."

The chili is hearty but the conversation is meager. "You

should hatch some production dedicated to ice fishing," I venture. "Remember some of those musicals we concocted in high school? We had *South Side Story*, with songs like 'Mr. Boobird's On My Shoulder' and 'Two-Bit Tito's Sundown Cantina'? How did the 'Tito' lyrics start: *Clouds in your eyes; we sympathize. Slob by the door; clean up the floor. How's it outside; Stan needs a ride. Team didn't score; ain't that a bore. Is it is it is it important if it's if it's if it's imported?*"

Gayle almost cracks a smile. He puts down his spoon and holds his head. "I'm having frequent, intensely unsettling nightmares," he announces.

"You've just been spending too much time with Johnny." I munch a saltine. "You've become concerned about his health, and now he seems like more of a responsibility than a monstrosity?"

"He's a fucking big pig-sucking louse." Gayle's gaze becomes more penetrating, as if his brain is sharpening its focus. "I lied to you."

I'm gripped with dread that he's surmised I'm not being candid about Maynard's situation. "Shading the truth is basic to social survival," I grant.

Spaatz takes a gulp of Merlot. "Back in October, Johnny derived my identity at the Tosa Team T Squared office. He rushed me as soon as he recognized me. I didn't tell you because I was afraid you wouldn't come up to Pleasant Lake, and I needed your support."

I nod with empathy. "Now you remind me of old Holden Caulfield. You really do."

"Yeah, you big phony?" He plays along with the analogy.

"You're vigorously questioning what you want." I attempt to exude tenderness. "That's the way we grow and move on."

We finish supper, I issue a salvo of doting goodbyes to Maynard, and Gayle accompanies me out to the Yukon. A forlorn look reappears on his face. I open the SUV door, look back at the cottage and titter. "Remember for a while in high school we had a saying: The only good Bustelich is a dead Bustelich."

"I think I'm really getting tired of this tohubohu." Spaatz's tears appear to freeze on his cheeks.

"Don't do anything drastic," I insist. "Hang loose, and we'll punch our way out."

"Yeah, sure." He scuffs his foot against an ice chunk.

I place my hand on Gayle's shoulder. "Johnny and I have discussed the prospect of buying him off. I think he'll go for it, so we can prevent him from turning us in to the authorities. I'm confident I command the funds necessary to close the deal."

Spaatz grimaces and backs away. "No, it's my party, Lisle. I can't let you pick up the tab. I won't hear of it."

"Killing him would be the practical alternative way out, and I don't believe either of us honestly wants any part of that." I try to display a cagey grin. "The only catch is we're going to have to shelter somewhere he can't find us for a while, because I'm dead certain he's too stupid not to try to cross us with some kind of retribution."

"Hide for how long?"

I shrug. "A couple of years."

"Guy I used to work with in collections moved to the Portland area. I've spoken with him a few times since, and he keeps raving about how phenomenal a place it is, encouraging me to go out there."

I snicker. "I know people who swear the same thing about Zamboanga."

"Have you ever considered traveling around the world?" Gayle wipes his face. "How about backpacking through Africa?"

"I think I'd be more likely to end up *backpedaling* through Africa." I shiver conspicuously. "I'm only too aware, as things are now, how dangerous the world is. I also suspect such a course would be slightly too strenuous a walk for Maynard."

A pensive twinkle clouds Spaatz's eyes. "I'd start at Lake Victoria in Tanzania and wander farther down from the equator. That's the topic of one of the books I had in my footlocker."

"You could bust out an entire life reboot, maybe attach yourself to a Chimanimani mama."

Gayle doesn't appear amused. "Thanks again for the victuals, Lisle. I'll start Johnny on his naturopathic diet as soon as I get back inside."

I climb into my bug-free Yukon. "When I come back Tuesday or Wednesday, we'll make sure his health has improved and flesh out our exit strategy." I glance at the cabin as I shut the SUV door. I start the engine and wave to Gayle intermittently until I've reached the end of the driveway. I start down Pleasant Road while a little lingering light is left in the day.

I spend most of my ride home contemplating options and priorities. None of my options are optimum, but at least I can identify some prospects for Maynard's medium-term accommodations. It's more than slightly ironic that I now have reason to see the Bustelich transformance experiment continue. My priorities are far less murky. If any doubt lingered, the way I want to quintessentially define myself solidifies. My ultimate allegiance belongs to whichever being has shown me the most love. These are dog days.

I RETURN TO work early Friday morning and get busy deconstructing glycan structures for a growth factor project to influence stem cell development. I find Kelly at one of the mass spectrometers. "Did I miss anything in the huddle yesterday? Was it a singular sensation?"

"They postponed it until early next week." She gestures that I should lean closer. "I asked Sandee about our increasing frequency of scrums getting scrubbed, and her exact words were, 'Most everything around a bio lab is disposable.'" She eyes me intently. "Something wicked this way comes."

"They'll probably reschedule it for Wednesday at eleven." I snicker. "That's when I'm set to start my second round of sensitivity training sessions." Ideally our team meeting will be held on Monday and I can arrange for enough midweek personal time to patch up the predicament at Pleasant Lake.

I spend every moment at Ideal Allele not dedicated to

the glycome pondering what fresh accommodations I might procure for Maynard. I can probably prevail upon Spaatz to prolong his tenure as dog-sitter, but only for another week or so. Even if I could find a commercial dog-sitter not subject to Capno-phobia, I refuse to leave my dog in the hands of strangers. I have my own variants of jitters. If I can't recruit another caretaker that I know and trust, I'll rent a furnished abode to which I can move the dachshund temporarily. It would be prudent to situate him somewhere beyond the scope of Milwaukee and Waukesha where I still feel the heat of the surveillance spotlight. Acquiring a safe house is an unattractive stopgap. Beyond the expense, it'll leave poor Maynard with countless lonely hours. But I need to be prepared. I don't know what sort of law-enforcement watch list I might have landed on, so a sanctuary property would be best rented under an assumed name. That means I'd require an alternative ID. Spaatz would probably lend me his; it's likely that he's still holding Bustelich's as well. Wouldn't that be cute to pose as Johnny? But even their names are perhaps on a watch list. My best bet would be to select one of our high school alums from the list of precocious decedents and transform myself into him. All I'll require is a subversive freelancer with a flair for photography and forgery. Gayle has always contended that the overcrowded graphic designer marketplace "retches with radicals."

The long-term resolution of my canine protection program will depend on what sort of compensatory settlement I'm able to structure with Bustelich. I presume he'd be amenable to an initial payment of fifty thousand dollars with monthly installments of ten thousand dollars over five years. The threat of forfeiting his cash cow should be enough by itself to dissuade Johnny from blowing the whistle on us or carrying out reprisals. But just to insure that I'm able to maintain solid leverage, I'll describe the pathogenic penalty he'll incur upon betrayal in horrifically palpable terms. He'll need to be paid until I can disappear, and it will be my intention to accomplish that act as expeditiously as possible.

Before I leave the building, I request personal days off next week Tuesday and Wednesday. Sandee responds that the team meeting has still not been rescheduled so I should check back Monday.

A few moments after I arrive home, a cargo van stops in front of my house and my Nile crocodile Companion Piece is delivered. After a quick pea soup supper, I lug my two huge newly acquired cartons downstairs and establish the croc's habitat in the sauna. The length of the automaton is four meters, over half of that consisting of its mighty tail. Assembly proves to be more laborious than I'd hoped, as stretching the lifelike synthetic skin over the frame requires special dexterity and perseverance. I'm finally able to curl the tail in an authentic manner which allows the entire body of the crocodile to sit comfortably in the sauna, and I gradually learn how to control the animatronic movements. It takes me well into Saturday afternoon to declare the project complete, but the finished product is worth it. Two seconds after I turn on the welcome lights by opening the sauna door, the croc blinks and snorts, lifts its head and torso off the floor, hisses and charges three steps forward opening its mouth wide. Now all I need is some pretext to induce Trish to come over and enter the sauna.

I carry my two empty Companion Piece boxes up to the attic and store them for future use. I gaze out of the peephole and spy a black SUV with tinted windows that was parked down the street this morning. I throw on my puffer parka, saunter out the front door and head toward the suspicious vehicle. As I approach, it takes off. Two hours later, I see the neighbors who live behind my property leave, as they do on most Saturday evenings. I emerge from my back door in an old Adirondack barn coat, vault the back fence, hustle through my neighbor's yard and march down the next street over. A black SUV cruises by and I'm almost sure it's the same one that was parked on my street. I make a mental note to re-engage Handy Andy on Monday.

Sunday morning after church, I drive to Bruce Neichi's strip mall and purchase a pair of burner phones from the Zhen Dianxin store. Following a little lunch and reflection, I place a desperate test call to Pasadena, Texas from the back lot on one of my new devices. "What's the good word?"

"I'm getting by." Delmar doesn't sound delighted to hear from his old benchmate.

"How's the dream job?" I persevere to elicit an inflection.

He snorts. "The distressing fact is I'm in jeopardy of losing my gainful employment. I've been censured and am currently on disciplinary report."

"Not further fallout from Maitai?" I pause but get no response. "Not another Companion Piece incident?"

"I've learned from your mistakes in those areas," he assures me. "I developed another customer for a slightly adulterated stack of hormones and I was caught in a surveillance audit gleaning the goods, so they put me on official notice. Their view of me was already shaded because a while back the little enzyme department in the rear annex caught me plundering dead mice for snake food." He grunts. "I'm fundamentally guilty of being a capable capitalist. Even an old socialist like you should be able to appreciate a scrounger culture that saves things from going to waste."

"My pink period faded," I remind him, "about the time I stepped off campus and started working a real job. If equity embers flared up every now and again, you terminated all potential to backslide when you couched wealth redistribution as 'your opportunity to pay the way for the grandkids of the women who rejected you.'"

"The paradigm of economic cuckoldry," he spouts. "As I keep trying to impress upon all you poppers, socialism is nothing but the new feudalism. Where there are no private property rights and one cannot amass wealth and transfer it to whomever he pleases without interference, we're all just vassals to the state, the only difference being that instead of a blood aristocracy, our overlords are a politburo and its cronies."

"I'm glad there was no issue of inappropriate conduct with your wild Malaysian honey," I reiterate. "It might be a knottier proposition to get Nancy to give you a fresh reference."

"You zucker, I was scooping you a shovelful." He emits a protracted gurgle. "Nancy never gave me a reference. I just told you she did to sway you in taking the proper attitude toward her."

I'm flabbergasted to realize I'm not sure what to believe.

"Delmar, everything you've just told me now is the absolute truth?"

"Hang your top hat on it." He smacks his lips. "And therein lies the real tragedy of Maitai. She's an entrepreneur after my own heart. But she found herself an exchange student with a proa, and I postulate a proa trumps a mountain bike, so my chance for intimacy there is near nada."

I hiss. "If she should ever favor you with another date, remind her that our hunter-gathering ancestors often faced starvation, so a skipped meal is an essential part of the paleo diet. Failing that, remind her how primitive the ancestral tableware was and challenge her to use a knife and fork made of stone."

"Our potential for a physical connection endures," he states flatly. "She's offering her eggs for sale, so if I can find a uterus to rent, I might still procreate. Money is tight now, but I'm scraping together the credit to buy one ovum and freeze it."

"She *is* colorful." If I were God, I believe I'd flood the world.

"She dyed her hair mauve." Del sighs. "It looks freakier than the teal."

I suppress an acute groan. "Did you ever recover your pet snake?"

"The building maintenance guy who cleans the vents found a dead little rattler. Of course, I didn't make any claim to it."

"How would you like to rent a real pet for a while?" I pause so he's not overwhelmed by my overture. "You'd be doing me a tremendous service, and I'd make it worth your while monetarily. I'm going to visit my sister in Zamboanga, and I need someone to keep Maynard for a few weeks. It sounds like you might have some extra time on your hands in the offing. You liked my dog when you met him, didn't you?"

Vecsey emits a nasal tone. "I'd love to help you out, pardner, but there are technically no pets allowed in this complex. A snake I can sneak by the watchkeepers, but not a dog."

"You indicated you were having some trouble affording one of Maitai's gametes. By how much scratch are you short?"

"I said I'm earning egg credit. Mai is working on a vasopressin immune system booster, and I agreed to take part in a human challenge trial. So if you never hear from me again, you can extrapolate that the trial went horribly bad."

I rub my neck. "It must be past time for you to upgrade your digs, isn't it? I'll pay you enough to help you make the status dream of ranch house ownership a reality."

He groans. "That's not the point. I like this neighborhood. There's a curvy woman who jogs by every morning. I've finally been able to get her attention. It's kind of odd. I was making fun of her because she's a bit waddly when she runs, and she chatters into her Megalophone nonstop. I originally nicknamed her 'R.C.' for Running Commentary. It turns out she's in constant contact with her daughter, who she home schools and is subject to falls and accidents. R.C. wears an accelerometer when she runs that feeds data back to her daughter, and they count her steps. The goal is twelve thousand per day. She could stand to lose a few fatty cells, but that's why she's waddling, and as I say, she got quite the curves. The last time I saw her, I bandied the subject of running with her."

He can't honestly believe that such an activity would have a long half-life. "You could walk Maynard jogging alongside her. You could suggest that she help you move as an exercise of stamina and bonding."

"R.C. figures to have a trophy uterus, so I'm not going to make any crazy, desperate moves that could ruin my destiny. Furthermore, I don't want to get stuck with the regular maintenance chores and yardwork that come with a single-unit dwelling. Really, Lisle, how would you like it if I requested that you move?"

"Say where." I survey the nearly empty parking lot. "I wouldn't ask if it wasn't dire, Del. I really believe I need to get out of town. I might've made the wrong people's enemies list."

"You're a smart boy; you'll work it out. I really gotta go."

"Just one final item. The latest gossip suggests that Anele is struggling a bit. Your company wouldn't by any chance be hiring, would it?"

"No. As far as I know, we're solid to the point of bloated."

I titter. "You couldn't ask anyway while they consider firing you if they'd consider hiring me, could you?"

"Sorry, Lisle, I'm meeting my buddy Bob. I'll get back to you sometime soon." He terminates the connection.

I expel a thoroughly frustrated breath. "I guess joining you in Texas is officially off the board as an option."

I drive home with the regret that I didn't offer to add my Nile crocodile Companion Piece to Delmar's dog-sitting perks. I may anonymously send him the reptile replicant anyway.

Monday morning, Sandee pressures me to accelerate the pace of my stem cell programming project, and I reach the cafeteria later than usual. Serge Kenower of the CDC is on TV providing a Capno crisis update. "Every bit as important as preventing further transmission of the infection," Kenower maintains, "is preventing further transmission of misinformation." The point man confirms reports that the outbreak zone has expanded into Colorado. "But there is still no evidence that Capno spreads human-to-human through airborne droplets. The key to containment remains compliance."

Further news accounts describe the growing movements of people demanding the mass extermination of dogs. Incidents of people murdering their neighbors' pets are presented. A man in Ohio who'd been going around his neighborhood killing dogs was found murdered. Another health official who attempted to seize a dog in Indiana was shot and killed. I share the lunch table with Spencer. "You're lucky you don't have your dog anymore," he submits, "or you could get caught up in shit like this." The death count from super-Capno cases surpasses 150. The death count from Capno-related incidents approaches 70.

Before my lunch period is over, I walk the premises and leave Handy Andy a message soliciting her services as a countersurveillance consultant. It occurs to me that her value needn't be limited to locating deleterious gadgets. She could rent a house for me in her name or subcontract the task to some golden opportunist like Rudy.

I finish my glycome project late in the afternoon. I leave work with no decision reached on when the highly anticipated team meeting will occur. But Sandee promises that a joint team huddle conducted by Nancy is imminent.

I begin my workday on Tuesday with insectary duty to maintain and nurture the Allele stocks of honeycomb moths, vinegar flies and beetles. I contribute a dead-on Ed Sullivan impression but nobody appreciates it. Nancy calls a joint team meeting for three o'clock, but at two she postpones it until the same time tomorrow. I grow anxious because I haven't received a call from Andy. Or Gayle. While engrossed at my desk compiling statistical blips, I'm startled by a ringing phone. The call proves to be on Skinny Jean's line, and our eyes meet when she hangs up. "I haven't heard a call come in on Delmar's old line in a while," I remark.

"They finally got around to terminating it at the end of January, chief," Sleepy Gene volunteers. "Didn't they clear it with you?"

I spend Tuesday night at home further training my crocodile as I anticipate the conclusion of the Bustelich experiment. Johnny will require assistance concocting an excuse for his four-month absence, or his wife will sue him for abandonment, and the foul truth will come oozing forth. Campbellsport, south of Oshkosh, is almost on the way to Pleasant Lake. The village is known as the UFO capital of Wisconsin, so Johnny might be released there with a story of having been abducted by aliens. More plausibly, Johnny could be found wandering around Pleasant Lake claiming to have suffered a blackout. He remains clueless about his current location, so he could be blindfolded, driven around and deposited at his own cabin oblivious to the notion that the one next door had any involvement in his ordeal.

The aftermath of the situation promises to be even more problematic. No matter how dreadful a pathogen I dangle over Bustelich's head, it'll only succeed as a deterrent temporarily. As

Johnny reaches middle age, his life is bound to get more progressively wretched, and he'll be looking for outlets to blame and punish. He'll habitually squander his hush money before he receives it and demand more. I return upstairs and plunk myself down in my low-profile chair. Maynard may never see this house again; as quickly and quietly as possible, I'm going to have to unload it. Campbellsport might be an ideal area to begin looking for a shack to rent.

I START TALK therapy sensitivity training at King Kryczek & Rohr-Kisslinger Counseling Solutions LLP with Dr. Arthur King. I expect DeRae might remark "Nice to see you again." She acts as if she doesn't recognize me. Dr. Rohr-Kisslinger momentarily pauses behind the partition to interface with her, and he deftly manages not to make eye contact with me. Perhaps the clinicians are trained not to risk an awkward moment by acknowledging people in the waiting room. All social situations seem to be potentially hazardous for mental health practitioners. DeRae glances over at me, and I suppress the impulse to ask about Dr. Kryczek. She looks away again before I can achieve a firm smile.

A few minutes later, she ushers me into Dr. King's office. She leaves me in a comfortable striped barrel chair to watch a video, in which King lists his educational credentials, mentions some professional associations and diagrams his basic treatment philosophy. He's bald with prominent browridges but has a much fluffier beard than Kisslinger. His method refines core beliefs and liberates them to promote desired behaviors. His modality requires clients to graduate to the immersion tank.

Dr. King enters and reintroduces himself in the flesh. "I've reviewed Dr. Rohr-Kisslinger's notes on your sessions, but I like to start fresh with a client." He seats himself behind his desk and cocks his head. "How many close friends do you sincerely think you have?"

I consider Maynard and pause to reflect further. "Can I count Kisslinger?"

King fixes me with a condescending squint. "Do you want to get better?"

"I look at every day as a self-improvement odyssey. I'd like to give a good account of myself on the voyage."

The liberator leans closer. "Let's try it this way. How many people do you have in your inner sympathy circle that you could count on to stand up for you if you experienced serious trouble?" His lips curl into a wry smile. "We'll even cheat and let you count relatives, neighbors and coworkers."

I tap my pinkies together. "How tight is 'inner'?"

"Ah, zero total," he infers. "Our first call to activation gains definite pitch." A gleam settles in his eyes. "When a client asks for my input about a particular person they're considering as a romantic partner or otherwise accepting into their inner circle, my first tip is to ascertain whether the candidate has any close friends already, or any friends at all. If the answer is no, then I can confidently assure them that this person is a bad risk and should be avoided."

I nod. "That sounds like a perfect solution for destroying a subclass of people in dire need of the benefit of close companionship."

"You miss the point," he makes scant effort to disguise his disgust. "There's a reason why this person is without friends. There's a fluid, self-correcting veracity in relational dynamics."

I emit a self-conscious laugh. "So now people who have trouble making friends will have the added burden of experts like you warning their charges to play keep away. It seems like the moral equivalent of kicking someone when they're down."

The liberator expels a heavy breath. "People tend basically to seek their own interest. If they sense you have value to offer, they'll naturally gravitate to you. They'll want to be your friend."

"Red flags emerge with the friends someone has, not with any friends they don't have." I wish I could splash him. "You should get a job in some progressive school district as clique organizer."

He refers to his Notemaster. "Dr. Rohr-Kisslinger believes you suffer from an extreme case of bovarism, which is an inflated estimate of yourself, or simply put, conceit. Horribly misplaced conceit. He suggests that a metacognitive impairment hinders your ability to assess the validity of your own knowledge and exhibit self-doubt."

"Is that a legitimate reason to advise my employer that I'm some sort of security risk?"

"You fit the profile. Do you feel as though you're not valued by society?"

"I don't," I concede, "get much love from the rest of the

humans. When that's the case, you go on an indiscriminate killing rampage if you're a complete piece of garbage. A decent person seeks love elsewhere, like in the obliging nature of his dog."

The doctor pauses to scrutinize me. "What really bothers me about that statement is your use of the qualifier 'indiscriminate,' as if to suggest a killing rampage could be justified."

"Don't be bothered," I comfort him. "Kisslinger certified I have poor execution function."

He refers to his Notemaster. "I can see why Dr. Rohr-Kisslinger repeatedly cites your belief that you don't have a problem as the key to the self-defeating behavior which leads to your ill outcomes."

I smile archly. "But you prefer to assess for yourself."

"Dr. Rohr-Kisslinger integrates alternative therapeutic modalities into his techniques. He pays more attention to formative childhood episodes." The liberator rises to his feet. "He and I do agree, however, that one's ability to hold and manipulate abstract ideas is the best indicator of whether they can and will be helped by any type of cognitive therapy. What do you think you learned from your sessions with him?"

"Mostly," I report with candor, "Kisslinger and I used to sit around and argue about which of us was more mentally ill."

"Your lack of intellectual depth may be correlated to insufficient social engagement. Even a little social connection serves to reduce neuron death and cognitive decline."

"Ouch, let me give myself a hug." I clamp my hands on my shoulders. "In fact, shaman, pour me a stiff ayahuasca, will you, and let's see if we can't expand my sociability the old-fashioned way."

"Do you know what the term 'alexithymia' means?" The doctor reseats himself. "It's a way for a clinician to suggest that a client needs to work on his self-awareness, to understand and interpret his motivations for resistance. Dr. Rohr-Kisslinger indicates that you wandered from one academic discipline to another in school and wound up in an unsatisfying professional situation, that you suffer from confusion about your sexual orientation, that you're filled with self-loathing, particularly in regard to your appearance, and you battle exhaustively to stave off depressive episodes and hopelessness."

"But everything else looks good?"

"Do you wake up fatigued even after getting a full night's sleep? Do you wake up earlier than you want to? With a cramp? You obviously have a problem with irritability. You're most likely suffering from a magnesium deficiency. I see that Dr. Rohr-Kisslinger already advised you to increase your consumption of eggs. You might add to that a few more leafy greens."

I stare into the eyes of the beholder. "The hunt for self-awareness waits not for nourishment nor slumber."

"No romantic partner. No prospects?" King hisses. "If I may speak boldly, Dr. Rohr-Kisslinger indicates that you've exhibited some of the dark personality disorder traits that foster an inured incel." He underscores the observation with a cold squint. "Meaningful sexual activity can rejuvenate the brain. Do you ever aspire to the dominant role?"

"Save the petty power dynamics for your dungeon, psychopomp."

The doctor grins triumphantly. "A trigger point exposed." I begin playing King, telling him I've become consumed with amorous feelings for Nancy Buetow-Detweiler. "A workplace liaison with your married supervisor? You couldn't flirt with disaster any more flagrantly, Lisle. You consider yourself a moral man? A Catholic, no less?"

I shrug. "I know I'm too agreeable. But her husband neglects her, and he's been divorced twice previously, so her crippled coupling begs for an annulment."

"You need to abolish this idea from your mind." He pleads with his hands. "I cannot emphasize strongly enough that this should be your prime takeaway from today's session."

I nod. "I'm not suggesting I wouldn't rather play with my dog, tend my houseplants and drink alcohol. Did you ever try hot cocoa mixed with Merlot?"

"Tell me if Dr. Rohr-Kisslinger understood you correctly. Is this dog still central to your emotional well-being?"

I don't trust the code of counselor confidentiality preventing King from passing information to one authority or another. "My beloved dog Gus died when I was a kid," I relate. "The local archbishop visited our parish shortly thereafter, and as he was circulating, I stopped him and asked if I'd find my dog again in heaven. The bishop smiled condescendingly, patted me on the head and said, 'Don't worry about dogs. Instead, pray for the starving children of the world.' I was a painfully timid kid, but as he turned away, the passion welled up in me and I snapped, 'What the *hell* kind of answer is that?' He looked askance at me with a twinge of indignation, and he moved on. His cassock-clad, cope-clutching attendant clipped me upside the temple. 'You don't talk to His Excellency like that!' he scolded." Nothing like this incident ever occurred, but I'm positive that the intellectual hack Bright Art the Brain Fart will scarf up the episode like a Schaum torte, and it'll draw his attention away from Maynard.

"He was undoubtedly trying to instill some emotional maturity in you by way of empathy for your fellow man." King smiles condescendingly. "Looking back, do you believe he should've lied to humor you?" He grimaces. "You never really gave a rip about the starving children in the world?"

"I believe in putting my own house in order first. I'll make sure the personal reason I have to cherish the world is provided for before I go out and save the rest of it."

"Do you find that thoughtlessness, mindlessness, that is, keeping conscientiously clueless, pays benefits in shame avoidance?"

I grunt fervently. "Let's burrow far beneath the virtue-signaling, Doc, for a reality check. I should forsake those beings who gave me nearly unconditional devotion and essentially dedicated their lives to me in favor of someone who's closer to me genetically and who wants my material support but would find me as mutually intolerable on an everyday basis as I'd find them?"

"How ironic to employ the expression 'reality check' on this issue." He steeples his hands. "If I'm hearing you correctly, you're suggesting you're as good with animals as you are bad with people."

"It's unfortunate that people generally don't have as fully developed a concept of purpose, of what's expected of them, of what's essential and meaningful, as animals do."

King scoffs. "What a childish Weltanschauung. A willingness to accept things the way they are defines maturity."

"To accept things the way you figure they are?" I lean forward. "I think it's precious that you respect yourself enough to see your opinion as obviously valid."

"Your frivolous digressions disintegrate into absurdities." The doctor rises. "You scrupulously avoid guilt trips by taking tortuous excursions into magical thinking. The idea that a being dead for ages could reconstitute and be the same entity is woefully irrational."

I stand. "There's an elite class of people where I work who think like that. They can't believe anything could exist that they couldn't deduce how to dissect. Maybe your body is less a sum of its parts than an avatar for your total being."

"Take a being and radically modify it." The liberator reseats himself. "Amplify a human's intellectual and sensory capacity but remove their interest in carnality, give them wings or the ability to pass through solid surfaces, and you're trying to tell me that this will be the same consciousness as before alteration?"

"Isn't your therapy transformative?" I drop back into my chair. "In the rare instances it actually changes someone, isn't that metamorphosis a fundamentally better version of the same person that started therapy with you?"

King pouts. His questions and comments become curt and he remains morose for the remainder of our session.

When I return to work, Sandee assigns me a project to reproduce the results of a series of experiments measuring the ability of resveratrol to directly activate longevity-boosting sirtuins. "Today Nancy is going to announce an initiative," she expounds, "to promote workforce flexibility for the sake of resource optimization and to keep techs from getting bored with any particular task." When my colleagues and I rise to tramp upstairs for the joint huddle five minutes before the appointed hour, Sandee detains me with pedantry about caloric restriction. The rest of the team proceeds without me. Ultimately, Sandee hands me a large envelope. "Want to first take this up to N.B.D.'s office, Lisle?"

Nancy's door is ajar. I knock and enter. "Please shut it behind you and sit down." The Duchess furrows her brow as I hand her the envelope and seat myself on the receiving-end of her desk. "Hello, Lisle." She assesses me as if I'm lying in the I.C.U. and she's obliged to put in an official appearance.

"I'll have whatever you're drinking," I try to defuse the tangible tension.

Nancy folds her hands and leans forward. "I'm afraid you may need one after you hear what I have to say."

My survival mechanism manifests itself as a cocked eyebrow. "Then make it a double?"

She stiffens her neck. "It's well-known that the past year for us at Ideal Allele was disappointing. We've been embroiled in disputes regarding our intellectual property rights and have incurred significantly stark losses. Though we have several patent applications pending and a pipeline full of promising candidates, the company has only one product on the market and limited instruments by which to generate revenue. Therefore, in order to conserve sufficient capital to fund our operations for the next twelve months, we're compelled for the first time in the firm's 13-year history to reduce payroll. We're going to lay off ten employees, including three research associates from the Healthpath team and three from the Healthspan team. The W.T.P. rating system we use for technicians, as you yourself have pointed out, can be somewhat arbitrary, and has formally never been anything but advisory. So we've decided that the most equitable method by which to declare departmental surplus is by least seniority, meaning those affected on the Healthspan team will be: Leah, Spencer and you. I like to think it's a testament to what a great place this is to work that you have seven years of service and you're third from the bottom in seniority."

"Techs who don't thrive here generally don't stick around for more than two or three years," I observe. "There must've been at least two dozen of those since I started."

"Even more in Healthpath," she affirms. "All three of the bottom people in their group have less seniority than you. We're going to combine the teams, so you'll be the first tech eligible to be recalled."

I can't let the Duchess off with no challenge. "Sleepy Gene has only been slumping around for five years," I mention.

"Gene Napolitano does have less seniority than you, but as senior research associate he's covered under a separate title at a different pay grade, so he has immunity to this force reduction." She forces a diplomatic smile. "I want to make sure you understand we're not picking favorites, and it's nothing personal. Your job performance is satisfactory. And I can hardly express how much I hate to lose Spencer's smarts; he's such a talented analyst, and he brings so much positive energy to the floor."

I nod. "Positivity is the thing to bring to inquiry."

Nancy sighs. "Of course, Sandee and I are heartsick about Leah as well. She's so measured, such a good listener and so likable. She has a young child and no supplementary income source. Her 'out' designation made Lillian in H.R. cry."

I rub my hands together. "Rank compassion is commendable. Lillian's leaky faucet is especially remarkable for someone cryonic."

"Do expect to be recalled at some point." Nancy reasserts her lofty bearing. "It may be only a matter of weeks. I recognize you'll be exploring other opportunities, and I really hate to risk losing you. Aaron is working diligently to raise additional funding. We have grant applications pending and are weighing a possible collaboration agreement. If I might make a recommendation, Lisle, this could be a perfect occasion to address your sensitivity training."

"I actually had a session this morning." I flash a deferential smile. "That's why I was away for two hours."

"Great, then you can focus on further growth and development of your personal skill set." Nancy opens the envelope filled with helpful guides to unemployment issues and has me sign a couple of documents that would make it difficult to sue the company. She thanks me for my service and my gracious attitude toward its cessation and sends me packing. As soon as I emerge from her office, a security guard stationed outside the door heads down the hallway toward the conference room, presumably to summon the next body to be downsized.

The Duchess offered me the rest of the workday to clean out my workspace so I could condole with other team members at the conclusion of their joint huddle, but I complete my evacuation in less than fifteen minutes. I don't need to hear Spencer squawk, and I'm anxious to leave the premises behind. I'll probably send Kelly a message from beyond in the next few days. As I toss my two boxes of work paraphernalia into the back of the Yukon, I realize that I neglected to turn in my ID badge. If Anele really wants it, they can solicit it. Far from being depressed or demoralized, I feel invigorated and indeed liberated. I speed home to collect a few essential items and head up to Pleasant Lake. One such item will be a gift for Spaatz in the form of my spare burner phone. I don't know why I didn't think of providing him with a convenient communication device the last time I visited. My criminal skill set is in further need of growth and development.

I turn onto my street to find a red tape stretched around the perimeter of my property and a team of space commandos tearing my residence apart again. This time their biohazard suits are blue. I angrily hop out of the Yukon and duck under the red tape. "Yes, blue is far less bilious!"

Mr. Lancaster comes storming out of his front door. "What is going on over there? It sounded like gunshots before!"

A brawny man in an N100 mask and a baseball cap saunters toward the perimeter. "The investigation is ongoing," he advises Lancaster. "There is no immediate threat to the surrounding area." A grey shirt, grey tie and grey suit lapels are visible beneath his partially open blue duty jacket. He veers toward me. "Lisle Amonor?" He produces a document from his pouch and deposits it in my hands. "We've been waiting to meet you." The document is a search warrant. "Now let's meet your dog."

Three space cowboys perform field tests on areas of interest around my house. Another emerges as if on cue from my front door handling a German shepherd on a harness. I point to the working canine. "It looks like you have your own."

He hisses. "If that animal has to be terminated for exposure, you can claim prime responsibility. That'll include financial responsibility."

I nod. "They've sent me an old softy, huh?"

He exhibits a subtle scowl. "You work at a lab so you must understand as well as anyone the critical health hazard that harboring an animal carrying a potentially lethal, transmissible pathogen poses to society. We'll ask you politely once more to turn over your dog so a scientific determination can be made about his level of infection."

I notice my two burner phones atop my laptop in the small pile of personal possessions on the front porch. "The only thing around here that's infectious, commandant, is my sick sense of humor."

The grey man notices Lancaster still watching intently at the red tape. "Please return inside the safety of your own home, sir." He turns back to me. "We might make more progress with a private conversation." He pats me on the shoulder. "A reasonable, amiable chat." He summons a large space cowboy. "Greg!" He points at the beige pickup truck across the street. The grey man takes my sleeve between his thumb and forefinger and gently tugs me toward the truck. Greg produces a pair of biohazard bags and saunters to the red tape. He removes his gloves and head bubble while standing in one of the bags and peels off his coveralls.

"Am I under arrest?" I snarl.

The grey man grimaces. "Not yet, Lisle, but you're working toward it."

Greg catches up with us beside the truck wearing an N100 mask. "I like the color," I admire the vehicle. "It's the same earth tone as the automated gene sequencers we have at work." The windows are open and reflective strips accent the tops of the box panels.

The grey man pushes his credentials into my face. "I'm Erik Coyle of the U.S. Marshals Service and this is Dr. Greg Slimak of the Centers for Disease Control and Prevention Epidemic Intel Service."

I turn to Slimak. "You get to hang with Kenower? You like to be called 'Gort'?"

The two men convey me into the rear seat row of the cab between them. "This is cozier than your breezy reefer," I volunteer, "although it's good for us all I keep trim."

"I've observed your initial interview with D.H.S. and reviewed the transcript." Coyle extracts several pages of documents from his pouch. "Some of your responses aren't congruous, Lisle."

"What kind of a lab do you work at?" Slimak jostles me.

"It's not your serendipity jab lab." I won't mention my layoff. "It's an ambitious molecular lab, working with genes and proteins, cells and organelles, some intact organisms. We mostly test how much structural integrity these entities maintain under pressure, the amplification of complexity."

Coyle cringes. "You must be a whiz at that last part." He

offers a wry grin. "You're still going to maintain that your dog is dead, Lisle? That he was struck by a train?"

I hang my head. "I'm going to maintain what happened."

Coyle adjusts his mask. "Even though investigative teams found no footprints in the snow. They found no body parts, no blood, no DNA near the area you claimed to have found the dog's severed hindquarters." He subtly leans into me. "You profess that you wandered onto the train tracks around three in the afternoon in full daylight not seeing, hearing or feeling the vibrations of an oncoming freight train. Neither you nor anything like a dog appear on any of the several surveillance cameras or were seen by anyone in the area in question." He scoffs. "What's the dog's name again?"

"Maynard," I mutter.

"Maynard." He shivers. "You're pretty fond of Maynard?" He nods with me. "And yet, as soon as you discovered the dog's remains, you turned around and went off to work." He expels an exasperated breath. "I'd expect you to be kind of upset, as would anyone who gave a damn about their pet."

"One second he's there-" I focus on what's at stake. "I walked up the tracks calling his name. I found- So raw red. I placed my hands on his legs. I walked up the tracks some more. Calling his name softly. I stopped and turned back. I didn't want to see- Just pure pain. I drove around aimlessly for a long time. Such a fuck-up, such a loser. House too empty. So alone. Nowhere else to go."

Slimak applauds. "I'm ashamed that someone who pays enough attention to detail to work at a research lab can't come up with anything more plausible than that." He eyes me incredulously. "Even in that pack of nonsense, you missed incidentals that might've strengthened your claim, like you were wearing earbuds, high on some controlled substance."

"Anything like that you neglected to mention?" Coyle pats my knee. "You just suddenly found yourself in shock?" He pauses but I don't respond.

"A telltale symptom of this heated up Capno infection is cognitive problems," Slimak relates. "Trouble remembering. Your immune system overreacts causing neuro-inflammation and tissue damage resulting in a brain fog. Maybe we need to check your cerebrospinal fluid for elevated levels of immune proteins to see if that's what's going on with you?"

I hiss. "My problem, epidemer, is I remember too well. I don't need to submit to any more worthless invasive procedures."

"See, Lisle, your major problem is this." Coyle slaps several pages of computer printout into my lap.

I look down and see a sheet with a lot of numbers, mostly zeroes. "I have no idea what this is supposed to be."

"I'm going to tell you what it is," the marshal snaps. "Read it in detail. You might've noticed the posts along the tracks. There are surveillance checkpoints that record train traffic. This is that record. One Canadian Pacific freight train was the only train that passed along that stretch that afternoon. And it was two hours earlier than you said your interaction was. How do you account for that?" He sneers as I remain silent. "And the train was southbound, not northbound as you claim. Allowing that you were disoriented, you've been unsettled and confused, a shell of yourself, let's try to re-create the event. Think back carefully before you answer. Was it earlier in the day? The train was actually southbound, heading toward Juneau Boulevard, wasn't it?"

If I learned anything from my skirmishes with Kisslinger, any deviation from my original account will create a crack in my defense wall subject to being ripped open wider and wider. "I wouldn't be mistaken about this."

"Every train has a headlight cam, and we've watched the video from all eleven trains that passed along Village Park on the Sunday in question, the Saturday before and the Monday after." Coyle leans in. "We've slowed it down. Nobody like you shows up anywhere. Again, Lisle, your tracks are nowhere to be found. There's no trace evidence. We've exhausted a lot of time, effort and resources in this." He hisses. "Let's not strain our relations further insulting each other's intelligence, Lisle, okay?"

I suspect that the marshal's records are spurious. "We came up the ballast to the tracks at a sharp angle, just as the engine passed. Maybe traffic noise from North Avenue dampened my perception of its approach. Maybe there was a mechanical failure with the electric eyes. Then there was more snow, and it got colder and iced over. Ask the coyotes and crows what they know about it." I fix my gaze on the academic. "I can only give you the data set, prosector. I can't explain the 'why' and the 'how.'"

"Maybe it was a ghost train," Gort contributes.

"But we know you're not a ghost, Lisle, and we can demonstrate it." Coyle reaches into his document pouch and produces a grainy photo of the Yukon. "Here we have highway cam video of you traveling in Oshkosh County Sunday morning. Where did you go?"

I notice "01-19" in the numerical label beneath the shot, which suggests it may have been captured on Monday. "I only remember driving up there Monday morning. But driving nowhere has been my pastime even before- I do it a lot. In the hours after losing Maynard, I just happened to go that way toward Oshkosh." I slap Coyle's papers onto his document pouch. "Going to pull some bamboo shoots out of there next, E.C.?"

Coyle shivers. "You just wandered way up north and came right back. Where did you turn around?"

"Omro, I guess," I counter crisply with the first city I reach traveling west on Highway 21.

"You're driving nowhere fast now, Lisle," the marshal advises. "You have no other option but to cooperate. I don't know if this is some desperate, misguided crusade to cling to your sick dog, or if you get stimulated messing with the big, bad government, or you hate humanity that much. But whatever your twisted motivation, you cannot be allowed to put the world community at risk."

"Your situation is spiraling out of control, like the infection," the health officer adds. "If you function in a scientific environment, you're familiar with the protocol of having to sacrifice animals for a higher purpose. Your dog's situation must be resolved; it cannot fester as a clear and present danger any longer. It's not hyperbole to suggest that a shitload of human suffering hangs in the balance!"

I nod. "Getting pounded with this altruism trope makes me think about all of the people in my life who've disappointed me, ridiculed me for things beyond my control and cast me aside like some vile debris." If I won't fight to the bitter end for the one who loves me, what is left worth fighting for? I slap my hand on Coyle's knee. "Instead of you guys, why didn't they send me a team of wind-up, blow-dried, manicured little autocratic man-dolls like they seem to have running the FBI these days?"

"You'll get them next." Coyle emits an exasperated breath. "Or something better. Trust me, Lisle, when the Hazardous Materials Response Unit takes over your case, you're going to wish they'd just work on you with bamboo shoots. Once you fail their polygraph, they'll have reason to believe you're harboring Maynard, and someone is going to sit on you until you quit jerking them around. You understand what that means? You're going to forfeit your right to privacy. There's always going to be someone watching you, listening to you, following you. Want to live like that? No matter where you have the dog stashed, you're not going to be able to see him. You're never going to be able to enjoy any time with him again. Why not save yourself that agony, and possibly save countless lives in the process? Come on, Lisle, it's time to let go."

"Wait and see how quick I sue you for harassment," I snarl.

Coyle and Slimak both snicker sardonically. "You're a douche, Lisle," the marshal explains. "Whatever stupid game you think you're playing, you can't win. We're aware that you acquired, apparently inherited, a fair amount of financial assets. The government employs hosts of lawyers who specialize in filing motions and injunctions for the purpose of bleeding opponents dry with legal fees. And your assets may simply be frozen, so you'll be unable to touch your money for years. Yep, they'll investigate every facet of your life. Maybe Lisle isn't so squeaky clean in other areas either."

I allow my teeth to chatter. "It sounds like you'll be holding yourself a regular recom recon, huh, Marshal Law? You should watch the news instead of just me. I see the public mood turning harder against this campaign every day. There are revolts all over the place-"

"The optics are why we've slow-walked you to this point!" Coyle snaps. "This is a campaign to prevent misery and save lives, dog lives as well as human, if you're more moved by those. You're in serious, serious trouble, Lisle, if you continue to lie and impede this investigation." I don't respond. "While you're thinking about it, who knows how many other people or dogs Maynard is going to infect?"

"How would you like us to put every house within a two-block radius under a shelter-in-place order?" Slimak chimes in. "We can declare a biohazard and condemn every property within a half-block area. You think your neighbors scorn you now? You'll see how they really feel when you've ruined them financially and they express their gratitude with a firebomb through your window at three a.m." He stretches his arms back and tugs lightly on my hair. "You're a fly that's about to get swatted. Be smart and save yourself while you still can."

"Under the Patriot Act, anyone who knowingly possesses any biological agent, toxin or delivery system is subject to imprisonment of up to ten years." The marshal blows his steamy breath in my face. "By harboring your exposed dog, you qualify for exactly that. We know you're not really such a bad guy, Lisle. Yet we have no choice but to declare you a bioweaponeer, a domestic terrorist. You think Maynard will still be around when you get out?"

"*He's not around now!!*" I slam my hands into the seats in front of us. "Haven't I suffered enough? I have nothing more to offer you sadistic pricks!"

"Where's the damned dog?" Coyle demands.

"How many times," I utter, "do I have to tell you bubbleheads?"

Slimak pats my forearm. "Look, Amonor, we can cut some deal by which he's put in a special quarantine program for several months. You have the extra money to pay for it, and we'll pull some strings for you. And then you're allowed to go on with your life."

I don't believe for an instant that the offer is genuine. Or that Maynard could safely navigate such a situation. I begin hyperventilating and force a laughing jag. My laughter grows hysterical, and I convert the emotion to a crying jag.

"Zip it!" Slimak orders. "Get a grip!"

I begin twitching and throwing soft elbows. Coyle's hands become fists, and I anticipate a sharp rebuke in the face, but he smiles wryly and pats me on the shoulder. "You're being a fool and a loser, but you've made your decision, Lisle. No one is going to help you now."

Slimak opens his door and scowls at me. "You remain in this vehicle until further notice. We'll advise you when our investigation is complete." He jumps out.

"A giant thank you to you, too, Gort," I reply.

Coyle handcuffs my wrists behind my back. He gets out of the pickup truck and gets back in. He starts the motor, turns on the heater and closes the windows. "I hypothesize you're holding me now?"

"That determination is being made." He gets out of the pickup again. "Sit still." He slams the door and marches back onto my property and into my house. He returns intermittently and asks if I'd care to revise any of my statements. I disappoint him every time.

Shortly before six o'clock, Coyle uncuffs me and escorts me inside my house for a supervised supper and bathroom break. I try to ignore the general commotion. I cook a medium frozen pizza. I offer to fix a large one for the entire investigative team, hoping that my hospitality might result in less wreckage, but they decline. When I've consumed my meal and recuperated sufficiently, the marshal directs me to return outside and remain in my own parked vehicle. I detect a faint scent of ammonia and other indicators that the interior has been scoured. However, nothing seems to have been confiscated. About an hour later, the investigative team emerges from my front door and tosses the items they piled on the porch into a trash bag.

Coyle approaches the Yukon and shines a flashlight into my eyes. I open the driver's door. "We're finished here for the time being, so you can return inside your residence." He flips his card into my lap. "Wise up, Amonor." He follows the rest of the investigative team in the second of two black minivans, and they speed away. The beige R1T pickup truck remains on the street unoccupied.

It's almost nine o'clock when I regain access to my abode. I feel extremely violated, and I subject every square foot of the dwelling to several rounds of inspection. The new framed photo of Maynard in the hallway has been turned crooked, but at least this time the rummagers left it hanging on its nail. The two rooms that are the most jumbled are the study and the sauna. Books and other objects litter the floor of the former, and the latter is ripped board from board, with the Nile crocodile Companion Piece on its back in a twisted heap beneath bench planks. I straighten Maynard's picture. I return outside and bring the Yukon into my garage. I'm positive there's someone close-by ready to hop into the beige pickup should I try to venture anywhere at this late hour.

I'm too agitated to sleep, so I head downstairs and angrily begin reconstruction of excruciation station. I restore the interlocking zip tiles of the gym floor to their approximate original position. I flip the bench press onto its legs and tighten some loose bolts. I remove bent nails, broken screws and spent anchors from the sauna lumber. I'm able to salvage most of the studs, and I organize neat piles of bench planks and wall boards. I test the infrared heater. The underbelly of the Companion Piece is cut open to expose some framework and the guts of its electrical circuitry. Did they fear that Maynard might be hiding inside or that the crocobot might've eaten him? I turn the croc over and find two suspicious holes between the eyes and another at the junction of the left forelimb and trunk. I find two holes in the floorboards and two matching pits in the concrete below. I scrutinize the area and find another gouge in the basement floor. The commandos shot my Companion Piece! I feel even more violated, but as I continue tidying up into the night, I'm equally infuriated by how my persecutors have forced me to turn my life into one humongous lie.

I AWAKEN AT dawn, having notched close to two hours of sleep. I gaze out of my picture window and find the street empty. I stuff two protein shakes and a change of clothes into my gym bag. I'm operating on a one-item agenda of getting up to Pleasant Lake as soon as possible. I venture out to the garage and find the door open a crack. I always close it tight, and I'm pretty sure last night was no exception. I toss my bag onto the front passenger's seat of the Yukon and return inside the house. I scramble upstairs and peer out of the attic peephole. I spot the beige pickup truck with its distinctive strips of reflective tape on the corner of my block. I take a shower and consider how to proceed. I get dressed and retire to the kitchen to fix myself some bean soup and coffee. I shuffle back to the living room peeling a tangerine. The beige R1T is parked in front of my house. I throw open my front door and tramp out to the vehicle. A black man with a shaved head is seated in the driver's seat. He smiles and waves. I take a juicy bite of my fruit. He lowers the passenger's window. "Are you planning to harass me all day, officer? Would you like some coffee? I pledge to hold the lye."

"That's a stirring idea." He starts his motor. "I could go for a bear claw as well." He takes off, and the truck disappears around the corner.

I retrieve my two boxes of personal workspace items from the Yukon and return inside to play the waiting game. I'll stay put until the bank opens in an hour and then withdraw sufficient earnest money to wave under Bustelich's nose. I peruse designs for an impenetrable residential secure room on my old work laptop as I finish my breakfast.

I finish restoring most of the ground floor of my home to its pre-invasion condition. I turn on the TV and drop into my low-rider chair. It's something akin to miserable not having Maynard beside me. Serge Kenower of the CDC is on the screen. He admits that the gold standard test to verify the presence of the super-Capno pathogen "frequently" requires a postmortem but promises that a "less-intrusive" method is imminent. I get up and gaze out the picture window. I spot no sign of any surveillance detail and proceed to the bank. I initiate the withdrawal of twenty thousand dollars in cash. After a lengthy delay, I'm permitted to pocket my money.

I drive to a home improvement center, and I catch a glimpse of a beige pickup tailing me. I resolve to rebuild my sauna as a fortress that doubles as a safe room able to withstand a combat onslaught. I cannot believe that a court would permit another raid on my residence, but if one occurs, those conducting the breach will have to work like mad dervishes to trash the place. I'm going to expand the dimensions of the secure sauna to 12 X 8 by reducing the adjacent excruciation station floor space. Specifically, I'll eliminate most of the stretching area – I'm naturally supple – and separate the sauna from the outside wall of the basement. The wooden studs are not only going to be placed closer together but reinforced by a steel frame inside them.

I arrive at the D.I.Y. superstore eager to acquire applicable building supplies. However, I find the staff blatantly unhelpful so I purchase only a few packages of fasteners. I spot the beige pickup again, and I return home.

I venture downstairs and complete the cleanup of the area. I inspect last night's sauna renovations and weigh upgrade schemes. I'm going to situate a bench in front of the door. The more inconvenient the room is to enter, the more inconvenient it should be to breach. To enter the sauna, one will need to either vault the bench or squeeze through the narrow gap between the back of the bench and the wall. I return upstairs and start watering plants. Even the teddy bear cholla is too dry. I wonder whether Spaatz tried calling me at work this week and I become overwhelmed with anxiety. I have to get up to Pleasant Lake.

I march out to the Yukon and travel to Bruce Neichi's strip mall. I buy two more burner phones at the Zhen Dianxin store. I cruise around the back lot, call Handy Andy and leave an urgent request for assistance. I honestly contemplate strolling around to the front lot and stealing the Charger. My old car fob conveniently rests in my hip pocket. I wander to the front of the mall. I purchase junk food orders from two fast food restaurants. I don't spot any surveillance detail but I strongly sense I'm being observed. I return to the Yukon and eat my lunch. Unbearably restless, I call Andy again. She answers but laments that she's too busy to rescue me today. I whine fiercely, and she agrees to meet me at three o'clock behind the loading dock at another home improvement center in West Allis.

I arrive at the D.I.Y. superstore two hours early. I venture inside and order all of the building supplies I'll need to fortify my sauna. The walls will be attached to the concrete floor with heavy-duty sleeve anchors designed to adamantly resist if removal is attempted. The frame will be staggered studs and the top and sides of the room will be wrapped with thick steel mesh. The crown jewel of the project is to be the security door, and I'd hate to be the shoulder or heel of a man who tries to break through it with sheer physical force. Consisting of two hickory slabs with a fiberglass armor plate sandwiched in between, the door will sit in a steel frame and employ six deadbolts. And just in case some intrepid surge is able to penetrate that, I'm installing my current mahogany door inside of it. If nothing else, the room will serve as the ideal storm shelter should a particularly vicious tornado wend its way down my street.

The store guarantees delivery of my custom construction materials within three days. As an appetizer, I order two dozen more framing studs for immediate pick-up, which also buys me access to the loading dock area behind the store. I return to the Yukon and wait for Andy.

The pink *STRAIGHT A's Assertive Measures* van appears

twenty minutes early and rolls straight to the lumber yard gate leading to the loading dock. Andy gains entrance and swings around the back of the building. I wait five minutes and head to the gate. I present my lumber order to the attendant and advance. I find Andy parked beside the court retaining wall, standing outside her idling vehicle in oversized aviators talking on her cell phone. I pull up behind her and jump out of the Yukon.

"Thanks for seeing me." I produce a thin roll of $100 bills. "After the feds raided my house again yesterday, I've spent most of today working to reverse the ransacking. I know they're following me, and I'm guessing they've planted another tracking device on the SUV." I rap the idling Yukon.

"Screw you, Rudy." Andy terminates her call and evaluates me. "What are you into anyway? Pot, shrooms, tryp?" She scoffs. "I don't want to know."

"I think they're trying to use me to catch up with Gayle Spaatz," I submit. "Some tax problem, I presume."

"I've always had a sweet spot for Spaatz," Andy confides. "He's mostly seemed kind of lost." She assesses the Yukon. "I don't have a lot of time. I should be able to transfer the jamming device on my van to an OBD port on your vehicle without too much fuss. You realize, of course, you'll be generating a wave bubble that's not strictly legal."

I sweep my hands over her van. "How would you like to save yourself any fuss for the present? Would you switch vehicles with me for the day? You can take the Yukon and install a jammer in it at your convenience."

A sly smile crosses her lips. "You're really banging to beat the heat?" She walks around the SUV and opens the liftgate. "The fact is I could use a vehicle like this tomorrow. How about if I bring it back by your house on Saturday morning?"

"It's a deal." I peel five bills off my roll. "Five cenotes up front enough?"

"Let's think about this." Andy snatches my cash. "Give me your coat." She pulls down her bib overalls and removes her hoodie. We exchange outerwear and she places her aviators over my nose. "Stay low in the cockpit."

Andy's hoodie proves to be an oppressively tight fit as I help her transfer her creeper and tools to the Yukon, but we swiftly get the requisite items resituated. I open the driver's door of the pink van and hand her my key fob. "I might have another job for you. Of a more exotic variety. Would you be interested in renting a cabin for me under your name? Or would Rudy? I'd pay you handsomely."

She eyes me suspiciously, and for a moment I fear she's going to nix the vehicle swap. "That sounds like something up Rudy's alley. He's going to be heading down Nawlins way so he might be interested in some extra waddage. I'll check with him."

I climb into the *STRAIGHT A's* van and plunk my gym bag onto the passenger's seat. "Thanks, Andy, I really appreciate your cooperation." I pass her tow sack through the open driver's window.

"You go give Spaatz cover, and I'll bring your hardened Yukon back over to your house Saturday morning." She withdraws her key fob from the tow sack and tosses it to me.

I salute her, pull up to the dock and get my lumber loaded.

At the exit gate, I scan the parking lot for the beige pickup or other likely surveillance vehicles but recognize none. I rumble out of the parking lot in the *STRAIGHT A's* van, head east and hop on Highway 41 to head north toward Pleasant Lake.

I'm confident I'm not being followed. The interior of Andy's van appears tidy, although it reeks of cigarette smoke. She has a laminated sign on the glovebox that says *SOVEREIGN CITIZEN OF THE U.S.A.* The heater doesn't work particularly well, and I finally resolve it's too cold to keep the window partially open.

I take a short detour to West Bend to fill the gas tank, and I discover that the vehicle has no license plates. I can't believe I overlooked a detail that could so easily lead to a brush with the authorities. Maybe I'll make use of Spaatz's mock license plates after all, but I have to make it up to the lake first. I stop at an outdoor outfitter store and purchase a Sherpa-lined, hooded cragsman's jacket along with insulated work gloves.

Sweating in my new cold weather gear, I continue my journey up Highway 41 and exit at Oshkosh without incident. I squint through Andy's tinted glasses into the setting sun as I roll west on Highway 21. The area appears to have recently received light flurries. I intend to beg Spaatz to keep Maynard for just a few more days. If he won't, I'll stay up in these parts until I've found an alternative safe house to rent. I spot a couple of candidates as I pass through the snow-blanketed streets of Redgranite. I'll try to coax Andy to bring Rudy up to the hinterlands. If she refuses, I'll have to figure out another ID workaround. Being laid off gives me the luxury of time.

I wonder if any government entity put pressure on Anele to cut me loose.

I spot a police cruiser three vehicles behind me as I near my destination. I turn off the main drag, hoping the cop doesn't follow and pull me over. He continues west on 21. I park on a slick side road, gulp down a protein shake and wait for about 15 minutes.

The sun has set by the time I reach Coloma, and I travel the final five miles in gathering gloom. I'm so anxious to see Maynard and soothe Gayle that I overshoot the Bustelich cabin property and pull into the Ryscavage driveway. I hop out of the van and trot to the side door of the cottage. The inside door is partway open. I surmise the boys are out back, but I knock twice and venture inside anyway.

"Gayle?" I step into the parlor and spot what looks like a dark sweater or towel bunched up on the floor. I detect slight movement, and a bolt of sheer horror pierces me. I rush forward and crumple to my knees. "Oh, God, no!" Maynard lies on his side softly gasping. His eyes are glassy. "Please, no!" A stream of blood issues from his nose. There's a slight tremor in his rear leg. "No, no, my God, no!" He seems to recognize me and his tail twitches. I remove my gloves, cradle him in my arms and rub the side of his head. He chokes and gurgles. I pull him further into my chest. I relax my hold and his head slumps lifelessly over my arm. A cascade of blood flows from his mouth. His eyes stare blankly. Hot tears stream down my face onto his neck. He has a cut over his left eye. His belly is swollen, and it feels as though he has broken ribs. I rock back and forth with him in my arms. "Maynard, oh, my boy." I lay his body gently on the rug and run my hands over him softly. "Oh, my boy, my pal, my very best pal." I feel the heavy atmosphere of the room pressing on me, the walls closing in, crushing me.

The door swings open, and I stagger to my feet, turning in a fog of agony and rage to demand an account of what happened to my dog. John Bustelich steps into the parlor carrying his braided rope wound in loops. He wears a thick green flannel vest and hip waders. His right hand is bloody with puncture wounds. "*You!!*" he roars. He rushes at me, extending a taut rope segment. I lunge and throw a wild elbow at his head as he reaches me, our knees colliding solidly. I'm able to hold two fingers between his rope and my windpipe as he draws the loop tight around my neck. I rake the fingers of my free hand across his face and gouge his eye with my thumb. He spits and turns his dark red face toward my restricted hand, tucks his chin and begins butting my face with the side of his massive cranium, as he applies further pressure on the rope. He directs another knee me at my groin but strikes mostly thigh. I claw his ear, club his temple, spear his neck, gouge his eye again and yank the hair on the back of his head.

We twist sideways. I wedge the fingers of my free hand against his throat, and he releases his noose. He clutches my wrists and sinks his teeth into my chin. I thrust my knee into his groin, and he loses his tooth-hold. He swings me around but I'm able to force an extra pivot before we hit the floor, and I land on top of him. My forearm slams his temple before he rolls us over so he's on top of me. I grasp his hair in one hand so he can't rise to a full mount, and I try to shield my face with my other forearm as he rains short blows on the sides of my head. I try to throw him off with a bridge but cannot and I lose my hold on his hair. He hammers both of my cheekbones, and the blood sprays as he smashes my nose. He sweeps his fist outward and rises to wallop me but slams the back of his head against the bottom edge of the oak tabletop. I deliver a palm strike to his chin, shove him off me and slide to the side. I crawl and stagger to my feet. He grabs one of my ankles, twists my foot and pulls me back to the rug but I kick him in the face with the bottom of my other foot and break free. I climb back to a standing position and stumble to the wall. I try to clear my vision and catch my breath as blood oozes from my mouth and displaced nose.

I turn to see Bustelich pluck the Welrod pistol off the table and fire a shot past my shoulder. He ejects the shell casing and awkwardly rotates the bolt as he advances. I lunge forward and he points the pistol between my eyes. "Bye, asshole!" He fumbles with the grip safety and the gun doesn't fire. I swipe at the barrel, and I run for the door. A bullet splinters wood of the doorframe beside my head as I push the outer door open.

I run through the snow toward the slope. I hear the dull crack of another shot. I head down the slope toward the lake in the trail of muted footprints beside the icy, slop-covered stairs. I hear another subdued pop and an unintelligible bellow. I stumble, lose my footing and slide farther down the slope. I scramble to my feet, expecting to find Bustelich nearly on top of me. But I can't spot him. I continue surveying the slope as I move gingerly downward. I finally discern his supine bloated form writhing in the snow. I can't tell in the darkness whether he still has the Welrod. Every grain of good sense I possess calls me to keep running. But my passion over Maynard wells up, and I clamber back toward Bustelich. He's clutching his chest and breathing heavily. I still don't see the pistol. I charge the final few steps and kick him in the ribs. He moans. I make a desperate visual search for the gun. I place a foot on his neck, and he suffers a coughing fit. If I spot the weapon, I'll want to shove the barrel into his mouth and pull the trigger.

I take a step back. "Chest tight," Bustelich gasps. "Medic mer-" I stand over him and look up the slope. I try to wish away the slaughter inside the cottage. If I'm not there to look at it, then maybe Maynard isn't dead. In my mind's eye, he licks my face as his tail slaps the davenport, he catches a tennis ball and his nails click against the floor as he brings it back, in so many little ways providing me with refuge from a bleak, dismissive world. But the truth ineluctably reimposes itself without mercy. I painfully attempt to readjust my broken nose. I expect that Spaatz is dead in the cellar.

Bustelich's coughs decrease in frequency. Breathing heavily through my mouth, I begin hauling him back up the slope by his leg. He makes one weak attempt to kick me with his free foot but the strike glances off my shoulder and he makes no further attempt to resist. He paroxysmally holds his chest or his stomach. I survey the surrounding area. Our commotion wasn't noisy, and there's a good chance no one noticed us in the dim twilight. The pain of uphill exertion is exceeded by my stark emotional agony. I continually lose my footing and stop to rest. I purge the notion that Spaatz could be barely alive and bleeding out. The disposition of Bustelich remains my triage priority. I feel as though I've been dragging his bundle of blubber for hours. He rubs his knee, mumbles something about the dog and chuckles. I kick him in the head, and it won't bother me if I've killed him. But he's still breathing as we reach the level ground of the backyard. I drag him across the driveway and observe that the glass in the outer door of the cottage is cracked. I insert a tissue in my nose. I open the door, yank Johnny up the step and back inside. "*Gayle!!*" I call out. I snatch the braided rope. I glance at Maynard and I bind Bustelich tightly.

"Gayle?" I shout. "Gayle?" I proceed to the kitchen counter. I find my old tactical flashlight in one of the drawers and hustle downstairs. "Gayle?"

The door is open and the lights are on in the wine cellar. The room harbors nobody alive or dead. The shock collar lies on the floor along with the remote control a short distance from the iron web. Nothing else seems out of place.

I employ the flashlight to investigate the narrow space behind the wine cellar. A stack of buckets sits right around the corner supporting a cluster of cobwebs. In the dusty area beyond, the furnace and electrical panel protrude from the outside wall while items such as a displaced door and replacement windows are propped against the inner wall. I trudge back upstairs.

Bustelich is unconscious but his breathing doesn't appear to be labored. I return to Maynard. I collapse beside him and cry effusively. I stroke his body gently. He's already cold. The minutes crawl by. Distress churns inside of me. How could Spaatz have let the situation get so far out of control? What the hell happened to him? I finally get up and look out the window. The night is cloudy. I stumble to the bathroom and strain to observe my face in the mirror. Both of my cheeks and my nose are grotesquely swollen and blotches of purplish discoloration ring the slits of my eyes. Blood from my nose has pooled atop the flap of skin torn loose from my chin and trickled down the front of my new coat. I try to resituate the patch of skin on my chin. I insert a fresh tissue in my nose. Every tooth seems to be intact, my uneven bottom row appearing far more stained than the uppers, and my jaw aches terribly.

I step outside to relieve myself, fetch water and ensure that nobody else is close by. I lock both doors when I come back, and I resume my vigil beside Maynard. I hear Bustelich snort and groan. I turn to find his eyes open, assessing me. His face bears several substantial cuts and his right eye is beet red and grotesquely swollen. He opens his mouth but has trouble speaking. "Ha, ah, had series cornry out there, Lloyd," he finally rasps. "Get me medic."

I rise and walk over to him. "Where's Spaatz?" I get a silent gaze. "Where is Gayle Spaatz?"

Bustelich titters. "At the bottom of the lake." He coughs and laughs maniacally. "Fetch me a doc or fetch me a drink."

I crouch beside him. "Exactly what happened here?"

He clears his throat. "Lowell, you need to know what it's like to be propped up on that web." His breathing becomes more rapid. "I'm thirsty! Bring me some water, at least." I don't flinch, and he coughs some more. "I guess your buddy Spaatz, he was afraid, after he killed your mutt. He took off."

"Bullshit!" I spring to my feet and kick Bustelich in the

hip. "You are the dumbest fuck that ever walked the face of the Earth!" I kick him in the ribs. "We could've all walked away from this whole." I want to stomp him to death. "You have bite marks on your hand!" A tear runs down my cheek. "My dog was like my kid."

Bustelich snorts. "There's nothin' in your life that isn't totally pathetic, is there, Amonro?"

I place my full weight on his sore knee. "For once in your stinking life, you're going to tell the total truth, you sack of shit, or I'm going to hop in my vehicle, drive down to Milwaukee, heave a firebomb through your window and shoot your goddamn wife and kids as they come screaming out into the night!"

"Yeah, you motherfucking bitch." He winces. "You cling to your delusions. Spaatz was getting off on putting his little shock collar on your dog and zapping the shit out of him. All that cruelty didn't sit well with me after a while. But he wore his batteries out, and that's how I got loose. Your dog must've thought I was trying to choke him when I took the collar off him, and he bit me." I step back onto the rug. "I don't know what happened. He collapsed. I brought him upstairs to tend to him."

I hold my head for a couple of minutes. Could Maynard actually have succumbed to SC01? I provide a cup of water and press it against Bustelich's lips until he drains it. "More," he demands. I plunk the cup on the table, snatch my flashlight and head back to the wine cellar. Could Johnny's account be rooted in the truth? I examine the shock collar and the remote unit. The collar battery appears to be nearly dead. I slowly move the light over the collar. I drag the collar over the Sherpa lining of my coat. Some tiny Sherpa fibers cling to it. I scrutinize the collar in the light once more. I don't spot a single dog hair. Does that prove anything? I grab a bottle of Merlot and return upstairs.

"My throat is real sore," Johnny alerts me. "I'm cold, and I have to piss."

I display the wine bottle. "We could both use a little Merlot first." A subtle gleam appears in his good eye, the triumph of having hoodwinked another diffident dupe. I smack him across the face with the bottle. "I just verified that you're a fucking liar. So I'm going to punish your family for it, but with elegant restraint." My glower outlasts his smirk. "I'm going to tag along on their Saturday morning trip to the grocery store. You know I work at a lab equipped with all kinds of interesting decomposition devices. We have a caustic compound, a mixture of sulfuric acid and hydrogen peroxide, called piranha punch. It can cause horrific skin burns. Think how much fun we've had over the years joking about my disfigurement. How about if I walk up behind your daughter in the grocery store parking lot and throw a cup of piranha punch in her face? I'm sure you're eager to see her again, so I'll try to get it on video. But better yet, one of the prime areas of research at my lab deals with killing tumors with toxins, and I have access to a venom bank. Snake, arachnid, wasp – we can get anything. A crazy potent marine toxin that comes from the Irukandji jellyfish causes intense abdominal cramps, an overload of stress hormones with a sense of impending doom and high blood pressure, often leading to a fatal brain hemorrhage. Spaatz said you like darts. I have a dart gun. How about if I load some darts-"

"Just shut up!" Bustelich snaps. "All right, Amonor." He shuts his good eye and generates an odd plaintive sound. "If you have any decency-" He shakes his head. "Please leave them out of this."

I crouch beside him again. "The more deceit you throw at me, the worse their chances."

He emits a heavy sigh. "The part I told you about the shock collar batteries is true. I'd felt the current get weak before. Spaatz got off on zapping me, but he was lax about recharging his batteries. He zapped me as he prepared to take me off the web and rope me up to walk me around the room, and I didn't feel much jolt but I pretended I did. I faked a leg cramp, and he freed my feet first. He had the gun tucked in his pants. He went behind the web and uncuffed my left wrist and barred my arm in its rope sleeve, but when he uncuffed my right wrist, I made a grab for the gun. He zapped me, but it had no juice. I got hold of the gun but I dropped it at my feet. He held the rope tight behind me so I couldn't bend far enough to reach it. I kept trying to balance the gun on my foot and pass it up to my right hand. Spaatz finally scrambled around the web and made a dive for the gun, but I kicked him in the face and snatched it. I tried to fire a warning shot at him but I couldn't get the damn thing to shoot. He grabbed my arm, but I kicked him and pistol-whipped him and threw him to the floor. I kept dicking with the gun, and I got it to fire as he got back to his feet. He turned and ran out of the room shrieking."

"Don't stop now." I return to a standing position. "You almost have me believing you."

"I'm giving you the lowdown, Lisle," he insists. "I heard

Spaatz scramble upstairs, and I hold the gun barrel between my teeth as I fight to free myself from the rope. I don't know if he has another gun or what, and I hear him rummaging around, like he's desperately looking for something. I hear a few other clunks and clatters before I finally get loose, and I slowly approach the bottom of the stairs and wait there with gun ready expecting him to appear at the top of the stairs. But instead, I think I hear the front door slam. So I wonder if you or someone else has come in, or what, and I wait longer. I don't hear anything for a time, except it's getting colder, and it seems like a door is open. So I slowly make my way up the stairs pointing the gun ahead of me, still expecting Spazz to jump out at me." He sneers. "You get no more of the pure dope, Amonor, till I get more to drink."

"You don't make any rules," I scoff.

He eyes me intently. "Come on, dude, my throat is raw."

I trudge to the kitchen counter. I'd like to believe that Spaatz put up a more valiant struggle and I suspect that Bustelich dispensed more brutality than his narrative would indicate, but I deduce that the gist of his revised account is reasonably accurate. I pull a corkscrew out of the drawer, open the bottle of Merlot and fill a glass. I return to Bustelich and delicately pour the wine into his mouth. "So you made it to the top of the stairs," I prod.

He takes a series of deep breaths. "And I look outside and get distracted because I can't believe I'm up at Pleasant Lake." He titters. "All this time we were up here, and I'm finally free and I'm about dazed, and all of the sudden the dog jumps out at me." He looks askance at me. "I didn't mean to hurt him bad, Amonor, really. I just kicked him out of the way, but he came right back at me growling and snarling, so I kicked him again. And he came at me again, so I slammed him down on the floor. And I left him and went outside still looking out for Spaatz. I made for our cabin next door to get some real clothes." He groans. "I had to break into my own place and settle for this fishing getup cuz that's all I could find."

I carry the bottle of Merlot to the opposite side of the room and plunk myself into the recliner in front of the flatscreen TV. I have no desire to exact more grisly details of Maynard's fatal beating. "The funny thing is we've been thinking of selling our place for over a year!" Bustelich volunteers. "We weren't using it much." I take a swig of wine. "How about a bathroom break, Amonor?" I take a sip of wine and stare into space. "Going after a wiener dog does nothing for me!" I sip more wine. "I promised you a world of hurt if you didn't let me go, didn't I?" I stare into space. "*Help, anyone!!*" he shrieks. "*I've been kidnapped!! I'm being held against my will!!*" I tape his mouth shut and reseat myself.

Bustelich tires of banging his head after a while and falls asleep or lapses into an episode of dormancy. Every few minutes I look over at Maynard. I don't drink much more wine. After a while, I get up, change the bandage on my nose and inspect the bedrooms. Spaatz's blaze orange backpack, camouflage duffel bag and black travel trolley suitcase are gone. Johnny's gowns are heaped on the cot. Most of Gayle's clothing, including his coat, appears to be missing. A few articles, notably underwear, socks and washcloths, are strewn across the floor. I return to the kitchen. It looks as though some dishes and utensils are missing, but I can't be sure. I surmise that some nonperishable food staples that should be present aren't. Gayle's game player seems to have disappeared. His footlocker, drawings, books, art supplies and novelty items, however, remain scattered about the cabin.

I venture outside shortly after dawn. The world stands in the grip of a surreal stillness. I walk around the van and continue to the front door of the cottage. A series of footprints and two thin ruts in the snow like those a trolley suitcase would make extend from the front porch diagonally across the yard and into the road. The tracks continue toward Coloma. A line of dachshund tracks also run from the front porch, crisscross the yard and return. I head back to the slope behind the cabin and conduct a painstaking search for the Welrod but don't recover it. I return inside and make coffee. I notice that Spaatz's indispensable lucky yellow traveling mug is nowhere to be found.

Bustelich escalates his level of gyrating and moaning on the floor. I indelicately remove the duct tape over his mouth. He pleads for an opportunity to relieve himself, and I drag him into the bathroom, boost him into the miniature tub and pull down his hip waders. After a few minutes, he begins bellowing, so I again seal his mouth with duct tape.

I sit at the table and sip coffee for a couple of hours. I'm not hungry, but I decide I need some nutrition, so I have a bowl of stale cereal with almond milk. I camp beside Maynard's body for a while. I cry over the past and for the future.

I head down to the wine cellar and rummage around in the cabinet drawer. The handcuffs remain locked to the web, and my search for their key proves unsuccessful. I do, however, find the charging cable. I retrieve the shock collar and remote, gather a couple of buckets and a roll of paper towels and head back upstairs. I take the buckets out to the hand pump and draw water. The sky has turned dark, and flurries swirl in the heavy breeze.

I charge the shock collar and remote to full capacity. I return with them, the paper towels and a bucket of water to the bathroom. I suffer a coughing fit. "You have to be the most rancid, foul-smelling thing that ever polluted the biosphere," I congratulate Bustelich. "I can't breathe through my nose, and you still leave me gagging." I fasten the shock collar around his neck and remove the duct tape from his face. He assails me with a string of raspy expletives. "Let's test your garter." I send him a major jolt, and he twitches and moans. "You're not faking again? My old dentist used to say 'Are you feeling this or just anticipating?'" I zap him again, and he emits a subdued screech.

I retrieve my tactical flashlight and return to the bathroom. "I'm going to free your hands, John E. You clean yourself up and then tidy up the tub." I brandish my instrument. "Touch your collar, and I'll turn your lights out." I loosen his wrist bindings, and he extricates his hands and begins indolently wiping up his mess. He begins panting and demands water. I nod. "When all's squeaky clean."

He ceases his activity. "The thing is, Anomor, the shit you're in isn't all that deep yet. I'll have to tell the cops my false imprisonment was mostly Spaatz's doing. If you just let me go, you won't ever have to put up with me again. A good lawyer should get you off with no jail time."

The bathtub drain is clogged, but Bustelich finally completes his task. I help him crawl into the parlor, and I give him the open bottle of Merlot. I place Spaatz's footlocker on the table. I have the vague notion of wanting to seize any object to which Gayle could be connected. I begin gathering his abandoned drawings, art supplies and assorted books and pile them beside the door. I return to the wine cellar with the Rex Wrex tote bag and collect leftover drugs and paraphernalia. I leave the badminton set. When I get back upstairs, Bustelich has nearly untied his feet. I give him a series of long, hard jolts, and he flops onto his side. I grab his feet, flip him onto his belly and securely rebind his ankles and wrists.

I snatch a pair of towels and a sheet from the bedroom. I wrap Maynard's body, take it in my arms and gently lay it in the footlocker. There are bloody stains on the rug where Maynard died. I stare out the window for a long time. The snowfall appears extremely heavy, and I wonder if it'll affect the fishing tournament. I take my pile of Gayle's possessions out to the van. I return inside, shut the lid of the footlocker and carry it out to the van. The snow is already up to my ankles, and I'm grateful to discover a battered shovel in the back of the vehicle. I carry it back into the cabin along with my supply of protein bars. Bustelich frees one of his hands and tugs on his collar. I whack him in the knee with the shovel, and he flings the empty Merlot bottle at me. "Since you're such a pip, I'll fix us some lunch."

I find sufficient ingredients in the depleted kitchen to make a decent shepherd's pie with ground beef. I tie Bustelich in one of the chairs at the oak table as I go about the business of preparing our meal. I fetch another bottle of Jose Rose from the cellar and serve lunch. "What kind of poison did you put in here?" Johnny challenges. I take a few bites of his portion, and we dine. "This is better than most of the shit Spazz gave me," he compliments me. "You might still make someone a good, little wife." He attempts to initiate conversation several times, but I sit silently. "Whatever you think you're planning, Amonor," he croaks, "I will not be hung up on that web again."

After lunch, I secure Bustelich on the rug and carry our leftovers out to dispose of them in the outhouse. The snow shows no sign of diminishing, and I recognize that travel today would prove impossible. I spend an hour shoveling snow off the driveway, but it reaccumulates so quickly I can hardly tell that I'd made any effort.

I return inside the cabin and suffer something akin to a panic attack. I'm overcome with the compulsion to just get the hell out of the cabin and never return. I calm myself pacing, staring blankly out the window and considering how little I have left to lose.

At supper time, I toss Bustelich one of my protein bars. He remains relatively docile throughout the evening, but I have no doubt that he's evaluating me for some kind of weakness or waiting for some opening. It's long after dark when the snow stops falling. I take a pillow from Gayle's bedroom, toss it at Johnny and leave him on the floor for the night. I sleep intermittently.

Shortly before dawn, I get up and check on Bustelich. He has succeeded in loosening the bindings of his feet and attempts to leg-whip me. I fall back against the table and give him a series of solid disciplinary jolts. He demands a toilet break, so I loosen his leg ties further and conduct him to the bathroom. "Wipe me gently, Auntie Lisle," he snarls. He finishes his business, and I deposit him at the table. Our breakfast consists of stale cereal, tepid coffee and soft apples. Johnny chucks an apple and grazes my forehead. I resecure him on the parlor floor and head outside. I begin shoveling knee-deep snow off the driveway. It's a partly cloudy day, not bitter cold, but stout wind blasts drive light drifts over the frozen surface every few minutes. I keep the hood of my cragsman's jacket wrapped tight around my tender face.

Exhausted after about ninety minutes, I hop into the van and start the engine. I clutch the new burner phone I intended to give to Spaatz. I'm not convinced that a caller's location couldn't be traced when using it. I call Andy but she doesn't answer. I clear all of the snow I can reach off the van and return inside the cabin.

I have a nervous tension headache which doesn't improve as Bustelich begins venting his litany of grievances. I tape his mouth shut and make myself hot coffee. A little past eleven, a rumble shakes the cottage. I jump up and look out the front window in time to spot the snowplow cruising past, leaving a wall of high white mounds along the roadside in its wake. I throw on my cragsman's jacket and return to the driveway with my trusty shovel. A few minutes later, the plow passes again on the other side of the road heading east.

I climb into the van and call Andy again. "Is he psychic as well as psychotic?" she opens.

"Saying Rudy?" I infer.

"You!" she scoffs. "I just pulled into your driveway. I

plucked two more tags off your Yukon. I don't see my van. You on the road? You close?"

"I'm afraid I'm stuck up north. It snowed pretty heavily here. What's it like in Waukesha?"

"We got a few inches." She snorts. "Come on, pussy, you're not going to let some snowflakes run your life, are you? I don't mind waiting here till noon."

Her sincerity level is harder to gauge than Delmar's. "There's a fishing tournament scheduled hereabouts this weekend, so the county must be moving heaven and earth to clear the roads. A plow has made an initial pass, so as soon as I can dig out, I'll head in. Until then, why don't we take advantage of your strategic location by having you conduct another thorough bug sweep of my house?"

"Seriously?" she grumbles.

"The cops visited again." I fidget with her oversized aviators.

She sighs. "If you want to spend the money, I'll scour your place from attic to basement."

"You'll find the spare key beneath the plastic trash bag in the receptable outside the back door." It troubles me to allow her free access but desperate times call for a suspension of paranoia. "By the way, Andy, I made the curious discovery that your vehicle sports no license plates."

"Did you get pulled over?" she snickers. "If you're not snotty about it, the cops usually will let you slide."

I refrain from inquiring whether she or Rudy are privy to any recent word from Gayle. The last thing I need is for Vito to call the sheriff and report a missing person. "Okay then, we'll plan to swap vehicles early tomorrow morning."

"Bank on it, mercaptan, or I'll charge you rent on it." Andy terminates the connection, and I put on her glasses.

I clear snow from around the hand pump, fetch a bucket and draw water. I return inside and offer to remove Bustelich's gag and let him drink if he can keep his mouth shut afterward. He guzzles four glasses of water and launches another vituperative rant. I tape his mouth shut again, check his bindings and head back outside with Spaatz's counterfeit license plates. I attach the plates to the van. They don't quite look authentic, but after I've peppered them with snow, I'm willing to bet everything I'll get away with it.

As I shovel snow off the driveway in earnest, the snowplow makes two more passes. I climb the huge snowbank at the approach, start reducing it, and an old pickup truck rolls quietly down the road. In the next few minutes, two more vehicles confirm that the roads are open. I fall off the snowbank. I resume clearing the rest of the driveway. I believe I hear an idling motor in the road a short distance beyond the Bustelich cabin. The heavy squeal of a snow blower follows shortly. I climb back on the snowbank to get a good look, but all I see is a massive, swirling cloud of snow. I tenaciously cut a narrow path all the way into the road and I gasp and stagger backward as I'm accosted by Bustelich in a red lumberjack coat. He eyes me dubiously. "Problem, bud?"

I recognize that I'm fronting Markie or Duckie. "Come closer at your own risk," I reload. "I've been down with Capno; I could still be contagious."

He takes a small step back. "Yeah, you really look gruesome. When my brother gets done with our driveway, maybe we can bring the blower over here and help you out." He points to his cottage. "Someone broke into our cabin." He takes a step forward, and I grunt sympathetically. "You see any shit go down?"

"I've been pretty occupied over here." I adjust the aviators and try to hold my head at an angle that best conceals my facial injuries. "Something get stolen?"

"Why would you say that?" He's a stout man, a bit taller than Johnny.

I shake my head. "Why else would he break in?"

He seems puzzled by the question. "To be an asshole." He places his hands on his hips. "Why do you say 'he'?"

"What's your preferred pronoun?" I take a crowhop and thrust my shovel into the snowbank.

"Name's Doug," he offers. "You over here alone?"

I nod and discard snow. "I'm Rudy." A snow-caked electric blue pickup truck crawls up the Bustelich driveway and parks behind the broken utility trailer. Duckie points to the pink van. "What does this business – Straight A's Assertive – do?"

I intensify my shoveling. "We renovate and conceal safes, build secure spaces, panic rooms and bomb shelters. We design household booby traps."

"Booby traps?" He emits a raucous chuckle. "We might be able to use something like that, or a bomb shelter. What's your contact info?"

"You can get it off the web." I cough and monitor him over my shoulder. "But the owner has been turning down business because of our backlog."

"Hey!" He points his finger at me. "There's something not quite right about you."

"Touche." The temptation to cold-cock this fathead with the shovel and run over him with the van besieges me.

"Our nephew came up here recently and found tire tracks in our driveway," Duckie volunteers. "Someone told him they'd seen an SUV over here a couple times, like an Escalade or a Yukon."

I shrug. "Install a booby trap."

Brother Bustelich shuts off the snow blower. He and Duckie exchange grunts and arm signals. Duckie turns back to me with a pouty sneer and produces a cigarette. "I may be back over in a bit." He strolls up the road to his driveway.

I shovel for another minute, but I have to tackle my main task. I'm not going to try to wait out these troglodytes. I return inside the cabin with Andy's shears. I haul Johnny into the bathroom. I pull the oak table to a corner of the parlor. With great difficulty, I'm able to extract the rug from beneath it. I systematically move all of the parlor furniture to the corner beside the oak table and chairs. The rug is nearly as big as the parlor, probably 12 X 18 feet. More importantly, it's thin and fairly flexible, so I have little trouble folding it over to 12 X 9. I hustle down to the basement and return to the parlor with the snorkel and fins. I drag Johnny onto the folded rug and rip off his gag tape. "What the hell do you think you're doing, Amonor? You fruitcake!"

I brandish the snorkel. "Open your mouth and rely on this thing if you want to keep breathing." He keeps his lips tight and mouth shut. I elbow him in the groin and jam the mouthpiece through his moan. I finish the roll of duct tape fastening the snorkel in place. I cut off the long tail of the rope with the shears. I don't know why I brought up the fins, but I wedge them along with the cardboard tape holder beneath Bustelich's knees. I roll up Johnny in the rug. The end of the snorkel tube extends beyond the roll, and I hear breathing. I tie up the roll with the rope segment.

I hear the whine of a snow blower nearby. I look out the front window and observe Duckie demolishing the remainder of the snow mound in the Ryscavage driveway approach. I restore the original furniture arrangement in the parlor. Duckie finishes clearing the approach. I'm so physically exhausted, I'm tempted to present him with a bottle of wine for the labor he's saved me. He glances toward the cottage as I stand in the front window, and I offer him a gesture of approval. I don't know if he sees me. If he starts up the driveway, I'll meet him beside the van and offer to buy him a drink at Horsepower. But he saves me the trouble by dragging his snow blower back to his own property and up his driveway.

I hastily prop open the side door and drag the rug holding Johnny onto the driveway. If Douggie returns, he can help me load his brother into the van. It would almost be worth getting caught to see the expression on his face. With all the strength I can muster, I tug and boost the roll into the back of the van. I hustle back inside the cottage, grab the shears and my protein bar wrappers, take one last look at the spot where Maynard died and relegate the place to my nightmares.

I stride to the van, jump in and start the engine. I back down the driveway as swiftly as the sluggish vehicle will allow. As I start forward, Duckie trots to the end of his driveway. I slow down as I approach him, gesture positively and drive onward. I don't stop watching for an electric blue pickup in my rearview mirror until I'm out of Coloma. Then I start looking out for cops.

I'm coughing with regularity, and my willingness to be pulled over changes from moment to moment. I just want to get home and try to get some rest. The traffic moves slowly, but nothing on the roads obstructs my forward progress. The sky is a blackish haze by the time I reach Waukesha County.

Four snow-covered skids occupy my front yard, and I can't help but think that Maynard was still alive when I ordered these construction materials for my sauna renovation. I back Andy's van halfway into the garage. I enter my house through the front door and proceed to the rarely used side door which connects to the garage. I toss the stacked recyclables baskets and houseplant accessories aside and open the door. In the darkness of the garage, I withdraw the makeshift cocoon containing Johnny Bustelich from the back of Andy's van and maneuver it through the hallway and down the stairs to the basement. I lug the Johnny roll to the open area of excruciation station.

I return upstairs and find a note from Andy on the kitchen table. She reports that she found two more bugs and guarantees that the house has been "disinfected." I squeeze her van all the way into the garage, shut the door and make sure all of the house doors are locked. I head back down to excruciation station. Bustelich squirms out of his rug before I'm able to completely unfurl it. He leg-whips me and I land on my back. I climb back to my feet, roughly tear the tape off his face and extract his snorkel. He sucks air in a series of harsh wheezes, and I help him to his feet. "You motherfucking bitch!" he hails me. He attempts to head-butt me, and I shove him back to the floor mats and zap him.

"You're still alive and kicking, Johnny." I snatch a nearly fresh roll of duct tape, restore his standard gag and rebind his feet. "You complicate everything."

MY CRITICAL PRIORITY is to arrange temporary lodging for the man who disdainfully rejected my repeated attempts to facilitate his release and murdered my dog. The obvious solution is to make a few alterations and convert the safe sauna I was revamping to keep what's undesirable out into a safe sauna to keep what's undesirable in. I'll want to nullify noise, too, so I move the room about a foot back from the outer basement wall. I had already planned to upgrade my reimagined model with a staggered stud pattern between 2 X 6 plates in order to deploy thicker insulation, and this arrangement should provide a soundproofing dividend as well. I reframe the walls with two extra feet in both horizontal dimensions. I craft California corners for more stability and add reinforcement blocking between studs. I use nails, screws and bolts a size larger than their predecessors and I attach the bottom plates to the floor with permanent wedge anchors.

Still wrapped in Spaatz's rope, Bustelich spends his first morning in my basement affixed to the base of the squat rack with cable ties. I take a bottle of water to him. "Thirsty?" I tear the duct tape off his mouth.

"Tell me where the hell I am, Anomor!" he rasps. "Is this your stinking house?"

"As I said last night, you're in my comfort zone." I take a swig of water.

He snickers maniacally. "Now I'm *your* hostage."

"You're being detained as a potential health menace, Johnny." I spill a fair amount of water as I hold his head and stiffly guide the contents of the bottle into his mouth.

He spits his final gulp into my face and sustains a coughing jag. "If you can chill, I'll let you go ungagged for a while. Maybe I'll bring you a banana." I return to my sauna project.

"You think you're building me some cage over there, Lloyd?" he snarls. "Some torture cell?"

I'm able to adroitly reconfigure the electrical connections. "You've ripped me a new one, Lisle!" Bustelich bellows. "But go any further now, and you'll have me hanging over your head for the rest of your god-awful life!" I spread a new waterproofing membrane on the floor. "What about that deal you kept pushing up at the cabin, that buyout where you'd pay me to get lost? Let's do it for real, and you'll never have to fret about me again!"

"That was a time-sensitive offer!" Lumber and locks seem to be my main material shortages.

"So this is all really just about the dog?" Bustelich squawks.

"Plain, simple spite? You loon, go to the pound and get yourself a new dog!"

I retape Bustelich's mouth, throw on my old green canvas coat and head out to the Yukon. Andy appeared shortly after sunrise this morning to swap vehicles and present me with a plastic bag containing the two tracking devices she plucked from my vehicle plus the two listening devices she purged from the house plus my bill. She designated me as a most favored trading partner. I'm able to procure the studs and locks I need to complete the sauna at the home improvement center, and I consider stopping at a sporting goods store to pick up a more robust weapon for better captive control. I had a Glock 19 pistol in my wall safe, but the joint shock troops confiscated it on their second raid and never returned it. I decide to stop at a drive-through instead for hamburgers, fries and shakes.

When I return home, I free Johnny's right arm. I offer him a burger. "What'd you do to it, bitch?" he challenges.

I unwrap the burger and start eating it. "You have my word I will not poison your food." I toss him another burger and stand over him with my unoccupied hand poised at the shock collar remote.

He scoffs but devours his burger. "Another!" he demands. I toss him the bag containing two burgers and a boat of fries. "What's the master plan here, Lisle?"

"That has yet to be determined." I finish my burger, remove the shakes from the other bag and set one on the floor for him.

He eyes me intently. "It's a wonder you and I weren't buds." He chomps some fries. "You were really never so bad. It was Spaatz that stood between us." I groan, and he glares. "You've never stopped to realize how he would always fuck you up just like he'd always fuck me up." He finishes his meal without further comment and chucks his garbage at my feet. "I need a bathroom break bad, Lisle. And a little privacy too?" He begins undoing his leg bindings.

"No, Johnny." I place my hand on the collar remote. "You're going to remain tethered to the squat rack until your accommodations are ready."

"Am I your new dog, Lisle?" He continues loosening his leg wraps. "You've got to let me lift my leg." I give him a jolt, and he crumples backward. He grabs his collar, and I pull one of the safety pins out of the squat rack, letting the Olympic bar with a 35-pound plate drop onto his chest. I press my foot on the bar. He moans and places his hand limply at his side. "Let me take a dump!"

I lift the bar, replace the pin in the rack and add another 35-pound plate. I recruit a large terra cotta planter saucer to be Bustelich's makeshift bedpan and cut the bottom out of a plastic milk jug for his urinal. I pull down his waders, and he awkwardly twists and relieves himself. He cleans up with napkins and offers no further resistance as I resecure his arm and leg bindings. "See what a good boy I am, Lisle?" I return to the sauna. "Woof! Woof!" He roars. "Build me a fancy doghouse, dude!"

I install new stone wool insulation and I'm able to reuse most of my cedar boards. I use bench planks for molding at the wall junctures and reinstall each of the original carbon fiber heating panels. The most significant new feature is the double-wall design, where four interior walls will stand as bare frames inside the exterior walls and be wrapped in heavy duty steel mesh screwed into the studs with tamper-resistant fasteners. The mesh will also span the ceiling. I retrieve my new lumber from the Yukon and finish laying the floor planks. I form my reinforced interior frames inside the sauna and stand each in place 16 inches inside an exterior wall. I cover them and the ceiling with the stiff mesh. While I had originally intended to attach my mahogany door to the interior wall, I now reassign that honor to the new high-security door with its six deadbolts, and I reverse the steel frame. I unite the mahogany door with the exterior wall and install two deadbolts and a safety latch on it.

I build a single-tier bench against the back interior wall of the sauna. It should make a dandy bed. I deposit a balance disc and an exercise mat on the bench to function as pillow and blanket. I cut Bustelich's zip ties with my safety scissors and drag him into the sauna. I utilize some leftover planks to construct a four-foot bench, and I fasten it to the floor at the front of the room 20 inches inside the interior door. The short bench will serve as a utility table and an obstacle to keep the occupant from taking a running start and throwing his weight against the door in an effort to break containment. Notwithstanding the six dead bolts, I recognize the security door as the weak point of the fortress.

"This is your think tank, Johnny." I plunk down two buckets beside the utility bench, spilling water from the larger one. "You'll have the freedom to pace around and reflect on the sorry trail of personal destruction you've left in your life." I remove a plastic cup and a roll of paper towels from the smaller bucket and place the items on the bench. "Use your toilet kit; foul this place, and you're the one who'll have to bear the fumes."

"How long?" he snarls. "Where does this lead?"

I approach Bustelich with the safety scissors and roll of duct tape. A look of alarmed confusion replaces his pouty sneer. "I'll save you the trouble of ripping this off." I remove his shock collar. "Hold still." I wad duct tape around both of his hands. I tape his ankles together. I cut the rope in five places and reel in the segments. Bustelich tries to roll into my legs but I hop over him. I collect the loose objects and head for the door. "Disrespect your new retreat hole by damaging it in any way, and I'll crank up the heat." I watch him voraciously tear the tape from his hands with his teeth. "Even better, I'll restart your hormone treatments. We may make a nice girl out of you yet." I slam the door behind me and lock the six bolts. "See you soon." I shut and lock the mahogany door.

I proceed upstairs, drop into my low-rider chair and turn on the TV. It's late Monday night. I automatically reach down to pat the head that isn't there. It's been over 100 hours since Bustelich was bitten, and he'd be exhibiting signs of sepsis, such as fever, dizziness and vomiting, if he was infected with super-Capno. Ironically, after praying so hard for almost a month that Maynard wasn't infected, I now desperately wish that he had been, even if he infected me, too. I doze off and wake up shortly before midnight. I jump up to take the dog outside. I tend my plants instead. I cry myself to sleep.

I awaken early Tuesday morning to the sound of thumping in the basement. I hustle down the stairs and peer through the sauna exterior door window. Bustelich is stomping around the floor, hurling his hefty mass into the mesh in one place after another. I open the mahogany door. "Stop it, Johnny, or I'll bring the heat!" He continues with more fury. I set the thermometer to 60 degrees Celsius and activate the sauna. "Settle down right now, or you don't get fed today!"

"Fuck off, Anomor!" He shoulders the mesh once more, rubs his forearm and sits down.

I lock the exterior door, return upstairs and prepare Bustelich a positive-reinforcement breakfast of bacon and scrambled eggs, sausage links, blueberry muffins, mixed fruit and pineapple juice. I arrange the meal on paper plates and include rubber cutlery. I find him awaiting delivery directly inside the interior door. "Sit on your bed while I bring this in, dragon-breath." He doesn't move. "Do it right now, or you don't get fed and I leave the heat on." He grudgingly withdraws to his back bench and seats himself. I enter and place his breakfast on the utility bench. "Put your garbage in your waste bucket and leave it beside this bench. I'll take it and give you a new bucket next time I come down here."

"Can't wait to see your face again," he grumbles.

I fix myself a can of chicken soup for breakfast. I have little appetite, and I force myself to consume an apricot protein bar to maintain my strength. I have a headache, a scratchy throat and I feel exhausted. The vibrations of intermittent pounding and muffled shouts reach me throughout the day, and I keep scurrying downstairs to monitor the security status of the retreat hole. I perform some light exercises and blast lively music through the excruciation station sound system in an effort to temporarily efface the detainee.

On Tuesday night, I serve Bustelich a dinner of petite sirloin steaks, baked potato and stuffed pepper. When I return to collect his garbage, he requests personal hygiene items. My paranoia kicks in, and I stay downstairs for a while to ensure there's no design flaw in the secure sauna that would allow one an easy escape. I end up napping for a few hours on the gym floor, but no noise emanates from the retreat hole, so I return upstairs.

Wednesday morning I bring Bustelich cinnamon pancakes with pitted cherries and Florida punch, an extra-large bar of soap, an extra bucket of warm water, a washcloth and the baggy artist's frock that Trish tossed into the laundry bin and never reclaimed. I notice that his knuckles are raw and his fingernails are cracked, as if he'd been trying to remove screws. He complains of boredom, and I promise to give him a project. Late in the afternoon I head out on a shopping excursion. Upon my return, I proceed downstairs and present Johnny with three coloring books and a box of crayons that I purchased. "Learn to be creative instead of destructive." When I return an hour later to serve him a fried chicken dinner, the books and the crayons remain in the same spot on the floor where I tossed them.

The next morning when I bring Bustelich his breakfast burrito and poached eggs with herbal tea and cranberry juice, the coloring books and crayons are stacked beside the utility bench. He springs to his feet and rushes me, causing me to spill his tea before backpedaling out of the hole and slamming the door shut behind me. I'm able to lock one deadbolt before he arrives at the door, and I rapidly lock the rest as he pounds on the door. "*Let me out of this hellhole, you deranged, psycho son of a bitch!!*"

"Color," I recommend, "and calm down." He pounds the mesh as I leave. I turn on the heat.

I return at noon to find Bustelich lying prone on the sauna floor wearing Trish's smock coloring his garden-themed picture book. He looks at me, sits up and holds the book open to exhibit his work. He has intricately colored a bee pollinating a rainbow carnation. "This reminds me of snatching the wasp's nest from our garage rafters in eighth grade to stick in Josh Bjorklund-Puderbaugh's backpack."

"What was your problem with Puderbaugh?" I can't resist inquiring. "His screwy name?"

Johnny shrugs. "I expected they'd clear out the classroom, call in pest control, and we might all get some time off." He snickers. "I wound up getting stung in the nose and jamming the nest in Dylan Spangler's backpack by mistake." I turn off the heat.

Later, I serve Bustelich a dinner of baked ham with green bean casserole. After I come back to collect his garbage and change his water, I install the poor man's alarm system at the retreat hole: empty cans stacked on an aluminum baking sheet outside the exterior door. If he escapes and flees the house, I'll likely cooperate with the authorities. If he escapes and – more likely – assaults me as his first order of business, I believe I'll have the wherewithal to kill him with my bare hands. Of course, an early warning never hurts. I leave six cans on the baking sheet, one for each day he's been my houseguest.

I water my plants. The leaf ends of the comely Madagascar palm are brown and curled. I've reached the days where my prime function is to raise the shades and open the drapes each morning and lower the shades and close the drapes each night. Suicidal impulses torment me, tempt me, tug at me. The tears that escape are fewer but no less bitter. My gut still churns. The sense of vacancy in the house overwhelms me. Contemplating how such a little guy could fill such a large area suffuses my wan spirit with the gamut of emotions. I long for my loyal friend to know that I never abandoned him.

The doorbell rings. My void insinuates itself in the lack of barking. I'm positive that Bustelich can't hear the doorbell over the heavy metal currently engulfing excruciation station, but I discern unexpectedly ragged vibrations. I observe a black SUV parked in front of the house as I trudge to the door. I find two bulky figures on my front porch, one of whom is tall and familiar. I open the door and couch my profound irritation in a wry salute. "Detective B. Cybyske of the Waukesha Mounted Police."

"Mr. Amonor, we meet again." Cybyske flashes a perfunctory smile. "I have someone here I'd like you to know." He nods to the husky adolescent boy beside him. "Tell him your full name, Chad."

"Lucas Chadwick Bustelich." The teen gestures to Cybyske. "He says you're the kingpin of missing persons."

The detective grimaces. "He means to suggest you're the lynchpin of the missing persons case involving his father."

I step out onto the porch. "Afternoon, kid." I shiver and fold my arms tightly against my chest. "Megan Borsak your mother?"

"You're well-versed on the situation." Cybyske looks like he thinks he's achieved a breakthrough.

Chad steps uncomfortably closer. "You knew my mom?"

I shake my head. "I knew who she was. I give Johnny credit; I didn't realize he wifed her up."

Chad sneers. "The old man made me take his name after he took me in."

"Do you have bruising around your eyes?" Cybyske scrutinizes my face.

"Things in my bedroom get moved around by investigators, and I trip over them in the dark." I step back and blow on my hands. "I got the impression last time we talked, Officer Cybyske, you were off this case and onto public health crises."

"Our conversation rekindled my interest." Cybyske places a hand on young Bustelich's shoulder. "Tell Mr. Amonor what life is like for your step-mom, for your little brother and sister. What are their names?"

"Phineas and Sasha." Chad exhibits a pouty sneer. "Jan struggles to find someone to watch them while she's working. Sometimes my grandma will, but they fight about what's fair to expect of her. I find Jan crying a lot. She wonders, 'Did Johnny desert us or did something bad happen to him?' The hardest part for everybody is not knowing. It's often painful to hang around the house there for the emptiness."

I emit a bizarre laugh. Cybyske has brought this next-generation lowlife to my door to evoke sympathy and gain tractability, but all I can do is fixate on the punk's thick neck, painfully aware that it was his jackass traffic stunt that incited Spaatz to concoct the entire transformance escapade, the upshot of which cost me Maynard. I don't dare look down, but I'm sure my fingers are twitching.

"That was a peculiar hoot," the detective evaluates my response. "It sounded rather disturbed."

I gaze at Cybyske intently. "May I rot in hell if this isn't the absolute truth, Detective Busy B. I have no idea where Gayle Spaatz is. He owes me money, so that's not likely to change soon. He talked about traveling, out West, even to Africa."

"When did you last speak with him?" The detective rubs his hands together. "Can we continue our conversation inside your house?"

"How considerate of you guys to ask my permission this time," I snarl. "*I'm* busy looking for a new job. Someone got me canned from my old one. You wouldn't know anything about that?"

He furrows his brow. "I can assure you I had nothing to do with it. Unfortunate. May I ask the reason they offered for your termination?"

"Does this have something to do with my pop?" the youth huffs.

"Nothing at all, junior," I assert, "and that's precisely the point!" I turn to Cybyske. "I don't know what evil monger is feeding you what warped information, deputy, but I should've never popped up on your radar. Since I did, you seem to have taken an unwarranted personal dislike to me, and maybe if nothing else, you've set your sights on punishing me with the process."

"What's unwarranted is your defensiveness." The detective rubs his chin. "We're just out trying to collect information, and you've just signified you have information to collect."

The youth bumps me. "You know something about my old man, shithead, you better give it up-"

Cybyske locks his arm around young Bustelich. "Not the way to go about this, Chad." He turns him and walks him down the driveway. I open my door. "We'll continue this conversation at a future date, Mr. Amonor!" the detective calls over his shoulder. "You can rely on it!"

I return inside and slam the door. "No need for a paternity test on Chad." As soon as I'm satisfied that the black SUV won't return, I place African violets in the container of the mandarin tree that's taller than me, grab an empty can and carry the items downstairs to the retreat hole. I slide the tray aside and add the tenth can to the stacks.

I find Bustelich naked on his stomach coloring. "Go to your corner, Johnny. You're getting a pair of roommates." He drops his crayon and eyes me agape. "We're going to liven up your environment with some houseplants." He grumbles, indolently gets up and waddles to his bench. I unlock the interior door and carry in the plants. "There's insufficient light in here for these to thrive, so you'll only have a few days to appreciate them. I inherited these African violets from my mother." I display the little plants teeming with delicate pink flowers and set their plastic pot on the utility bench. "I've tried to honor her memory by taking meticulous care of them." I slide the mandarin tree past the utility bench. "And this tallboy is special because I've grown it from a tangerine seed. Be careful of the nasty spikes on it. But it's also got a bud, which is rare for a 3-year-old citrus tree."

Bustelich pops up and rushes me. I knock over the mandarin tree backpedaling out of the hole and slam the interior door behind me just as Johnny arrives. He pounds on the door and whoops raucously as I lock it. "How can you move so fast on those skinny stork legs, Amonro?" I step outside the exterior door. "Wait, seriously, Lisle, you like working with plants? Cuz they can't tell you're hideous?"

"That's right, cankle king, plants rarely break your heart." I hear him howl inside the hole. I turn on the heat.

When I return two hours later with his hummus dinner, the tree is still lying on the floor. "You'll get fed," I propose, "after you stand the tree up properly."

"You knocked it over, dropkick." After a standoff of several minutes, he flips the tree upright. I shut off the heat and serve the dinner. I wait at the exterior door as he inspects it. "What's this shit?"

"Today I wasn't able to spend the entire afternoon toiling in the kitchen."

"Do you have a job, Amonor? You're awfully handy. You seem to be around all the time."

"I'm your major-domo." I fold my arms. "And don't you remember? I'm also a doctor."

Bustelich prowls along the wall. "So when do we expect our old pal Spaatz to drop in?" He snickers sardonically. "He ran out on you, didn't he? How does he excuse himself now?" He punches the mesh. "This entire shitshow with me was *your* brainstorm, wasn't it, Loyal, and Spazz dumped on you! He got out so quick he must've been ready and set to go. Left you holding the feed bag? You still in contact with him?"

"Eat pita, Johnny."

"I got a few fistfuls of Gaylord up at the cabin!" he persists. "I choked him like he choked me, kicked and punched him.

He seemed to almost get off on it. I figured he would end up shooting me and then turning the gun on himself. Is that the way it's going to end with you, Amonor?"

I rub the crook that Bustelich put in my nose. "I don't need a gun." I slam the door behind me.

I hear a strong, rhythmic thumping in the basement early Tuesday morning. I find Bustelich seated on the utility bench kicking the security door with the bottoms of his feet. "I don't generally reward outbursts, Johnny, but I have an epic headache, so I'll give you some perks if you mellow out." I bring him some of Spaatz's drawings and caricatures of our schoolmates. "You might get a charge out of these. See how many you can identify." I give him Gayle's pastels as well. "Flesh out the ones that could use finishing touches." I serve apple frangipane galette with coffee liqueur for breakfast. When I return to collect the garbage, Bustelich is still pacing restlessly and pounding mesh. At dinnertime, I serve him five-minute meatloaf. When I return, Spaatz's illustrations are scattered haphazardly across the floor. "Those have sentimental value for me. Pick them up and treat them with some respect."

Bustelich refuses to retreat from the mesh. "This whole snafu is really just about your selfish aspect, Amonor. You get more butt-hurt when I needle you about your appearance than any business with the dog! You look at things like a 10-year-old, like my boy Phin. His interests are limited to himself. Anytime anything goes wrong, he has to find someone else to blame. Pull on your big-boy pants, Lisle! Attach yourself to some wretched ratchet as frightful as you are and bone her brains out! Join some porcupine people support group to find her if you have to."

"Is that where you found yours?"

"It's your chance to find acceptance." His smirk returns. "A real man wouldn't settle for a pet. A dog is a mindless beast who can only react. He can't love anything. He's your captive, same as I am now. Just too dumb to know how miserable his life is."

"When I was a younger man," I confide, "I knew a couple of girls who I would've blissfully dedicated my life to trying to please. After each rejection, what bothered me most was the notion that I'd never know what it's like to have someone willing to be completely devoted to me. But now I realize I do know. That's right, I accepted my lot and took my love where it presented itself, a pure, platonic love, faithful, unconditional and enduring."

Johnny squints with confusion and disgust. "I'm pretty sure you just got dragged into this mess, Amonor. So just let me the hell go! I promise I won't do anything to get back at you! I don't even want any of your goddamn false imprisonment money! I swear I won't tell the cops you had any hand in this. I'll lay it all on Spaatz where it belongs! I'll even get you a new puppy. You'll probably like him better than the last one."

I nod. "Your wife will probably soon find herself a new husband and your kids a new father, and unless they're crazy, they'll like him a lot better than you."

He shakes his head. "It sure must suck to be you."

"And there's nothing you could offer me right now to make me want to trade places with *you*." He returns to his bench muttering expletives.

Bustelich awakens me early the next morning with continuous shouts and screeches. I march downstairs and poke my head into the retreat hole. "Shut up, leather lungs!" I turn on the heat and fill the basement with contemporary rap. Johnny seats himself on the utility bench and begins kicking the security door again. The bench collapses and he crashes to the floor alongside the African violets.

He staggers to his feet sporting a gash on his left wrist. "*Bring me a bandage, dipshit!!*" The flower pot is cracked and violets are dispersed. He kicks the mandarin pot and dashes the tree to the floor. "Come in here so I can do you a solid and tear your face off!"

I return in about two hours with a stack of dried frozen waffles, a paper shot glass filled with blackberry syrup, a cup of cold coffee and a small adhesive bandage. Bustelich grudgingly withdraws to his back bench, and I place the items just inside the security door. "Your food has been too elegant for a waffle house," I advise him.

I head upstairs, flop into my low-rider chair and watch TV. I find live coverage of a press conference being conducted by Serge Kenower of the CDC. "We want to emphasize once again that our containment efforts have been cumulatively successful and there's no cause for alarm. We're dealing with a recombination event which has resulted in the horizontal transfer of genes between different species of organisms, increasing the pathogenicity of *Capnocytophaga canimorsus* and rendering it neurotropic. I can confirm now that our data does not support transmission of this infection between humans through airborne droplets. Transmission occurs from a dog host to a human or another dog or possibly other animal."

"Social media is rife now with lab-sourced mechanisms of

regulating gene expression," a reporter submits, "you know like restriction enzymes, heat shocks, transposons-"

"Jumping genes," Kenower relates. "Our modeling has successfully re-created a natural scenario by which ducks in Minnesota lakes and brackish lagoons have consumed bromide-rich underwater weeds coated with cyanobacteria. These weeds produce bromine-based toxic compounds which vitiate the ducks' strength and energy, causing them to be easier prey for duck hunters. The cyanobacteria contain syringes that allow them to easily inject their contents into the extracellular environment, and they would've exchanged genetic material with *C. canimorsus* bacteria carried by the dogs retrieving these ducks, resulting in a transformation event giving Capno a greater capacity to modify antimicrobial binding targets as well as enter the bloodstream of a host organism and cause a more lethal infection, leading to not only sepsis but vacuolar myelinopathy, whereby holes are created in brainstem tissue."

"Could the climate crisis be a significant factor in driving this merger?" a reporter suggests.

"That's a great point," Kenower concedes. "It's quite plausible that warmer temperatures drive mineral fluxes switching dormant genes on or adding genes that result in a virulence factor gain of the microbe. Water pollution may also increase the likelihood of DNA oxidative lesions inducing a mutation that gives the Capno pathogen more competence to take up extracellular cyanobacteria genetic material."

"Never leave home without packing your bag of excuses full of global warming," I remark.

The afternoon indeed finds a balmy winter thaw settling

over the region, and I take a slow walk through the park and around the neighborhood. When I return home, I proceed downstairs to change Bustelich's water and collect his garbage. The moment I step inside the hole, Johnny leaps to his feet and pelts me with dark, little balls. I backtrack beyond the security door and lock it. I find one of the projectiles squashed on the bottom of my shoe and examine it. "Fecal balls, Johnny, really?"

He hobbles to the mesh. "If you had a family, with kids, you dildo, you wouldn't be soulless enough to keep me here like this."

Shortly after five o'clock, I serve Bustelich his dinner of macaroni and cheese. "I recall in high school, Johnny, you likened my complexion to a pot of melted cheese. We'll designate this as our popular nostalgia meal. Expect to see a steady diet of it." When I collect his garbage, I leave a twelfth can in the stacks.

Late the following morning I bring Bustelich a brunch of canned albacore on a plate with saltines, a side bowl of noodles and a tumbler of weak lemonade. Maynard had a penchant for tuna, so my cupboard is filled with it. I'm struck by the tidiness of the retreat hole. The mandarin tree is upright and the surviving African violets are back in their damaged pot. Every other item seems to be arranged in a neat pile along the wall. Johnny is wearing Trish's frock and working on Gayle's illustrations. He looks up and smiles archly. "Hey, dingleberry, remember this one?" He holds up a half-colored picture of Zoe Fallone. I can tell by the trademark knit cap.

"Old Zoe," I acknowledge. "She had a ready sparkle and a reputation for being approachable."

He grunts. "She had a rep all right, jackalope. She'll go down in the annals of slutdom as a real crowd-pleaser. You, of course, recall the time I was exploring her easygoing nature, and Spaatz yelled at her, 'Zoe, why don't you get yourself a boyfriend who can tell you apart from his lunch?'"

A slightly embarrassing memory of the incident presents itself. "I only went to one school social besides the prom," I muse. "She was the first girl I ever asked to dance."

He snickers in a surprisingly empathetic way. "She show you some fancy moves?"

"Hell no. She politely declined my invitation. I returned to my table shattered."

Johnny shakes his head. "Aw, poor wallflower Amonor. You spent the whole rest of the night in the background sobbing?"

"I had a good sulk for a while," I admit. "Then Kiki Kuecherer came over and took me by the hand, and we danced."

"Kooky, kinky Kiki." He rises. "A freak, but the kind, considerate sort."

"Yeah," I sigh. "A little later, I asked her to dance again, and she politely declined."

Johnny nods. "Zoe married and divorced some lawyer. Last I heard she was living in a mansion in Genocide Depot. It pays to be buxom." He opens his frock and fondles his man boobs. "Sometimes." He approaches the wall. "You're not going to keep me in here forever? End this shit, Amonor!"

I believe that Bustelich and I might be developing a rapport. He wantonly murdered the best friend I ever had, and I'm not sure I can retaliate. Whether I force myself to dispatch him or force myself to release him, I'll despise myself. I didn't create this unholy mess, and I tried to resolve it, and now I'll be stuck with the final residue. I'm going to have to count on some divine mercy.

An afternoon shopping junket takes me to Bruce Neichi's strip mall. I buy a new burner phone at the Zhen Dianxin store, I stop at Xaman's crafts shop for a packet of sealable transparent archival display envelopes, and I pick up a bundle of practical suits with accessories at Arma-Garden Preppers.

Late Thursday night, I drive down to the casino. I play the slots for about an hour and consume one orangeman to stabilize my nerve. From the Yukon in the casino parking lot, I place the urgent call I've been postponing. I know that she rarely works on Friday afternoons. I'm also aware that she doesn't answer calls from unidentified sources, so I resolve to overcome her reticence with brute-force perseverance. On the sixth attempt, she picks up. "Hello! Hello?" I'm not sure whether she identified me before she terminated the call, but I try again and she engages. "Di, it's high time we made peace."

"Make peace with the creep who terrorized and defiled my child?" My sister's wrath radiates unsparingly from Zamboanga.

"Might your take on my custodianship be a bit severe?" I smack my lips. "You don't realize how much that kind of hyperbole hurts me."

"Hurts *you*? My son is receiving gestalt therapy to treat the trauma he suffered at your hands."

"I apologize from the bottom of my heart if I was in any way tone-deaf to his special issues." I endeavor to advance the conversation. "You might be pleased to know that *my* head too, is back in the hands of a competent mental health professional.

Dr. King artfully reduces my self-esteem so I'll be more amenable to the behavior modifications he suggests."

"He has his work cut out for him because you're an awful person."

"And because my fragile psyche, as you know, is so easy to bruise. But seriously, Dinah, I did not discipline Angelo for his malicious mischief anywhere near as sternly as Dad used to ramrod us when we got unruly."

"And look how you turned out." She hisses. "Your 'discipline' may be pardonable. Introducing my pubescent boy to depraved rough porn is not."

"What are you talking about?" I suppress the inclination to verify whether she's referencing what we found her doing at the hotel.

"You skeeve! What's your technical term for it: hard-core techno-gore; manhandle-and-maul fantasy? We found Angelo on a rape-and-rip gaming site that he admitted you exposed him to." She ignores my grunts of denial. "Fitsal tapped Angelo's MP web history, and he visited the site hosting this horror show for the first time on the Saturday night he stayed at your house."

"He spent some time in his room with his phone after we came back from the supper club, but-"

"What was the only instruction I gave you when I dropped him off? Deny him his Megalophone! But you were too soft or obtuse to honor my wishes!"

"You might've tipped me off that I should withhold the toy from the boy for prurient concerns. But, trust me, Angelo is telling the quintessential self-preserving fib if he claims I facilitated his foray into any sort of sordid material."

"Trust you?" She emits a scornful howl. "I've taught my son to be perfectly forthright and I've never had an occasion to doubt anything he's told me. You, on the other hand, have firmly established yourself as Lisle the liar."

"Be fair to me, Di." I snicker indignantly. "You need to appreciate that your little darling is not as innocent as you want to believe."

"Patterns of lechery define you," she asserts coldly. "You were keeping a woman, weren't you? Were you giving her a stipend? Did you salvage her out of some strip bar? What was her name again: Sinnamon with an 'S'?" She huffs. "You sure do pick the winners."

"That's the thing you've never quite understood, Di. I never got to have my pick like you did-"

"Is that the hidden agenda of this call?" she objects. "To load me with more misplaced guilt for going out and finding myself? I'm sorry, am I also supposed to apologize now for being ambitious and successful? I made my own breaks, and you could've done as much if you didn't channel your drive into chronic self-pity and bitterness."

"Dinah, please." My voice cracks. "Please, you're the only person left that I can turn to." I emit a deferential breath. "Your family is your last refuge. There's an important reason for my call. Please help a brother out."

"You overdramatize everything. What's the matter?"

"I could be in some legal trouble, big, complicated trouble. I may need to get lost for a while." I'm not quite sure what I want to ask. "Maybe you could help me find digs near you, or else suggest somewhere I could vanish, and assist me in stealthily moving my money out of the country?"

"Oh, no!" she gasps. "No, really? Don't tell me you harmed Sinnamon? You begged her to come back, and when she laughed in your face, you got physical, things got too rough, and you didn't mean to do it?"

A sudden wave of distrust sweeps over me. "I was just having some sport with you there, you gull of a girl." I force a chuckle. "Not a bad deadpan, huh? I really had you going."

She expels an irritated breath. "You really put people off when you put people on."

"Is that why the quality women reject me?"

"Honestly, Lisle, what do you have or what have you done that would impress an attractive and accomplished woman?"

"Are you kidding?" I chafe. "I'm weird and wonderful. I'm the perfect gentleman. I was always pleasant and respectful to the girls you had over, wasn't I? You used to tell me they'd remark on how sincere and polite I was."

"You were so ultra-polite, you were cringeworthy. You always tried too hard to be too nice, and you came off looking needy, even desperate. Quality women tend to view men as success objects. If you have none of the one, you'll get none of the other."

"I'm tired of going through life feeling like I have to apologize for myself to make people like me." I rub my brow. "Once upon a time, we were pretty close. I loved you dearly, and I firmly believe you were fairly fond of me, too."

Her silence cuts through several moments. "You've undoubtedly deduced that I'd like to be a lot happier, more fulfilled than I am." She takes a deep breath. "But it's not something I want to get into over the phone."

"Maybe we could meet up at some resort in Mexico." The urge to find refuge overwhelms me. "Any chance on the horizon of you escaping from the 'Pines?"

"The use of that term for this country by an outsider is extremely offensive," she carps.

"How so?"

"It's like 'Pinoy.' If you're not a citizen, it's arrogant and obnoxious, and you have no business using it."

"Don't I have privilege by proxy through you?" I can't believe how pretentious she's become. "Sponsor me for citizenship. In return, I'll lend my wizardry to fixing your daily problems."

She groans. "You're not capable of fixing my problems. Try fixing your own instead. You complain that you're stuck in a job that's beneath you. Go back to school, finish your degree and make something of yourself."

"I don't want to jump through some goofy academic hoops, do some stale exercises and suck up to some pompous professor." I opt to spare my sister a briefing on my employment status. "I'd like to commit real, meaningful science."

"You want to evade pressure and criticism," she charges. "Like always, you cower before risk. Work on not kowtowing to your peers and being such a cream puff. You're the one who lacks personal discipline, you boob!" She terminates our connection.

My hopes of taking temporary shelter in the Philippines and adopting the identity of Filippidas Pinatubo Grossnickel are dashed. "I guess if and when the time comes for us to declare an armistice, sis, you'll let me know, provided you can find me." I start the engine of my vehicle and head for home. I'm sure that Dinah has no regrets. The thing I always admired most about her was how true she was to herself. Being true to others has proven to be a sticking point.

Friday morning, I bring Bustelich his breakfast of slimy oatmeal, dry waffles and cold coffee. He objects to the quality of the meal and barely touches it. "What happened to our genial Johnny from yesterday?" I challenge. At lunchtime I serve him a plate of canned albacore with a pair of dog biscuits on the side. "Maynard loved tuna, and I'm not going to let the biscuits I have on hand go to waste." When I return with his dinner, I find him sitting quietly on his bench holding his head in his hands. I set his macaroni and cheese on the floor inside the interior door.

Bustelich fixes his sullen eyes on me. "For God's sake, Amonor, I'm begging you, will you please let me out of here?"

"Are you suggesting you've found religion in the slammer, Johnny?" I titter.

He bolts at me. I retreat outside the door, slam it behind me and lock it as he hurls his bulk against it. He continues pounding on the door and the mesh, wailing and cursing me, for several minutes. He throws his dinner against the mesh. I turn on the heat and some classical music. When I return later with a bucket of warm water and fresh roll of paper towels, the African violets and mandarin tree are smashed on the floor. "I promise you, Johnny, conniptions will get you nowhere."

Late Friday night, I get into the Yukon and drive into Milwaukee County past Ideal Allele. I continue down the road and park in the lot behind a professional building two miles east of Innovation Drive. I turn off the engine and sit in the SUV for over an hour. The underlayer of one of the outfits that I purchased from Arma-Garden Preppers and a touch of anxiety induce a light sweat on the unseasonably warm night. I discern no activity in the area. I take my black briefcase, slip out of the Yukon and traipse the scrub along the fence separating the lot from the adjacent county park.

Keeping briefcase in hand, I climb a tree that's collapsed over the fence and drop onto the wooded side. I reflect heavily on Maynard's death as I scramble over the mushy hills beyond the woods. I question my faith. Any life strategy other than to maximize pleasure and minimize pain, I reason, is insanity for one who doesn't believe in God. Matters get more complicated for the rest of us. I derive no pleasure whatsoever from holding Bustelich prisoner. I resolve that the next time he rushes me, I will not retreat. Should he get the better of the ensuing skirmish, he could lock me in the hole and I might never escape. He could even facilitate my demise by setting the house on fire as he leaves. "Keep Maynard foremost in your thoughts," I exhort myself.

Traffic is light, and I feel nearly invisible as I scurry across the six lanes of the dimly lit road in my onyx puffer parka, black jeans and rubber boots. I proceed beneath the expressway bridge and complete my 40-minute march to the border of the Allele premises. I pause amid three pine trees, crouch down and survey the nearly empty parking lot. If the desired opportunity doesn't present itself, I'll classify this outing as recon and return another night. If I must, I'll even try to use my ID badge.

In less than an hour, the Chantilly Food Service truck pulls into the loading bay, green-lighting the mission. I wait for the driver to enter the building and the dock door to be raised. I doff my boots, parka, jeans and sneakers. I pull my hood over my head, leaving me in my full charcoal grey biohazard coverall with booties. I hear the plate extend from the dock and the truck door opening. I remove the duct tape from my briefcase and tape my gloves to my cuffs. I step back into my outdoor boots, pack the rest of my clothes in a large black plastic trash bag and stow the bundle beneath the tree branches. I don my biohazard face mask. I trust that the driver has had ample time to wheel his cart amid the honeycomb of work stations, and I head along the ridge at the edge of the parking lot. I turn squarely toward the side of the building and stride briskly down to the loading bay.

I toss my briefcase onto the floor ledge, perform a poor man's muscle-up onto the dock plate, kick off my rubber boots and propel myself into the building. I move cautiously through the storage area and reach the main laboratory floor. I stop, take cover behind the fermenters and breathe deeply. The task will succeed or fail quickly. I move furtively among the work stations. I don't see anyone as I make my way to the rear of the building and the biocontainment suite. I discern movement on the other side of the floor and I crouch behind a biosafety cabinet. I identify the maintenance man. I crawl to the second-last cabinet before the biocontainment suite. The station is lit but no one is in attendance. The workspace is cluttered with plates, pipettes, glassware and a shaker. It appears that human hair follicles are being cultivated in a growth medium. I advance to the next cabinet, reach beneath the counter and find the Guest Researcher ID badge. The maintenance man has disappeared, and I discern nobody else in the area. I stride to the stainless-steel biocontainment suite door, present the ID badge to the reader and enter the key code: 8-8-8-8. It's rejected. It must've been changed. I try the next option: 9-9-9-9. It's rejected. One more unsuccessful attempt and I believe I'll trigger an unauthorized entry attempt alarm. The 7-7-7-7 combination releases the lock.

I open the door and find myself in the vestibule. I key the 7-7-7-7 code into the gallery door, and I gain entry to the area with the aquariums and terrariums. My mask becomes a bit foggy, and it's all the more reason to work fast. I hustle past the ongaonga shrub to the gympie-gympie plant in the back corner. I place the ID badge in my briefcase and withdraw a Phillips screwdriver. I remove the Plexiglas plate. I squeeze through the lacuna into the display case. I remove Spaatz's illustration of the nude Stephanie Recktenwald from its sealed archival envelope and hold it against the briefcase. I produce my shears and tube of glue. I harvest three thumbnail-size leaves from the gympie-gympie plant and affix them to Stephanie's image at the same three strategic points where Vecsey placed cones on the Companion Piece Nancy. I return the picture inside its envelope, reseal it tightly and replace it in my briefcase. I step out of the terrarium and reattach the Plexiglas plate. I place all of my tools in a heavy plastic bag, wrap it tightly and drop the package into my briefcase. I believe that I hear footsteps and crouch behind the coral tank. How stupid it would be to get caught now. I advance cautiously to the gallery door and discern no activity. I return to the vestibule and place my hand on the outside door. I consider the possibility that the researcher has returned to the hair growth bench. I open the door, head onto the main floor and replace the ID badge. If I'm spotted, I'll scramble for the exit. The food service man pulls his cart into the area ahead of me, and I duck into a prep room. I open the fridge and find it loaded with goodies, including three vials of Q-fever causing pathogen *Coxiella burnetii* on the top shelf. I decide to push my luck and take one of the vials. I emerge from the prep room, scamper past the food service man as he busily tends his vending machines and creep back to the storage area. I dart back to the dock, jump down, climb back into my rubber boots and march briskly to the pine trees on the border of the Allele premises where I left my clothes.

I empty the trash bag and quickly refill it with my bio-hazard suit, face mask, gloves and briefcase. I slip back into my jeans, sneakers, parka and boots. The only items I retain outside the bag are Stephanie's enveloped illustration and my vial of *Coxiella burnetii.*

I wrap the trash bag tight as I stride up Research Drive. I turn onto Innovation Drive and deposit the trash bag in one of the dumpsters behind one of the quaint office buildings. I trek triumphantly back to the Yukon and return home.

Early Saturday morning, I bring Bustelich his breakfast. The retreat hole remains a mess. He is seated on his bed with his head down. "I gather you're a little sick of waffles," I chirp.

He raises his head. "I'm sick of *you.*"

"You shouldn't be; I fixed you a stack of buckwheat pan-cakes." I backtrack outside of the interior door, and he slowly rises. "If you're sick of pancakes, think of these as flapjacks."

When I return to collect his garbage, half of the stack of pan-cakes have apparently been consumed, but the remainder have been dumped on the floor in front of the back bench. The dog biscuit I placed at the bottom of the stack also lies on the floor. He snatches the biscuit and hurls it at the mesh. "How's your coloring going, Johnny?" He glares and grumbles unintel-ligibly. "I have another special treat for you: another stack of Gayle's drawings. Some need to be finished, others are just to be admired. The four that I believe he considers his master works are sheathed in archival display envelopes. I'll trust you to be particularly careful with them. That means no smudges. Don't remove them from the envelopes or tamper with them in any way. Also, this was Gayle's." I display Spaatz's blaze beret. "You might like to wear it like he did while working with his pastels."

"I hurt my knee, and it's getting worse," Bustelich utters. "There may be some structural damage; I really need to see a doctor." I offer a pouty sneer. "Then I need to contact my family!" he snaps. "If you have any decency, you'll at least let me tell them I'm alive."

"How does a guy who's given me so much grief feel entitled to make demands?" I wonder. "Give me a decent half-day's work and maybe we can discuss small favors, starting with your grub. How would you like to build cultured mouse-meat tacos?" I leave the set of drawings and beret inside the door and head upstairs.

I return in the late afternoon with Bustelich's dinner. The beret and drawings that I presented in the morning are still where I left them. Johnny is lying naked on the floor. "Who's ready for mac and cheese?" He rolls over to show me his backside. I open the door and plunk down his dish along with an herbal coffee substitute. "Actually, it's liver and onions, but don't expect to be rewarded again for wasting time." I check on him two hours later. He's reclining against the back bench, clutching his knees. The paper plate that held his dinner sits empty beside him. "Want to bring your garbage up front?" He raises his head and glares. "Still feeling grumpy, Johnny? Did you have to wrestle your supper?"

"I feel like shit." He lowers his knees and grasps his stomach. "I feel like you look."

I nod. "I found the liver at the back of the freezer. Maybe you'll gain a new appreciation for your mac and cheese, hmm?" I leave a fourteenth can in the stacks outside the sauna.

Late Sunday morning I bring Bustelich brunch. "You don't seem to be finishing your waffles, so today I've given you a smaller portion. If it's not enough, I've included a bowl of cereal on the side. Technically, it's kibble from an old bag of dry dogfood that Maynard refused to eat, but it's likely just about the same ingredients." Johnny approaches his meal and picks up the bowl. He sniffs it and dumps it on the floor. "That's the way to put yourself on a menu of worms and cockroaches." He flings the bowl at the mesh, kicks over his cup of cold coffee and limps away muttering expletives. I work out for two hours and recheck the retreat hole when I've finished. "Corrective labor is the key." I toss Bustelich a bunch of green bananas and turn up the heat.

Four hours later I hear heavy pounding and a series of shouts and screams. I dash downstairs and find Johnny vigorously rubbing his hands. His face blazes with fury. "What the hell have you done to me, you son of a bitch?"

I observe Stephanie Recktenwald's picture on the floor lying across its envelope and the three gympie-gympie leaves discarded at short distances. "Didn't I direct you not to open those envelopes? Where does it hurt?"

He holds up his hands. "*Make it stop!!*"

"It might help if you dip your hands in water."

He grabs his dirty water bucket and douses himself. He shrieks. "*It's worse!!!*" He frantically rubs his arms and face. "*Please, please, make it stop!!*"

"I'm afraid the pain is bound to keep escalating, perhaps for days. The removal of Stephanie's modesty leaves exposed you to a condition which originates with a dangerous Australian bush full of tiny toxic needles."

"*Do something, you fucking douche!!!*"

I raise my hands. "I feel helpless, Johnny. As helpless as I did when you were attempting to shoot me. *As helpless as my dog must've felt when you slammed him against the floor and broke his neck!!*" He stomps and shrieks. "Maybe if I turned up the heat, I'd create a baseline against which the pain wouldn't feel so intense."

"*It burns, it burns!!!*" he screeches.

"All right, I'll review the literature and search for some kind of antidote." I shut the outer door as he strafes me with his foulest expletives. I blast generic headbanger music through excruciation station and head upstairs.

Pounding and screaming unrelated to the music stops in a couple of hours. I cook a frozen pizza for dinner. I wash my dishes and head back downstairs.

The spectacle of Bustelich lying in ringlets of blood is

gruesome. I gaze at his motionless body for several minutes until I'm positive that he's dead. Dots of blood lead from the mangled mandarin tree to the spot where he collapsed on the floor. Perhaps he began stomping the plant out of pure rage and recognized that its thorns could be employed more expediently. He apparently used them to carve deep longitudinal cuts from his wrist to his elbow. I regard his expiration with no sense of elation, satisfaction or relief. I profoundly regret that circumstances brought us to this point. But he ordained his own destruction. "A life for indulgences predicts a death for indulgences, Johnny. But so much for your eulogy." I may not have met the moment, but the moment met me. I take my malaise upstairs and drop into my low-rider chair. I reflect on how Maynard could tell whenever I was dispirited and would sit quietly close by me.

26

THE APT THING would be to leave Johnny where I found him. I take the Yukon to the gas station and fill the tank. When I return home, I back the vehicle halfway into the garage. I don a fresh disposable biohazard suit and protective face mask along with old gloves and floppy boots that belonged to my dad. I move my bench press, super pullover machine and stationary bike. I retrieve the Ryscavage cottage parlor rug and unfurl it in front of the sauna. I tote a heavy-duty jumbo trash bag containing duct tape, a coping saw and an extra-large biohazard suit into the sauna. I dump the bag contents, tape my gloves to my cuffs and refill the bag with Stephanie's picture and archival envelope, the three gympie-gympie leaves and virtually every other loose object in sight. With a little difficulty, I pack Bustelich's body into the extra-large biohazard suit and tape shut the empty sleeves. I drag the body onto the rug. I deposit the snorkel and fins I brought home from Pleasant Lake on

Johnny's chest to potentially scramble the eventual discovery scene. I roll up the body in the rug and secure the bundle with Spaatz's rope. I cut apart my mandarin tree and stuff its trunk, branches and root ball into another heavy-duty trash bag.

I work deliberately. The later tonight I hit the road, the lighter traffic should be. I load my adjustable hand-pump sprayer with bleach and begin the exhaustive process of decontaminating the sauna. When I return, I'll replace the bloodstained floor boards. I doff my biohazard suit, face mask, gloves and boots and discard them with my tools in another trash bag. I affix the mud guards over the wheels of my DDbeLL XXL7 and charge its battery along with the remote unit. I conduct a final survey of the basement and kitchen and fill another bag with the buckets, jugs, cups, the shock collar and the terra cotta saucer that had contact with Bustelich. I stow the trash bags inside the sauna to await transfer to an ideal disposal site. I decontaminate my squat rack and excruciation station floor mats.

I arduously lug Bustelich up the stairs. The task seems to require more effort than dragging him up the slick slope behind his cabin. I maneuver the cumbersome bundle out the side door and into the unlit garage. I open the Yukon liftgate and bit by bit boost the Johnny roll into the back of the vehicle. I return inside the house. I put on my parka, black knit hat, gloves and rubber boots. I stow my bag of gadgets including my motor skateboard and remote beside Johnny.

It's after eleven o'clock when Johnny and I begin our drive up to Pleasant Lake. There aren't many vehicles on the road, and the night has turned hazy. Once we leave the lights of the city behind, the fog gets heavy and the expressway curves become difficult to follow. I pass through patches of extremely dense fog where I depend on the faint taillights of vehicles ahead of me to keep me on course.

Any incident that takes my vehicle off the road now takes what little there is left of me with it. If the story of Bustelich's last stand ever becomes public, I'll be labeled as another "troubled loner," a socially maladapted monster. The media will dredge up the fact that I was seeing a shrink and suggest that my therapy wasn't intensive enough or didn't include the proper medication. Johnny will be portrayed as an upstanding family man with a forlorn wife and devastated children. Reporters will find a few sources from our high school who'll recall him as a great friend and me as a woebegone outcast. The topper will be the revelation that I risked exposing my fellow citizens to the plague. I'll be deemed fit only to endure the deservedly severe punishment that society will mete out, the logical conclusion of its energy to rid itself of me, to incrementally dissolve me throughout the years.

I concentrate on the road hard enough to give myself a headache. It's increasingly difficult to discern the lane markers and the road signage. I almost miss the Highway 21 turn-off, and I desperately hope as I head west that visibility will improve. A couple of vehicles come up behind me, and I pull over to let them pass. I can't fathom how they can see the road well enough to zip through the fog.

A few miles beyond Redgranite the night clears. An SUV comes up behind me, and I strongly suspect that it's a cop. He stays on my tail. My foot twitches on the accelerator, and beads of sweat collect at my hairline. As I grapple with the glare created by the bright lights of an oncoming truck, the red lights begin flashing behind me. "Go down swinging, Lisle." I increase my speed slightly but then pull over to the side of the road.

The cop hesitates for an instant and speeds past me. I watch his red lights fade in the distance. I sit for a few moments. I don't feel a sensation of relief, only a reduction of irritation. "Johnny, oh, Johnny." I continue on my journey.

I reach Coloma, turn south and slowly pass Horsepower Pub. The sign is dim, and I can't tell if it's still open. The moment I'm out of town I encounter more fog, but I spot the crossroad and head west. Crawling along in the dark, I finally spot my turnoff and head south. After I've driven over a mile, I realize I'm on 3rd Avenue instead of 4th Avenue with no direct access to the lake. I curse Andy for disabling my navigation system, but at least I have a more respectable excuse for having gotten lost. I turn around and agonizingly make my way back toward 4th Avenue. I don't believe I've ever despised Bustelich more. I find my turnoff, and as I head downhill, the fog becomes terribly thick. I somehow locate Pleasant Road and drive through the sinuous dips at walking speed with the windows open listening for the sound of gravel beneath the tires. I can barely see the road, but I can make a fair estimate of the distance I have to travel. I stop, get out of my vehicle and walk a short distance down the road. I spot the decorative windmill on Ryscavage's front lawn.

I hustle back to the Yukon. I feel for the Bustelich cabin driveway and pull into it. The trailer is gone. Remarkably, most of the snow has melted in the previous two weeks. I'd feel better if I knew that Markie and Duckie weren't just sent staggering out of their favorite tavern and liable to return here at any moment. I also hope that I didn't inspire them to set up some sort of booby trap or security camera on their property. I shut off the engine. I step out of my SUV, slink around the cabin and search carefully for any signs of activity or surveillance. The fog is now my ally. I return to the back liftgate of my vehicle and awkwardly unload the Johnny roll. I grab my gadget bag and place it atop the bundle of no-joy. I shut the liftgate and start tugging.

I feel the strain of every step. There are only about two inches of snow cover, and the rug doesn't slide well. I'm tempted to simply prop Johnny up on the Bustelich outhouse seat and be done with him, but it seems too much like what he would've done with me. As I start down the slope, I find a couple of squash-size rocks. I take the garden pickaxe from my gadget bag, work the rocks loose and tuck them inside the Johnny roll. I pull tenaciously, and with some slips, I convey Johnny to the lake in a little under an hour.

The air temperature has dropped since I arrived, and the fog seems thinner. I can see a short distance onto the lake, and there are some red flags discernible starting about twenty meters out indicating dangerous thin ice. I produce my tactical flashlight. The ice crust is rather bumpy and I spot a few more red flags. I target a pair of flags about thirty meters out in front of what appears to be a stretch of open water. I survey the area a final time for interlopers. I cut Spaatz's rope with my electric knife and unroll the rug. I place the rope in the bag. I unzip Bustelich's biohazard suit, perform some strategic cuts and remove it completely. I discard the sections in the bag. I find another squash-size rock. I place it along with the other two rocks and the snorkel and flippers on Johnny's chest. In the shadows of the night, he appears to be smirking. I'm able to roll the rug back around the body fairly tight.

I carry my DDbeLL XXL7 and remote onto the lake ice. I point the board between the target flags, switch on my remote, select low power mode and accelerate. The wheels claw for traction and advance two meters toward the flag before I cut power. I drag the Bustelich bundle out to the longboard and try to boost it onto the deck. The wind picks up and I hear a subtle cracking as I attempt to balance Bustelich on the board. With the bundle drooping off the back, I finally believe I've succeeded. I take a deep breath, push start and press the low power button. The wheels spin and the board fishtails. I reorient the skateboard toward the flags and select high power. The DDbeLL wheels struggle to grip the ice, the board shoots four meters forward, drifts off course and spins out. Light snow flurries begin whipping around me. I reset the board to account for some drift, select low power again and steadily accelerate as I lug the rear edge of the rug forward. I lose my grip and fall flat on my chest but the longboard and its load continue their advance. On my hands and knees, I watch the XXL7 drift past the target flags. I consider the awful possibility that the bundle could make it all the way across the lake to the public beach on the other side.

I hear subtle cracks and a decisive splash, and my mission is accomplished. I snatch the remote and climb to my feet. I estimate the point of entry to be around fifty meters out. If I'd had to cut the hole myself, I would've chosen something in that range. I expect Johnny to get swiftly separated from the rug and the rocks as well as the board, but the longer he stays submerged, the more degraded and chaotic the recovery scene should be. If I can return home without attracting notice, any evidence linking me to this case should be as thin as the ice that gave way under Johnny.

I start toward the shore, the ice cracks and I'm plunged into the water. Totally submerged, I can't feel the bottom of the lake, but I bob up and grab the edge of the broken ice. As I cough violently and gasp for breath, it feels as though a carving knife is attacking my lungs. I try to flatten my body and lift myself onto the ice shelf. The ice breaks off, I drop beneath the surface again and become inverted. In full panic mode, I lunge upward, grope for the new ice edge and pull my head and shoulders out of the water. I feel as though a burning electric current is running throughout my body. I take a series of deep breaths and shift my position to the other side of the hole. I pull, thrash and kick my way back onto the ice. I roll away from the hole, orient myself and crawl to the shore.

I stagger around dazed. But I manage to retrieve my gadget bag, and I start back up the slope on the slick stairs. I've strained my lower back. Icicles form on my heavy, saturated pants. I realize that I lost the skateboard remote in the lake, and for a moment I believe I've lost the SUV key fob, but I finally locate the latter in my parka pocket. Ice crystals form on my face and in my hat and hair. A burning numbness pierces my extremities, and I fear I'll collapse on the steps. I stumble and fall several times, but I keep bouncing to my feet and keep moving. I finally reach the Yukon. I climb in, start the engine, switch on the heater, jump out, strip naked, get back in and toss all of my wet clothes behind the front seats. I sit, shiver and seek my lost composure for a solid ten minutes.

The snow flurries appear to be getting heavier and sticking to the ground. If I'm pulled over, my nudity can only bolster my claim to a mental defect. Shuddering with an intensity I don't believe I'm capable of surpassing, I back out of the driveway and head up Pleasant Road. Visibility has improved, and I hope the accumulating snow won't become an impediment to travel. I roar triumphantly when I reach Highway 21, but I continue shivering all the way home. Only a trace of new snow graces my driveway. I pull into the garage, stagger into the house and collapse beneath a hot, cathartic shower.

I make it to bed and sleep past noon. I'm awakened by an awful dream in which I open the door of the Bustelich cabin outhouse to find Spaatz with his throat carved open. For a sweaty moment, I believe that Johnny's death and disposal were also a dream, but reality swiftly reasserts itself. With a weak cough, slight case of the sniffles and extremely stiff back and neck, I sit down gingerly to a brunch of mixed fruit, hot cocoa and waffles. Pain be damned, I plan to spend the afternoon cleansing the basement. The doorbell rings, and I find two bulky men standing on my front porch. I open the outside door. "Detective Busy B., how short has it been?"

Cybyske grabs the door handle. "Mr. Amonor, I have someone with me who needs to come in and speak with you." The two men press me backward and shut the door behind them. "This is Lt. Diatchenko of the Milwaukee Police Department. He's taken over the John Bustelich missing persons investigation."

I extend my hand. "I might've guessed you were Johnny's uncle." I nod toward the davenport, covered with assorted mail and my old green canvas coat. "I'd invite you guys to sit down, but even the areas that escaped my official ransackings are a mess."

"We'll get right to the point." Diatchenko eyes me peevishly. "We were able to trace a call that you placed to a Mr. Delmar Vecsey in Pasadena, Texas. We contacted Mr. Vecsey and upon questioning him learned that he supplied Gaylord Spaatz with a stockpile of hormone drugs, a portion of which were paid for by you. Mr. Vecsey believes the drugs were intended for use on John Bustelich. Does this sound familiar?"

"Gayle and Johnny, hmm?" I sigh. "Who could've called that one?"

"So that's an admission of what exactly?" Diatchenko snarls.

My cantankerous gaze meets his walrus mustache. "When Gayle began transitioning, he mentioned Johnny as a himbo he aimed to seduce. He couldn't wait to see the expression on his face when he revealed his identity." I smack my lips. "But they sort of turned on to each other on the way."

"What kind of crap are you trying to push, Amonor?" Diatchenko scoffs.

I sneer. "Isn't that heteronormative enough for you, Sarge?"

"Cut the shit, Lisle," Cybyske snaps. "Where is the body?"

I take an uneasy sidestep and expel a long breath. "Follow me." I grab my canvas coat and lead the policemen back outside.

"Are you listing?" the detective references my tight, uneven gait.

"I have a recurring spine issue," I acknowledge. "Ask Dr. Neichi." We arrive at the freezer in my garage. I grit my teeth, gently remove the article wrapped in plastic and place it on the floor.

"What's this?" Diatchenko huffs.

"The real point of your visit, isn't it?" I fix my beleaguered eyes on Cybyske. "After Maynard was struck by the train, I made up the shit about finding him dismembered on the tracks. It was my way of dealing with the fact that you're going to hand him over to be examined by butchers."

Diatchenko snickers sardonically. "We don't care about the damn dog right now, Lisle. Where is John Bustelich? Where is Gaylord Spaatz?"

I face the lieutenant squarely. "As I alluded to before, Johnny wanted to do some steroids as Gayle was transitioning. They were holed up in neighboring cabins the Bustelich brothers have at Pleasant Lake in Waushara County." I turn back to Cybyske. "Chad can take you up there. I visited them a few times, and they let me briefly stash Maynard there. I bought them some vitals, including a selection from Delmar's medicine bag. I even took them some toys like my skateboard and toboggan." I mention the skateboard because I suspect they'll ultimately find it and link it to me and I invent the toboggan as a diversionary device. "It's a bit awkward being around bondage buddies. They'd get off on playing with this antique pistol – it's called a Welrod."

Diatchenko pokes me in the chest. "You're suggesting that

if we went up to this Pleasant Lake right now, we'd find John Bustelich and Gaylord Spaatz living together in a cabin?"

I furrow my brow. "No, unfortunately. I should've taken their wanderlust talk more seriously. They said they wanted to go somewhere more tolerant and welcoming, even if it meant leaving the country. The last time I went up there, they'd clearly vamoosed."

Cybyske edges closer. "Bustelich is just going to drop out without a word to his wife or kids or his mother or brothers?"

"Do his brothers know?" I shrug. "I didn't really talk to Johnny that much. I still don't like him. He's a bad influence on Gayle, but it's Gayle's life. Gayle told me Johnny is embarrassed by his feelings, and he's going to make the announcement to his family in his own time in his own way. I took that to mean from long distance."

"Why didn't you disclose any of this in our previous conversations?" Cybyske demands.

"I told you Spaatz owed me money and was looking to travel!" I exclaim. "I promised I'd guard their privacy, even though I don't approve so much of their kinky lifestyle. And I'm no lawyer, but there's a confidential medical issue involved."

Diatchenko stares at me agape. "Mind if we have a look around?"

"Around here?" I chafe. "Open house is over!" I point toward my front hallway. "Your weasels smashed the glazing on my picture of Maynard, and it took me two days to remove all the glass shards from the carpet! And where's my Glock 19 that you bustards never returned, Viktor? If you want-"

"Otherwise," Diatchenko interrupts, "I could drag you

downtown and conduct your interview there!" He produces his handcuffs. "You might think of me as *your* bondage buddy."

Cybyske takes charge of Maynard's body. Diatchenko hauls me to the District 1 police station in Milwaukee and grills me for two hours. I offer him no information relevant to his investigation beyond what I outlined in my garage. He suggests that he could place me under arrest for obstruction, and I hint that I might speak with an attorney who's an outspoken advocate for transgender rights. The lieutenant releases me with a warning to remain available for further questioning. Should he garner the intel to place me at Pleasant Lake earlier in the morning, I'll admit to having made a final unsuccessful foray to recover the recreational equipment I'd lent the lovebirds.

I sit in the King Kryczek & Rohr-Kisslinger Counseling Solutions LLP anteroom in preparation for my fourth session with Dr. King. I finally engage in polite badinage with DeRae. "You might call this my second act here. No second act though for Ivanhoe, hmm? I keep hoping he might materialize on your shoulder." She gives me a miffed look as if she believes I've insinuated I wish the bird would defecate on her. I roll with the flow. "He would probably be aiming for Kisslinger."

I return to the immersion tank. "Here's a man in queue to achieve a fluid oneness with the universe," King celebrates my progress. "Perhaps this tool will temper your irritability as well."

"I usually add colloidal oatmeal to my baths at home," I volunteer. "It seems to improve my skin." I sense his befuddlement. "I mentioned in our last session that some of the oral meds I take can be rather unkind to my gastrointestinal tract."

"That's right, you disclosed that you regularly wake up constipated, didn't you?" He studies his Notemaster. "I'm sorry, you stated that your stool is often loose and oily. Do you have daily diarrhea?"

"I have projectile diarrhea," I retort.

King huffs. "Your voice becomes nasal when you confront stressors. You should practice frequent irrigation, both nasal and rectal."

Soaking in the tank suppresses my inhibitors. "These helpful hints will set me up to squeak by better socially?"

"They'll make you feel stronger, and you will consequently project strength. They'll make you feel like you care, which will make you appear as though you want to belong and contribute. Many people will respond favorably. But even if they don't, isn't it incumbent on you to make the effort?"

"You know me and my strained history with society. When I try to connect, we always end up with people regarding me as woefully inadequate and me regarding them as woefully obtuse. It seems that when I try to be kind or helpful, they resent me even more for it. Naturally, that applies to no demographic more than thoroughly modern women."

He groans. "If you dedicated the energy you burn nursing your bitter wounds over past rejections to pursuing other romantic partners, you might just roll up some numbers."

I give the doctor a rare peek inside my head. "I guess my default comfort zone has always been to flit from one innocent, little crush to the next, the girl du jour often unaware, letting my tender feelings burn themselves out with or without her complicity."

"Such a juvenile resignation," the liberator titters. "You need to build the courage to resist your panoply of fears and weaknesses." He leans forward. "DeRae noticed that today you're walking funny."

I retain my limp from my Pleasant Lake plunge. "I recently had a slight slippage and fallage."

"Is this a common occurrence?" King rises. "Do you fall down often?"

I grunt. "Seems to happen a little more frequently when there's ice on the pavement."

His Notemaster lights up. "Have you recently taken a direct blow to the back of your head?"

I rub my head. "I can't recall any."

He shakes his foot. "That's a likely indication that you *have* been the recipient of a blunt force trauma. There could have been significant damage to your cerebellum, or perhaps you have bilateral vestibulopathy. You really should have a video oculography and full brain scan."

"I'm waiting for my lab to come out with that home test kit," I quip.

The doctor reseats himself. "A part of my evaluation process here, of course, entails threat assessment. Would you say you pose a danger to yourself or others?"

"You can't rule anything out," I reason. "After all, I'm a timid white male, a loner with scientific training and a grudge against society, so I fit the profile, don't I?"

"Let's revisit your scientific training," he pounces. "Why do you refuse to complete your degree, a capstone which might serve as a springboard for advancing your career?" A mighty sigh serves as my response. "This would be a prime example of exchanging your scarcity mindset for one of abundance. You're only two semesters short, aren't you? Why didn't you gut it out in the first place?"

I have another bad moment in which I offer complete candor. "I felt I was struggling to keep up. There were some stupid, little lab incidents. I recall one in which I was rushing to finish an experiment, and I spilled something like sulfuric acid on a girl." I blow bubbles in the water. "Just a few drops on her lapel, so the fabric steamed slightly. She hit the emergency wash and made a stink. She was a real bulldog. She kept rehashing the event for other classmates. I overheard her discussing it with an Indian guy and this flakey hippie babe, and they joked that she could've ended up looking like me."

King takes a deep, contemplative breath. "What bothers me most about this anecdote is how you describe these other people. Why is his nationality or her cultural orientation relevant?"

"Because individual differences that set someone apart from others are sorted by my neural processors as effective identifiers and organizers?"

"Are you threatened by diversity in the work environment?" he prospects.

"By certain microbial diversity," I concede.

"Do you believe that men are essentially superior to women?" he perseveres.

"Smarter," I assure him, "and the proof is in the predominantly female trait of preselection. Women presume that other women are reliable arbiters of value. Men are bright enough to recognize that other men's views most likely suck."

"You mentioned a particular frustration with 'modern women.' Are you troubled that you're progressively unable to rely on societal norms to stunt their independence and provide barriers to their ambition?"

I gasp. "Not by the life of Eunice Newton Foote!"

"If a reckoning troll has a point to make," the liberator exhorts, "he ought to couch it in speech that's not too inane for his audience to interpret."

"I've always found it adorable," I reload, "to see a woman that I'm in love with eschew my company in favor of some slug who's pleased to make her his next cum dumpster."

"Doesn't paying tribute to your own victimhood at some point grow old?" King challenges.

"You're right, that rant made me sound like a feminist comedienne."

"Don't you see that you won't even try to accept responsibility for a basic flaw without spewing venom at someone else? Stop to consider whether your failures might be a by-product of your own crippling insecurity, which itself is perhaps a function of the inadequacy of your traditional values to confront the challenges of an enlightened world."

I deactivate my personal force field once more. "I consider the devotion my grandparents seemed to share, of the respect and admiration with which each of my grandmothers spoke of her husband in the years after his death. Most of today's sisters-in-arms would be too sophisticated for such feelings. Modern women have their own fancy job titles and their own money. They don't need anyone else. I believe with that goes a diminished capacity to love. Romance seems to be reduced to a power proposition. At the end of it all, does the uber-feminist really believe that her careerism soothes the soul more than a man who would cherish her?"

"Not by any well-rounded, optimum standard." King's condescension fills the float room. "You've previously dichotomized the baser natures of men and women as infidelity and hypergamy, respectively, which illustrates perhaps your fundamental fault: You need to stop segmenting and get in the habit of considering people as a whole. You must be familiar with the expression: We're all in this together."

"With props to Orwell: Some people are more all in it together than others. I prefer the expression: Keep your friends close but your enemies closer."

He scoffs. "In these days of elevated social awareness and layered oversight, perhaps terms such as 'enemies,' even 'bullies,' are a bit too strong. In a previous session, you carelessly lobbed the term 'evil,' but by evil you should understand that you simply mean those who have temporarily succumbed to destructive influences and need treatment or those who've made poor decisions and need behavioral intervention. Bad folks are generally good folks having a bad day."

"I mean bullies and enemies," I charge, "who through gross selfishness or willful malice seek to rob you of qualities beyond material considerations, such as your ability to trust, basic sense of security and self-respect." I fret I'm on the cusp of revealing too much. "Like your colleague Kisslinger, when I was at his mercy. I resented his constant assaults on my belief system and all he thought I stood for."

"Respect is something that must be earned." King consults

his Notemaster. "An argument you perceived as detrimental was very likely a valiant therapeutic effort to provide you with the finesse you need to manage your life. According to your ex's notes, you have extreme challenges regulating your emotions and you're overwhelmed with negative affect."

"I'm probably just too aware that we live in an age without heroes," I reason.

"You must make the conscious decision that disillusionment is not an option," the liberator explains. "Even in the face of extreme despair, you must choose to be happy."

"Oh, I've usually chosen happiness, but it often hasn't chosen me." I grab the float-pillow rack and propel myself from side to side of the tank. "I consider those who've filled the moments of my life, how dear I held their companionship, and how easily and frivolously they cast me out of their lives and moved on. I wonder if I should treasure them for the special memories they've given me or resent them for ultimately deciding that I was no longer worth their time."

"If you camp in the shadow of misery, those around you will be chilled by the shade." King exudes aplomb. "Stop swimming and you start sinking, and those around you will fear you're going to drag them under with you. Your lack of contentment and fulfillment will impact anyone close to you."

I nod. "As Dr. Dave used to say, 'It's important to cultivate friendly relations with all people if for no other reason than you'll be putting yourself in a far stronger position to inflict heavy psychological devastation when you ultimately turn on someone or abandon them.'"

"We therapists often overestimate our clients' intellectual

capacity to process nudges not rendered in plain-speak," the doctor croaks.

With about a quarter of my session left, I take a powder room break. When I return, King gives me a vexed look as he helps me back into the tank. "Do you have chronic cold feet and hands?" he inquires. "Do you often experience problems with your balance? Are you a bit clumsy, accident prone? Do you frequently sprain your ankles?"

"Do you install sandboxes as a sideline?" I dismiss his probe. "It seems like we've recently covered this ground."

"The traits that I've identified are inveterate precursors of neurodegenerative disease, in case an underlying medical issue may be responsible for your cognitive infirmities." The doctor consults his Notemaster. "As a little more time has elapsed, are you coping better with the loss of your dog?"

"I'm still working through acceptance, and I'm adapting." I've advised King that Maynard ran out of my yard and was struck and killed by a passing car. "Last weekend I was able to put away his dishes." This alternative narrative should allow me to contact-trace the spread of my confidential information. "Having dealt with the similar death of my boyhood dog Gus, I thought this one might be a bit less painful, but I guess there were more distractions in my life when I was younger. I've felt this one more acutely."

"Perhaps you gave this dog too much emphasis and thereby limited your other opportunities." The doctor sounds smug. "I believe you'll recognize with some introspection that it's not the individual dogs themselves but the times gone by of which 'the dog presence' was a limited part that you really miss."

I emit a silent growl. "You couldn't be more wrong. Dogs have their own personalities, and it's the shared experiences, the unique bonding, that makes the individuals themselves significant and precious, just as it would be with another human. They give and receive love. In fact, they have a lot to teach humans about unconditional love, and even more about loyalty. Dogs are not just some quick loneliness fix, and they're not some commodity to be replaced."

The liberator titters. "Some of us strive harder than others to anthropomorphize them."

I nod. "I would think there are many days on which God is challenged not to consider them his favorite creation."

The doctor twists in his seat. "Are you still someone who identifies as religious, or has that become a fluid social construct for you?"

"I'm still a believer. I still consider myself a good Christian and will attend Mass and partake in the sacraments that I believe have divine sanction. My faith is not blind. Outside of going comic book, one can only conclude that the miracles described in the New Testament narratives had to be performed through God. How do we know these narratives depict real events? The common people we encounter in the narratives are too real to be contrived. They're selfish, egotistical, petty, scared, lazy, overly inclined to keep asking 'What have you done for me lately?' and are entirely too human. The exact ethos of the scribes and Pharisees can be seen today in our cultural vanguard and virtue-signaling elites. Governing officials are more concerned with clinging to their authority than the trifles of the powerless little people. In the long view, common people have common sense and don't lie like elites. They obviously believed fervently that the acts were genuine or they would've averted their own subsequent persecutions. And the arrogant remain quick to mock the religious when God appears to have abandoned them."

King expels a frustrated breath. "You don't resent your God for not protecting your dog?"

"I don't claim to understand why such a tragedy would occur, why my only close friend was taken from me. The crucified Christ stands as the ultimate symbol of what man has done to God and what God has done to man. It signifies that this life is a gallery of grief, guaranteed to leave the bearer with heartache and pain. I won't trade a few more months or years for a chance, just a solid chance, at permanent joy. To whom else would I go?"

The liberator clears his throat. "Do you ever seek spiritual counseling from your church?"

"I'm not that holy," I submit. "I tend to keep the clergy at arm's length. Too many of them have twisted themselves around to a place where they identify pleasure as pain and pain as pleasure. Ridiculously enough, many of them also espouse a political ideology which renders the church itself obsolete as a social organ."

He leans forward. "Then logically why do you stay?"

"I look at it as having a venerable acquaintance whose friendship you wish to cultivate, and he takes a bride with a beastly affectation and progressive battle-axe tendencies. You make an effort to get along with her to maintain your relationship with the friend."

"So you're going to blame the wife?" King roars. "I don't claim to be an expert in Judeo-Christian theodicy, but that sounds like an awful perversion of the fundamental doctrine. I'm fairly certain the tradition makes no provision for animal rights either. You're quite the shrieking heretic, aren't you?"

I resent his tone. "In my experience, you can try to please people or do the right thing, but often not both. In his treatise *Answer to Job*, psychology icon Carl Jung posits that Christian ethics inevitably lead to 'collisions of duty.'"

"Jung is engaging high theater," King contributes. "His views are a philosophical exercise of little practical therapeutic value."

"Could that be a little tarot envy talking?"

The counselor rises. "Perhaps the divine will would be appeased if you weren't so quick to expect trouble and catastrophize, if you showed less hostility and more charity to your fellow humans, and if you weren't content to desperately cling to the memory of a dog?"

I straighten my posture. "The theologian Will Rogers said 'If there are no dogs in heaven, I'll ask to go where the dogs are.'"

"I sincerely hope your life isn't going to the dogs. With more time, you'll likely be able to find closure for the passing of your Maynard and go on to expand your horizons."

"If you believe in the resurrection and an afterlife, there is no closure. Only a pause to reflect, to regret and maybe request more divine mercy."

King groans. "I'm a man of science."

I discharge diplomatic guffaws. "You're a shrink!"

I trudge home from my sensitivity session in an uncomfortably pensive mood. The top-billed counseling partner isn't as confrontational as Kisslinger, but he weaponizes his humanity and influence in more subtle ways. Jung would say he "prates loudly his liberal-mindedness."

Our sessions have turned destructive in another manner. I'm afraid that King has liberated my psyche to the extent that my feigned romantic feelings for Nancy Buetow-Detweiler have grown genuine. I strive not to think about it because I'll be back at Ideal Allele facing her in an hour. She stopped by my house yesterday because I couldn't be reached by phone. Apparently, one of the research associates from the defunct Healthpath team rejected the realignment and resigned, prompting the Duchess to invite me back. I'll undergo a re-entry interview this afternoon and reorganize my desk so I can officially end my three-week layoff and return to the job tomorrow. Nancy mentioned that Van Leskosek praised my work ethic and expressed an interest in having me assigned to his project of developing a therapeutic remedy for super-Capno.

I jog my Megalophone and catch the news report of another Capno outbreak in Oregon. I sincerely hope that Spaatz opted for the Bwindi Impenetrable Forest over Mount Hood. If Diatchenko ever locates him, I'm not sure what the upshot will be for me but I don't anticipate it being positive. Do I owe Gayle a profound apology or does he owe me one? I hope we're someday afforded the nose-to-nose opportunity to sort it out. How guilty do I remain about what became of Bustelich? I won't deny that I guided his demise, and I'm sorry if his loss made his family even more miserable than they started out, but it was an impossible situation that caught me in its gears and resisted my best efforts to mend. I refuse to believe that what I suffered with Maynard wasn't more than punishment enough.

Johnny's bloated body is bound to surface at the lake soon – maybe one of his lovable brothers will happen to reel him in on a hook – but I don't believe the circumstantial evidence against me will rise to the probative level as long as I staunchly stick to my liaison fable. Discovery of the Welrod shouldn't point to my involvement either. My immediate to-do list includes retaining a good criminal defense lawyer, surreptitiously moving funds offshore and keeping a finger on viable escape routes.

I'm leaning heavily toward sending my nephew Angelo a Companion Piece replicant of myself. It's a gesture that could burn my final bridge to Dinah, but its potential to restore my self-respect makes it highly attractive. The automaton will have the language capability to say: "Ask your mom for another spanking"; "Be ever vigilant for ways to shake down your teacher"; and "Tell your pop and uncles you feel like a big girl and want to have a baby."

I pause at a tree in the park where we stopped many times on dog walks. Maynard arranged his four blankets into a nest in front of the heat register at the foot of my bed and probably hid one or two food tidbits among them. I don't anticipate having the wherewithal to pick up the blankets for a long time. Growing movements of dedicated activists across the country are determined to rid society of dogs. A mob demanding mass canine extermination is preparing to protest in Portland tonight. I have arranged to purchase a fleet of nontraceable preowned drones through Andy, and I will convert my secure sauna into a secure BSL-3 complete with negative air pressure and HEPA filters. I intend to produce pathogenic agents in my personal lab with which to dust anti-dog demonstrators. I feel as though I've already completed a Phase I trial on the gympie-gympie plant neurotoxin, and I may try mixing it in a cocktail with the *Coxiella burnetii* bacterium that I took from Allele. I view working to eradicate the *Capnocytophaga canimorsus* plague during the day and working to eradicate the anti-dog warriors at night as a fair exchange. I cut across the athletic field. A lonely girl pedals her bicycle in ovals on the vacant tennis courts.

ABOUT THE AUTHOR

Richard Fendry lives in Wisconsin. He believes that the world would be an awfully bleak place without our canine companions. *Anomie* is his second novel. He published *Flyte of the Century* in 2021.

9 781736 441626